SEER QUEST COVENANT

BOOK THREE

LEGEND OF THE ANCIENTS

THE BOOKS OF LOCURNIA

DEONNE DANE

Published by Black Onyx Publishing

Copyright © 2023 by Deonne Dane

ISBN: 978-1-7385831-0-2 (Paperback)

ISBN: 978-1-7385831-1-9 (Epub)

ISBN: 978-1-7385831-2-6 (Kindle)

Cover Image by: B King

Edited by: Rascon Revisions

*Seer Quest: Covenant is the third book in The Books of Locurnia series & the first book in the Seer Quest Tetralogy - Legend of the Ancients. The books of Locurnia are LGBTQ inclusive and contain explicit material. This series is intended for adults 18 and over. This book is written using British English.

To Anne for all her time so freely given and her unstinting kindness

PART ONE
The Quarry Found

CHAPTER ONE

Shimmering Fields, Locurnia

With every breath, Meran tasted the metallic tang of blood and sweat. It tainted the air and set the small arena abuzz with anticipation. He surged to his feet with the rest of the audience, all eyes affixed on the downwards arc of the fighter's blood-stained sword.

"He's going to kill him!"

The phrase echoed through the throng like threads of fate.

Meran's fascination pulled up short at the expressions on his companions' faces. Ellom's grey eyes haunted, Jon's lips pressed together tightly. At the arena's centre, the felled combatant staggered to his knees, the colour rapidly draining from his features. His shield dropped from his grasp as he clutched at the spurting stump of his mutilated sword arm.

With a thud, the mail-clad champion released his own shield and knocked the helm from his opponent's head. Winding fingers through the defeated man's sweat-slick hair, the victor jerked his hand back, his sword grazing the man's exposed throat.

Meran's dismay echoed Ellom's gasp and Jon's stunned expletive.

"Don't do it," Meran shouted, his words consumed by the noise of thumping feet, pounding hands, and voices that roared their desire to see the vanquished man slaughtered. The light of the berserker burned bright in the victor's eyes, as if poised on the precipice of giving in to his nature.

The black-cloaked enforcers drew their weapons and stepped from the shadows.

"The Mavish. The Mavish. The Mavish." The crowd roared the warrior's name over and over as if demanding he finish what he had begun.

Meran swallowed, his mouth dry.

"Stand down." One of the surrounding enforcers advanced on the

Mavish.

The warrior ignored them and, with a wicked grin, caressed the edge of his blade against the vulnerable flesh beneath his opponent's jaw. His intense gaze challenged the crowd, incited them, playing them until they bayed for the blood that only he could give them.

Meran pushed forwards, his heart hammering. "Mercy!" he yelled.

The enforcers' bows pulled tautly. The crowd's excitement ratcheted higher.

"Mercy!" His shouts were as effective as a whisper in the face of a gale…until a warning arrow whistled, and blood bloomed across the Mavish's cheek.

"Mercy!"

Meran's shout reverberated across the arena as all else turned to silence.

Heads shifted, curious eyes turning his way. Embarrassment flamed in his cheeks, the hands of his friends jerking him back protectively. Chin jutting, he masked his emotions, feigning confidence. He was Meran Durante, scholar and seer, and he refused to cower before anyone.

That included the warrior in the arena below.

The Mavish rose to his full height, shoulders broad, stance threatening as he tossed aside the unconscious man like a discarded rag. The limp body fell into the awaiting hands of several healers who had rushed to his side.

The warrior fixed his sneering gaze on Meran. "I see you," he called ominously as he swiped a hand over the wound on his face. Blood smeared across his rugged cheek.

Meran swallowed hard, the reality of the man more intimidating than any recurring vision he'd had of this sandy-haired giant. Visions that had haunted him since that fateful day in spring. The day that had turned Meran's world on its head.

He stiffened his back and gathered his determination. His purpose could not be deflected by his apprehension.

The Mavish bent, grasped the severed arm, and flung it. With an audible gasp, the crowd surged aside as meat and bone flashed through the air.

Ellom ducked, and Jon cursed as he jumped clear. Trusting the warrior's aim, Meran held his ground, though his stomach churned as the grisly limb landed at his feet.

"A trophy for your mercy, little brother." The warrior grinned. Ignoring everyone, he collected his shield and made his way through the enforcers and his fellow competitors. Without a backward glance, he disappeared through the darkened exit beneath the spectators' stand.

Meran kept his eye upon that phantom, the echo of the man's presence like a shimmer of heat. "I see you too, man of Mavish," he whispered, "and I am not afraid." The telltale tingle of admiration built within him as he thought of the warrior's forceful bearing. Still, it spurred on a rising unease.

Fate commanded he come to the Shimmering Fields to hire this sword—and what a sword it was—but why would such a man as this bow to his demands? They were not clan and far from equals.

Men of the Mavish's ilk were their own masters. Meran knew from bitter experience, they were oft self-absorbed and untrustworthy. But his quest demanded the presence, the allegiance, of this warrior, or it was doomed to fail. That could never happen. Ever.

He ignored Jon's annoying snort and the even more infuriating concern in Ellom's eyes, but he refused to allow past humiliations to deter him.

"Is he really your only choice?" Ellom stepped out of the way as a young lad pushed past him, bent on retrieving the severed limb. The healers' acolyte grimaced in disgust at his gory prize before disappearing into the surrounding throng.

Meran watched it go, its disappearance at least easing one of his tensions. "You know very well—"

"Yes, yes, of course we know," Jon said before Meran began berating Ellom again.

More and more of late, irrational irritation with his lover led Meran to harsh words that he ended up regretting. Ever since he had discovered the identity of the man from his vision, a nagging unrest unsettled him.

"The prophet might have ordered you to find this man, but he should come with a warning." Jon's brow furrowed in concern.

Meran stared at his friend in surprise. Few people ever ruffled Jon Reko's feathers. Why, even patrons buying his art, only to besmirch them as depraved, had not stirred his ire. If Jon worried, perhaps so should Meran?

But after all he had witnessed over the last six moons, Meran knew that the Mavish was the one he had been looking for. Amazing. Powerful. A warrior and a champion, he wore his victory like a badge of superiority. Such confidence stirred Meran's fascination.

"I think that display is warning enough," Ellom said. "To win, all he had to achieve was first blood. We are *Voce*, not the barbarians of Velkor. He did not need to cut off his opponent's arm."

"But the prophet has spoken." Meran patted Ellom's hand.

Despite the tightness in his chest and the persistent memory of arrogant men and their hubris, Meran found himself enthralled. He should not. Prudence demanded he crush every errant feeling, the escapade with Rune Gratian having taught him that lesson well. Still, his cheeks flushed with a wayward heat that not even past mortification could douse.

"I cannot ignore it," he continued. "I will, however, endeavour to step warily. That is a promise."

"How?" Ellom asked, his voice rising. "How can we even dare approach such a one?"

"*We* won't have to."

Before Ellom could demand clarification, a little man at his right shoulder shushed them all. "Be quiet, be quiet. 'Tis the chief magistar."

Meran turned to see a richly robed man stepping to the podium at the edge of the official's gallery. The magistar's words honouring the victor in one breath and chastising the crowd's call for savagery in the next rang out, but Meran heard hardly a word.

With the absence of his target, his agitation grew. More than his reputation's loss rode on his success. Though they did not know it, the fate of all the *Voce* of Locurnia stood on a precipice.

He had no choice.

Without the Mavish, Meran's quest could not succeed. This was his only chance to confront the warrior before the man returned to his clan lands and put himself beyond Meran's reach.

Ill ease or not, he had to seize the moment.

"Hear me. You two stay here. I'll see you back at the lodgings."

"No," Ellom said. "You can't go after him alone. What would your father say?"

"I don't care."

There was no doubt his father would be furious to learn that Meran intended to consort with a man of such base temperament as the Mavish. His sire had allowed him to attend the Festival of Etta only because his friends had accompanied him. They were expected to keep him from trouble. That same forbearance would not extend to a journey to Locurnia's savage hinterlands nor a delay of his return to his home in Dun if he had to give chase.

But, Meran suspected, his father's displeasure was not the root of Ellom's protest. As his own dissatisfaction with their relationship had grown, Ellom's had become more demanding and desperate.

Yet, there came a time when every man was forced to take control of his destiny, and this was Meran's. He was a seer, for the gods' sake, and one day all would acknowledge it. Even if how he achieved his current goal presently eluded him, Meran was confident he would succeed. He had already foreseen the outcome.

"Please, do as I bid and stay here. Have your fun. I have things to do, and they will be best accomplished alone."

Protest roiled in his lover's grey eyes nonetheless, and Meran's heart softened. "Stay," he said, infusing his voice with reassurance and sealing it with a kiss. "I will see you later. We'll celebrate the day with some of that imported wine and a meat platter of all your favourites."

"But when?"

"Two turns of the dial; two, and all should be sorted." Yes, two hours would surely be sufficient to secure the Mavish's agreement. After all, Meran had a damning weapon in his arsenal of persuasion. He shored up his courage and pushed through the crowd.

CHAPTER TWO

Reaching the exit, Meran set up watch on the dusty street outside the high stone wall of the theatre and awaited his quarry.

The touch of Ellom's farsight tingled in his mind and shivered down his back; a whisper of unwanted attention. Frustration returned with the further evidence of Ellom's festering insecurity and lack of faith. This was Meran's quest, and it required his full focus and fortitude to see it through. He needed Ellom's support, not a grip that threatened his ability to take the necessary steps towards success.

With a herculean effort, he shook off the indignation of having his privacy invaded and turned his attention back to the issue at hand. Finding the Mavish and convincing him to take up the cause.

Before he had time to consider his predicament further, Meran spied the band of burly men exiting the competitor's underground rooms. Except for Ellom's magic clinging to him like morning mist, Meran all but forgot his lover in his rising anticipation.

As he had suspected, the warrior and his clansmen left before the entertainment was over. The Mavish stood head and shoulders above his fellows, as legendary in appearance as the tales of the Serpent War had painted him. Meran's heart hammered with a sudden tattoo of nerves. Raw, animalistic power and a fierce will came coupled with that greater size, and Meran had to steel his nerve.

Following them to a large ramshackle building filled with noise and the pungent odour of sweat and ale, Meran kept to the shadows. Settling in a small booth alongside the door, he sought his prey in the gloom and dust of the Broken Sword tavern room.

The band of men pushed through the revellers to reach the dark-stained wooden plank that served as a bar, patrons skulking aside to give them their due. Who could blame them? The warriors were rough, hale, and wearing aggression as thick as armour. Giants amongst men. Fighters all, they had gained their expertise in the most recent and infamous of wars ever to touch the *Voce* of Locurnia. Only grim determination had Meran preparing himself to step forwards.

But catching Meran off guard, his target veered towards a table at the back of a gloomy alcove. Three figures filled the booth. A lad and lass, and a man with perfectly coifed greying hair and wearing a long cloak. The Mavish hauled the latter from his seat.

Clutching the heavy chain about the man's neck, the Mavish dragged his captive through the establishment, the fellow's protests bawling breathlessly.

Ignoring the other patrons, the warrior threw his victim from the premises. "Get gone before I rip off that filthy little prick of yours."

"You cannot do this!" The man tried to re-enter, only to be met with a growl and a fist that shoved him back through the doorway.

Meran's shock transformed into unbridled curiosity.

"Do you know who I am?" the smaller man demanded. "I am Lord Marshal Belton, and a man of the House of Jordan Orr, the chief magistar—"

Gods, this man held rank. Meran started to rise from his seat.

"*Pah!*" The Mavish blocked the entrance. "Do you think your title has me aquiver in my boots? My own is equal to it, and my demesne of far superior value. Think again, little man, for the bone I have to pick with you is far from settled."

Alarm rose in Belton's voice. "You are not a chief magistar. You have no such authority."

To Meran, the Mavish appeared unperturbed by the declaration.

What did he know of Belton that made him behave in such a daring manner? And why was Belton not with the head of his house at the arena?

No one else moved to intervene, and Meran gritted his teeth with indecision. Any altercation could derail his plans. If the Mavish stepped beyond his bounds and found himself arrested, what could Meran do to save his cause? Should he attempt to placate the pair?

"I know you." The Mavish strode outside, yet his words slipped through the hush that had fallen over all the tavern's patrons. "You are vermin. I smelt your foul stench the moment I stepped past your two guards here. Their disguise did not fool me, and neither do you."

Guards? Meran had seen only a couple of men with greasy hair and dirty faces. They had worn layers of dull, torn garments and lounged against the tavern's outer walls with a look of desperation to have what they could not afford. He had never suspected anyone loitering outside was not what they seemed.

The harsh thuds of flesh being pounded floated back to Meran, the savagery tightening his gut with unspoken excitement. He should not relish the unleashing of more violence, but wasn't that what he needed? Strength, action, unstinting resolution, daring.

Meran refused to move from his spot as some of the other patrons did, hesitant to see how it ended.

Shrieks and groans followed the clattering of a sword falling to the ground. The brutal thud of a club connecting with bone trailed after whining protestations. An uproar of cheers followed from the rougher men clustered at both the doors and glassless windows.

"Get you gone, you corrupt bastard, and take your scum with you." The muffled sound of one final kick and a resultant wail preceded the warrior's return, his expression grim but satisfied.

Many congratulated the Mavish as he dusted the residue of the fight from his clothes and turned his attention back to the booth. The youth had risen as if he wished to follow his now vanished companion, his face flushed red and desperate.

The Mavish placed a forbidding hand against the boy's skinny chest. "Go back to your ale, lad, and save your companion the heartache of discovering your bloodied corpse on the morrow. You'll get no coin from that one. He pays for his pleasures in blood. Here, save yourself the trouble this eve. This is enough for a further drink and a spiced sausage pie...for the both of you."

A small brass-coloured disk flipped through the air and was snatched up, the lad's eyes shining with gratitude.

Meran stared wide-eyed at this unexpected act of kindness. Perhaps the brusque man was not as harsh as his previous behaviour suggested. The very possibility eased the tension of Meran's taut muscles, though he kept caution close to his chest.

"Sir, my thanks...but I do not fear to earn my keep." The lad's eyes were almost longing as they rested upon the harsh face of his unexpected benefactor.

"*Gah!* Be on your way. You are not my preference." The Mavish edged the boy from his way with a disconcerted grunt. If it was for the lad's forwardness or surprise at his own generosity, Meran could not tell.

What sort of person would please this harsh, and apparently, noble man? Certainly not the young fellow's female companion huddling in the deeper shadows of the booth. By reputation, the Mavish held no penchant for the ladies, though Meran had heard he was wed.

Furtively, Meran studied the Mavish's companions. They all had that same tough confidence and aggression. Hardened fighting men. Were they comrades or preference?

He shook himself. What did it matter? It would not be him. He could not afford to be seduced by the base and animalistic trappings of lust. Not again.

Returning to his companions positioned at a leaner that offered them the best prospect of the room, the Mavish took a long pull of the ale they offered him. He then immersed himself in their conversation and the bawdy laughter that followed, no doubt at the expense of Lord Belton and his ineffectual guards.

They did not seem to consider that the lord might send the constabulary to arrest the Mavish for his disrespect. But that could, of course, raise questions as to why Belton was consorting with rent boys instead of attending to clan business.

The chief magistar of the Midlands had recently augmented closer ties with Meran's father. From all Meran had observed, Jordan Orr appeared to be a decent man, and such behaviour would likely strike him as intolerable.

But now it was Meran's turn. If he hesitated longer, his nerve would fail and he would never take up the reins, as he must. Not alone for country but for the devastation he had seen afflicting his own family.

Six moons back, the vision of his elder sister's glowing hazel eyes, dull in death, overshadowed him, stabbing him to the quick.

"What ails you this morn?" Patrice had asked, "You look at me as if I sprout a second head." Concern enlivened her expression as they shared a breakfast of cucumber and hard-boiled egg.

Hopelessness and denial alternately assaulted him putting paid to his hunger. The clarity of the premonition—her rich blonde hair dyed brilliant red with blood as she lay abandoned amidst carnage—stole his voice and struck at his heart. He could admit to nothing other than he was under the weather.

Since then, his dread burgeoned to wretchedness at the flurry of portents that flooded through his dreams. She could not die. Could not leave him devastated as Beorn had, cut down by the machinations of a despicable enemy. He'd felt his soul wither, grief baring down on him even as visions hounded him with her beautiful face made unfamiliar by the brutality of an enemy that had to be stopped.

He shivered at the foreseen devastation coming, carnage and flames consuming his people. He had to change this lethal outcome. And he would.

Boldly, he strode forwards.

CHAPTER THREE

"You are Leon Ricci of Mavishtown," Meran declared, offering the big man a confident stare.

"I am *the Mavish*," Ricci responded.

Meran nodded. This was Ricci's fighting name and one no one would easily forget. But, even if Ricci had not introduced himself as such, he too held the title of a lord marshal.

As either, he was infamous.

Though Meran had never met him in person, his father, Lord Marshal Durans, had known of him. His disapproval had been obvious.

Yet, here stood a man of at least fourscore and ten years who looked little older than Meran himself. Of course, with the Voce frequently reaching three hundred years of age, Ricci could, after all, still be considered young amongst them.

Meran's gaze skated over the bulk of muscle that marked Ricci more warrior than man of title. Power and potency brewed within that large frame, and yet each movement Meran had ever seen was fluid grace. *Fascinating.*

Gaze sliding higher, he took in the rough as granite features, only to find himself captured in Ricci's hawk-like stare. A glare so intense, it set Meran's face afire. *Caught and gawping like a mute, star-struck fool.*

Meran shook off the flush of embarrassment though his heart hammered in his chest. Now would come the condescension he often saw in the eyes of fighting men for those of academia.

It did not follow.

"You remind me of someone," Ricci said, a twitch of recognition and intrigue tugging at the corners of his lips and teasing his brow as he cast his own appreciative eye over Meran.

This, more than the look the Mavish had given him earlier, heated Meran's every nerve. He had been subjected to that same greedy gleam in men's eyes before. And one in particular.

Rune Gratian was a sensual man; composed, controlled, and cultured. Tall, broad, and imposing, like Ricci, his soft fair locks also fashioned in the short-cut style of Velkory. But his eyes, the colour of wild honey, had looked at Meran with desire…and lied to him.

The Mavish's piercing, pale blue eyes exuded the truth of the man behind them—a warrior of dangerous, animalistic barbarity kept in check by little more than an indefatigable will.

And yet, Meran's visions of Ricci had revealed nuances of authority, surety, confidence, and, in person, that magnetism bordered on irresistible.

Excitement and fear alternately plagued Meran. He could so easily lose himself to this brutal, masterful stranger. But no matter the temptation, that was not his plan. He would keep himself at arm's length.

"You were at the arena this day," Ricci continued.

"Aye, sir, that I was." Meran signalled to the wench behind the bar to bring him a pitcher of ale. Although he preferred wine to the yeasty brew, he hoped it would be cool enough to douse the flames of awareness assaulting him.

"Who are you, my bold lad?" Ricci asked. "A steward?"

Meran had expected a rebuke, but Ricci's tone seemed more amused than affronted. Pleasure and anticipation rifled through him, and he thrilled at his temerity. "Meran Durante of Dun." Chin jutting, he held out his hand in greeting.

Ricci took it with a quirk of his brow, his grip firm and powerful.

Meran steeled himself. "And I am no steward, but a scholar, and a herald of truth."

The lord marshal's eyes again flashed amusement. Meran cringed, hearing the echo of his own pretension.

"And what truth have you for me, that you approach me amidst the celebration of brawn's superiority?" Ricci held Meran's hand tight as if daring him to pull free.

Meran refused to be intimidated. He leaned in confidentially. "Nought that I'd care to share in such company, but a proposition that bears promise of future change, and with it, recognition beyond the winning of a few tourneys."

"Oh, I'm sure I have reputation enough," Ricci said, his eyes smouldering.

Meran found his hand freed.

A nerve ticked in warning. If he did not watch his tongue, his quarry's interest could wane before he had a chance to say anything useful.

"But you find me in a good and curious mood," Ricci added, "so I shall deign to hear you out."

Tension fled at his relief. Meran allowed the lord marshal to lead him away from the leaner and his ribald companions.

The back of the establishment sported a few darkened alcoves that offered what little peace and quiet were to be had amongst the sotted patrons. After sending a secluded booth's occupants on their way, Lord Marshal Ricci seated himself across from Meran, eyeing him with interest. "So, tell me, what is this momentous titbit of gossip that is too good for any ears but mine?"

At the tone of condescension, a flash of anger flamed Meran's face. "Not gossip, but a vision."

Ricci nodded, though scepticism sparkled behind his eyes.

"You think me a charlatan?" Meran tamped down his ire and considered the lord marshal's cynicism. "Yes, I will admit it, a true seer has not been seen in Locurnia for many a century, but you may take my word for it, the gift is not lost." The lord marshal's aid would be garnered at the Shimmering Fields, and on this very day, Meran did not doubt it.

However, Ricci remained frustratingly silent, as if Meran's boast was mere entertainment.

Meran sighed. He had swum in the River of Time on that blessed ethereal plain called Elysia. He had foreseen Ricci's hand wrapped around the ultimate prize and felt the future course through his body. Yet here he was, the preeminent medium, having to prove himself again. But Meran could overrule Lord Marshal Ricci's every doubt.

He smiled, his eyes flashing a challenge. "There is a glade, an isolated spot amidst Farnham's thick forests, though within walking distance of your hometown. In summer, its verge is lined with tasty mushrooms; small, hard apples fall to moulder upon the ground from the gnarled fruit trees dotting its course. There is one spot amidst the tall grasses that bears a flush of borage. The seeds were in her dress—"

Surging from his seat, Ricci grasped a fistful of the clothes at Meran's throat and yanked him upward as easily as if he were a child.

Meran clasped the lord marshal's hand as it dragged him closer to his furious expression. The Mavish's aggression burned from behind Ricci's pale eyes.

Meran tried not to panic.

A hum of chatter rose from their surrounds, followed by the clatter of furniture and the scraping of chairs. Ignoring all, Meran leaned into the Mavish's harsh grip. "Prove me false," he said.

He stared into the daggers of the warrior's gaze even as a maelstrom of disbelief and uncertainty swirled within to tie Ricci's tongue.

"I know the names of those to whom you brought misery." Meran would give Ricci no choice but to believe in his veracity.

"You will be silent, you lying pissant."

"Eain and Loni," Meran continued. "I have seen the misfortune that befell that man of your township… A man you had called friend. A man you would have called more if you could—"

Hostility as dark and dangerous as a fiery tempest rolled through the Mavish's eyes. "You. Will. Be. Silent!" The warrior's fingers imprisoning Meran by his shirt collar slid over his skin, stealing his voice.

Fear hit.

Oh gods! The revelation had been madness. Meran quashed his rising panic. He was far from helpless. Hooking one of the warrior's constricting fingers, Meran wrenched it backwards.

"Curse you, bastard!" followed a resounding snap. Meran reared free from the Mavish's loosening grip, though a thundercloud of ominous rage rolled over the warrior's expression. His fists clenched despite the pain of his broken finger.

"Lord Marshal Ricci. Hold!" Meran raised arms in supplication. He could not retreat, no matter how his instinct screamed for him to do it. He could not let the confrontation degenerate into a fight he had no hope of winning. That would not help his cause. "Hold, I beg. Despite what you think, this is not the reason for my coming here."

"Who put you up to this?" Ricci demanded.

"No one—"

"I'll have that name. See if I don't. No one threatens me with such libel."

"I am here of my own volition…" Meran may have spoken only the truth, but it was an unwelcome one, and he cursed himself for his misstep.

Ricci lunged.

Meran flung his hands high, the heavy table between them his only salvation.

"Sir, I am not here to slander you but to offer a chance for you to save the world." Meran modulated his tone to the pleasant timbre that held many of those he knew in thrall better than any magic. "This is a matter of the greatest import. A quest of the most extraordinary proportions which must fail without your aid. I am here to make you an offer."

"I am no mercenary. I am a lord marshal, and I will have the name of my accuser or do not think to leave this place in one piece."

"Damn you, man!" Meran banged his fist on the table. "I am he that accuses you. I am a seer, by the gods! You dare to threaten me."

His success seemed impossible now, even though Meran had assumed the victory assured. How? How had he managed to persuade this obstinate man to secure the future he needed to save those he loved?

"Get out." The command echoed coldly through the silent room. The weight of a myriad eyes prickled at Meran's neck, and he found himself surrounded by Lord Marshal Ricci's men, their presence an unspoken menace.

"If you know what's best for you," one of them said, "you'll do as told."

Blood rushed to Meran's face even as he strained to keep his expression controlled. He could show no weakness in the face of this defeat. For the sake of Patrice. For all those dearest to him, this was something he had to win…but not at this time and in this place, it would seem.

"Till we meet again, Lord Marshal." He saluted boldly and backed away with as much dignity as possible. With what felt like a ramrod of resolve up his back, he sauntered through the crowd with his composure intact.

Until he made it outside.

Humiliation crashed through him, his pride collapsing beneath the onslaught of shaking limbs and a rush of nausea. *Fool!* To make such an enemy.

The impossibility of gaining an accord with the lord marshal of another clan, Meran had accepted as given. He was a nobody, despite his father's position. But to hire the Mavish's sword? He had felt sure that would appeal to the warrior's ego. Especially on a quest of such import to their people. But he had wrecked his own chances with his overinflated pride.

His knees trembled with every faltering step he took down the dusty street. Dropping his gaze, Meran avoided the accusing eyes of the swarming revellers. It felt as if they knew what a fiasco he had made of the meeting. All he wanted to do was hide.

"Meran, Meran." The urgent call cut through his self-castigation. Ellom darted through the crowd, heading straight for him. *His ever-faithful Ellom.* Meran's dark humour eased, for once glad of his lover's unstinting attention. His safe harbour amidst a plethora of brutal men.

Ellom gripped and lifted Meran's jaw. "I saw what that bastard did," he said, examining the bruises that throbbed about Meran's neck. "You should not have gone alone; I knew it would not be safe."

Meran grimaced. "More fool me that I did not listen."

"Well…" All ire fizzled from Ellom's expression at the admission, and he tucked himself beneath Meran's arm. "You're hurt. Shall we repair to the lodgings for its healing?"

"*No!*" At this moment, Meran could not bear to see the disappointment in his friends' eyes. He had told them of his mission and used them to divert his father's scrutiny, but the subterfuge had been for nought.

"Pray, why not? Jon won a bet at the games and has shouted the lads a barrel of ale… and Ormand has finally arrived from Dun with news from your family."

Doubly no! Ormand, a former manservant and his dear friend, had become a factor for Meran's father on one of his trade vessels. He could not bear news of home; of Patrice, or even his younger sister, Sofie. News of lives immersed in the mundanity of villa life. Peace fated to end. Meran's attempt to sway Ricci had failed.

CHAPTER FOUR

As the door to the Broken Sword slammed behind Leon Ricci, the desire to hit something escalated tenfold. The venue had only served to remind him of the confrontation with a certain young charlatan from the previous eve that he was wont to forget. That incident had already blackened his mood, even before he agreed to meet Jordan Orr there.

Now that his audience was finished, Leon's mood soured even more, his jaw aching beneath gritted teeth. The encounter had not gone as well as planned.

Shrugging the hood of his cloak over his head at the persistent rain, he headed into the night. Gloom persisted like fog over the small township. The inclement weather, settling in at dawn, had caused a raft of cancelations. The festival's revellers now chose to indulge in the comforts of their accommodations, the streets nearly deserted.

Many a street merchant was no doubt cursing the weather gods at the loss of their revenue. If he had any belief in them, Leon would curse them too. The previous day's gains from the tourneys had been a handsome sum for Clan Ricci, and today's would have been the same.

The sudden urge to drown his sorrows in drink overwhelmed him. His clansmen awaited him at the Wrestler's Arms. No doubt with a couple of barrels with which to slake their thirst and ease the passage of time until his return. Leon quickened his pace.

The lamps on either side of the porch at the inn flared and hissed, fighting against the rain. A sheet of water cascaded from the slanting roof as Leon drew closer, blurring his view of a shadowed figure in the shelter beside the closed doors.

The man moved to hail him. Tall and rake-thin, the hood of his cloak covered a smooth, balding pate. Thagn Regis.

"What goes on here?" Leon demanded, a snarl returning to his features.

Immune to Leon's sharp tone, Regis replied, "Mistress Neve wished for me to give you this." He handed over a gilt-edged scrap of folded paper.

Taking it, Leon read the invitation scrawled in his daughter's firm hand. His passions gentled, a sudden warmth vanquishing the last of his temper.

"And my lady would have news of the negotiations with Chief Magistar Orr. What shall I report?"

Leon snorted. Olivine was a canny woman and the most sensible that had ever crossed his path. The shame of it all was that he'd had to marry her. "He listened. Made the appropriate noises, agreeing on principle, but we have no accord yet. He'll make no move until he sees fit, damn him."

Orr had been more interested in the affront Leon had caused Belton than in the proposal he had presented regarding the Prince of Atena's outrageous river tolls. Tolls that needed to be lifted if the people of Locurnia's mid and highlands were to prosper.

"Ah, that is unfortunate."

"How so?"

"Despite my lady cautioning him, Magistar Jacobi has sent a shipment of aqua vitae."

Leon cursed his twin. *That calculating little bastard.* "So he refuses to undertake negotiations on the matter himself, leaves me no recourse but to approach Orr knowing full well this will cause delay, and then sends a shipment anyway? The difference between them languishing in the warehouses of Farnham and those of Dun is the cost of those blasted tolls."

Equally, Leon cursed Ivo Dee. At the death of their king and in the absence of an heir, Locurnia's former thane had proclaimed himself the *Voce's* first primoris. Many things had changed since that day.

Though Leon had been Farnham's earl in the days of King Voltan, Dee had been duped by Jacobi's sycophantic manipulations into making him Farnham's Chief Magistar instead of Leon. If that position had been his, Leon knew he could have persuaded the Quorum of Chieftains to his cause without the need for a covenant between his clan and Orr's Midlands.

"Perhaps he thinks to beat the winter storms," Regis said. And who could argue when they both stood in the current downpour.

"You know him as well as I do. He does it to thumb his nose at me." Fate had made Jacobi the younger by half a turn of the dial, a situation Leon's twin had come to despise.

"That I do, my lord, having wiped both your snotty noses more than once as children."

Leon scowled, abhorring the reminder. Regis had often rescued Leon and his various siblings from the foul temper of their dam. More than once, the retainer had scrubbed the tears from Leon's cheeks when his mother's ravings and subsequent punishments had gone that one step too far. Being admonished to pull himself together eventually fired Leon's temper enough to have him hide his true face behind a mask of stoicism. Jacobi, on the other hand, had learned to fawn and wheedle. They had both become experts.

Regis took a deep breath and forged on. "Regrettably, my lord, Jacobi has not seen fit to provide funds for the toll should it still be required."

"That horn-headed bastard." Either Leon succeeded in having the levy lowered, or he had to fund the toll himself. *Gods!* Besides wanting to strangle his self-absorbed twin, Leon wanted that drink more than ever. Drink, and the company of real men…

"What shall I tell my lady?"

"Is the shipment already at the docks?"

"No. My lady has requested it remain at the crossroads north of here to await your instruction."

"Good," Leon said. "Have a messenger sent. Tell them they are to take the normal route through the Brua gorge. All is not ready here, and I'll not be importuned to pay for the Magistar of Farnham's impatience."

"And the other matter?" Regis indicated the paper in Leon's hand. "If I fail to take back your response, Mistress Neve is wont to make garters from my gut."

Leon smirked. He had spawned a feisty woman. A woman now of marriageable age and with an eye set on a suitor, it seemed.

"Tell me, what does the Lady Olivine think of this prospect?"

"I believe she is most content with the match."

The thought tasted like bile. It seemed like forever since his position as earl had required Leon to breed an heir. He would never otherwise have suffered a wife, and his disdain for all things female at that time had not made him a good bedfellow. It had been a miracle that the marriage had been consummated. A miracle that the singular fumbling attempt he had made produced his one and only child.

The small squalling thing had petrified him, but there had been a vulnerability about her that had soon fired to life his every instinct to protect. She owned a part of him, and none would dare bring harm to Neve Ricci as long as he lived.

"Tell her I would not miss this opportunity for the world." Even to his ears, it sounded more threat than acquiescence. He would meet this upstart that dared to court his Neve midafternoon on the morrow and decide whether he was good enough.

Bidding Regis farewell, Leon banged through the small wooden doors, complete with their pretty squares of leadlight glass, and hurried to his rooms.

"How went it, my lord?" The question greeted him as he ploughed into the well-lit triclinium, spying the four strapping men before the fire.

"Don't ask."

Orr's last words reverberated through Leon's memory. *"You will not approach Belton again on any matter. Do not fling accusations at him nor exact punishment for crimes for which you have proffered no solid evidence. I would have you confine your antics to the theatre."*

Clearly, Orr had known what had occurred the previous day. That he had resorted to a warning rather than sending a guard to arrest Leon meant the chief magistar was not completely fooled by his kinsman's version of events.

Yet, Orr had done nothing. Belton, the vile snake, still lived under the chief magistar's protection, safe from the justice Leon knew he deserved.

A depraved predator, Belton only feigned the demeanour of an innocent maid, but Leon could almost see the foulness writhing beneath the man's fawning façade. Could almost smell it like rot from the core working inexorable fingers of decay to the surface. Leon knew that man's perfidy, as he knew his own darkness.

If he did nothing, who would?

Yet he was not ignorant. He sought a boon from Orr. To at least go as far as taking his suggestions to the Quorum of Chieftains. Leon could not afford to insult the Midlands' chief magistar. He knew where his priority lay.

He had taken his leave before his ill temper forced him to a course he knew he would regret. Justice would have to wait, but he did not doubt it would come. Men of Belton's persuasion could not help themselves. He would strike again.

But Leon determined thoughts of Belton would not ruin his eve. The smells of warm dark beer and roasted goose with herbed gravy accompanied the aroma of yeasty rolls, and hunger rolled through him.

Hunger for more than the food and the foaming tankard Del held out to him. He relished the comradery of his men, their loyalty and indomitable spirit. He appreciated the sounds of their boisterous conversation and the rumbles of drunken laughter that flowed easily between them. But more than that, he savoured the scent of their sweat and their masculinity.

"We'll save that for later," he added as he joined them. He took the offered tankard from fair-haired Del, swinging an arm about his clansman's neck and pulling him in for a hard kiss. Del responded. Pure lust and the tang of beer blasted Leon's senses.

These were the kind of men he needed. Hard-working, hard-drinking, hard-fighting, hard-playing. Brash and base and physical. He immersed himself in it for hours until exhaustion and overindulgence left him senseless.

Much later, Leon roused with a groan, the banging on his door finally louder than the thudding in his head and the last vestiges of disturbing dreams best left to fade. Blearily he took in the open bedchamber and the triclinium beyond, the evidence of the night's revelry strewn across the table and floors.

Captured by bedlinen twisted about his body, Leon looked over to see his bed occupied by more than just himself. With a meaty slap to a firm naked buttock, he pushed his companion from the warmth. "Get the door, will you, and put a stop to that infernal racket."

Abel, his titular deputy, groaned almost as loudly but tumbled from the blankets. Despite the thudding torment of liquor, Leon gave one appreciative glance at Abel's fine physique as he disappeared into the vestibule. Then, he fell back against his pillows, cursing whoever so insistently disturbed him.

Too soon to be a messenger from Orr; perhaps it was Regis returned.

He heard the door swing open with a protesting squeak and the muffled murmur of Abel and another. A young lad.

Impatient, he called, "For the love of the gods! Who is it?"

The door slammed, and Abel padded back.

"'Tis a missive for you."

Leon eyed it warily, his mind and eyes fuzzy from his intemperance. It could be anyone. "Read it," he ordered with indifference and closed his eyes. A pleasurable ache burned through his body, and distractedly, he wondered what had become of Del, his prick twitching at the memory of his clansman's talented mouth.

Silence preceded Abel's grunt.

"Pray, what?" Leon sighed.

"It is a request for an audience…from Master Meran Durante."

CHAPTER FIVE

Leon came fully awake, the mention of that name burning like acid reflux. The spectre of his confrontation with Durante rose again to torment him. Memories so arresting they had dared afflict his drunken dreams with desires best abandoned. The beauty, the horror, that heightened pulse racing beneath his palm...

Heat flashed across Leon's flesh.

Oft lads threw themselves in his path, glamoured by his fame and the air of danger about him, but Durante had been magnificent. His glorious blue eyes glaring so fiercely at Leon, his exquisite silver-white hair glimmering in the gloom like a long fall of silk. The perfect mix of haughtiness and vulnerability, of courage and determination, and a body made to be bent over.

Instinct demanded Leon wrap his fist about those luscious locks and claim Durante's submission. Those eyes would worship him even as he forced that bold mouth to worship his cock. Until Durante spoke, releasing those damning words...

Gods forbid, the young fop continue to sow those ill-gotten rumours. All Leon had worked for; his clan's reputation, his legend, his daughter's prospects; even Orr's tentative cooperation; all could be lost.

No. He did not wish to be reminded of Meran Durante but to erase the taunting ghosts his pronouncements had let loose.

"Isn't this the young fellow who would hire your sword?" Abel asked. "That pretty lad from the tavern with balls as big as his purse?"

"Aye." Leon kept his face as bland as possible and tried to relax back into the bedding as if he had not a care. "Is he here?"

"No, but he would have you attend him at—Well, well... 'Tis obvious this Meran's balls are prodigious."

"And gall to match, to insist I call upon him."

Abel smirked at Leon's petulance. "Like I said. Balls!"

Leon glared.

"Hear him out," Abel said, tone reasonable. "He seems polite. He asks only if you have had time to reconsider his proposition and requests your attendance at the King's Reach for further discussion. 'Tis a fine establishment. We currently sojourn there as Magistar Orr has an exclusive wing for when he passes this way."

Leon grunted and gave him a dark look. "I wonder that you gave up such comfort for a night spent in the company of your erstwhile earl."

"I wonder that myself." Abel crawled back on the bed, straddling Leon, and pinning him beneath the covers. "There are perks to being in the employ of a chief magistar, but a large, skilfully applied cock is not one of them. Now, as for this bold young fellow…" Abel cast him a speculative gaze, as if Leon would care to enlighten him.

He did not care but gritted his teeth against his reluctance. "If he is a Durante as claimed, then aye, the lodgings would be appropriate."

After the lad's absurd assertions, Leon had expected to find him a born liar. But if he were not a Durante, then how could he afford rooms at the Reach? Leon had heard of their patriarch, Durans. A lord marshal, and from Dun, and no admirer of his. But Durans Durante was not the kind of man to pay for such a ruse.

Being the man's son could explain the youngster's audacious behaviour. Instead of approaching Leon again with cap in hand, this supposed Durante expected Leon to drop everything and call upon him. Disrespectful and reckless. No matter his apparent privilege, such attitude tempted Leon to put Durante in his place.

"That name rings many bells." Abel looked intrigued. "Didn't one of them fight in Aleia?"

"The eldest son, Beorn. You must remember him. Not a man to our taste," he gave a soft flick to Abel's dangling prick, "but a good man to have in a fight. Died in the massacre at Ustra's Isle."

"Bastards!" Anger flashed before Abel sobered. They had all lost companions on the fiery shores of Aleia's lava river to the snake people. He gave himself a distracting shake, a frown of curiosity growing across his brow. "Seems to me I heard somewhat more of the Durantes. Was there not some scandal circulating a few years back?"

"Aye. You recall the lord marshal whose wife absconded with the bastard, Belvin?"

"Ah, yes. It infuriated the primoris. Del said Jordan has not long signed an accord with the Lord Marshal of Dun. They are setting up negotiations of trade, I think, between Dun, Atena, and the Midlands."

Stunned, Leon reared upward, his movement knocking Abel from his position. Jordan, it seemed, was already manoeuvring. Yet he had chosen to say nothing at their meeting. *The whoreson!* Did he think to cut Leon out, to sideline Farnham while their two clans made agreements with the Velkor? "And you thought only to bring this to my attention now?" His voice rose.

"Leon?" Abel held his hands up in supplication as he rolled to the side. His features showed no fear, only the desire to maintain civility. Abel was good at that, always able to calm the thunder that rumbled across Leon's brow.

Right this minute, the muscles of Leon's face ached from the ferocity of his displeasure.

"I found out only yestereve and would have told you at once if you had not already been in the mood for distraction."

Leon could not deny the truth. His reticence to divulge what had been said between himself and Orr had stopped all discussion in its tracks. His men had only followed his lead.

"Such agreement does not preclude his reaching a similar covenant with you, my lord," Abel added.

Also true, but Leon did not like the secrecy. He let out a resigned curse and flopped back to his pillows. "So, what needs doing is still to find out exactly who this fop is and put a stop to his attempts at coercion." He would brook no interference from any corner when it came to the plans for his clan.

Abel shrugged, assuming the question was rhetorical. His deputy knew him well and waited as Leon tried to master his anger. His equilibrium dangled on a precipice, a lump of grief threatening to tighten his chest. He tried ever to keep the memories of those bygone days locked away, the madness of his past pressing like darkness to the edges of his vision.

He could not afford to be overcome by those ghosts; he had to remain calm and focused and conquer the threat Durante posed.

Long and hard, he considered, but nothing was as simple as running a blade through that youthful chest.

It would not be difficult to come and go from the King's Reach, unseen and undetected, and unleash his vengeance. All *Voce* had magic in some form or another, but Leon was endowed with a talent that no other had ever had. Still, the furore that would follow should the youth turn out to be affiliated with the Durantes would need to be avoided.

Almost like a gift from the gods, a sudden thought occurred. Two birds, one stone. If Durante needed silencing, then Leon needed a scapegoat. Evidence that pointed to someone else to leave in his murder's wake, and he knew of just the man. A man with a chain and a deep-seated perversion that led him repeatedly to brutality.

"When?" Leon focused his full attention back on Abel. "When does he demand audience?" Already he felt lighter, his head clearer with the germination of a plan. Now, he wished for a more memorable interlude than the frenzied sating of flesh of the eve before. His companion's body, a hard, muscular delight, set Leon's desire stirring against the sheets.

"It seems he is impatient for your presence." Abel referred to the rescued parchment that had fallen to the sheets when he had climbed back on the bed.

Leon raised an inquisitive brow.

"He wishes to conduct this interview within the next turn of the dial. '*If you should find it in your heart to be so kind*,'" Abel quoted, his curiosity now even more obviously inflamed.

Well, he could be curious all he liked. Leon did not wish for company on any visit to the presumptuous and impatient scholar. If he was a scholar at all.

Leon would take the day at his leisure. The thought of putting Abel in place and taking his fill tempted him. Enough that he refused to forgo it. He cast a leering glance over Abel's magnificent body, a warrior's, hardened and honed to perfection. He deserved Leon's undivided attention and time enough for Leon to stir him to his peak. There was no greater achievement than a man who succumbed to Leon's touch, to the power of his body rendering them insensible.

"Here," he directed, but Abel held the parchment out towards him. Leon plucked it from his fingers and tossed it aside.

As quickly as the lust took him, so did the thudding in his head, his belly roiling. Grunting, Leon threw the blankets aside and strode to the table. Sniffing disdainfully—a headache could not compare to the determination of his cock—Leon shuffled through the cups, and finding a couple still with dregs, he poured the ones into another till there was enough.

He swigged the vile liquid down.

Abel said, "Hair of the dog, eh? I could do with a dram myself." But he did not follow. Instead, he headed for the pile of his clothes and began to sift through them for his britches. "Will you attend the bathhouse ere you head for this rendezvous? I would not say no to company."

Leon wrapped his hand through Abel's hair and brought him to a halt, jerking his head backwards until understanding flared in his dark eyes. "I would have company now. On your knees."

Abel dropped his clothes, his lips parting with a knowing leer. "Not this time, I'll be bound." He pushed against Leon's hold, the thick muscle of his arm contacting those tightly lashed across Leon's gut. A growl, feral and eager, escaped Leon.

Such power, such beauty in hard muscles beneath taut skin, Abel's body wearing its history like a map to confrontation and bravery. Unlike most *Voce*, he had scars, the consequence of battle and sharp blade. Nigh on two decades previous, he had survived the rigors of the Serpent War down in Aleia, where healing magic had failed. Where all *Voce* magic had proven fallible. Abel was a worthy suitor for Leon's attention, but the Mavish would never yield his superiority.

Leon held tight even as Abel surged to his feet, pulling him close and keeping him in place with a firm hand grasping his answering erection. Baring Abel's neck, Leon leaned in to admire the thick cords of his throat and to graze the vulnerable skin.

"On the bed," he whispered in Abel's ear and started to herd him.

Leon got as far as the edge of the bed before Abel laughed. Scissoring his legs about Leon's hips, Abel took him down to the mattress in a mass of flailing limbs.

Wrapping his arms about the body that pinned him, Leon jerked Abel's head forwards until lips crashed against lips. Abel was caught, his mouth plundered in an all-consuming wave of lust that rumbled from his throat. The hot silky feel of Abel's flesh stroked against Leon in a parody of fucking even as he slid his hands the length of Abel's back, easing down his crease.

"No, no, I will not have you win."

Both grinned as they fought like a couple of tomcats, flesh meeting flesh, tumultuous and titillating as they battled for dominance.

Leon smirked as the heat rose with every stroke, every tussle. He was the tempest lashing the shore even as Abel rose like the jagged cliffs of Land's End and laughed at the pounding waves. But the

Mavish was stronger, power and passion an irresistible force in him that pumped his limbs and swelled his loins.

He tossed Abel, capturing him beneath his weight, a prohibitive hand planted to the back of his neck, keeping him restrained and submitting.

Even as he leaned to the side table and the little bowl of oil, Leon's leer broadened as Abel struggled to turn his face from the pillow. After a quick dunk, Leon's finger fell to the warm crack between Abel's arse cheeks, daring him to change those growls of frustration to gasps of anticipation.

He sank deep, quick, and fast.

"*Argh... ah, ah,* you bastard."

Leon persisted until all resistance faded and Abel began to moan.

A hearty rumble escaped as Leon palmed oil along his prick and, without hesitation, plunged deep into that welcoming body beneath him.

Passion surged. A carnal storm shook Leon with no calm to soothe the rage in his breast, no relief from the pounding. He had vanquished all defiance, had worn it down beneath the supremacy of his assault. Only the frenzied rolling of Abel's hips meeting him again and again, and the huffs of bliss breaching his lips, told of the joy of his submission.

Leon finally rolled free and collapsed to the bedding. His body glistened with sweat, and his lungs sucked air as if he could not get enough, but his cock and his vanity were well-sated.

"You are the biggest fuck-bastard that I know," Abel said as he moved to his back and threw a feigned punch.

"Aye, and you enjoyed every moment of it."

"I would have enjoyed it more had it been my cock in a virgin hole."

"You may dream. I can assure, it will never happen."

Abel snorted, no hint of surprise showing on his face, but he did not look unsatisfied. "Shall we repair to the bathhouse? I might not prefer your company this minute, but you have your wee fop to see to."

"No, first I need to sate a more mundane hunger... I may not sojourn at the King's Reach, but the Wrestler's Arms's kitchens produce a worthy spot of spiced meat, pickles, and gravy that beckons after such activity. Then to the baths...and then I have a mind to ease the dregs of liquor's malaise with a little sport of the wrestling kind."

Abel's brow rose.

"At the arena, my good friend, not in a bed."

After that, he would visit his daughter, where he might be able to discover the truth of Meran Durante, since her new prospect also hailed from Dun. And, despite the magistar's prohibition, Leon considered having words with a certain degenerate marshal from the House of Jordan Orr. He could pretend an apology and, if the opportunity were ripe, relieve Belton of a certain unique piece of jewellery...as a precaution.

"Ah. And your scholar?"

"I will deal with him all in good time."

CHAPTER SIX

"Ah, Papa, you are finally come." Long, lean arms wrapped about Leon's neck, firm softness flowing into his embrace, his nose filling with the tantalising fragrance of rambling rose and citrus.

Leon breathed it in like balm and found himself settled as if by magic. "Vixen." Only she could do this to him.

She pulled back with a playful slap to his chest and a broad grin. "Now, none of that. I'm grown old enough that such endearment is endearment no longer."

Leon rolled his eyes and took in the sight of his child. She was her father's daughter. Tall and rangy, with his light blue eyes that gleamed with stunning intensity, and waves of dark, sandy-blonde hair. Her features were well-defined, yet they possessed a softness inherited from her mother. Pretty she was not, unlike Olivine; striking and handsome described her better. "Neve."

"I began to wonder if Regis had delivered my message."

"He would dare not."

"Well, let us not tarry here in the cold vestibule. Come and meet Helios."

Helios? *Ye gods! The pretension.* Already Leon harboured a predisposition to dislike everything about this young man, even should he have answers to all his questions about Durante.

Leon took in the splendour of a deserted atrium, walls painted claret and adorned with swirls of golden filigree. Slanted rays of the afternoon sun danced on the still-damp tiles of the drainage pool, and candle stands flickered with extra light. A row of columns led to a small triclinium at its end, where a table sat, set with various delicacies to tempt the taste buds. Olivine sat demurely to one side while a strapping, handsome fellow lounged at the other.

Leon sneered. Olivine might consider this Helios suitable, not alone for Neve but for their clan, but the ability to hire such a domicile could not satisfy Leon. Not being a Ricci, the boy's wealth and clan would demand its own loyalty. Leon would not allow Neve's allegiance to fracture for the love of some pampered fool.

"The festival is fabulous, is it not?" Neve continued. "Well, except for the rain. I wish we had thought to visit before now."

As Leon drew near, Helios jumped to his feet, his hand outstretched. His smile looked forced, and his confidence feigned. Wariness dulled the resplendent beauty of unusually emerald-green eyes. "My lord. Well met."

Leon grimaced. Shades of the damnable scholar's behaviour confronted him. If Helios tried to finish the greeting with a kiss on Leon's cheek, Leon might punch him out of sheer pique.

Helios did not but resumed his seat with a gesture of invitation.

Leon turned his attention to Olivine, taking her hand and kissing the tips of her fingers. "Wife."

"My lord." She dipped her head and offered him an open and beguiling expression. No one would suspect the fierce, almost ruthless heart that lay beneath, the loyalty that had him believe her the only person he could trust with anything. He had always felt it a pity she had not been born a man, but then there would have been no Neve. And that was unthinkable.

"May I just say, sir, you put up a most stupendous performance the other day," Helios said once Leon had seated himself on the other chaise lounge. "I must congratulate you."

"Is that so?" While he might be pleased with the praise, he had not come here to be fawned over.

"By the gods, yes." Neve's ready agreement took the storm from his sails. "We all thoroughly enjoyed the spectacle. I have never shouted so much in my life; I cried myself hoarse… and you should have seen Aunt Linny."

"Emlyn?" Leon's sister was here? He threw Olivine a questioning glare. "You brought her with you?"

"She called your name as loudly as any," Neve intervened.

He expelled a grunt of amazement. *A miracle.* His sister had few words for any, wont to live in a world filled with invisible friends and a language none but she could understand. Such injury, not even *Voce* magic could hope to heal. *Gods damn his bitch of a mother.* If she were not already dead, he would take great pleasure in killing her for the abject misery she had caused.

"Yes," Olivine said. "However, she rather overexcited herself, and I have sent her home with Regis. By the bye, he has passed on your instruction, and the shipment has been directed to Brua's Pass."

"Thank you."

Leon could see she had questions about his conversation with Jordan Orr. Yet she respected the look he sent her, patient enough to await a more suitable time and place, away from present company, to discuss their endeavours. He turned his attention back to Helios, noting how Neve and the lad sat close and twined their fingers together.

Brilliant green eyes looked at his daughter with adoration, but did they also harbour the respect a daughter of Clan Ricci deserved? Before he left, there would be a need for a private word with this fellow. If one hair on her head came to harm, one feeling crushed, Helios Byzane would have the Mavish to answer to, and he needed to know it.

"So you are from Dun," Leon said. "Tell me of yourself, your aspirations."

Helios smiled for the first time, his confidence appearing genuine, and launched into a spiel that laid his life and intentions bare. Yes, his family was patrician, but he had joined the academy and trained in combat rather than gone to Dun's university. He could fight, hunt, guard, kill if necessary. He could protect those he cared for with his life...

All things that Leon felt deeply, but he could not view such a life with glasses so rose coloured. And if Durante's accusations became known, what then for Neve's attachment? Would the Byzanes view Neve and Clan Ricci as tainted by the furore it would cause?

"Do you know the Durantes, perchance?"

"Who in Dun does not?" Helios's grin broadened. "I see why you ask, and yes, that bold fellow begging for your mercy was indeed a Durante. The youngest bar one."

"We met him once, did we not, Mama?" Neve added. "At that infamous showing at the Civilus Gallery some years back. The pieces on display were stunning, and the artist was a close friend of his, although not of the same circles. Jon...*hmm*...something." She looked pensive for a moment before shaking off her memory's failure. "I'm sure it will come to me... but I can vouch, he has a formidable talent."

"Word from Dun's temple labelled them debauched and not fit for public airing," Olivine said, yet she did not look perturbed.

Neve made a rude noise at her mother's teasing. "The *Summus Sanctus* is a wizened old man who would be hard-pressed to locate his own jewels."

"Neve!" Olivine's tone held a subtle warning as if she considered their daughter's forthrightness unfit for present company.

Leon could only cheer her on and stifle his own laughter. He had once met the priest and agreed with Neve's assessment. Uncaring of her forthrightness, her beau still favoured her with a tolerant, love-struck blindness that spoke of his continued infatuation.

"I say only that he is not in wont of fun and would prefer none else have it either," Neve said. "I myself found them amazing." A pretty blush bloomed on her cheeks, accompanied by her laughter. "You should have seen them, Papa. Oh my lords, they were lewd, and beautiful and perfect, and everything dissolute bound together. And as for Meran Durante? Let us not forget him. Never have I seen a man so pretty, and clean and soft—"

"Not soft," Helios interrupted. "He near bested me at one of the open wrestling forums. Sometimes what is within can be masked by the outer façade."

Neve waved his criticism off. "I meant only that he was not as rugged and handsome as you. With all those silver tresses, if he were not *Voce*, I would think him an elf."

"I thought you were quite taken, myself," Olivine said.

"Mama!"

"Pray, what? You spoke with him for half a dial turn and could not stop talking about him."

"Yes, well." Neve pouted. "He was tall. You do not know how difficult it is to find a man whom I need not peer down upon. It was but a passing fancy, nothing more."

"And, of course, he is too young and *fraego*, which will undoubtedly portend many a broken heart in his future. And not necessarily his."

So there it was. The upstart was indeed a Durante and sullying the very name with his attempted extortion. To rid himself of the threat would not be as simple as Leon first anticipated. The Durantes had many friends and connections. Prudence demanded Leon discover if this Durante worked alone, and what he wanted, before deciding on his final course of action.

His next port of call then had to be at the King's Reach.

CHAPTER SEVEN

"Pretentious." Leon's scorn slipped free as he entered the King's Reach.

Marble steps dropped down to a widened vestibule before him. Glowing candles festooned the ceiling's large pendant fixtures, and ornaments in polished silver and bright ceramic decorated the reception area. Creepers smothered in brilliant cerise flowers covered an entire wall, their tendrils trailing to the dull granite and polished obsidian tiles of a sunken floor.

No match in pretension for his prospective son-in-law's dwelling, but frivolous and a ridiculous waste of money. Jacobi would doubtless approve of it. Leon's lips curled with disdain. The same disdain he felt for the young fellow expecting the coming conversation.

"...*I have seen the misfortune that befell that man of your township... A man you had called friend. A man you would have called more if you could...*" Durante's words circled in Leon's head, turning his stomach sour.

Though dulled by time, even now, desolation still had the power to tear through Leon at the memory of Eain. A man who had sparked a confused youth's raging hormones. Desperate lust had turned to aggression with the addition of blinding jealousy when Eain had taken Loni to wife, and it had all led to tragedy. A secret Leon determined he would take to his grave. But if Durante was a seer, then what hope had he?

No. Leon did not believe it. Seers were as mythical as the centuries-old tales of the Ether and humanity's crossover into the world of Locurnia. This Durante was no more than a brilliant swindler, but that did not explain where he had heard Leon's secret.

Bah! What did it matter? That he thought to extort a lord marshal and a renowned warrior meant the youth had earned the sharp edge of the blade concealed on Leon's belt.

He would listen and then decide if Meran Durante fronted a rival's intrigue. If so, Leon would find out the whisperer of such accusations and ensure no further secrets fell from their traitorous lips.

"Can I help you, sir?" An attendant stood on the top step, at the edge of the sunken floor, his look disdainful as he took in Leon's muddy boots and weather-stained cloak.

Leon stepped closer and looked into his eyes, even though the concierge stood two steps above him. Unease began to filter behind that haughty expression, regret already tainting the servant's superior tone.

"Leon Ricci, Lord Marshal of Farnham. But I am also known as *the Mavish*. I am expected."

The servant's eyes flared wide at that name. It alone was enough to strike fear into the hearts of most men.

"Sir…I humbly beg pardon." The concierge bowed his head and clasped his hands to still their sudden trembling. "But Magistar Orr and Lord Belton are from the premises—"

"My business here is not official," he interrupted. "I come to see Lord Marshal Durans's son."

"Master Meran?" The attendant sounded surprised, but nodding nervously, he gestured for Leon to follow him. "This way. He is to his rooms, sir. Allow me to show you the way?"

"I need no such company," Leon said. "I am capable of following a few directions."

"Of course, of course…" The fellow stopped at Leon's cold stare. "Um… Follow the western colonnade, my lord. The young master's rooms are on the right of the first juncture."

Grim-faced, Leon strode down the wide, covered terrace until he came to a halt before the final pale wooden door. It swung wide at his thunderous knocking to reveal a face made unfamiliar by tresses stained a dull-coloured witch-hazel. Cut short, the once glorious pale locks curled about Meran Durante's ears and brushed at his collar.

Leon glared in silent astonishment. What had he done to himself?

The tension fled from Durante's strained features as those stunning blue eyes alighted on him and flared with relief. "Welcome, Lord Marshal," he said and stepped aside to usher him in.

Leon entered the bright room, surprised the young fellow wore nothing more than a silk robe. Despite himself, more than Leon's curiosity stirred at the sight, and he abruptly turned to study the apartment. Extravagant furnishings met his gaze.

A bevy of young men surrounded a table laden with copious bottles of wine and platters of fruits, breads, cheeses, and cuts of cold meat. Others lounged on chairs covered with thick golden dusters. All eyes turned to him, and the chatter to silence as a wave of interest and judgement prickled over Leon's skin.

One lad stood scowling thunderously, his look familiar. This one had been at the arena, and Leon could see a fire of resentment burning in his grey eyes... But not at him. They blazed at their host.

That fire turned molten as Durante dismissed the group. "Lads, I do apologise for the interruption, but as warned, my guest has arrived."

"Best late than never." Another fellow smirked as he picked up a platter. "Here, do you mind if we take a selection of the victuals?"

Durante nodded impatiently.

The gathering abandoned the room in the way of all young men. Loud and rambunctious, and filled with a verve for life that came from being a part of the Festival of Etta. Except for the familiar youth who trailed them. He glowered over at Leon before directing his words at his friend. "You should at least have one of us for a witness."

Leon almost laughed at the lad's attempt to stare him down, awaiting the inevitable suggestion of nominating himself for the position.

"Ellom!" Exasperation filled Durante's tone. "What did I say?"

"That *the discussion is a private matter should the bastard ever show up*," Ellom quoted with a baleful glare.

Irritation settled over Durante's expression as he flung an arm about Ellom's shoulders and walked him towards the open door, talking in a low, confidential tone. Just the right pitch of depth and masculinity, authoritative and yet with an appealing touch of youthful insecurity and exasperation to please Leon's senses.

Ellom capitulated but not with good grace. Leon sensed his frustration and perversely flashed him an unrepentant smirk over Durante's shoulder. Yet he knew without a doubt, should something untoward befall Meran Durante, this was the friend Leon would need to placate.

No easy task.

Leon knew well the look of obsessive jealousy; he had once seen it in his own looking glass. Such mistrust would be dangerous and unwavering. Ellom continued to scowl even as Durante shut the door in his face.

And that's when Leon had him.

CHAPTER EIGHT

Knocking Durante back to the wall, Leon's weight imprisoned him, a broad forearm pressing across his throat before he had the chance to catch his breath. His smile predatory, Leon said, "You should have listened to your friend."

Durante pushed back, a fascinating flush of fury climbing his neck to glow in his cheeks.

Leon's superior strength held him in place, Durante's heaving chest and hips bumping against Leon unwittingly seductive. Accusation and belligerence filled those brilliant eyes, though Leon couldn't care less. Perhaps none before had ever denied the pampered Durante his every wish, but there was a first time for everything.

Leaning in and brushing his lips against Durante's cheek, Leon whispered, "Convince me why I should listen to one so ready to slander his betters."

"I have told only the truth," Durante said, voice hoarse from the pressure on his throat.

Heat burned from the body beneath Leon. Beautifully taut, the sleek muscles rippled with tension. Young, lean, unblemished, but the youth's handsomeness would not sway him. Contempt surged for Durante's righteous tone, his obvious privilege colouring everything. He was nothing more than shades of Jacobi with a vision tunnelled by cosseted self-absorption and lack of respect for the precedency of clan. This brother disgraced Beorn Durante's memory.

A sharp, ringing blow caught Leon full on the ear. Durante's fist drew back to deliver another. Leon jerked from its way, an unexpected spark of delight burgeoning in his chest as Durante lashed out, up for the fight.

A hard undercut hit Leon in the side of the ribs, and he lost a breath. Movement flashed low, Leon barely intercepting the knee heading for his groin.

Perhaps he had been too hasty in his judgement. Durante did not hold back. Leon grinned and gripped the offending limb and twisted, flipping him to the floor. He was no match for a real fighting man.

Durante managed to roll and spring to his feet, the fleet move impressing Leon. Yet foolishly, he remained within reach.

Leon's fist defied Durante's defensive block and clipped him across the chin. Another blow sent him reeling back, catching his balance on one of the golden chairs.

Durante gnashed his teeth and propelled himself at Leon's midsection. Leon caught the charge, lifting Durante, and slammed him to the wall, pinning him like a fly in a web. "Convince me," he ordered, ignoring the flash of enticing flesh as Durante's robe fell open.

"You risk your fingers again." Durante reached for Leon's hand at his throat.

Leon's middle finger cracked beneath that promise. Unflinching, he lifted his chin and ground his teeth, dismissing the injury as if it were a mere pinprick. His lips twisted into a smirk. "I have ten. Do better."

A new fear filled the young man's eyes, though it failed to dampen his determination. Those shapely lips pulled back in a fierce grimace, and the tussle continued, elbows, fists and knees employed to weaken Leon's hold. Each was battered away, blocked, or answered until the youth had almost fought himself free of his robe.

The brutal dance took the combatants into the room. Their movements, a concise choreography of blows and jagged thrusts, their music a symphony of grunts and ragged huffs beneath the merciless battering of flesh. Chairs crashed in their wake as they fought. An urn smashed to pieces as Durante hit the floor, the fury glowing on his face, as did the realisation that Leon outweighed and outmanoeuvred him. This time, Leon picked up the near-naked man and shoved him cheek-first against a tiled wall, one arm wrenched behind his back.

"My lord, please…"

With his blood high and pounding from the brawl, and his nerves vibrating with life, Durante's breathless submission was music to Leon's ears. In that moment, he smelt deliciously like prey, the most beautiful and tempting of beings. His skin was perfection, his essence a heady combination of masculinity and resoluteness, arousal, and pain.

Leon pressed in, shoving his knee between Durante's legs, spreading him and increasing his vulnerability. His voice brushed the shell of that beautifully sculpted ear with a caress of inevitability. "You put up a good fight, scholar. I am impressed, but you have yet to convince me. Tell me why?"

Leon could feel his opponent's struggle, his anger still evident in the taut back muscles trapped beneath his chest and the grimace crinkling the corner of his one visible eye.

"Because I have need of you," he cried. "Damn you, man. Only your magic can save our people. Only you stand between the *Voce* and war."

A derisive snort escaped at the blatant attempt to flatter his ego. It would take much more than that to garner his interest. "I have experience enough to know one man and his magic will never be enough to turn the tide—"

"Voltan did. The Serpent War would not have stopped but for him."

An undeniable truth that still stirred anger and loss deep in Leon's heart. Carl Voltan's ultimate sacrifice had ended the conflict with Aleia's snake people, as no one else's could, but with the king's passing, Locurnia's loss had been greater. "I am neither king nor Voltan." Leon had always been willing to die, but the difference between all other *Voce* and any of Voltan's line had been, and would always be, vast.

"Still, I beg, please, for all our sakes, you must listen."

The plea echoed with sincerity enough that Leon took a measured step back, Durante's resolve impressive. Whatever compelled him to confront Leon certainly outweighed a young man's foolish pride, but Durante remained undeterred by his resounding defeat.

Released, Durante refastened his gaping robe, though not before flashing Leon an inadvertent view of his stunning physique, from his pampered feet to the tips of his dyed locks. A spike of lust betrayed Leon as his attention snagged on Durante's thick prick—appealing even in its flaccid state. The desire to handle it surged, unbidden in Leon's nethers. A heat he ferociously tamped down.

As tousled and exciting as he might be, Durante deserved no such interest.

An awkward silence filled the space between them, Leon's attention locked on his new nemesis. "Heal yourself," he directed. "And then we may talk."

After only a moment's hesitation, Durante obeyed. Leon watched as the euphoric expression of self-healing suffused those defined features. Even before it could take up residence, Leon erased from his mind the wonder of what this man might look like in the throes of passion.

With a flick of his will, Leon healed the injury that swelled large and aching in his own hand. While all *Voce* had the magic of self-healing, it came easily to him, easier than to most except if they were marked out to be a healer. It should have been his calling…if his true nature had not gotten in the way.

All the time, Leon kept his eyes on Durante, observing as his injuries faded. He proved himself a lightweight, already woozy from the little he had accomplished, slumping onto a chair at the table to catch his breath.

Ignoring the food, Leon took up the nearest bottle of wine and a couple of clean goblets. Pouring himself a significant measure, he handed another to the youth. "So, war comes, you say."

Despite his attempt to tone it down, condescension rippled through Leon's voice.

Meran frowned. "I do indeed."

Leon waved his glass in Durante's direction. "You know this how?"

The youth's full lips thinned. "How many times must it be said? I am a seer."

"Please. Enlighten me."

"I need not your mockery, my lord. I need your belief."

"I await convincing." Leon leaned back against a column and crossed his feet. "So, talk while you still have my undivided attention."

Durante took a deep breath. "Over the last six moons, many visions have inundated me, both from the dreamlands and the river. Coming war and its horrifying aftermath are the most preeminent."

"A war with whom?"

Durante closed his eyes as if conjuring the images. "I see a man armoured in black, carrying the banner of the Prince of Atena. There is a vast army to his back and a red mage at his side."

A rude noise escaped Leon. "What nonsense is this? He would never dare." What could Prince Rane hope to gain? Why take more land at the expense of his people's lives when he had already gained that, and wealth, by virtue of his allegiance? Unless more of his countrymen wished to move from the Summer Isles of Velkor to settle on the mainland of Locurnia. In all his negotiations, Leon had not heard tell of that.

"I swear on my life," Durante said, hand over his heart. "It is the truth, and thus my mentor has bestowed a quest upon me. One that is destined to stop the war in its tracks. One that can only succeed if you are with me."

Raised brows and pursed lips accompanied Leon's surprise. "And this quest?"

"We go to steal a treasure."

Did Durante take him for a thief? There were many and varying treasures to be had in Locurnia and its surrounds, and his specific form of magic seemed particularly suited to it. Yet, not once in his life had Leon succumbed to the temptation. However, his indignation could wait until he knew more of this treasure and the identity of Durante's intended victim. Leon did not interrupt.

"They will insist on retribution for their loss," Durante continued, hand going to his dull, stained hair and running his fingers through the shortened locks. "Who would you rather their wrath fall upon? Us or the Velkor?"

"I should think it obvious."

"So, a disguise is called for," Durante said. "Do you know their language well enough to speak it without accent?"

Speak it? Of course. Had he not lived through wasted years of dissipation and madness in the city of Atena? The very heart of the Velkor's settlement in Locurnia. Leon shook off the sudden overwhelming despondency. He would not dwell on those bleak years. Not here, not now. "Who are they that you expect to fool?" The treasure could not be in Locurnia. Leon considered his face too recognisable.

"It is not I that expects you to fool anyone." Seriousness intensified in Durante's eyes. "The quest is a call from no less than the prophet."

"The prophet?" Leon's interest turned to frost, revulsion banding every muscle.

"Aye, the prophet." Durante nodded, seemingly oblivious to the sudden strain radiating from Leon's every pore. "My mentor and guide in the ways of seership."

Leon thumped his goblet down, his lip curling in contempt as a fuming rant of words rang in his mind. *You'll do as told, you little brat. We know what's needed for the likes of you.* This had always preceded a vicious shaking until his teeth rattled and fear exploded, his cries of rage and desperation going unanswered. *Holy Seus says little snakes must crawl on their bellies. Crawl, worm, into your hole."* And then darkness had always followed.

The memory had been carved into his then young and malleable psyche.

Never would he do the work of the followers of some capricious deity. He would lift not a finger for men or women of such singular blindness. This quest? If it turned out to be some damn-fool crusade, it was not for him.

CHAPTER NINE

For a moment, Meran thought he had been getting through to Ricci despite the lord's permanently patronizing sneer. But then Ricci moved, the door banging open, and he prepared to step through.

Meran threw himself against the wood with a startled *"No!"* and tore the handle from Ricci's grip.

Pinching fingers trapped Meran's jaw, his skull thudding against the now-closed door. That scowling visage breathed clouds of rage that he could almost taste as it bathed his face. The Mavish stood before him, magnificent but scary as all the hells put together.

"You dare attempt to detain me?" the Mavish demanded.

"My lord," Meran said, barely able to get the words out through the prohibitive hold, his thoughts frantic. So much for his hope that the warrior might consider the Reach neutral ground. Meran's course had not changed, but it had seemed dangerous to repeatedly accost the lord marshal as he went about his business.

Hope of success had teased him when Ricci had finally turned up at his door, but again, he had blundered. *Gods damn!* He had to bring Ricci onside. It was imperative, now more than ever. Sofie's muffled screams from last night's vision still rang in his head. The first he had seen of her in the coming confrontation, and it had filled him with terror.

Anger grew sharp and hot. He did not understand what had brought out this savagery. He gripped the Mavish's wrist and dug into the tendon until the hand involuntarily flexed and Meran gave it a furious tug. "You gave your word we would talk. Does it mean nothing?"

"I do not associate with fanatics."

"I am no fanatic—"

The Mavish growled. "Any who believe they see visions is either a zealot or a simpleton. And now I see which you are."

"So, you would risk the pillage of Locurnia, its men slaughtered, and its women raped and murdered, all because you will not accept the truth. You bastard!"

The sights that Meran had never been able to scrub from his memory came back to feed his fury. Dun consumed by billowing smoke, the rumble of horses and war machines crunching upon the cobbles, the pounding of feet, and the piercing screams. And now the sight of his little sister, barefoot and running in her nightclothes through oppressive darkness, had joined the array.

The panic flaring in Sofie's golden eyes, red curls streaming behind her, damp with anxious sweat as footfalls thudded ominously from behind, taunted him. She was but eight years old. Her screams, as a sack covered her head and strong mail-clad arms lifted her and roughly threw her over a stranger's shoulder, pierced his heart.

This future could not happen. Ever!

"You selfish prick!" Meran raged. "You consign my family to abduction and death. But it will not just be my sisters who will suffer; it will be your family, your clan. Everyone you hold dear. The enemy will spread like a plague. In blood and violence, the world as we know it will end. You can trust me on this."

"You will tell me now, what have you heard? Who dares threaten us? Speak or be damned as a conspirator."

"*Gah!* It is not whispers or gossip or intrigue. I have seen it." Meran slapped the side of his head, his chest heaving, eyes hot with frustrated tears that he refused to let fall. "It is seared into my mind. By your disbelief, you damn us to decimation."

The lord marshal stiffened at Meran's accusation, the baleful eye of the berserker fading, disbelief waging war behind his pale eyes. Beneath the hauteur bloomed a spark of real fear. It shook Meran to the core that Leon Ricci feared anything. Somehow, Meran had hit the spot, yet he did not understand how.

Meran tempered his anger and took command of his voice, pitching it low and earnest. "Was it not your express intention to hear me out? Please. Until my tale is done, I beg you, have the grace to listen."

Ricci's expression hardened, unbreakable as steel, his stare like shards of ice. For moments that seemed to drag into eternity, Meran held his breath and stilled his tongue. His heart raced so rapidly it beat a tattoo in his throat as that razor-sharp gaze contemplated him.

"Tell me, which god does your mentor favour, scholar?" Ricci asked, dripping disdain. "Are you an adherent of Hesi, Dion, or Seus?

Or do you follow Seidon or, indeed, the despicable Hads?"

Meran drew back at Ricci's vitriolic tone. Where did it come from?

Most *Voce*, while giving lip service to those traditions, professed to have outgrown the old ways and the old gods. Caught in a miasma of apathy and a smattering of common sense, they were more likely to adhere to the Voltan Doctrine. A doctrine of self-control, opposing excess and violence, and elevating consideration and the sanctity of person and soul.

That did not mean there were no lessons to be had from history— or myth—if Ricci preferred to think of it that way. There was much-needed wisdom inherent in the ancients' teachings. Who better than Meran to know?

Stomping down every angry retort, Meran grasped Ricci's arm. Ignoring the tension in those rigid biceps, he encouraged him back into the room and to the table. Ricci stood stiff and inflexible, but to Meran's relief, he did not make to leave.

Making himself comfortable on one of the chairs, Meran began gravely, "None of these. Please, please take a seat, and I will make plain."

After a moment, Ricci dropped onto a chair opposite and balanced himself on its two back legs, resentment rife in his posture.

Trying to ignore the peevish expression, Meran feigned calm. "As I have told you, I am a seer, and there is but one giver of visions. Only one that welcomes his followers to the wonder of the Elysian Plain and to the presence of the older gods. Yes, they are real, my lord. Scoff all you will, but I have felt their presence. They are like suns, radiant and fierce, but there is only one who has a care for this world. Philo Janiusz, the ultimate prophet of the Lord Who Keeps the Gates, has shown him to me."

Ricci snorted, "Philo? A prophet and a madman, and dead over a millennia ago. That is an interesting mentor."

Meran's hackles raised. "And yet you have heard of him." His works were some of the oldest volumes in Dun's university's possession. "Tell me who of *Vocekind* has not?"

"I'll admit," Leon said. "A few of my clan during their own collegiate made mention. As did my nursemaid of an eve telling bedtime stories of a ragtag bunch of survivors running from the wrath of the Ether's most renowned warriors and led by this heretic. Spare me the reiteration of such fantasies."

"They are far from fantasies."

Disdainful eyes pinned Meran in place, even as his own uncertainty threatened to choke him. How could he convince such a corporeal man to the cause when he did not believe?

Ricci suddenly brought the chair's feet to the floor with a startling bang, his eyes narrowing as he leaned closer. "Tell me, scholar," he said, his tone at once reasonable, although Meran did not trust it. "Why should I follow this prophet of yours when he is never mine? When these asinine ramblings lead you to conclude that extortion in any form is acceptable?"

Ricci's reproach hit Meran hard, his face heating at the reminder of his error. "It does not. Not ever." He leaned his elbows on the table as he stared imploringly, the intensity of his gaze made sharp in hopes of shattering the lord marshal's reticence. "What is done is done, and the price you have paid is yours, but what has come from it, what has been learned, that is what I need."

For a moment, deep in Ricci's eyes, a figment of memory flashed. Not the Mavish's nor the lord's nor even the man's, but a scared boy's. Vulnerable. Fleeting. And then gone as if it had never been. Had Meran imagined it? The possibility ached through him for what it might mean. Did Ricci regret what had happened? Though it sickened Meran— both for the violence and injury—through it, Leon Ricci had become whom Meran needed now.

Meran reached for Ricci's hand as it rested upon the table, racked with excitement at his presumption. The vibrations of his daring set his senses alight as he risked the familiar touch. He smoothed his fingers over the harsh knuckles and sinewy ridges, the potential for savagery as palpable as a sharp blade.

Lifting his eyes, Meran met Lord Marshal Ricci's turbulent gaze as he shifted beneath Meran's intent stare. Lips twitching, Meran realised he had again caught the lord marshal off guard.

He took a heady breath. "You have strength that I could never hope to own. But it is also beauty, a fierce and ferocious force, and I have need of it. Where I seek to go, there can be no mercy, no hesitation, for there is all possibility such would end in death."

A spark lit in those glacial eyes, the first hint of interest Meran had managed to induce for his quest. Cautiously, that chin tilted in question. "Where would you have me go?"

Here now, he took his chance. "To the north, my lord," he said.

"To Draca. The treasure I seek hides in the inhospitable climes of Nord's desert."

His words appeared to light a fire of suspicion in Ricci's eyes, the ridges of his near-permanent scowl rising to meet a wayward lock of hair. In the moments before emotions crashed across Ricci's face, Meran felt the irresistible draw to smooth the strands aside.

"You have found it?" Ricci asked.

Found it? Confusion crinkled Meran's brow. What did Ricci speak of? Did he already know of Meran's mysterious gem? *Impossible!* Blue and diamond-sharp, encrusted in crumbly black rock and filled with radiant and formidable power, his vision revealed the gem being recently dug from the arid wastelands of Draca. The natives named it *Anigema*, and Meran's mind filled with the enticement, the wonder of it.

But being so newly revealed to the Dracan, what then could Ricci think Meran had found?

He knew King Voltan had sent Ricci to the north on some secret mission at a time before Meran had even been born. Rumour had it that Ricci had returned empty-handed, the object of his quest a mystery to this day.

Could Ricci be thinking Meran had discovered the whereabouts of whatever that treasure had been?

According to the prophet's writings, there were only a few known objects of power in Draca. A fabled cursing staff and the missing Orb of Janus, *Amplion*. But Philo's stipulations regarding the latter's revelation remained unfulfilled.

Yet, what if Ricci, being ignorant of Philo Janiusz's writings, did believe Meran had discovered this very thing? To let him remain under this impression could only work to Meran's advantage. He could not risk Ricci's refusal. Anigema was what the *Voce* had to obtain, or the future Meran had seen would devastate them.

He chose his words with care. "I know not of what you think I have found, but I assure, this treasure we seek is power beyond imagining." Let Ricci think what he would.

Speculation played across Ricci's face. Meran had obviously struck the right chord. Here now was the catalyst to cooperation.

"Lord Marshal, if you accompany me, your reward will be the ultimate authority in this life, and glory, not just for now, but through the annals of history." He spoke the truth. This man taking up the gem was pivotal.

"Your name will be writ large in the stars and in the rapids of the River of Time. A name to be deemed great should you proffer me aid in this one endeavour. Isn't this what you fighting men want? To die and never be forgotten?" He squeezed that frozen hand tighter, demanding, begging… "So, what say you?" The sweet nectar of victory mixed with the tart taste of uncertainty sparked across Meran's tongue as he waited on edge for Ricci's response.

A wolfish grin spread Ricci's lips. That expression said Meran had done enough to give him hope.

"How can I say you nay," Lord Marshal Ricci replied. "Tell me more."

And here, at last, was Meran's opportunity. He leaned forwards eagerly and began to speak.

CHAPTER TEN

His adversary's breath grunted out as Leon threw him to the dirt. A meaty stomp to his centre back finished the job. Leon straddled the prone body, chin grasped in hand and head yanked back.

Victory at last. *Let him get out of that.* Leaning in, Leon ran a quick tongue over the crinkles of defeat lining the man's temple. Salt and the pleasure of conquest mingled in his mouth as he rumbled with almost malicious mirth.

Abel conceded with a growl that turned to a yelp as Leon bit down on his ear before releasing him.

"Ye gods!" Abel rubbed at the injury and turned a vexed scowl Leon's way. "You're in a vicious mood."

Leon's grin broadened as they both pushed to their feet.

After a sleepless night, the victory came as a surprise. A competent opponent, Abel had taken his frustration and made him strive hard for every advantage.

For a half turn of the dial, they had wrestled skin to skin. Sweat ran in rivulets across their flesh as they wrapped arms and legs about each other, each trying to force the other into submission. Now, for the first time since leaving Meran Durante, Leon felt the tension ease from the back of his neck and shoulders.

He snaked a quick smack against his disgruntled deputy's naked, sand-dusted arse.

Abel slapped him off and started towards the practice ground's singular palaestra. "I take it things did not go well with the scholar."

Leon grunted. "He changed my mind." Drastically.

The excitement that had careened through Leon at the mention of Draca and a power-filled treasure still vibrated through him.

"And?" Abel encouraged, curiosity overriding his previous pique.

"Let us freshen up first." Leon moved to allow the bathing attendant to lather his body with oil. The man scraped the dirt free with quick strokes before Leon dove into the warm water of the deep central pool, ignoring Abel's grumbled assent. But the bathhouse had ears, and the matter was of import too great to relay without regard to privacy.

The current slipped through his sweat-slick hair and rippled over him as he swam its length. Situating himself on a ledge at the far end, he let Abel catch up with him, watching appreciatively as his second's sleek muscular strokes sliced through the water.

Reaching Leon's side, Abel settled against the smooth tiled edge, his expression easing as the warmth soothed every ache. He surveyed their surroundings. "So, now that we are alone and you have worked out your foul humour, what did Duran's son want of you?"

"Not foul." *Agitated, annoyed, exhilarated.*

"As you say." Abel offered him a disbelieving look. "Anyway, please proceed."

Leon pursed his lips and mulled over the interview. "He wanted my sword, as we already knew. But more, my knowledge and experience."

"Sensible."

"Yes, he is no fool, even if sometimes he lets stupidity rule him." Durante was calculating and canny on the one hand, but on the other, impulsive and inexperienced. "But he made an interesting proposition. A quest that he says will not succeed without me."

Durante considered Leon a vicious tool to be employed for selfish ends. So, if he took on the quest, and considering what he suspected awaited at its end, there was no doubt that he would, Durante would need to reconsider that stance. The Lord Marshal of Farnham bowed to only a very few, and the Mavish to none.

"And the quest's objective?"

Leon snorted but refrained from answering as others began to trickle in, dirt-slicked and boisterous from their training. With a nod in the direction of the steam room, the pair rose from the pool and padded across the tiles towards the more private enclosure.

Abel tossed water on the coals, producing a hiss of steam, and Leon, wrapping a cloth about his hips, settled back to let the heat sink in. Sweat beaded across his skin as every muscle relaxed.

He gave Abel the more interesting facts of the proposal, his part to play in navigating their destination, along with his complicity in a daring theft.

Abel huffed a laugh. "He said 'annals'?"

Leon's lips twitched at the memory of Durante's earnestness. "Aye. A scholar and a poet together. He could charm the tits off your granddam, that one." His amusement turned a little sour. Durante's words fell sweet as honey, but Leon suspected the offer came with a sting.

"Best you go," Abel smirked with a playful backhand to Leon's bare chest, "for seems to me, from that gleam in your eye, the lad's charmed the cock off you too."

"I think not." Yet there was magnetism inherent within Meran Durante. Neve had been right. The youth was enticing with that ethereal beauty. He possessed the capacity to turn Leon's reticence on its head if he were not careful.

No matter how he argued with himself, his curiosity had already tipped in Durante's favour as soon as he had come in contact with that firm body. But he was little better than an elf in Jacobi clothing. Privileged, self-serving, fawning; all things that smacked of Leon's brother.

That such a person offered Leon this opportunity twisted his gut. That mysticism played a part did not ingratiate Leon to the cause either.

"He is certainly bold for a pup," Abel said, brow raising. "But I've not known you to back down when it comes to such a tasty morsel."

"I would be more likely to despoil my brother than I would be to take this one to my bed." Leon's skin crawled at the thought. An appealing body was no reason to lose his wits. Leon had a purpose and a goal, and he would not let wild and mistaken cravings turn him from it.

"That is an unpleasant prospect, but surely there is no comparison. Durante is young and unjade—"

"And I have much to teach him," Leon interrupted. "Not the least of it, to drag that silver phallus from his arse. He will learn, or he will die. That is a promise." The southern desert of Draca demanded caution. The tribesmen were warriors, hunters; hardened, cold, unwelcoming. "As it seems our mission is in aid of preventing war, and the retrieval of this treasure central to it, he will have to endure my command."

"So you have sworn a covenant with him, then?"

"Not in blood." To do so implied a trust that Leon did not possess. "Come now, what need?" he asked at Abel's surprise. "Are we not more civilized than that?"

"You don't believe that."

No, he did not. But, until he knew everything, Leon would not give such an oath. He would not have the Riccis and Durantes at each other's throats as a consequence of breaking a blood covenant.

"Durante does," he said, and that was all that mattered. But whether the accord they had signed saw the inside of the Covenant Registry, Leon doubted. Durante would likely give his copy to Ellom Marius. Should Leon fail to uphold his end of the agreement, there was enough bile in Marius's heart to see vengeance met, anyway. Not that Leon feared Marius's retribution, so long as Durante had not shared Leon's secrets with him.

"But this treasure you think is *Amplion* found at last?"

"For all that I baulk, I do." What else could it be? Ivo Dee had often petitioned the king for its recovery ever since reading that the smooth white orb's magic had facilitated their ancestors' crossing over from the Etherworld.

"And you consider it possible? That he has discovered the whereabouts of this fabled conduit?"

"Dee said the prophet wrote of it in his damn scrolls. If Carl Voltan believed, who am I to disagree?"

It had been fortunate that diplomacy rather than *Amplion's* mystical magnifying powers had won over the Velkor as allies, for Leon had failed in his bid to find it. A fact he preferred not to think on.

But, if they secured it now, Locurnia would never have to bow to any threat of invasion ever again. That was the only reason he had gone as far as he had in agreeing to Durante's plan.

"Then why will you not sign a blood covenant?"

"Because, unlike Durante, I do not claim to know the future. I will not willingly limit my autonomy."

Abel considered Leon's position. "A prudent stance," he agreed. "The Dracan are already wary of outsiders as it stands. They will be incensed at such a theft. It can only mean war."

"Let us hope they know not the potential power they possess," Leon said. "Or they may set the world on fire. But, according to Durante, our enemy is our own Velkor allies."

The prudence of Durante's disguise now appeared twofold. Should they succeed in obtaining *Amplion*, it would set the Draca and Velkor at each other's throats and distract Rane from attacking them. Leon had to concede its brilliance.

"You believe Durante a seer?"

"No, of course not. That talent is myth, not reality. There's been none to claim it for over five hundred years."

"That does not preclude—"

"The lad moves in privileged circles. I don't doubt he has overheard many things of interest, this being one of them. His father and Prince Rane have a close tie due to their proximity, and perhaps similarly, the prince has the same to Draca."

"But Prince Rane? He would never. His sister is married to our very own primoris."

Leon found his lip curling. "And is that not an abomination in and of itself, but I am not privy to the exact words the young Durante has overheard nor the identity of his source."

"And yet you must believe at least some of it?"

"I do."

"This news will slay Tark, you know this?"

"I would hope its finding will end his self-imposed exile."

Leon had not seen Tark in over twenty years. Not since Ivo Dee had sent his clansman on a mission from which he had not returned.

Leon had missed Tark's presence on the fields of battle in Aleia. He had missed his support in the years that followed as all of Locurnia turned to turmoil without their king. He had missed his calm demeanour and sensible words as Leon had tried to navigate the uncharted waters of Ivo Dee's new administration. And he had missed his warm companionship. They had been friends in the way that only those without the distraction of physical attraction could ever be.

But Tark's failure and subsequent descent into the pit of guilt had kept them separated. With the finding of *Amplion*, that situation could end.

Abel's expression remained sceptical. "Will you take him with you?"

Rubbing the back of his neck, Leon considered. "I will send him a missive. He is best placed to secure all that we need for the journey once we reach the shores of the Meith, but..." Leon would not risk Tark's reaction should they again fail in their objective. Leon needed to see the man in the flesh before he could decide on the best course of action. "For now, we will need transport downriver. Do you know of a captain who will ask few questions?"

Abel shook his head. "Not I, but Dak is well-travelled. I can enquire of him. He is currently in the employ of Magistar Orr...at least until civilization gets the better of him."

Leon nodded. Tark's nephew possessed the feet of a wanderer; taciturn and restless, he oft proved as nomadic as the people of Southern Draca. None could blame him with what he had lived through. "Yes, get him to get me a name, and we can enquire after a berth."

"Shall I accompany you on this quest?" Abel asked. "Seems to me another set of hands would be of worth."

"Not this time. There is still much to be done here. You will stand as my deputy and hold the copy of my accord as security against Durante's deception. You will also stand in my place with Farnham's Chief Magistar."

"And what of the Lady Olivine?"

"I will speak with her, of course." For all intents and purposes, it was her direction that Abel would have to follow. Wise to Jacobi's artifice, she knew him better than any.

But Jacobi would never entertain a woman's recommendation, though she possessed the most astute of minds. Abel had to stand as Olivine's voice. His steadfast presence and unwavering loyalty would ensure Jacobi saw sense, even if it took twisting his arm…a little. "You will accompany my lady and Neve back to Mavishtown and assure their safety."

"I will request release of my oath from Magistar Orr immediately. But what of the others?"

"They will stay. Tell Del, I wish Jordan watched, he and Lord Marshal Belton both. As for the latter, if evidence of his perfidy should come to light, all the better."

Of course, it was improper of him as a lord marshal to ask his clansmen to break the oaths they had sworn upon entering the magisterial guard. Oaths that demanded their impartiality. But they were innately Ricci's. It had taken years and much convincing to have so many of them in one man's service, but their stalwart nature had proven their worth again and again. Yet, when push came to shove, they would ever defer to him, their former earl. Leon would not give up that advantage.

PART TWO
Amidst Challenge

INTERLUDE ONE

City of Ormanca, Northern Draca

Dira felt to the depths of her bones the sudden hush that fell across the Holy Nord's great hall. The assembly within quailed beneath her resolute and unwavering disdain. She, their most powerful and infamous scroll master, had been charged to lead the procession through the cathedral's magnificent entranceway and to Nord's garish altar. She sneered. Ormanca. The city of misguided pretensions.

Trailing her, the honour guard's boots crushed the plush carpet runner, and to her right hand, the Princess Cielo let her grief steal her dignity. Tears that she had not stopped shedding since the disastrous incident from two moons previous muddied her complexion, scouring streaks through her artfully applied powders and creams.

Spread out before Dira, the well-to-do aristocracy shuffled in their seats. Their accusatory gazes followed the sorrowful procession as if it were a spectacle—a curiosity—to be gawped at and made fodder for gossip.

The prickle of latent magic stroked her palms as her gnarled fingers curled tighter about the draudwood staff. Thudding its resonating beat in time with her defiant stride, she set her wrinkled face in lines of dignity as befitting the occasion. A memorial to a dead princeling. And one they all assumed she had killed.

It was true. But it had been a mercy.

Ahead of her, a page held a cushion upon which sat a silver urn. Reduced to fragments of charred bones and ash by crystal venom, the princeling's remains sat within. All that survived of his corporeal self. The young lad carried the receptacle with grace and dignity to the altar and placed it on the golden platform.

Jedro stepped forwards, bedecked in his priestly finery. A state he affected more for the fact he served the family of the forbidden prince than that he served either the Holy Nord or the people of Draca. His expression struck Dira as reminiscent of the holy man who had turned all her plans on their head. She had been so sure of herself, but the evidence of her miscalculation now sat in a chalice. A monument to her apparent incompetence.

Dissatisfaction fomented in her belly, and her lip curled, but none would take any note. Weathered and wrinkled, the power of her beauty had long since vanished. Her notoriety now lay in her wisdom gained through decades of study at the fortress university of Alatim, and in the earth magic that she bent so easily to her will. Or it had, before her visit to Catana Keija's Outlier two months prior, where Curia Venner had made her a laughing stock.

That he had put her in her place still rankled. But she would have the last laugh. The fate of her people rested in her hands and not that upstart usurper, though he thought to sway Anigema to his purpose.

He would not.

Dira had read the scrolls, the portents, and not alone those written by their beloved Hezro but also the ultimate prophet of the *Voce*, Philo Janiusz.

Venner, a backwoods priestling of a backwoods tribe, would not be the one to awaken the power within the gem. That would take a special kind of man.

And one, it proved, she had yet to find.

She drew near the altar, taking up her position at the head of the honour guard, and awaited the eulogy.

Jedro's black gaze shifted to her staff, eyes gleaming with calculated greed. Dira gritted her teeth. It would not surprise her should he make his play for its possession. The clergy could be persuaded her reign as the most eminent scroll master had reached its end with the death of Prince Brokos bloodying her hands. Apart from the now resurrected Anigema, her draudwood staff was the most powerful talisman the Dracan possessed, and the priesthood would long to have it back.

If Jedro came for it, however, there would be a little surprise in store for him. Jedro had no earth magic, no defence against the power with which she had imbued the staff and to which only she had immunity. She almost wished he would.

The staff was useless to the priesthood other than as a symbol of authority. Authority came with its own rewards—influence, obedience, deference, power to have his word become law. But Dira determined Jedro should have no more power than he already possessed as a man of God.

The eulogy said, the hymns of sorrow sung, and Nord's words read from the scrolls brought the ceremony to a close. The priest made a futile effort to pass through the throng clustering about the princess and the altar. With each pushing to pay their last respects with kisses to the silver urn and her sodden cheeks, the crowd stymied his intention.

Dira turned for the door, sweeping the draudwood staff before her. The congregation considered it with wary eyes, edging back to give a clear path.

She sent the agitated Jedro a smirk before gesturing to a familiar figure stationed just inside the entrance. Ormanca's own scroll master. Remo was tall and dignified despite the wiry hair clinging to his head like a fungal cap of black, bleached brown and silver grey. He followed her in silence as she made for the terraces on the temple's upper levels, away from the madding crowd and their curious eyes and gossiping whispers.

He drew to her side as she stalked the marbled balcony. "Pray, what happened?" he asked, expression rife with confusion and concern, his long robes flapping about his feet.

Dira stopped, peering out to the horizon. The cityscape sprawled before her, the skyline littered with a collection of buildings rising and falling in pinnacles and waves like jagged termite mounds. Sand and slop hard-baked together for the most part, at least for the poor who were forced to the walled city's extremities.

The folk of Ormanca scurried its paths like ants about their business. "And they know not what awaits them." She shook her head. The future? Greatness or annihilation? She knew which one she preferred.

"Maki?" he said, using her formal title.

"He was not the one." She sighed. Admitting her mistake tasted bitter. "All my study brought to nought. The great gem dropped into his hand and rejected him. I have never witnessed anything so soul-destroying... Unless, of course, you count every time I bear witness to my useless and degenerate son." She had seen that gloating expression on Eno's sneering face as her prince fell to the ground, writhing beneath Anigema's judgement. Magos Eno! A title he barely deserved though she had bestowed it upon him at his incessant begging, and still, he had revelled in her failure.

Shaking her head, she damned fate. Who could credit that the gem she had sought from the moment of reading about its impending return would be found by the very tribal Outlier she had banished him to?

"But, how? How could Prince Brokos not be the man of silver? One need only look at him to see his uniqueness. And he fulfilled the other stipulation, did he not? He *was* a descendant of the forbidden prince. I do not understand."

"I know not." Dira growled her frustration. Prince Brokos had indeed been unique. A man of pale skin and white hair and violet eyes that glimmered with shots of silver. Draca had seldom seen his like, and she had counted it propitious. She had been so sure, given his lineage. "Mayhap they are not one and the same. Mayhap we made an error in our interpretation. I wish I knew." She turned from the vista and began to walk away.

Remo matched her step. "Will you tell me what happened?"

Taking a deep breath, she recited Brokos's disastrous attempt to take up the jewel. "But," she said in conclusion, "Anigema was freed from a well by a half-breed. A most interesting boy, for it seems to me that his fate and ours are inextricably tied. Falric Mislan, a slave, but one allowed to attempt his rite of passage." She calculated for a moment. "He should be five days on his journey at this time. I have demanded his blood for a reading once he has returned, but I do not anticipate obedience, either from the boy himself or his Outlier."

If she felt inclined to lower herself and agree to her son's insufferable demands, she could persuade Eno to aid her. Perhaps the boy was important enough that she would have to bend. But first, there were other distracting concerns to focus on. "Venner has gotten above his station and is fomenting insurrection with his every breath."

"Surely the southern tribes do not plan to overthrow our governance?" Remo looked stunned.

Dira snorted. "They have not the numbers, and never will, but still, they use Catana Tane and his Outlier to seek out followers. They will be a danger, not least to themselves. If they follow this path, it will be a blood bath. Brother against brother, cousin against cousin, neighbour against neighbour, and Draca will be left weak and defenceless. Do not think that our neighbours across the waters will not take advantage."

"But if Venner is the new candicio, what can we do?"

"He is no such thing. He may think having been a silversmith before he became a priest is enough to make him the man of silver, but he will learn. The south will be annihilated by his fallacy."

"Then we are bidden to do something. We must wrest Anigema from his grasp and bring it to Ormanca."

"And have it fall into the hands of Jedro?" Not literally, of course. The high priest took inordinate care when it came to the safety of his own skin. And he would never give her the satisfaction of witnessing him succumbing to Anigema's deadly benediction, but he could be trusted to use its possession to his advantage. "I think not."

"To Alatim then, and beneath your watch?"

"Hmm. I have stationed men to watch over Becchus where Keija's Outlier winters and sent some to oversee Tane's endeavours. 'Tis safer where it is until the real candicio is revealed, and we can claim it with legitimacy. Venner's arguments will be dust and a civil war averted."

Remo nodded. "That is good." They walked for a few more steps before he hesitated. "On another matter. I have had word that the slavers are active again along the Meith, both buying from our people and stealing the unwary. Should I have further fighters sent to strengthen our borders and send them on their way?"

Dira growled. "Nord curse him. Chief Magistar Bosan and his men are the scum of the earth. I wish daily for a way to be rid of them. When Anigema is in our grasp, he best beware."

Remo flashed an agreeing grin. "And the fighters?"

"Yes. There is a guard stationed at Petrucci's Oasis that is loyal to Alatim. Send them a bird with your direction and my blessing. We will allow no foreigners to taint our soil."

Now that Remo had something to do, he seemed more settled. "And in the interim?"

"We keep looking. One thing I know for certain, now that Anigema has been found, the silver man will come, and we must be the first to find him."

CHAPTER ELEVEN

It had taken three days before Dak brought Leon details of a prospective captain.

Leon now sat before a non-descript-looking *Voce*, Abel standing at his back. With his second concentrating on the noisy crowd crammed into the gloom of the Drowned Tabby, Leon took his ease to peruse the captain and his one-man entourage.

Captain Mot might be small in stature, but the companion at his back was another matter.

"He is crew?" Leon asked, though he sat feigning unconcern as he eyed the dark-skinned man. The stranger's shining black hair was long and braided and scooped back to the top of his head. As if chilled, he wore a vest beneath a heavy coat and a pair of long drapey britches secured with a belt weighted down with varying lengths of blades.

Indisputably Dracan, he made for an unusual riverman with their reputed caution of water. But despite the array of weapons, the fierceness that Leon had come to expect in that people had succumbed to a noticeable melancholy. Defeat etched across the Dracan's expression, his life force a mere glimmer, as if the fight had been wrung out of him.

"Not officially." Mot interrupted Leon's assessment. "Dak brought him to me, and I have taken him beneath my wing. Though his look is savage, I assure, he is not."

Leon nodded, his curiosity piqued by Dak's involvement, but the opportunity to further the conversation was broken by another of Mot's crew approaching to receive his wage. From his looks, this riverman was of Velkor origin.

That Mot hired as many Velkor as *Voce* aroused Leon's interest. Had there been too few of his own countrymen available to make the numbers? But if the captain drew from the pool of those in this tavern, he may have had little choice. It hosted an equal number of both of

Locurnia's peoples. And now Mot had added a Dracan to the mix, proving himself a most unusual man.

Coins changed hands, and with the ledger marked, Mot turned his attention back to Leon, an apology etching his brow, the long grooves deepening beside his mouth.

Leon appreciated the deference, but there was no need. The crew took precedence, for what was a captain, or any leader for that matter, without loyal men. He interrupted the captain's apology with blunt words relaying his requirements.

"When next do you set sail? I have a few things still to attend, but haste is imperative."

"At dawn, my lord," Mot answered. "Should I ensure a berth is available for you and your young companion?"

"Aye, that should give me enough ti—" Even amidst the sounds of revelry that surrounded Leon, the purposeful advance of footsteps and the swift movement of Abel bent on intervention grabbed his attention.

One glance and Leon swivelled in his chair, taking in the unexpected presence of Durante caught about the arm by Abel's impeding grip.

"What by all the hells are you doing here?" Leon demanded. Did the boy have no sense? The difference between the King's Reach and the riverside hovel was as vast as Aleia's swamps and the snow-crested peaks of Farnham's mountain range. It was not safe. Especially with Durante painted and primped as he was, like some common bawdy trollop.

The last Leon had spied of his pending cohort, Durante had been ensconced in the dilapidated town library leafing through scrolls and sifting through ancient tomes. A far more fitting setting for a scholar, at least, if not for the son of a lord marshal. "Are you following me?"

"No, my lord." Durante sounded momentarily indignant, but, ignoring Abel's hold, he leaned closer, his anxious gaze catching Leon.

A feather of foreboding prickled across his nape; surprise buried beneath curiosity. "Pray?"

"You must come," Durante urged, a hand reaching out as if to drag Leon from his seat only to be self-consciously withdrawn. "Please, sirs, there has been a most dreadful…incident."

Any hesitation died beneath the imperative of Durante's supplication. His imploring expression, as much as intuition, told Leon no foretelling had forced the young man's approach. So unexpected.

Still distrustful of each other, they floundered in unfamiliar territory despite their agreements. What could have occurred to make Durante seek Leon out? And in such a wretched location?

Taking a deep breath and centring himself, Leon rose to his feet. "Tell me."

"A-a... I fear, foul murder." At the admission, Durante's face drained of its remaining colour.

Leon's jaw clenched at the instant assumption that came on the heels of those words. There were many cutthroats in these parts who preyed on the vulnerable and unwary; it might not be Belton up to his old tricks. Still, Leon's gut twisted at the possibility.

"Captain? You will accompany me." He glanced Captain Mot's way, unsurprised by the tension that rippled around the table, though their conversation had been little above a whisper. Tension that rolled out like a wave to drown out all revelry across the tavern room. A strained silence ensued, all eyes settling on the captain who, in these parts, would be recognised as having the ascendency.

Captain Mot acknowledged Leon with a nod.

Waving Abel off, Leon's attention fell on Durante. "Lead the way," he said, the order softened by a conceding gesture of his hand.

They hit the cobbled street behind Durante, the patrons swelling them to a crowd as he led them into the maze of streets of the township's River District.

"What are we doing?" Abel's confusion rang clear. "This is Belton's jurisdiction."

"More's the pity. But I refuse to send for that reprobate until I know the extent of the situation. I will not risk interference with my and Durante's plans."

Leon could feel the weight of Abel's curious gaze swinging from the figure they followed back to press against his consciousness. "That is Durante?"

"Aye. And going by the moniker of Zachary the Fisher for the duration."

"When did this happen?"

"The disguise?"

"Of course."

"Since last you met, obviously."

From the corner of his eye, Leon could see it had made an

impression as Abel nodded and murmured, "Rather stunning."

Leon scowled, floored by the spike of irritation that struck.

"I spotted him at the Tabby and had no notion it was him." Abel shook his head with a look of wonderment. "Thought he was just some highbrow dandy from Atena slumming with the great unwashed for a change of scenery. Certainly had enough of the Velkor drooling over him like he was spun candy."

Leon could admit the paint on Durante's face accentuated his blue eyes enough to make them pop like fallen fragments of sky and contour his face to that of an angel, but... "He is a strutting peacock." Something Leon refused to be taken in by. It surprised him that Abel was, especially by a look so distinctly not *Voce*.

If Abel had a retort for Leon, it died on his lips as Durante pushed his way through a restless crowd stationed at the mouth of an alley.

Wariness and anger hummed in the air as Leon followed, the crowd from the Drowned Tabby weaving together with those already in position. A mob in making if common sense did not prevail. Tension coursed Leon's back and tightened his muscles in preparation for whatever the circumstances called for.

The shadows grew longer. Chill fingers swept the dark stone as Leon surveyed the scene and the one man standing beside a pile of debris at the nearest intersection in the alley.

With his dirty blond hair, storm grey eyes, and tough physique, Leon recognised the fellow as one of Durante's close companions. The young man stood as a barrier to the crowd's curiosity. An urchin bent on defying that intent succumbed to the man's implacable grasp on his tattered shirt, though his protests filled the air.

Durante joined his friend, his features schooled to radiate a calm Leon doubted he felt. Affixing his gaze on the captain, Durante followed Leon's unspoken directive. They were surrounded by river folk, and Mot had no doubt hired many of their family and friends at one time or another. That Durante recognised the subtility in play impressed Leon.

"Good sir," Durante began his address. "I know that this is a most tragic situation that my companion and I stumbled across—"

"Don't listen to 'im. He's lyin'." The urchin abandoned his attempts with the blond fellow and gripped the captain's arm, scrunching the sleeve of his long coat in his distress. "I been looking for Bas for an age and I spied 'is shoe by yon corner and came in 'ere to see that one leaning o'er him, and he not movin'.''

"He would not tell us his purpose in being down Scutter's, sir," an older Velkor added for good measure, and Leon snorted. Not murder of a certainty. Durante did not have it in him.

But many bawdies were scattered hereabouts, though they fell far short of Leon's forgiving standards. They were unlikely to tempt the son of a lord marshal. Too polished, too pristine. Durante did not look as if a scrap of dirt had ever caught beneath his nails, nor a callus graced his palm.

The thought of sullying him up struck Leon out of nowhere, his face heating at the intensity of the image enlivening his imagination. He shut it down with all haste.

"I beg," Durante stepped aside without a beat missed, "you and the lord marshal, please inspect this for yourselves."

The crowd murmured at Leon's presence as if only now realising he was there. They did not seem to care that he hailed from Farnham. The title alone flushed them with deference.

"After you, Captain." Leon gestured.

People milled, muttering hushed whispers that echoed their horror and dismay as the captain bent to examine the remains.

The unseeing, unmoving eyes caught Leon, desperate in their vulnerability. He knelt across from Mot. The corpse's flaccid face, grey; a silenced cry of hopeless anguish forever marring those colourless lips.

There had been pain.

Leon pushed off further debris. There it was. The mutilation at the chest and groin, and if he turned the body over, there would be more, a telling tale of the depravity that the boy had suffered.

With his suspicions confirmed, anger rose in Leon like a furious force about to consume him.

Abel hissed under his breath, a hand massaging the back of his neck in a motion of self-comfort. "It is the butcher's handiwork."

Leon gave a curt nod. "There is evidence of injuries consistent but the fish and rats have been at him." Still, the authorities of the Shimmering Fields would have to be called, and that meant Belton. Where once Leon had thought to use the butcher's crimes as a cover to take out the threat Durante had posed, the reality left him cold and sick inside.

So often in his life it had been kill or be killed. He could run an enemy through with a blade without qualm or hesitation, but Durante did not have the right of him. The berserker did not rule Leon Ricci.

When his blood was high, and circumstance called for it, he let the beast in him free to rage. He became every bit his fighting name, and as the Mavish, he could hack an opponent to bits, make them bleed, and demonstrate his superiority. But Leon did not possess this monstrous capacity to render the innocent helpless and hopeless. Not like this.

Thank the gods, he believed Durante a threat no longer.

He scrubbed his face as if trying to dislodge the bitter taste, the fury that his hands were tied. What kind of a man was he that he let this perfidy go unchallenged? Yet, here again, he lacked the evidence to tie the butcher's handiwork to the lord. And would never if Belton were in charge of those sent to investigate.

"'Tis him, is it not?" the urchin called, trying to get closer, but Durante's companion again stepped in the way.

"No, boy."

The urchin fought against him, struggling and kicking. "Take your 'ands off me!"

Mot rose to intervene, gesturing to the huge Dracan who wrapped a big arm about the distraught lad, holding him steady while humming a soft lullaby into his ear. Mot knelt, bringing himself level as the boy went limp. "Tell me, how long have you been searching for your friend?"

Tears of misery streaked the urchin's dirty cheeks. "Bas's been missing come three days now, and I was so torn. It weren't like him, sir." The boy began to cry, the realisation that he would never see his friend alive again bright in his eyes. At a nod from the captain, the Dracan hefted the shaking body into his arms. As if the boy were no bigger than a babe, the big man carried him from the disturbing scene, still crooning and patting the lad's back.

Leon stepped up to the captain. "Send someone for the militia. Have them survey the scene and then send them to the Drowned Tabby. We will gather any witnesses there for questioning."

"And the boy's accusation?" Mot gestured to Durante's companion.

"It will not stand. The militia will discount his tale once they have seen the body. The poor soul has been gone for days ere either of these two stumbled across his remains. Besides, the tall one is Zachary. My ward, at least until I have seen him on his way."

"Ah." Mot nodded. "This is your companion? I did wonder at a Velkor coming to you in the first instance. It is unusual for them to trust a figure of *Voce* authority without the backing of the Ambassador of Atena."

And despite that Durante trusted Leon with his quest, he had never placed absolute faith in him either. There had previously been reticence to acknowledge Leon's leadership. Had instinct overruled Durante's reluctance? Unexpected pleasure flashed through Leon at the thought. Perhaps he would prove more reasonable than Jacobi after all.

But Leon needed this inquest over and done as soon as possible. He had agreed to Mot's price and would not allow the grisly find to delay them.

With that in mind, he directed the gathered river folk back to the tavern, and Mot sent one of his rivermen off to alert the constabulary.

Leon shot out a hand to detain Durante as he made to follow the horde. "You have done well to keep up the ruse that you are not *Voce*, but it is imperative that from this moment forth, you are Zachary." He included Durante's companion in his glare. "Every question, every thought comes from him."

"Understood." Durante nodded.

"Who is this butcher your companion spoke of?" the blond fellow asked.

"Someone that has gotten away with murder one time too many." Leon's scowl deepened. One day there would be a reckoning, but that would have to await the securing of *Amplion*. "For now, however, answer the questions as truthfully as you can without giving away Zachary's true identity, and then be on your way."

"Aye, my lord." The young man followed the retreating crowd.

Leon held on to Durante, the lithe bicep beneath his hand taut with tension. "As for you, I have yet to hear why the both of you were found skulking about in this dirty backwater alley and placing my plans in jeopardy…and it best be good."

Durante barked out a nervous laugh. "Nought easier. We were testing my new look," his cheeks flushed, no doubt pleased with his success if Abel's and the rivermen's reactions were to be considered, "and spotted you. Not wishing you to see me like this, we tried to make our escape unseen. But when… Well, I had to alert you."

A pleasurable burn of pride heated Leon's chest at the evidence of Durante's implicit trust. A foolish emotion; he quashed it with a deeper scowl.

"Hmph! Well, be at the docks first thing on the morrow. We have berth on the *Galacia*. Do not do anything that might hinder my plans further. Once I am free of the constabulary, I will meet you at the King's Reach to discuss this further. Be ready."

CHAPTER TWELVE

Belton's justiciar sent three stone-faced militia men to the Drowned Tabby to gather what evidence they could. The Velkor's ambassador had followed soon after, no doubt to ensure no miscarriage of justice came to pass.

Leon judged the Velkor an efficient emissary, commanding respect not alone from his countrymen but also from those of the constabulary. Durante, in guise as Zachary the Fisher, had charmed the man with his studious demeanour and that enthralling voice he possessed. He had garnered much attention to the point irritation curdled Leon's stomach. But it had facilitated an easy investigation for Durante, his disguise remaining intact through the entire process.

The added flick of powders and slick of kohl, Leon had to admit, worked to shore up the look. And Durante's speech, accent, and inflection were impeccable. A rival to Leon's own. It was all impressive, even though it spurred his resentment.

Durante's companion—the infamous artist Neve had found so intriguing—had not fared so well. One of the lawmen had taken an instant dislike to Jon Reko. Still, they had both been released an hour earlier. Thorough though he insisted it be, Leon had to suppress his impatience for the repetitive and interminable process to be completed.

No amount of investigation would ensure guilt landed where it should. Like a storm, anger and helplessness raged through Leon as he strode down the colonnade leading to Durante's rooms a turn of the dial later.

Reaching the colonnade's juncture, he heard raised voices and drew to a stop, cautious of what situation he might be walking into.

"...I want *my* Meran back," a voice Leon recognised as Ellom Marius declared. "And don't doubt that I will have him."

"I am not *your* Meran!" Durante's response came rife with

frustration. "You make us something we were never. Right from the start, I warned you not to do this."

"So I am nought to you but a tool to be used."

"No!"

"I say yes, and gods' be damned to you."

From around the corner, a door slammed, followed by angry retreating feet stomping the corridor away from where Leon lurked. *A lovers tiff?* Thank the gods he had not been a few moments earlier. In his present mood, he had no patience.

He waited a moment in the descending silence to see if Durante would give chase. He did not.

Leon grimaced. *Trouble in paradise.* Yet how could it be any different? Such possessiveness always led to difficulties. Marius had many lessons to learn if he wished to keep a man. To cling so tenaciously was not one of them.

Leon finally rounded the corner to find the abused door to Durante's rooms standing open. It had failed to click into place.

He did not bother knocking, expecting Durante to be drowning his sorrows in a glass of that magnificent wine he kept ordering, but the room stood empty.

The King's Reach, being of marble construction, rendered Leon's farsight useless in tracking Durante down. More silence met his low call.

Scanning the room, Leon headed for the tiled wall at the rear, a flickering glow of light illuminating the entrance.

He found himself standing in a private bath chamber, steam rising from a deep pool ringed about by a myriad of lit candles. *What had he here?* His curiosity rose as he took in the room's luxury.

Leon did not usually hold with the banality of seduction. A good fight and a hard fuck were all he needed. But even he had to admit this was a most romantic of rooms.

"Ah, finally, you are here." Beginning to shed his robe, Durante turned at the sound of his presence. "Lord Marshal!" He caught the garment mid-fall, a glimmer of embarrassment and vulnerability shimmering across his unguarded features.

Leon was obviously not whom he had been expecting.

Yet at the sight of enticing golden flesh, the unbidden beast of desire surged to the very extremity of Leon's skin. Meran's lithe and sculptured muscles and the taut and peaked orb of a tanned nipple called to him like a siren song. Here was beauty and possibility. A combination that promised to shut out the ugliness of all that Leon had seen that day, taking him down to the minutiae of need and distraction.

Before common sense caught up with him, Leon herded Meran into the corner, so close their breaths mingled. "Let it go," he commanded.

To his satisfaction, a fire of acceptance flashed behind Meran's eyes. He let it drop. *Ah, so compliant. What a treasure.* The beast growled within Leon.

He wrapped his fingers around Meran's chin, a firm and captivating hold, keeping him in place, to be subjected to his mercy. To be explored and admired and tasted. To be owned in that moment but never to be possessed.

The heat of their bodies touching freed in Leon an explosive need that blinded him to all but Meran's chest heaving as breath panted through those defined lips. Daring him to take, to kiss. A world of hope and sensation far away from the despondency and darkness of murdered innocence.

An audible swallow accompanied a shiver racking Meran's perfect frame. Leon's attention flicked to capture Meran's gaze and read fierce want there.

Meran pressed his body against Leon, silently clarioning his affirmation, his prick hardening along Leon's groin. But the mind behind those stunning windows to the soul shouted for caution. "Sir! Wha—"

"I wish to command you," Leon said, grazing his scruff-shadowed cheek against Meran's smooth one. "Will you bow to me?"

A small whimper was all answer he received to his seldom-asked question. The one advantage of having carnal knowledge with like-minded clansmen and friends, Leon knew them down to the letter of their smallest desire. This youngster remained a mystery yet to be solved.

"What say you?" He tasted the beads of sweat dotting the young man's jawline from ear to neck, his hand exploring in a teasing, featherlight caress over that firm chest. Gently squeezing, Leon plundered the bud of Meran's nipple. The resultant shiver and whine beneath that touch served only to urge him onward.

Leon bit back an enthusiastic growl, his gaze in tandem with his palm sweeping over the array of Meran's smooth, honed abdominals and tight, flat belly. Abel had the right of it; even in the midst of his disguise, Meran was stunning.

He swirled a finger in Meran's navel before traversing the trail of pale hair, so discordant with those on Meran's head. It thickened into a delicate cradle, shimmering in the candle's flickering glow like spun gossamer.

From that silver bed, burgeoned an impressive and tempting prick. Straight and generous, with skin as delicate as satin. Leon grazed its length with the back of his hand and felt it flex with anticipation.

Though he bit his bottom lip, as if to hide his natural response, Meran's breath quickened.

Leon grinned, determined to turn that plaguing hesitancy on its head.

He filled his palm with that glorious flesh, curling his fingers about its girth before he leaned in. Beneath his lips, the plush softness of Meran's trembled, yet only for the briefest of moments before Leon felt an answering curiosity.

The slow exploration became a fusion of greed and want, his blood heating as Leon tasted man laced with a hint of mint.

Lips imbibed and demanded. Teeth clashed, and tongues forged back and forth until Leon's skin tingled. It was as if ozone bursts danced like wild magic over his body, and he struggled against his deepest and most primal needs.

He was here, not to take advantage, but in recognition of Meran's patent submissiveness and his own penchant to dominate. He would open Meran's eyes to his specific form of tutelage, with a slow and steady hand.

Even as he drew reluctantly back from their kisses, Leon exacted a measured stroke from root to tip, the shaft warm and weighty beneath his hand.

"Tell me," Leon said, gliding back down again. "Say it." And back up. Firm and excruciatingly slow. "Tell me you want more."

Meran cleared his throat only for a groan to escape. "I-I...I...want..." The rosy flush of his cheeks deepened, his struggle appearing interminable. Leon continued the infernal dance meant to destroy all and any resistance.

In the depths of those amazing blue eyes, Leon saw want glow fierce, strummed to fire by the urgency of Meran's own rampant passions. Yet he looked wracked with indecision.

Leon cast about the bath chamber, gaze landing on a bottle of cleansing lotion close to hand. Deft moves had his palm slicked and returned to its administrations, allowing Meran little time to think.

A ragged, encouraging groan accompanied a shudder as palm and lotion glided along that beautiful cock. "Ah, yes…yes. Yes, please…more." Meran's thigh muscles clenched as if he battled the insistent desire to thrust into Leon's fist.

The death of caution flashed behind Meran's half-shuttered eyes. Hand and body fell into rhythm; one ruling, one begging. Leon cupped Meran's chin, holding him steady, gaze glued to the open-mouthed urgency, the flaring nostrils, the rolling eyes, and smiled victoriously as Meran began to come undone.

Bending at the knee, Meran forced himself in short sharp bursts through Leon's fist.

Satisfaction like fierce heat burned in Leon's chest as clear fluid flooded from Meran's slit and streamed down the back of Leon's hand. A testament to the extremity of his arousal.

"That's it," Leon encouraged, dragging his palm to the tip and twisting around Meran's glans. Repeating, he strummed faster, revelling in the phallus's sudden expansion. "Now, now. Give it to me."

An inarticulate moan escaped Meran's throat, his hips bucking. He raised a hand as if to grab Leon and hold him, but it fell away. Permission had not been given. Leon's pride swelled along with his cock at the sight of the fulsome strings of ejaculate.

Thrown back at the moment of release, Meran's head thumped into the wall. Pure bliss spread across his expression, his mouth slack, his pleasure sighing out in strangulated huffs that punctuated the air as each milky jet pulsed from his body.

Leon swiped his hand through the glorious mess, coating his fingers. Primal instinct insisted he press Meran up against the wall, spread his firm cheeks, and paint his delicious pucker. It urged him to forge inside with demanding fingers and ready Meran for the fury of his invasion.

Yet the desire for a slow and enticing seduction eclipsed Leon's impatience. Meran Durante was a canvas crudely painted. Leon had the ability to forge their connection into a masterpiece. His commands, like sweeping strokes, would blend passion with submission. He would teach and master, and Meran would revel in his supplication. Their reciprocal desires served only to heighten each experience to a level Meran had unlikely known before.

The possibilities danced like a craving through Leon's imagination. Gone was the want to experience a swift, plundering incursion. That was the Mavish's way, and Leon wanted more. They would be in company for weeks. What need was there of haste?

This prospect, Leon dared to seal with unhurried, wet kisses before pulling back with a possessive and satisfied leer. "Well, well, will this not make for an interesting adventure."

CHAPTER THIRTEEN

"Yes. Fuck me, own me." The plea shrieked through Meran's mind and tipped his tongue.

He looked into those sharp, turbulent eyes sparking with promised passions as they devoured him and ached for Ricci to take him where he stood. Any time; each and every day. His body vibrated with the intensity of his craving. That touch, those commands, fired Meran's blood hot enough to immolate him.

Yet he could not get the words past the alarming depths of his need.

He wanted to experience everything, drawn by the gathering of the potent ethereal magic that sparked to life at Ricci's tone, his words, his body overshadowing Meran. Power had surged down the length of Meran's spine like lightning streaking across the horizon, and he had bowed to it like an addict.

Even now, his knees trembled from the magnitude of his release, as if they begged to fold and drop him to the floor. He wanted more, wanted to offer Ricci his bruised lips and open throat this very minute.

But a persistent knocking came from the other side of the servant's door. "Master Meran?" A middle-aged maid popped her head around the opening in the far corner of the bath chamber, her quick gaze taking them in.

Meran stiffened, the consuming haze of lust clearing like windblown fog.

Ricci stepped back, cool air rushing to fill the gap where once there had been only heat, and turned his daunting attention on the woman. "Who are you?"

"I have come to attend the young master, as he requested." Her expression remained unperturbed by Ricci's ominous tone.

"Holy Janus." Furious heat flushed Meran's cheeks.

She turned to him. "If you are indisposed, I can return."

"Ah… No, no. Now is timely." Yet with Meran's spend still

spattering his thighs and across his belly as well as dotting his pubic hair, she could not fail to realise what she had interrupted.

Meran pushed past Ricci, his blushes refusing to dissipate as the woman nodded and set down her bucket, looking expectant.

Could he do this in front of Ricci without his embarrassment becoming complete? The lord marshal might think him craven.

He had known Ricci would attend him after finishing with the constabulary, but Meran had thought to be finished with these particular ablutions before then.

He cast a furtive glance Ricci's way. Curiosity burned back at him.

"Timely?" Ricci asked, his quizzical gaze sweeping over the maid, the bath, and Meran.

"Yes, very." Meran chided himself for being a fool. More than anything, he wished for the time to reciprocate, yet part of him knew the interruption had been propitious.

He could not afford to throw himself again into the path of a dangerous and dominant man, the outcome of which would only facilitate his greater turmoil. He needed time to breathe, to ponder the consequence of such an unexpected turn of events.

"For what, may I ask?"

"Um…nought. Just something I had thought of earlier." Flustered, Meran grabbed his discarded robe and wiped himself clean. He swallowed hard. Dare he ask for a bit of privacy? But Ricci now squinted at him with eyes of suspicion and the look of one determined to stand his ground.

Meran gave in. What did he have to hide after what they had just done? Nothing.

"I am ready," he said to the maid.

She came to him, a thick foam of soap, linen, and a thin sharp blade gleaming upon a platter.

Meran submitted to her as she lathered his chest, trying to ignore the sceptical twist to Ricci's lips as he observed the goings-on. Ricci offered no comment as the woman began to slick the blade over Meran's few chest hairs, her hand deft and steady, and they were gone.

"And this is in aid of what?" Ricci finally ventured.

The blush returned with such ferocity Meran wondered if he had any skin left on his cheeks. Yet guilt bit deep at his libidinous reaction to a Velkor riverman's attentions at the Drowned Tabby. It was an attraction that sang to his soul in a life that had become cloistered and lean, Ellom's expectations haunting him.

From the very outset of their relationship, he had warned Ellom it was not to be exclusive. Notwithstanding, the more time passed, the less Meran felt at liberty to indulge. Even his liaisons with Ormand had petered to nothing in deference to Ellom's displeasure.

For both their sakes, Meran could not allow this to continue. In the guise of Zachary, freedom beckoned him. So, why should he not think to indulge?

Meran sighed. He considered admitting nothing of this to Ricci, whose frown evidenced his resolve to get to the bottom of this apparent mystery. But why should he hide anything? "My disguise, of course."

He and Jon had visited the Drowned Tabby on the premise of gathering further information that Meran had failed to learn from his studies. Moreover, he had wanted to test the effect of Jon's embellishments, the success of which had confirmed that the disguise needed to be more… *thorough.*

The possibilities afforded a primped-up Zachary had thrilled through Meran like a child rushing through fields of hay. Like sunshine and fresh air and uninhibited joy in the freedom to play.

Upon his return and before his inevitable altercation with Ellom, Meran had asked the attendant at the reception to send someone to complete his transformation. If Zachary's fancies ever happened, Meran could not risk the disparity of his hair above and below giving him away.

"Your disguise demands you shave?" Ricci asked before enlightenment filled his eyes just as the maid directed Meran to perch on the edge of a tiled ledge and open his legs. "Ah."

Amused laughter rumbled through Ricci's Cheshire grin as she began to deal with the hairs about Meran's loins.

Meran had never felt so exposed; his lascivious intentions laid as bare as his body. It was something he had never intended the lord marshal to see for fear of the advantage it would lend. Especially with what he had just allowed to happen.

When Ricci retreated to the triclinium, taking his laughter with him, fear that he would take his leave had Meran on edge. He stifled the urge to follow, admonishing himself that he must trust the covenant they had forged between them. Even if it had not been sworn in blood, Ricci had given his word.

Meran's heart only settled at hearing the clank of glass and decanter meeting and the slosh of wine pouring. The creak of the chaise beneath Ricci's weight followed. Then silence, as if Ricci's patience was eternal, while Meran himself indulged in frivolousness.

Yet Ricci's amorous attentions had come as a shock. As had his declaration. *"I wish to command you."* He had asked, demanded, ordered. And Meran had capitulated without thought, as if Ricci's voice had the power to bend him to his will.

Ricci was more dangerous than ever Rune Gratian had been.

Gratian had been regal, intense in his interest, and reasoned in his dominion. Harmless with his machinations, or so Meran had assumed when he'd given up everything. But he had been the very reason Meran had chosen Ellom to fulfil his unexplainable desire for submission. Ellom was safe. There was no safety with such men as Leon Ricci. Especially with what lay ahead of them; and what Meran had allowed Ricci to believe the goal of their quest to be.

Though the body in the alley had revealed a deep-rooted instinct to trust Ricci, the lord's penchant for taking command stirred Meran to caution. As seer, he had to control the narrative. He had to straighten the record or at least set them on the path of mutual equality.

Meran shivered with anxiety as the maid ended her ministrations with a dab of balm over his tender bits.

"Is there anything else that I may attend?"

"No, no. That is all, and most satisfactorily done, thank you."

She took her leave, and Meran's stomach clenched in turmoil. The coming conversation sat heavily upon him. Still, he was no coward. It had to be done.

Ignoring the strangeness of his denuded skin, Meran pulled on a pair of long breeches and a tunic that covered every other inch of his body. Affecting a demure cast, he exited the bath chamber.

With his colour high and an air of reluctance, Meran seated himself opposite Ricci, who wore a self-satisfied smirk in the placement of his usual scowl.

Meran gathered his courage and forced down the guilt that he must destroy such an uncharacteristic semblance. "Ah, Lord Marshal... I must apologise if my behaviour"—he flicked a shame-faced glance towards the abandoned bath chamber—"has given the wrong impression, but...I think it best we take no further what was begun between us."

The goblet froze mid-motion on its trek to Ricci's parted lips as if he had been struck speechless. Whate'er had produced the smug, congratulatory look died beneath a shard of hurt and disconcertion that flashed across the lord marshal's expression. A reaction that took Meran by surprise.

A thudding heartbeat later, Ricci's impressive brow descended like a thundercloud, accompanied by an ember of irritation sparking in those sharp eyes.

Meran held his breath. A shiver coursed his spine at the terrifying prospect that the Mavish would awaken to mete out his displeasure.

Gods have mercy, to poke such a bear. But what else could he do? His position must be made clear for all their sakes.

To his relief, Ricci did not explode from his seat, though his voice rumbled like damnation, "What say you? You beg me for release and once given—"

"No, no. My lord. It is not like that. I-I… You…" Meran shook his head at his own inconstancy. He could not afford to cower before the rogue demand to capitulate to such a man as this, no matter its insistence. The quest's objective was too important. Chin raised and jaw firm, he hardened his resolve. "I am not in the habit of taking my pleasure and offering nought in return, but it was a mistake, my lord. With what is before us, I will not have you deem me servile."

Ricci's eyebrows shot high as a sharp note of offence escaped his throat. "Servile?"

"Aye. Such attitude…it places me…us…in an awkward situation, can you not see that?"

No more awkward, of course, than Meran's obvious rejection. And at Ricci's glower, he began to fear his attempt to pull back had ruined everything.

Ricci might now abandon their plans in a fit of pique. Tentatively, Meran began, "As for the quest, my lord—"

"By the gods, man. I am not so affected that I will go back on my word." Ricci's lip curled. "I am not a dog to be whipped by such capriciousness."

Bathed beneath that flood of scorn, it was Meran's turn to be taken aback.

Ignoring Meran's discombobulation, Ricci forged on, his posture echoing his sudden impatience as he abandoned his cup to the low table. "As I've said, we travel on the *Galacia*. They brought with them a cargo upriver from Dun—"

"I know the *Galacia*," Meran interrupted, his own irritation snapping back.

"Oh really? From where?"

Meran licked his lips. "It belongs to my father." The irony that he started his unsanctioned adventure on one of his father's merchant vessels was not lost on him.

"You know Captain Mot?"

"I know of him, but until this day, we had never met." Due in no small part to his father still not allowing him into the family business after the scandal his dalliance with Gratian had caused. Gratian, too, was a merchant, and a competitor of the Durantes. Mot had appeared as fooled by Meran's disguise as had the tavern's other patrons. "I assure, my masquerade remains undetected."

"Ensure you keep it that way. I will not have the wrath of Durans Durante descend on my head should the ruse be discovered. My face is too well known on the southern side of the Meith for my guise to come into play until we reach Port Delmay and disembark."

Meran nodded. Though he had come overland to the Shimmering Fields, they had passed Port Delmay; it huddled at the great confluence where the Celari and Meith Rivers met.

"We will hire a small craft to take us up the Meith. I hope you are prepared for hard toil. It is no easy task paddling upriver."

"Anything." A churn of excitement overtook Meran's resentment at Ricci's warning. On the morrow, he ventured towards his destiny. No matter what he thought of Ricci, no matter his trepidation, in a mere few hours, his life was to change forever.

Ricci gave a sceptical grunt but offered nothing further on the matter. "Have you a definitive destination, then?"

Irritation curled Meran's lip. "Not of this moment…other than to reiterate what I have already told you." That Ricci had not recognised the description of abundant palms and surging water Meran had given from his vision had astonished him.

He had tried to find more information at the small township's library, but for all that the climes of Southern Draca were dry and inhospitable, the vast landscape contained a startling number of lush oases.

"Best I take care of that too, eh?"

Before Meran could protest, Ricci furnished him a list of things he would need for at least the first leg of their journey. "Two shirls, five copta, food and beverages, and a measure of salt," he read. "Sounds reasonable."

"Aye." Ricci affected an efficient tone. "The shirls will cover expenses once Draca is reached. The rest covers your berth on the *Galacia*. Take whatever other funds you deem necessary and any personal items but limit them to this." Ricci handed Meran a carry-sack. "There will be no room for trunks."

The prospect came as expected. The trip, of necessity, would have to be frugal, and Meran had already resolved himself to it. He began to tally all that he perceived needed and what he might be able to fit.

"Do you have a hunting bow?"

Meran nodded absently until the weight of astonished silence had him flick an uneasy gaze at his companion. "Pray, what?" he asked. "I also thought it pertinent to bring a hunting knife and hatchet." He was no imbecile, despite what Ricci might think.

Ricci's brow crashed down at the disrespectful tone, his voice cold. "Good. You will no doubt need it." Without preamble, he rose and took his leave.

Lost for a moment at the abruptness, Meran watched the door close behind Ricci before surging to his feet and beginning to pace. Despite what had gone on in the bath chamber, Ricci had returned to his derisive superiority with apparent ease.

While Meran had detected an initial perturbation at his snub, Ricci's evident disdain would certainly douse the flames of any attraction he might ever have contemplated. And that was what Meran wanted, didn't he? It was for the best.

He rubbed at the ache in his chest until the rustle of parchment against his clothes brought his attention back to Ricci's list. He shook his head at the futility of his yearning thoughts and came to a stop. "By the gods! I have no time for this. Meran Durante, stop acting like a pup whose bone has been taken, and pull yourself together."

CHAPTER FOURTEEN

Ellom's eyes were like freezing shards of ice stabbing into the back of Meran's neck as he and his friends strode to the jetty.

Beyond the moored *Galacia*, the rising sun cast pale fingers like tender caresses across the Celari River's dark waters, trying to warm the crisp dawn air. But Meran could see little dared thaw Ellom's petulance.

Any satisfaction Ellom had taken last eve when Meran finally sought him out quickly faded upon realising Ricci had visited Meran in his absence.

Although Ellom had continued to harangue him for details, Meran brushed the incident aside, his resentment blossoming at his friend's dogged tenacity.

He refused to be coerced or intimidated by the threat of love's loss that Ellom thought to incite. The more Ellom pushed, the more Meran held his ground. After all, Ellom failed to understand that Meran had no choice in the matter. Destiny called him. If Meran had to utter those words, *"You cannot come with me,"* one more time, he would have to throttle his friend.

"We are lovers, are we not?" Ellom demanded.

"Friends first, El, and then lovers when the passions move us, you know this." Meran flopped down on the bed. *"I care very deeply for you. I never wish you ill. Never! But—"*

"No, don't say it. Nothing good ever follows such a word."

Meran had acquiesced only to have Ellom treat him to a sullen silence for the remainder of their last eve together. Much remained unspoken, much Meran knew Ellom wished to accuse him of. Selfishness being his greatest sin.

Almost as punishment, Ellom had shared his bed. It had been a chill and fruitless cohabitation. Backs turned to each other. Any sympathy Meran might have had perished in the cold. Only an obstinate anger remained.

The sight of the flat-bottomed River Runner now called to him with the promise of freedom. The result of Ellom's obstinate attitude, though that obviously had not been his plan.

Nervous excitement joined his simmering irritation as the group clomped to the end of the jetty and watched the small number of Meran's provisions being loaded aboard.

Meran scanned for Ricci, finding him atop the rear aft cabin, standing like a godling of war, the Mavish manifest as he surveyed the activity. A morning breeze floating off the river played with his familiar brown cloak.

Only Captain Mot, his Dracan companion, and the urchin from the previous day hugging the big man's side braved the warrior's company. The captain stood with a puffed chest and straight back as if attempting to equal Ricci's inherent authority. It proved a wasted effort as the rivermen cast wary, brittle glances the Mavish's way before they scuttled about their business.

Meran's heart tripped a fluttering beat as he took Ricci in, nerves sparking to life through his stomach and down his spine.

No! There would be no repetition of yestereve's satisfactory—almost miraculous—coming. He had rejected any possibility of further advances and had to lie in the bed he had made.

Taking a deep breath, he turned to his companions. "Well, this is it." His voice vibrated with barely concealed excitement. What lay before him was an adventure as much as a necessity. "Thank you all for getting me to this place. Without your help, this quest would not be possible."

Each, in turn, stepped forwards to say their farewells with hugs and slaps for good luck. Ormand's farewell ended with him pressing a thick envelope into Meran's hand.

"From Patrice. I meant to give it to you earlier. I am sore sorry, but I got…distracted and forgot."

"You think she—"

"No! Well…she is suspicious, mayhap that there is more to your undertaking than visiting a festival."

Meran's heart fluttered. A little time in company and Patrice had always been able to intuit his every intention. The question was, if she had, would she tell their father?

"From my observation, your father still lives blissfully ignorant,"

Ormand said.

Such ignorance would not last. Nervous guilt tickled Meran's conscience for his friends. They stood to bear the brunt of Durans Durante's wrath until Meran returned, and yet, they had not hesitated.

And the very reason for Meran's defiance he now held in hand. Patrice's missive, words written by a woman who knew him better than any. A sister that loved him through all his triumphs, tribulations, and failures.

He conveyed his thanks with silent acknowledgment and a squeeze of Ormand's hand. The letter went into his jacket pocket, palm protectively over it, until time allowed for him to savour her words of wisdom. Or, more likely, her less than subtle instruction.

Ormand stepped back, and Meran found himself confronted by Ellom.

His grey eyes glittered in his pale face, no longer with petulance but grief, his lip tremulous. Meran's heart ached, and he took Ellom in his arms. "Don't say it, please. Let us not part on a note of contention but hope that we will be reunited soon, the prize in our grasp."

Ellom nodded against Meran's neck, the trickle of tears warming a track down his skin. Memories from past years flooded through Meran, of their idealistic hopes and dreams, their burgeoning friendship, and their love. Not the kind that Ellom longed for, but love, nonetheless. But even Ellom could not deny that their intimacy had run its course. It was time to move forwards, to forge their own destinies.

A sound clicked in Ellom's throat even as he breathed in Meran's ear, but no words of either encouragement or dissuasion followed. Fingers tangled in Meran's locks, the pull sharp. Ellom tugged him down, bringing their lips together in a kiss meant to remind Meran of what he stood to lose. But Meran tasted only vexation and bitter tears.

He could not bow to the unstated demand, his instinctual response cowed by the spectacle Ellom forced on him. Resentment washed away any last vestiges of possible pleasure, and Meran Durante, son and heir, took control where previously he had not dared.

He deepened the kiss. *He* pressed in with his tongue to claim and master. *He* ravaged his erstwhile lover, and a gasp of utter dismay escaped Ellom. He pulled back, his eyes flashing outrage and fear. Pushing away from Meran, he put distance between them, his body shaking.

Meran anticipated his fleeing the scene, but to his surprise, Ellom held his ground, his head coming up high, his eyes a defiant storm. Whatever wound Meran had afflicted would not be fodder for the amusement of others.

Last, Meran found himself caught in a fierce bear hug before Jon pulled back with a powerful slap on his back. Not quite enough to wind him, but nearly. "Don't worry for him," Jon said. "He will survive his hurt, and as promised, I will take him beneath my wing. You have my word."

"And you have my heartfelt thanks."

Meran paused, undecided if he should say more. But it boded best to be safe than sorry, and of all, Jon had seen what could happen to those that trod an unwary path.

"If you could keep an eye on Lord Marshal Belton too," he said, as memories of the boy in the alley sat heavily on his mind. "Truly, I'd much appreciate it. His lascivious attention was much turned on Ellom yestereve until I managed to drag him away. I know I cannot be all Ellom needs, but…I do not trust that lord's intentions."

While the butcher mentioned by Ricci's clansman and Belton could not be one and the same—not when he heralded from such a reputable family—still something oily and predatory shone through the lord's demeanour.

"Of course. Now go. *Your* lord marshal awaits, as does your adventure."

"Not *my* lord."

Jon's brows rose. "Really? For a lord, I deem him a far superior prospect, and perhaps that was the prophet's intention all along. There is more to a man than just the finding of him. You must also secure him. And what better way than he fall for you."

Face heating, Meran thumped Jon's shoulder in exasperation, stifling the instinct to cast a speculative gaze Ricci's way. "Menace," he said affectionately before turning from Jon, and his own tumultuous thoughts, to the rest of his friends. "Off with you lot and enjoy the rest of the festival. I will see you all back at Dun in…a moon and a half, all going to plan." *Surely that would be long enough.* "Farewell until then."

He showed them his back and strode aboard. Despite every misgiving, a swelling excitement bloomed brighter and more urgent in his chest. Finally, they were off. The gem awaited his claiming, and the future, his victory. Locurnia would be saved, Sofie safe, and the dread and bloody scene he had witnessed of Patrice would never come to fruition. And all because, with Leon Ricci's aid, he would not fail.

Leaning against the boat's railing, the deck rolling beneath his feet, Meran watched the jetty recede, confidence and anticipation filling him.

"Well, well," a deep voice rumbled from behind. "If it is not the young Fisher from the Drowned Tabby."

A warm hand landed upon his shoulder as a handsome man drew alongside. Meran caught a lascivious twinkle in the darkest of brown eyes as the Velkor caught his hand in a firm grip. Friendship, and more, flashed in his grin. "Is this not fortuitous?"

The Velkor's appreciative gaze of the previous day was easily dwarfed by today's reality. Appreciation, Meran returned, because why should he not? The riverman radiated a combination of exotic beauty and earthy roughness. Planes and angles, tight hard muscle, strong, sure, firm hands.

Meran smiled at the familiar face. "Ah. It is Willard...Garda?"

"One and the same." Willard drew Meran's arm up into the strange one-arm clasp that was the greeting of Velkory. Arms twined, fingers threaded, and the back of the hand presented to each other. Willard had used it at the Tabby, a gesture that allowed a friend to be pulled close or an enemy to be pushed away.

Gesturing to the two small figures left standing at the dock's verge, Willard asked, "A particular friend?"

Both Jon and Ellom stood like twin sentinels at the edge of the jetty, but Willard's attention came to rest on the latter. Of course, Meran and Ellom's parting kiss had been anything but private.

"We are close but not exclusive." Suddenly giddy at his declaration, Meran's spirit soared at the prospect finally realised. A future unfettered. He gave Willard's hand an allusive squeeze.

Willard's brows rose into the graceful sweep of his bangs, delight lighting his eyes as his tongue skimmed full lips, perfect for kissing.

Rising heat smouldered through Meran.

"Willard!" the captain bellowed in a voice like a dash of cold water. "About your business."

Meran followed Willard's wary gaze, noting the usual thundercloud upon Ricci's brow as he stood alongside Mot. Willard sagged under that dark scrutiny, his rich brown face paling as if Ricci's glare suggested he were about to crush a mouse beneath his boot.

Ere he could assure Willard that this was Ricci's normal expression,

Willard had released him and saluted his captain. "Your bag?" He held out a shaky hand and took the sack from Meran. "I will show you to your quarters."

"Most appreciated." Meran followed though he would much rather have stayed on deck and watched the boat's prow cut through the dark water. Equally, his curiosity needled him at Willard's pallid deference to Lord Marshal Ricci's look. *What is that about?*

Willard led him across the mid-deck and around the back of the aft cabin. A lone door led to a storeroom, replete with two hammocks and a short stand topped by a heavy metal jug and basin. A small looking glass hung tacked to the wall, and a dark-stained walnut trunk and a further carry-sack were abandoned on the floor.

"The captain had it prepared for the…the M-mavish's comfort," Willard explained, stuttering over Ricci's fighting name, his gaze flicking to the ceiling on top of which that very man stood. He swallowed. "I beg pardon, but I had not realised the lay of the situation, or never would I have approached you in such a manner. I thought, with what happened at the docks, your affiliation to the Mavish was a more conventional one."

"Pray, what?" The lay of what situation? That he and Ellom should have an open relationship? Or that it seemed he was to share the small space with his apparent guardian?

Exchanges in stewardship between the *Voce* and Velkor had been encouraged ever since Prince Rane had signed the accord with King Voltan. It meant closer ties and better understanding.

That he travelled as Ricci's ward was done only to shore up their necessary subterfuge until the lord could safely don his own disguise.

"I swear," Willard said, "I have no intention of stepping on anyone's toes…"

"Of what do you speak, man?"

Willard looked more than a little rattled, eyes again turned to the ceiling, "Why? That the Hell-spawn of Roth has taken you for a lover."

CHAPTER FIFTEEN

A bark of dissembling laughter escaped Meran. "He has not." Though, aside from his own insistence, the lord marshal might have done that very thing. "But mayhap keep that blunt descriptor between the two of us, eh?"

Hell-spawn of Roth! Ricci could either be incensed or flattered by the title. Roth was, after all, the Velkor's God of War, and the Mavish might relish the moniker, but not so the unbeliever. Best Willard not risk its general use.

"It is the truth." Willard's eyes widened, his voice lowering conspiratorially. "We all know of *his* legend. The Mavish, vanquisher of a thousand lives. There is none like him, either before his coming to Atena or thereafter. A beast of a warrior and without mercy. No injury touched him; no adversary overwhelmed him. He is nothing short of miraculous."

And the whispers had turned into a roar of rumour and speculation. Only one with divinity running through their veins could have been so triumphant. Yes, yes, even those of Locurnia had heard the myth.

"And yet it can all be attributed to skill, tenacity, and the basest of natures," Meran argued.

"He remains undefeated in our tourneys." A flash of indignation etched Willard's features.

Was that on the Mavish's behalf or that Meran had attempted to quash a fable that had taken on its own life? "I do not say this to undermine him, of course. It is no mean feat."

Recollections of the first fight Meran had ever seen reinforced the animalistic brutality of the Mavish. It had been both terrifying and exhilarating. But how much more barbaric without the limitations of Voltan's laws?

If Meran had been reduced to incite mercy, then how would he have withstood a match to the death? How would he have been able to watch a man, who he had started to consider honourable, commit ritualistic, brutal murder, whether it fall within the law or nay?

He understood Willard's reticence for further flirtation completely, but Meran refused to allow it. Being Meran Durante no longer, the shackles of his obligation to father and to lover were shattered by the mere fact of his new identity. As Zachary, he was Velkor, an adventurer and a free man. If he sought a dalliance, for the first time in forever, he was at liberty to indulge.

"Look, I assure, we are not lovers. He is not even an ardent admirer of mine. He is but a travelling companion until I reach Port Delmay and there meet with my friend, Cyro Maier, my companion for our further journey into the north."

Of course, Cyro was to be the lord marshal's alias, but none on the *Galacia* needed to know that.

Even though he nodded as if all had been resolved, Willard looked unconvinced. "Well, best I be on my way. I'll take my leave of you now, sir, and hope that your journey will be a pleasant one."

Willard left without a backward glance, and Meran felt his excitement fade. Flopping onto the nearest hammock, he covered his eyes and groaned for the passionless austerity of his immediate future. No Leon, and now no Willard. *By all the hells, what was he doing?*

As the swinging of his bed eased to a stop, a lump pressed against his hip. Shifting in the awkward space, Meran pulled Patrice's missive free. A part of him wanted to wallow longer in self-pity, but the thought of his sister insisted he pull himself together.

Breaking the seal, he unfolded the crinkled parchment, a silken package falling onto his chest.

The bow unfurled beneath his fingers, and the fabric opened to reveal a snowy-white swan feather he himself had shaped into a quill. The same feather that Sofie had used to set him free of the dreamland's tenacious hold two years previous.

Caught in the clutches of a recurring vision—a nightmare of the death of their brother—she had used it to trigger in Meran's sleeping mind a happy memory. Snowflakes kissing his cheeks. The distraction had allowed him to push from the dreamlands and back to reality. Choosing to emulate the process had placed the power back in his hands. It had been the first step on the road to mastering his gift of seership.

Curiosity piqued for what Patrice might wish to convey with its giving. Did she insist he write her back with his plans? Did she send it as a reminder of his obligations to his talent?

He turned to the neatly linked script and read.

Dearest Meran,

I hope this letter finds you enjoying your sojourn and that the festival has proven itself all that you and your friends hoped it would be.

I have not been to Etta in a long time, and it is an experience I am in much want of repeating when Sofie is of age.

For my part, I rather enjoyed the sparring, though some of the competitions turned brutal too easily, the resultant barbarism being a consequence I did not so much relish. Still, it allowed me the opportunity to meet with old friends unseen in many years, and forge new ones where I could. I hope you, too, have grasped this opportunity Father has graciously allowed and have not sunk too much into dissipation. It is not an easy temptation to resist, as I recall, but feel sure Father hopes that you have proven your character strong and have been able to resist. (As much as any man can in your situation.)

I must confess, when finding that you had taken Jon with you, to being a little miffed. From all that I'd heard, he is very close to the completion of your commission. Now, this adventure has served to push the unveiling out at least a further six moons. I was very much looking forward to seeing his interpretation of Beorn and his honouring of the fallen, as were many in this city. But, for all that he is a consummate flirt, he is a man of sense and a good influence…when out of his cups.

Dun has, of course, waited with bated breath these two years past for Jon's latest revelation, so I suppose they can wait a moon or two longer. So long as you find what you seek in this unexpected venture. Though what the Shimmering Fields can offer that you would, with such haste, insist you must go, I fail to guess. Still, my heart is with you, though it bids you caution for want of not losing another brother, and this time perhaps to recklessness.

I have enclosed here your quill. Not just in the hope that you will reply but that it offers you luck and peace with your talent on the path it, no doubt, demands you tread.

Your loving sister,

Patrice Tish-Durante

Obviously, Patrice knew he was up to something. He did not resent her advice nor her cautions, but neither would he stop. Silently, he thanked her for the timely reminder as to his venture's necessity and to not distract himself with his carnal desires. That had been a moment of madness.

Pressing the soft barbs of the feather to his lips, he gave it a kiss for luck and returned it to his pocket.

Meran turned back to the parchment and the less sophisticated scrawl that covered the paper beneath Patrice's neat hand.

Sofie's.

Dearest Merry,

I could not allow Ormand to take our sister's letter to you without adding my own salutations. What fun you must be having at the celebrations. So much to see and so many things to do and learn in these strange far-flung places. You must be so excited. But I do miss you, though.

Will you bring me a keepsake from your travels? Please, please, Merry. The little one you win from your tourney. It will be very, very special to me.

I so look forward to your return.

With the most love,

Your sister, Sofie

Warmth tugged at Meran's heart, even as a smile spread his lips. Such blatant affection laced with unintended manipulation. The gift of all children, he supposed, and yet it grounded him.

Though he had no intention of ever fighting in a tourney, either at the festival or anywhere, he would have to remember to bring her a bauble of some description. If for nothing more than to see the look of joy and wonder on her young face.

That he would triumph in his quest and, in the process, save her from danger were things she never need know. He would have her retain her innocence, and if she wanted a keepsake from what she took to be adventures, that is what she would have.

Once again feeling centred and focused, he left the small room and moved onto the mid-deck. His gaze skittered down the riverboat's sleek lines, over the forecastle to the taller bowsprit and the water beyond. Passing the single mast with its fitted square sail, he climbed the steps to the top deck and gazed restlessly at the rocky shoreline as it passed them by.

They were some days away from Port Delmay and time stretched out long and boring before him. He would need a distraction. Spinning on his heels, he ignored those who stood atop the aft castle, and he watched the rivermen about their chores.

He could offer to help, he supposed, and in doing so, perhaps he would have the opportunity to glean further information. To find out what the crew might know of Draca and its people. It would not hurt to ingratiate himself with them, and what time but now was better to start?

CHAPTER SIXTEEN

It took two more days for the natural suspicion of the crew to dissipate. Willard offered cautious glances and shy smiles. All out of the sight of Ricci, of course. Even Meran had noted the distinct difference between how his Velkor brethren responded to the lord marshal and those of *Vocekind*. They offered respect tempered with a healthy dose of dread.

By the third eve, Meran found himself a welcome part of friendly competition. With wind in the sail and the current on their side, ten of the rivermen not on duty set up a makeshift game. A wad of rolled fabric stood for a ball and a broken plank for a bat.

Laughing and jeering, they dashed along the deck, thrashing the ball from one end of the midsection to the other, endeavouring to cross their opponent's goal line. Not knowing all of the rules, Meran did his best for his side. He had been asked to join the Velkor's team, and he would not see them lose because of his ignorance.

"Catch, Zachary," one of the Velkor yelled in his own tongue as he hefted the ball towards Meran. With no way to catch it on his bat, he leapt for it. Shouts followed, and then mayhem. Thrown backwards, Meran found himself buried beneath a pile of men, the ball still in his grasp and his upper torso over the opposition's line.

Hoots of victory echoed through the huddle he was squashed beneath. The weight began to ease as the men scrabbled free. Meran's first breath came as a blessing.

Voce and Velkor slapped each other on the backs in a display of good-natured sportsmanship, and he laughed in delight at the joy that thrilled through the gathering.

"That was a magnificent catch." Willard pulled Meran up, throwing an arm about his shoulders and giving him his own victory slap.

"We won?"

"Aye. The first time in an age. You were an asset to our side."

Pleasure flushed through Meran, a foolish grin to match Willard's.

"Here," Willard added, a note of nervousness edging his tone. "We had thought to celebrate the game with a drop of ale. You are more than welcome to join us?"

"It would be my pleasure." Meran felt the acceptance inherent in the invitation.

"Here, two for us," Willard called to one of his countrymen filling battered tin tankards from the barrel others had rolled onto the deck.

Taking the offering, Meran leaned upon the railing, sipping in companionable silence as Willard took up the space beside. The eve before them seeped into night, a slow invasion, a star-studded expanse spreading across the sky. It drew him with its magnificence so reminiscent of the veil that hung between dreamland and the Elysian Plain.

What resided beyond the blackened vault so far above his head? In comparison to its vast and inexplicable reach, his concerns seemed small and insignificant.

But on the morrow, the *Galacia* would reach Port Delmay, and he would be forced to disembark with Ricci. Alone. From there on out, he had to ensure he did not succumb to a repeat of what had occurred in the bath chamber. The yearning for a replay niggled at him like an infernal weakness he could not shake.

Ricci had to trust him—respect him—as much as Meran had to return the favour. Alas, he still knew so little, his visions having failed to show him everything. It left him hanging by a thread.

He had thought to be gone for a moon and a half, but what if it drew out longer? Not knowing the exact location of Anigema, they could wander in circles. And that would be his failure. Visions were not like farsight, where feet and target could be brought together. His visions of an oasis in a parched desertscape did not enlighten him about its locale.

By the time he and Ricci found it, secured their prize, and returned, the lads would have resumed their lives back in Dun. Jon to finish the monument to the fallen, Ellom to his continued studies, Ormand back to sea as one of the Durantes' factors. All that awaited Meran in the port city was his father's incandescent fury for his tardiness. A prospect he pushed determinedly to the back of his mind.

The sounds of the crew embroiled in revelry behind them, loud and boisterous, played in counterpoint to their companionable silence until Willard cleared his throat, his expression pensive.

"I've heard you enquiring of the crew what they know of Southern Draca."

"Oh, aye?" Curiosity bubbled, but Meran contained his eagerness lest he suffer further disappointment. "Do you know something of it?"

"Not I, but my father. He told many an exciting tale in his long life. Some that might be of interest to you."

"And they are. Please, I am all ears."

"He spent a number of years as crew with the Ballan. You have heard of him?"

"Who has not? The infamous captain of the *Wind Maiden*." Meran wondered about the direction of this conversation. "Richest merchant to ever grace the Summer Isles and the Western Sea."

"Da was with him in the early years when first my cousin, Timmon Garda, joined his crew. The *Wind Maiden* ventured to the far north of Draca at that time."

Meran almost held his breath. "Aye, the Ballan made a name for himself amongst the northerners. Did he also venture south?"

"When he was a younger man, yes. Mayhap, around the time the Serpent War came to an end, but I'm not certain."

"Your father accompanied him?"

Willard nodded.

Meran could barely contain his anticipation. "And what did he say of them?"

"That they are nomads, those of the south, as you have undoubtedly already heard from others. They live in groups, each called Outliers. I guess because they, of all the Draca, remained in the south, even after Nord cursed them, while the bulk of southerners moved north. The Outlier is a gathering of families under the leadership of a catana—a chieftain."

"A chieftain?" Meran's target would doubtless be a catana. *Catana Keija.* The dreamlands whispered the truth of it.

Could this sudden knowledge aid him in his search? Excitement sparked in Meran at the possibility, and he wished to dash off to inform Ricci, but Willard had not finished.

"They have priests and magicians, one of which I have met on the trade routes to the west. He and another tribesman came from the desert to secure some barrels of good wine, but mostly they stay within their borders. I have heard that they are a most devout people." This time, Willard's eyebrows rose suggestively.

"Those rumours I have definitely heard," Meran said. They were one of the first things any man who knew anything was eager to impart.

"Bawdy, debauched revelries, the likes not seen in Velkor, or so I hear."

Meran shook his head in disbelief. No doubt old wives' tales to vilify those who were unknown and different. "It does seem to be on everyone's lips."

Willard smirked before he sobered again. "Da was not sure of its truth. Their men are all warriors, and the tribe means everything. Nothing but Nord is held in higher regard."

"Their god?"

"Aye, their god, and never a more jealous and bloodthirsty one has ever been seen."

"Unless you count our Lord Roth." Velkory's own vengeful deity.

"Hmm, yes. Unless you count Roth. But I am certain they do not. When you find them on this quest of yours, be wary," Willard said.

"I wish only to do what the Ballan has done in the Golden Vales of the north. Negotiate trade. They must see that it will be to their advantage."

"Still, they will be suspicious. If you get into strife, I suggest that you invoke the Protection of Nord. It's an old creed but may save your life until you use that golden tongue of yours to persuade them of your sincerity. I will teach you the words."

Meran turned his head to stare at his new friend, only to find dark eyes staring back and an expression filled with concern. "I'm sure...my companion will suffice to keep me in one piece, but thank you, I will not forget your advice." He had almost said *the Mavish*, but of course, none could know Ricci's further part to play in the venture.

"Good. You are too handsome to be fed to the desert, as is the way of the barbarians, Zachary Fisher." And with that, Willard leaned forwards and kissed him. A taste. A pressing of lips filled with want and promise, and suddenly Meran did not wish the excitement of the eve still thrumming through the air to be over.

His blood returned to its competitive high, adrenalin spiking through his muscles.

Meran followed up the deepening kiss with a salacious chuckle. There were pleasanter ways to work out the furore of his agitation than to only bend his elbow.

A speculative fire lit in Willard's eyes as he pulled back.

Nonetheless, he sent a questing gaze sweeping across the deck.

If he sought the Mavish, he need not worry. Meran spied both he and Mot distracted by some competition going on further down the deck. They could slip away if that was Willard's intention.

Should Ricci wish to know Meran's whereabouts, the ship's wooden structure could not hope to stop his farsight. Not once had Meran ever felt the touch of Ricci's magic invading his privacy, and he did not expect the discourtesy now.

"Do you think your guardian will make objection if we celebrate this eve's victory in a manner best kept from company?" Willard asked as the tips of his fingers caressed suggestively down Meran's back.

A shiver squalled the length of his spine at the possibilities.

Meran's gaze latched to those gorgeous, bruised lips as Willard wet them. He had only just sampled them, and he wanted more. If Willard could get over his hesitation in the face of the Mavish's reputation, then Meran wanted this opportunity to freshen his own palette. As Zachary, he could sweep behind him the denigrating yearning to be mastered.

"I assure, I need no permission to be allowed to *celebrate*."

Willard's grin broadened, a sparkle of anticipation answering in his own dark eyes, his hand slipping to take Meran's.

"Where do we go?" Meran asked.

"You will see," Willard said close to his ear.

Flutters of anticipation shivered down Meran's spine, landing in his nethers. He followed Willard as readily as Willard led him across the deck and down a ladder.

Dim and musty, the faint hint of bilge and old straw assaulted Meran's senses as they stepped onto the upper level of the two-level hold. Still, his insides danced with expectation.

A flame bloomed at the striking of flint. A lantern began to flicker, bright enough to see Willard had guided him to an area sectioned off from the rest of the hold by a metal grill. A straw-filled pallet sat on the floor, and down-stuffed pillows graced one end of it while a loose-woven rug lay strewn across the other. To one side sat an upturned crate, and atop it, a tin bowl and pitcher and a few other propitious items.

Meran could guess at the uses for such a space. Where the crew slept under the forecastle afforded little privacy, although some bold souls indulged, nonetheless.

Willard threw himself down on the makeshift bedding, his gaze like heat waves crashing over Meran. "'Tis ours for the next turn of the dial. I say we make the most of it." Willard waved him over, licking his lips, gaze slipping to the front of Meran's breeches.

His anticipation grew large and obvious at the mere thought of Willard's mouth on him, and Meran grinned, a boyish exuberance taking hold.

He was not Meran Durante but a young man of Velkor, flush from exercise and alcohol, and alive with expectation. Here before him lay a mystery. A foray into carnality. He flashed his companion a roguish grin and, with a laugh, leapt on him.

CHAPTER SEVENTEEN

Leon stood on the aft deck, looking down on the shenanigans playing out before him. The crew's spirits were still high from their eve's entertainment. The drink flowed, and their voices rose in crude wit and raucous laughter. Some sang a bold shanty, arms flung about each other as they rolled to the ripple of the wind and the current.

For the first time since leaving the Reach, the sullen storm cloud of Leon's spirits lifted. Even Orr accosting him as he'd stormed from the premises that eve and agreeing to present Leon's concerns had served only as a momentary distraction. He gave no credence that anger rode him due to Durante's rejection. He did not pine over lost opportunity like some lovelorn maid. After all, it was not his loss.

Regardless, twists of confusion muddied Leon's thinking until he stamped down any threatening regrets. Nothing would interfere with his hunt for *Amplion*, be they his own feelings. He was here for the glory of *Vocekind* and to stop any possible conflict with the Velkor from happening. Nothing more.

He smiled at the blended crew's exuberance and their appearance of comradery. *Miraculous.* But how long such comradeship would last if Durante's war were to start, Leon could not guess. Not long. Only peace favoured such integration.

Mot slipped up to his elbow, handing off a further tankard of the pale swill the men drank. Nursing his first drink, the captain watched the merrymaking with a benevolent eye. He could enjoy the prevailing good mood while retaining sense enough to command restraint should the revelry turn to a brawl. *Circumspect as well as canny.*

"Lord Durans does not mind that half your crew is Velkor?" Leon asked.

Mot shrugged. "If I succeed in getting my cargo from one port to the other undamaged and in a timely manner, what is there for my lord to mind?"

Not much, although Leon had little suspected Durans being so magnanimous with his authority. Yet the lord had assigned no factor to the vessel. Evidence of the trust he placed in this particular captain.

"Besides," Mot continued, "the excise master offers relief of at least half the toll should a man crew his vessel with equal *Voce* and Velkor."

"And Lord Durans reaps the benefit?"

"I may people my vessel as I see fit, and if it is to his advantage, all the better. After all, it is no hardship. At our next stop, we take aboard wool and bolts of fine fabrics for Atena, as well as a cache of foodstuffs and sacks of wheat for Dun. We cater to all of Locurnia. The profit is sufficient to make the trip worth his while, I assure."

Again, Mot proved himself a useful acquaintance to know, especially when next Leon approached Rane's tax collector. Perhaps after a new accord was signed between the *Voce* and Prince Rane, Mot would not have to split his loyalty. He could contract with the Ricci clan and people his entire crew with *Voce*.

"How do you find them?" he asked.

"They are pleasant enough and hardworking."

Leon snorted. "Aye? When they are not at play."

"Ah, but they did execute the sport with much energy and enthusiasm." Mot gave a tolerant smile, as if he had never barked orders, rebuked, or punished any of them. "Even young master Zachary put on a sterling performance, ensuring his team's victory."

"That he did."

Durante had been fast, strong, dexterous, beautifully flushed with excitement…and without apparent guile. Whether to bolster his disguise as Zachary or with genuine sincerity, he had integrated perfectly with the Velkor's team.

For their part, they had accepted him. But who could tell Durante's motivations? A man who claimed seership rather than reveal his sources. Delusional and yet so sincere in his insistence.

Leon should have felt relief at not falling beneath Durante's thrall. Someone so like Jacobi could only be expected to use any sign of weakness to his advantage. But was he being honest with himself? Was he being fair to Durante?

Guilt needled him.

Meran's dedication to his cause, the lengths he went to secure the safety of his family and people, were no reflection of Jacobi's narcissism at all.

"He is a very personable young man," Mot said, nodding in the direction of the railing where Durante chatted with an admirer if the heated gazes were anything to go by. "It seems Garda is much taken with him."

"Hmm." A river rat if ever Leon had seen one, and far beneath the note of a lord marshal's son, but what was the harm in a bit of flirtation?

Leon had every faith that it would come to nought—*because that might prove very awkward, and lords above, Durante could not suffer awkwardness.* Nor, it seemed, could he handle a real man showing him where his true preferences lay.

Servile! A bark of scorn threatened the back of Leon's throat. Of all the insults. As if the wonder of having come undone beneath Leon's hand would ever suggest such a thing. Abel, Del, or any of Leon's other bedfellows could not be labelled servile in any respect. Yet they all submitted to him, and not because he was their lord, but because they wanted to.

Abel might, on occasion, pretend otherwise, but he ever melted at the pleasure Leon offered, yielding his body in the most beautiful of acquiescence.

Leon grimaced at the pang of bitterness tainting his thoughts as he watched the mismatched pair. He had never counted himself sensitive. But now, a squall of resentment tried to feather through his belly as the bold fellow drew Durante away and out of his line of sight.

Firmly, he denied the urge to track them with his farsight, though a black storm threatened to wash away his satisfaction with the evening's revelries.

"You are well with this turn of events?" Mot asked, a hint of tension edging his voice. "If necessary, I will have Sem intervene."

"No. He is man enough to follow his folly where he wills."

When it came to sexual partners, Leon had found jealousy tiresome, dangerous, and futile. He could secure the attention of anyone he wanted if he so desired. Even Meran Durante.

Shivering with yearning, Durante's craving for a firm hand and a commanding voice had called to Leon across that bath chamber, almost vibrating visibly through the air.

Leon knew he could push his claim, lean in and kiss Durante at any time, and all conscious thought, all resistance, would crumble to dust.

But Leon no longer allowed his urges to rule him. If distance and disdain were what Durante craved, that is what he would get.

A fragile memory pricked at Leon's heart. A flame that dared to awaken and resonate with unwanted pain. In Eain's eyes, he had witnessed that same need; a man he had yearned to hold and command and fulfil every one of those long-held desires.

Both Durante and Eain had chosen to shrink from it. A learned response, perhaps? But a lover who doubted himself, his true desires, Leon would ever keep at arm's length. Rejection would never again send his life into a vortex of spiralling emotions.

He had made the right decision to step back, to stay away from Durante, even should the situation goad him.

"I'm sure they merely blow off steam, my lord," Captain Mot said with awkward consolation.

"Steam, is it?" A wry smile found Leon's mouth. They both knew it would be more than that.

Mot's cheeks reddened even as he cleared his throat. "There is no harm in letting the men have their fun whate'er its form." He waved his hand at the crew members setting up a box and two chairs on the deck below them. "It encourages their solidarity."

"Hmm."

Leon watched a big burly *Voce*, at least a half-head taller than his Velkor opponent, drop to opposite seats. Their glowering appeared far from friendly. Others of the crew gathered around as an arm wrestle ensued.

Faces darkened with effort on both sides, teeth clenching, muscles straining, shoulders rigid. Arm thrust over and down, the Velkor succumbed to the *Voce's* superior strength. There followed yells as the victor leapt about receiving the veneration of his peers and blossoming with his own praise. His defeated opponent slunk away to get himself a further drink and drown his displeasure at the outcome.

Though strong and fierce and driven, the Velkor did not possess the musculature or aggression of the *Voce*. It had been a futile way to resolve whatever their disagreement had been.

However, another Velkor stepped up, looking determined to take the loudmouth down a peg. Again, the *Voce* prevailed... Again and again, and his ego grew with each victory. "See, you have not a hope to beat us," he said. "That you took the match was only down to that pretty boy of yours graced with beginner's luck."

Leon bridled at the fellow's officiousness. If he were down there, he would show the braggart a thing or two about beginner's luck.

"He played better than you on your first attempt, you wretch," one said.

"And he was new to the rules," another added.

"We won fair and square," a further Velkor finished.

"Where is he, then?" the big *Voce* called back, meeting their objection with his aggression. "Get him here to face me, and I'll show you lot his true mettle."

The Velkor men looked around blankly while wide grins bloomed on each *Voce's* face, their farsight, no doubt, landing on Durante like a swarm of stinging bees. Streaking through the ether, Leon's own magic followed, smashing through the boat's wooden structure as if the planks were wisps, aiming for his target like an arrow for its prey.

Gah! Fool boy.

Again, Durante ran from himself, from the perfection of his true desires and the ultimate satiation his submission would afford. How short-sighted to throw himself into such inferior hands when he could have had the best.

The urge to pull him from his place and show him what he missed rippled the length of Leon's arms to his clenched fists, even as the breezes of sense blew through the storm of his affront. All the potential Leon could offer spurned for one blind to Durante's quintessential passions.

Purposefully, he uncurled his hands, crossed his arms, and planted his feet. As he had told Mot, Durante was a man. No one learned from their disappointments unless they experienced them firsthand, and he would let Durante wallow in his own folly.

The big *Voce* gave up a raucous laugh. "Ha. Too busy buggering to fight. 'Tis what's wrong with the damn lot of you. There's none of ye man enough to challenge me."

A volley of protest went up. So much for building solidarity unless one counted the unanimity of all against this one witless antagonist.

Leon's grimace morphed into a rumbling of satisfaction at Mot's gesturing hand that said, *"You are welcome. Be my guest."*

It would be his pleasure.

He was feeling inclined to put someone in their place. If it could not be Meran Durante, then this self-aggrandizing *Voce* river rat would do the trick.

CHAPTER EIGHTEEN

Meran planted his knees on either side of Willard as he urged the Velkor further up the mattress, all the time staring into Willard's sparkling eyes. Pinning him down, Meran claimed a kiss from those ready and waiting lips.

Heat and saliva exchanged bodies as Meran supped on the delicious nirvana that was Willard's mouth, an earthy and carnal desire shivering through his body. With each ensuing kiss, he grew hot within, urgency prickling his skin, and he rolled himself over Willard, even as Willard ground his hips back.

Yet the familiar spark remained unstruck. Encapsulated within his body and inflamed with fleshly passions, the sensations were strange. Urgent. Feverish and fervid and yet somehow magicless.

The ether weighed against his skin with soft touches of expectation, but the power that filled the air at the possibility of coitus lay flat and unmoved by this connection. He did not understand its absence.

Yet he still craved touch, sensation, satiation. The firmness of Willard's muscles, made hard from long hours of manual labour, were worthy of being experienced and explored. A veritable feast to gorge himself on, so did it really matter?

"Will you take this off?" He plucked at Willard's sweat-stained tunic.

Willard obliged, even as Meran discarded his own.

The flat planes and defined curves of Willard's chest thrilled through Meran, as did the lattice of muscle down his abdomen. His skin glistened, rich and velvet dark, split by a trail of enticing black curls leading into the band of his breeches.

"By the gods!" The allure of sweat and heat drew Meran to take one of Willard's tight little nips between his teeth and bite it seductively.

Willard groaned and jerked, pushing Meran away. "Ah, no. Too sensitive."

Meran raised a curious brow before trailing an experimental finger down his ribs. Willard twitched and jerked from reach with an involuntary laugh.

"You are ticklish? Well, is this not delicious?"

Meran spent a few minutes tormenting Willard until he cursed between laughs and toppled Meran from his perch.

Meran took that moment to discard the rest of his clothes before tugging Willard's breeches down his legs. They rolled, grappling with each other, a parody of aggression as they both revelled in the feel of skin on skin.

The soft hair on Willard's chest tickled against Meran's naked pectorals. The hard length of his cock was insistent against Meran's stomach.

"And you are not ticklish." Willard sighed his disappointment.

Meran laughed all the same, "As a child, I was, but no longer." And he kissed Willard again, as much to distract himself from the memories of Beorn, who had tickled him with affection, as to express his continued desire. Many little kisses devolved into desperate lashings of tongue. Willard's lips were big, soft, and exquisite as Meran nibbled and sucked and teased at them until they both could barely breathe.

Like two youngsters at their first experience, they drew back to stare into each other's eyes.

"So, you no longer fear the Mavish's response should we do this?" Meran asked.

Nervousness flickered in Willard's eyes for a second before desire burned them to dust. "It will be our secret. Come here."

Though Meran felt the compulsion to obey, Willard's words had been a want, not a command, and without the forceful timbre, he easily resisted. They were as equal as Meran had ever experienced. He shuffled forwards at the request, his knees to either side of Willard's head.

Meran gloried in the wet heat of Willard's administrations. Gloried as his balls were suckled, taint lathered, and a finger teased between his cheeks to stroke his sensitive flesh.

Willard took him to the root, a frenzy of delight surging up Meran's spine as the delectable suction consumed him. The girth of Willard's finger breached him, teasing and taunting him deep inside. What need for magic with such perfection?

Wet. Tight. A glorious tongue enacted flagellation over his prick's tingling, sensitive skin. Meran gasped beneath the indisputable exaltation. The sounds, the sight, the feel. Earthy and lustful, the sensations mingled into one heart-pounding moment of realisation. Passions overwhelmed his flesh, every muscle, every nerve roaring and roiling with ecstasy. He was grounded in his body and subsumed by its demanding needs, and it was beautiful.

"Ah, ye gods. You have a most delicious flavour," Willard said. "I can't wait to taste your seed."

"Not yet." Meran pulled himself free of the ecstasy. "I-I want to fuck you."

The demand astonished him. Willard, however, remained unperturbed by the declaration. He reared up, following Meran as he drew back. His teeth latching, Willard tugged at Meran's lip. "You may...and then I will fuck you in return."

Flopping back onto the mattress, Willard offered himself for Meran's rapt attention.

Fascinated at the play of light and shade on the richness of Willard's skin, Meran settled between the Velkor's open legs, exploring them in awe. The beauty of that body left him breathless. His lust spiralled unhindered, and he was determined to get every single pleasure he could from a man who wanted nothing from him but a sensual and pleasurable release.

He toured the length of Willard's body, so dark and gleaming. He touched and tasted. Every hill and vale explored as he made a slow map of Willard's legs. Drawing closer, the roundness of his hairy balls fell to the exploration of Meran's teeth and tongue.

Musk filled Meran's nose. Heat seared his lips. The seductive scrutiny forced Willard to roll his hips and hum encouragement.

The danger of it all, the novelty, spawned in Meran an even stronger desire to witness his already aching shaft spread Willard's enticing hole and be consumed. His loins vibrated with the eroticism of it all.

In his new guise, he could do as he willed, and he made his way up Willard's taint, over his heavy balls, to the scorching heat of his prick.

"Ah, holy Deter," Willard moaned, battering Meran's lips with the dusky purple tip as his shaft jerked and twitched with the desire to push into his mouth. Meran encircled the broad erection with his free hand and drew it in. With slow sensuality, he rolled it over his tongue until it hit the back of his throat.

He swallowed it down, sensing the jolts of ecstasy that rippled through Willard's body.

"By all that is holy, do it now," Willard begged. "Do it now before I shame myself." He directed Meran to the stoppered bottle of oil on the wood box at the head of the bedding.

Lathering himself, his lip caught intrepidly between his teeth, Meran placed the head of his prick at that tight pucker and edged forwards. Conquering any resistance, he sank into the headiest, fiercest tightness, a shuddering, animalistic urgency gripping him by the bollocks, and he began to move.

A thrusting, hammering dance played to the music of grunts and groans and the slapping together of sweat-laden flesh. The fist of Willard's body grasped him, teased, and tormented him. Rapture barrelled towards him as undeniably as a hurricane storm from the sea. It pounded him; battered, bruised, and annihilated him. Even the questing curiosity of his fellow *Voces'* farsight grazing him with ethereal fingers could not match it.

As powerless beneath it as Willard, both their voices rose and fell with demands and exclamations and grunts of disbelief at its wondrousness. Release thundered from Meran into the heated, insistent clasp of Willard's body. Seconds later, the white streaks of Willard's own spend spattered and beaded in blobs on his dark skin.

And with the sating of his flesh, realisation shattered Meran's satisfaction as easily as a bucket of cold water thrown over his head.

He yearned for the aftermath of the soul-engorging feast of magic that should now be glutting the ether. The emanations of which had always before proven more orgasmic than the sating of his prick. Alas, even from the beginning of this liaison, their connection had failed to trigger that mystical, effervescent shower of magic.

Hollowed out by disappointment, Meran licked his lips even as Willard smiled. "Lords bless me, 'twas magnificent."

By the gods! What had he done? In comparison to all that Meran had experienced before, he could only consider the episode satisfactory and that on a mediocre level. A *nice* way to have passed his time… Awkward could not express the depths of Meran's feelings.

Likewise, it seemed all the *Voce* aboard had witnessed that wretched finale. Had the lord marshal too? Meran did not recall sensing Ricci's farsight, but at that point, he had been a little distracted…

"Master Zachary?" a low, deep call came from above.

Meran's heart leapt.

Not Ricci, but an unfamiliar timbre. Lantern light flared at the top of the ladder, a hulking shadow looming from the open hatch. Sem's dark face came into view, black eyes peering into the darkness. "Willard? Are ye finished? The captain would have words w'ye."

Blue curses sizzled the air as Willard's fear-bright eyes latched onto Meran, and he began to scramble back into his clothes. "He knows."

"The captain?" But Meran could not remember the touch of Mot's magic either. And what matter? It was no one's business but their own.

"No! The Mavish." A sheen of terror glistened on Willard's ashen skin.

"So what if he does?" Though he felt anything but, Meran attempted to calm himself as he cleaned off. "I have told you. He is not the master of me."

"A fact he knows not, I tell you." Anger tightened Willard's voice, panic wild in his eyes. "He'll come after me now."

"He is not that kind of man." After the incident in Meran's bath chamber, Ricci had kept his distance both night and day, barely speaking, even when they were alone in the cramped cabin.

"Where is your head at?" Willard gave Meran a small push. "All know he has no mercy, and I am no fighting man. Why would you do this to me? To anyone? Especially when you knew my feelings on the matter."

"Stop!" He grabbed Willard by the shoulders, stilling him. "That is unfair. I was not in this alone. And neither did I lead you off."

Willard chewed his lip as if to stop an unjust outburst of protest.

"Lord Marshal Ricci is no longer the man who fought in Atena, Willard. Here in Locurnia, such savagery is never tolerated; or so I have found." Being of Velkor, Zachary would have no real authority on the subject. A fact Meran had to remember. "Being a man with the obligation to keep the peace, he of all people cannot be one to destroy it, or I should think he risks destroying himself."

Willard made a rude noise. Yet hope and fear vacillated from those dark eyes, wont to believe, even as the Mavish's legend still held him in its thrall.

Meran pulled the hesitant Velkor into a fierce hug. The resistance first encountered slowly melted beneath his persistence until, on a sigh, Willard went limp.

"Do you truly think so?"

"I do." Meran tried to imbue his voice with surety. "Besides, it is Captain Mot that seeks you. Not Ricci. And what do you have to fear from him?"

"Nought, I guess."

Meran clasped a comforting hand to the back of Willard's neck. "Then clean up and be off with you before Sem has to come further to fetch you and see the mess we have made together. A mess I will fix. Don't worry."

Willard huffed, giving Meran a push, his familiar grin returning, even as he turned to the basin and jug with its cold water and sliver of soap.

"Oh, and Willard?" Willard stopped, and Meran swung an arm about his broad shoulders. "I forgive your timidity this once, but do not let it happen again. Agreed?"

For a moment, Willard looked sheepish. "Aye."

"You know, I will grudgingly admit that his mere shade is enough to have many a man quivering in their boots, mine included. Now, does that ease your mind?"

"Somewhat, though I still do not know how you stand apiece with such a man for a guardian."

"Must be my boyish charms."

Willard huffed good-naturedly. Once their ablutions were finished, they dressed, and Willard headed to the patiently waiting Sem. Meran tidied the space, contemplating whether or not to return to the cabin and the possibility of Ricci's ridicule.

Cowardice or not, he found a space and a blanket beneath the forecastle and curled up, his back to the rest of the now-retired rivermen.

Lying at its verge, he stared at the sky until the star points blurred into a uniform blackness and sleep quashed every tumultuous thought. Cradled by the lullaby of snores, creaking of boards and lapping water, and the gentle rocking of the boat, he slept on… Until he roused to the arc of a vaulted sky so vast in height and breadth, it felt as a weight of dread on his soul.

The dreamlands, and not the river, confronted him.

Night encompassed his mind, stars chill in their clarity. He felt entombed in emptiness, a boundless landscape spreading out before him until he sighted a low ridge of darkness. A finger of rock pointed towards the empty void, the silver orb of a near-full moon glowing at its rear.

His heart fluttered. Though Philo mostly drew Meran past the dreamland's haunting landscape and onto the river, infrequent incursions still filtered into his sleep when at his most vulnerable. Meran recognised this harrowing vision, one he had suffered numerous times before, and shrank from it.

It did not release him. Urgency filled his every step, the pull from the familiar landmark irrefutable. He was alone, and that way lay his only salvation.

Fear and panic throbbed through every fibre of his being, surrounding, prodding, demanding.

Futility impaled his heart.

Lost. Not only was he lost, but he had lost something. Something of such import that he could not turn away.

As always, he began to run, his heart a thudding tattoo of trepidation, his mind yammering for him to quicken his pace. Meran put on a burst of speed, his boots flinging dirt and sand in little plumes behind him, his sight affixed to the solid ridge…

The land fell away into sudden darkness.

Pinwheeling his arms, Meran's heart slammed into his throat as he teetered on the edge of a precipice. Gravity called to him…only gut-wrenching fear pulled him back. He fell to his backside on the hard ground, breathless and shaking.

All about him, chittering and scuttling sounds teased his hearing. Heat flamed in his lungs as he tried to calm himself from the frenzied burst of adrenalin. He had not fallen in, but even as he gulped in a breath of relief, he knew that to get what he wanted, he had to step over that ledge.

Meran rolled to his knees, fear clawing at his chest, every nerve singing its dismay. Stricken, he crawled to the edge, the land dropping away into impenetrable obsidian. The sounds of chitinous feet clacking rose ominously from below.

A call startled him from his paralysis. It floated like a bubble caught on the breeze to burst with a shout before his face. There followed a stream of hoots, grunts, and bellows shimmering forth in gossamer spheres. Voices brought to him, even as movement writhed in the unseen depths and echoed across his skin in a slow and revolting crawl.

A multitude of eyes blinked open. Shining, they presented a disturbing parody of the night sky above. Meran drew back with a hiss, a roar of nausea rushing through his ears as sound swelled and heat bloomed, and the orange flashing eyes rushed upward.

CHAPTER NINETEEN

Meran sat up with a shout of protest, opening his eyes to a sudden, blinding daylight. The sounds of water skimming beneath the vessel, and the excited shouts of rivermen on the mid-deck, overrode the rapid tattoo of his thudding heart.

Praise Holy Janus! Hand to chest, Meran exhaled a slow breath of relief, though his limbs shook and his nerves jangled as he came back to himself.

That plaguing vision again. *Gods damn!*

This time he had travelled further than ever before, and he did not relish where it had taken him nor the incessant feeling he had lost something.

He tried to shake free of the anxiety stirring in his breast. It might not be his future. One could not always tell when madness slipped free of the dreamlands to infest sleep. They were random and could be anyone's thoughts or memories laced with violent or strong emotions. Perhaps more of the vision would tell, or even time itself. But not now, and not in this place.

He looked around to pinpoint the source of the commotion that had insinuated itself on his dream and brought him back to his senses.

Most of the crew were about their business or gathered on the mid-deck and in the midst of some kind of revelry. Ricci and another, fighting.

Meran scrambled to his bare feet and hastened down to join the throng surrounding the pair. His trepidation eased back when he saw Ricci was fighting a big *Voce* riverman. For a heart-stopping moment, he feared he would find Willard.

He sidled up to a Velkor. "What is all this in aid of?"

"After last eve and his complete humiliation at the hands of the Mavish, seems our boatswain wishes to reclaim his title as the biggest fool alive," the riverman replied. "He sprang a challenge this very morn before 'is lordship bare emerged from his cabin."

Pointing to the captain stationed on the aft deck overseeing the rivalry, he continued, "The captain thought it best to hold a tourney. He's offered a gold dagger from the city of Ormanca to the winner. I'd be tempted to own such a rare treat, but not if it involves wrestling with that man."

Meran nodded. "I understand your reticence."

He watched the two men grapple back and forth like two drunken louts groping at each other. Ricci got the big *Voce* to the ground and, using the boatswain's own belt, flipped him over. The boatswain found himself pinned facedown.

"What is the purpose here? How are points scored?" Meran asked.

"Simple. Relieve your opponent of his underdrawers without unlacing his britches before he manages to relieve you of yours, and you win."

Ah. Now he understood the reason for the participants only being half-naked. Serious wrestling bouts were always fought in the nude, but this was but a bit of fun.

Meran huffed a laugh in disbelief. He had not thought Ricci so playful. But it did make for a lot of grunting and grabbing and inevitable swearing as the sturdy cloth resisted the wrenching.

The surrounding crowd crowed and jeered at the gasping bellow of the boatswain as his underclothes tore. Ricci gleefully jerked them free at the expense of the poor fellow's balls.

Rising, Ricci paraded the greying linen for all to see as if it were a magnificent prize. The defeated fellow staggered to his feet, and in a show of defiance, grabbed his ruined garment, his face contorted in a sneer.

More fool he, if he thought to make an enemy of this lord marshal, Meran thought.

A clap on the back sent the man hobbling off amidst a round of jeers and booing, leaving Ricci the victor in the ring of men.

"He'll not live that down any time soon," Meran said.

The riverman laughed, "Couldn't have happened to a better man. The lads 'ill rib him for sure, but not I. Fool though he may be, to face the Mavish proves he be the braver man."

Ricci raised a hand to halt the cheering and derision. "A courageous lad," he said, "but I feel the challenge insufficient for me to accept such a magnificent gift as your captain has offered. Why, it lasted not even a full five minutes?"

At that, the rivermen tittered, although a wave of nervousness rippled through the crowd, suspicion sparking in many an eye at the direction this might be heading.

"I propose another," Ricci called, his eyes gleaming as he retrieved a corked bottle that sat on the deck beside his discarded jacket. "Shall we not level the playing field with a dose of this?"

Unstopping the bottle, he poured a stream of amber liquid into the palm of his hand. *Oil.*

"Let us see how I fare should my next opponent be doused in this. Who is up for the challenge?"

"It will indeed make him a slippery catch," Meran's companion said with a look of interest.

Meran cast him a worried glance, wondering if the riverman had changed his mind. But there had to be a catch. Magnanimity was not in the Mavish's nature.

"Come now," Ricci called. "I have bested the *Voce* this day. Now it is time for Velkory to stand their best against me. A champion from Atena willing to pit his skills."

Unease slithered through the sudden silence as each crewmember from Atena cast questioning glances at each other. Meran's companion grunted and murmured from the corner of his mouth, "I wonder who of these young fools will consider it?"

"Not you?"

"Nay." Even as the riverman spoke, he leaned away as if trying to avoid Ricci's roving eye. "Not even should he be disadvantaged. *Pah!* What is a bit of oil to *Roth's Hell-spawn*? Unless he be bound hand and foot, I would ne'er consider it."

"You are a canny man."

The riverman offered him a broad smile. "That I am. But what of you, my good Fisher? You are as near equal in measure for it not to matter. You might stand some chance?"

Meran shook his head. He might be the closest in stature of all on the *Galacia*, but he also suspected a bit of oil slicked over him would not save him from defeat. Meran had already earned enough of Ricci's derision. He would not give him more fuel to heap upon that fire.

"Anyone?" Ricci jeered. "Not even though I humble myself. What am I to think of you, my dear allies? You cannot all be cowards." He strode a circle, eyeing each potential candidate until his gaze landed on

Willard. A feral gleam lit his demeanour, a smirk stretching his lips. "You. What of you?"

For such a dark man, Willard paled under that scrutiny, his head shaking even as he stood frozen like an animal caught in the crosshairs. His gaze flickered Meran's way, not with accusation but desperation.

Meran's back snapped straight, head held high, sensing the pending threat. The way Ricci's gaze burned over Willard—menacing, lethal, incensed—Meran knew, even if he had not felt his farsight's touch, that Ricci had seen them.

Willard might have the strength to stand, but he lacked that innate spark of aggression to best Ricci in competition. Especially if the tussle awoke the darker side of Ricci's personality.

"I insist, Velkor," Ricci whispered. "Come test your skills on me, or are you not man enough?"

Meran reached Willard and pushed him aside. "I'll do it. I have little problem in taking you down a peg or two."

Ricci's eyes flared sharp and fiery as daggers heated on coals, even as he smirked. "You may dream."

Meran snarled back. "I see you, Leon Ricci, and I am not afraid." Yet, even as he curled his hands into fists, he felt them tremble. At no time had Meran come near to besting this man. This time promised to be no different.

Again, Ricci held his hand aloft. "And here is your champion. I can but thank our young Zachary for his volunteer. Here," he thrust the oil into Willard's hands, "lather him well, my fine fellow, or victory is sure to be mine in the next two minutes." With that, Ricci strode to the other side of the circle now formed from the *Voce* contingent of the crew.

The men of Atena rallied to Meran's side. He swallowed. Could he do this? Already he saw the division made by this small competition. Allies they might be, but they were not one people. His quest would separate them further and put them at enmity with their Dracan neighbours. They did not deserve this. What if they were killed as a result? He would be to blame.

Nevertheless, he had seen what he had seen, and without this plan, the Velkor would overrun his people with war and bloodshed. His hometown would be set afire, and Patrice would be savaged, her knowing hazel eyes dimmed forever. And Sofie, *ah ye gods.* Sweet, innocent Sofie... He shook the dread from his mind. Never, never could this happen. Gathering his resolve, he let Willard help him from his tunic before starting to smear oil over him.

"You do not have to do this," Willard said, concern furrowing his brow. "Mortification is not new to me. We all suffer it at one or another time in our lives. This is the Mavish. Mayhap having my drawers wrenched free by such a man would serve to make me famous."

Meran's heart softened at the attempted humour and grabbed Willard's wrist. At the touch, the assurance washed over him that Willard would not be part of the war to come. He had no idea of the reason, but that did not matter. Some things were what they were. "I would have neither you humiliated nor injured on my watch. What kind of friend would that make me? Besides, can you truly say that you trust him, that this game is all that it will be? Well, I do not."

"What if he were to hurt you? That is not my want."

"He will not." Of that Meran, was certain. "Embarrass me? Aye. But of the two of us, I think I will suffer the less bruising when all is said and done." At the look of doubt on Willard's face, Meran plastered on a confident smile. "Trust me." And he turned to face his grinning opponent.

Cheers rose, and a robust chant began, Zachary's name on every Velkor's tongue. He wished it could be *Meran*, but he applauded their intent. As he eyed Ricci, Meran only hoped he would not let them down too quickly.

For a moment, they circled each other, Ricci's arms spread wide as if he welcomed their inevitable embrace, his grin a leer, and his eyes bright. "Come to me, boy. Let us see your mettle."

Meran lunged, their bodies coming together with a blinding force, the wind almost knocked from him. He hung on, trying to take Ricci down to the deck, though he was all solid muscle and seemingly as immutable as a rock.

They grappled. Hands gliding, gripping, sliding. Oil painted a slippery sheen from Meran's body all over Ricci's.

Meran could find no purchase. He slipped from Ricci's grasp like a fruit squeezed from its skin.

Roars of excitement hammered at Meran. The addition of the oil had evened the prospects, and all knew it. No longer a matter of brute force, either of them could win.

Meran returned Ricci's grin and went for the waist of his pants.

Battered easily aside, he struggled to defend his own from Ricci's answering grasp.

They fell as they wrestled, Meran pinned beneath Ricci's heavy body. Every hard muscle pressed him to the deck with an intimacy bordering on salacious.

Meran felt Ricci's hand struggle to sneak down the top of his britches and latch on, but his arm was trapped beneath their combined weight.

Ricci huffed out a laugh, the excitement bubbling out of him like a boy with a new toy. The light in his eyes, so alive and foreign, could not fail to entrance. The hint of joy, the revelling in such a competition, seemed to transform him.

The feral eyes of the Mavish did not stare back at Meran, nor the authoritarian glare of Lord Marshal Ricci, but that of Leon himself.

Meran's hand, sliding over hot skin and ridges of muscle on the way to the firm mounds of Leon's arse, stalled in surprise. Here was a man savouring the fun.

Leon took advantage, throwing his weight to his back and hefting Meran aloft.

Meran scrambled back. Slithering from Leon's hold, he skidded on the oil that slathered over the deck's boards and almost planted his face in Leon's crotch.

Leon gripped Meran's waist and pulled him up. One hand went for his buttocks as the other threatened to slither beneath his waistband. The tight tailoring of Velkory defeated the attempt, much to Meran's relief.

He threw himself sideways. Leon, holding on like a leech, sent them rolling and fighting for the lead. Hands roamed free over each other's pelvises, intent on snatching the prized fabric from beneath. A dance of intimacy that Meran could not ignore, his nethers as effectively explored as if he were in mid-coitus.

His heart pounded, sweat breaking out over his skin and his breath coming in ragged pants. Affected as much by the exercise as by the thoughts that sprang to his mind, his loins stirred to life and a shower of magic flared into the ether.

And in his distraction, he found himself flipped on his belly, fingers slithering beneath the band of his britches and scrabbling against his flesh to find his underclothes. *No, no, no!* He was having fun, enjoying the tussle maybe more than he should, but he would not let Leon so easily defeat him.

He shot to his knees. Bumped off Leon's hold and flipped as he twisted his legs about Leon's hips. He slipped his hand beneath Leon's clothes with a bold forthrightness, only to be met with the firmest, hottest flesh that had ever taken him so completely by surprise. Leon's naked prick overflowed his questing hand, long and thick and startling.

Meran yelped and scrambled back. It had been so big and shocking when he had expected to feel linen. Yet the ghost of its velvety skin tingled across Meran's palm, and eagerness rose with an intensity unbidden. The want to see and explore that impressive phallus took his breath.

Leon laughed as he came to his elbows and eyed Meran, a curious glint in his eyes for the hand Meran still held aloft, his fingers splayed. "That is what a real man feels like."

"You bastard." Anger yanked Meran from his daze. "You are not even wearing any underdrawers."

Leon grinned, unrepentant. "Ah, that is too true. It seemed at the time of the challenge I was caught short and had accepted it before the details were made known to me."

Instead of the crowd being incensed at the deception, they burst into raucous laughter, Meran's face heating with a mix of fury and embarrassment. "By the gods! How was I ever to win?"

Leon rose and stood before him, a hand held out. Meran slapped it aside, springing up to confront him and ignoring the evidence of arousal still large in Leon's britches.

A heavy hand on his shoulder held Meran in place, Leon's voice low and rumbling, "No one but I was expected to win, so what did it matter if I had underdrawers or nay. Not everything is about you. Pull yourself together."

Ignoring Meran's discombobulation, Lord Marshal Ricci turned to his audience, feigning consolation. "That he even had a chance to get his hand down my trousers, which some might consider the greater prize"—some of the crew sniggered while others let out shrill whistles—"proves he is braver and more tenacious than any man here." He turned back to Meran while addressing the captain. "Mot, the dagger is his."

Captain Mot pressed the prize into Meran's shaking hand.

Meran kept the snarl of outrage to himself as the Velkor rivermen crowed and cheered and stamped their feet in a victory dance. He did not want Ricci's charity or whatever he thought this was. He wanted respect.

But he could not, for the life of him, think how he would ever get it.

PART THREE
A Path of Discovery

INTERLUDE TWO

Becchus Oasis, Southern Draca

Joram made his way down the stepped corridor hewn from the ground. His footfalls fell muffled beneath the low ceiling, the angry spirits breathing their displeasure from above at his invasion, death settling close to watch and wait.

This destination always sent dread shivers through him. Time had faded the wall's original paintwork to specks and shadows, enough to put him on edge. An edge he hid beneath a ferocious demeanour. One that no fellow tribesman would dare penetrate.

A gaping hole cut in the wall sat like a black maw about to consume all who entered. Determinedly, he strode to it. Beyond lay a tomb, stark and cold in its subterranean cavity. In spite of that, it made the perfect gaol.

"Has he spoken?" he asked of his father's lock as he stepped inside. If anyone were able to persuade the stranger to talk, it would be Adon. A man of both reason and silent force. A small, wiry warrior of calm collection, he possessed a wisdom that even Joram's father, the catana, ofttimes lacked.

Adon looked up at his entrance, his dark brown eyes for once smouldering with dissatisfaction.

Blood escaped from the corners of the captive's mouth and dripped from his nostrils as he lay crumpled on the floor. His eyes were swollen shut, his nose a contorted lump.

"Nay, and not likely to for the present." Adon pulled back on the fellow's hair and lifted his sagging chin. He let it go with a disgusted shake of his head at the strapping warrior at his side who had apparently misjudged the strength of his beating. The stranger's head lolled to the side, insensible. "His body is fragile, yet his spirit is fierce. He has refused to tell me aught, even unto his name."

Joram stood over the obstinate fellow, silently impressed. That the stranger had been up to mischief had been obvious. His furtive behaviour had given him away when one of the young warriors encountered him hiding above Becchus's Sabin Falls.

"Of what Outlier do you think he comes?" Joram bent to peer closer into the stranger's face, his knees snapping off hollow pops of sound into the oppressive chill of the dark surrounds. Ripples of nerves fingered up Joram's back, and he grimaced, hating that he was not immune to the belligerent spirits that haunted the place. Yet, more oft than not, fear of them had many a prisoner talk.

Bodies had once lain here on the chalky ledges, dry and desiccated in their swaddling. His people would not have come here had the tomb not already been raided and the bones left scattered. The Outliers honoured the dead, performing the ritual using crystal venom to return them back to the desert and to their most Holy Nord, just as He had commanded.

Men were not meant to lie mouldering, trying to take with them their most precious of possessions into the Otherlands. That was the old way, the way of the arrogant and privileged. Men unable to let go of what small riches they had attained in life for the glory promised in the presence of their gods.

Joram sneered at his own superstition. He feared no man, be he alive or dead. Ghosts were nought to him, he told himself.

He studied the slack face before sweeping a searching gaze across the captive's body. He, too, tended to small and slender, his skin nutmeg brown and his hair thick, black, and plaited into an extravagant, long tail. Like many of Joram's own countrymen.

Little identified who had sent him, but with what Curia Venner had in his possession, uninvited guests were no longer welcomed at Becchus. They needed to know from whence he had come and what his intentions were.

"He has no defining features. No clothing that is not a match to our own. It is as if someone has dressed him to blend in," Adon said.

"And yet he does not."

"No. There is consideration behind his disguise." Adon considered a moment. "I think me, we should bring the magos to assess him. This smacks to me of Maki Dira's want to keep track of what goes on here, knowing what our Outlier has come into possession of."

"A spy, you say?"

"Aye. See here, he has the studious cast of a learned man—soft of skin and soft of hand, as if pampered." Adon held up the man's hands. They were indeed unmarked, barring a callus along his index and middle fingers on his right hand, which showed he held a stylus for many hours. "But then he also has shown warrior-like courage." Adon screwed his face in thought. "He reminds me of the guards set to ensure the safety of Alatim. Their service remains unwavering to those they believe hold the real power of Draca. A loyal man."

"But not to our Outlier."

"No. His allegiance lies elsewhere."

"To the maki, presumably? And that can only mean she still hopes to usurp what is ours."

Adon did not answer, but his eyes held concern. No one wished to incite civil war. None of the south could afford such a conflict. They were nomadic, the poor relations of Draca, and until Venner uncovered Anigema's magic, they remained vulnerable.

Joram swore under his breath. This, they did not need. This was their Season of Rites. Their older boys were in the midst of their rite of passage to become men. The Outlier could not abandon the oasis until the Moon of Solitude had come to completion and the lads home again from their trial. Honour and prestige demanded it.

He took a deep breath. If they had found one agent, there could be more roaming free and able to take vital detail to those who would rip the power from them.

"We need to send all our available warriors to search the area. I will not stand for any threat."

Adon nodded his agreement and gestured to the young warrior in attendance. "Gather who you can and fan out from Becchus in every direction. Search not only for men but also for the signs of their passing and bring back to me what and who you find."

"Sir, what of Nairo?" the young warrior said, chin lifted in bold belligerence. "He languishes this moment, doing nought. In a hunt, he is a good man—"

"No!" Joram cut through the impudence, squinting at the insolent warrior, his look familiar.

He knew by sight most of the young men from the Tent of Warriors, and this one he placed as a sycophant that hung upon his half-brother, Nairo's every word. Baban, he thought him called. A man one step from the Tent of Servants but for that friendship. And perhaps one who'd had a hand in Nairo's scheme to subvert Nord's holy rite this one week past.

The irony was not lost on Joram. Falric, Nairo's intended victim, had been born into slavery. The catana had afforded him the chance to transcend that position should Nord show him favour during his Moon Rite. That Baban might have participated in circumventing to another the good fortune that he himself had received spoke to how misplaced that magnanimity had been.

A sneer tugged at Joram's lip for the conceit of his half-brother's plan. More than anything, this proved Nairo was far from being a *good man*.

"He still awaits the Quorum's pleasure. Not even for this will he be let from his mother's tent. Now be about your lock's direction or, despite Nairo's insistence that you were not party to his misdeeds, I might have you join him in his pending punishment."

Baban's expression grew sulky, but he had the wit to take his leave with a curt "Sir" to Adon and a disgruntled nod to Joram before Joram's irritation had him carry through on his threat.

The instinct to bash the lout's arrogant head against the lintel as the young man passed into the corridor beyond, Joram barely restrained. How the Holy Nord had favoured such a recusant, he could not understand, but he would never contend with his god on the matter. It was his duty to believe.

"I will have Beric oversee him," Adon said. "That one grows too bold for his sandals. 'Twould have been better should catana have called the Quorum together right at the outset instead of awaiting the rite's conclusion."

"Amata interferes." Joram's lip curled at the thought of his father's singular catanee. The Outlier would have fared the better should his own mother not have passed, leaving the self-serving Amata as his father's only wife. "She will not have her precious spawn labelled reprobate, but by his very actions, he has revealed himself devious and unscrupled."

The silence that followed this declaration grew heavy. Joram glanced over to where the lock stood beside their prisoner, his expression impassive. Whatever his thoughts, they would always be reasoned and fair, but Joram felt no such compunction. His father's youngest was a blight on the face of Draca, a twisted sword, useless to any hand and safer buried. He already knew what his vote would be.

The prisoner took that opportunity to groan softly, both men turning to ponder the rousing man. Breath whistled wetly through his nose, shivers setting up tremors through his body as he floundered on the cold stone of the floor.

"Shall I send for the magos?" Adon asked.

"No need. I think it fair to suppose he is under the maki's direction."

"What would you have me do with him?"

"Hmm." Joram pondered a moment. "Seems to me he has served his purpose in alerting us to her devices. I would send her his head, but that would only have her change tack."

"He needs to be silenced, though."

"Aye." Joram nodded in agreement. "Take his tongue and fingers or send him back to the desert. I care not which."

At that, the prisoner began to gasp, though not to beg. Not yet, at least. If the lock chose the latter, the crystal venom was sure to loosen his tongue. By the time Joram crossed from the oppressive corridor and back into the clear day, his spirits lifting, the man's muffled gasps had turned to echoing screams.

CHAPTER TWENTY

Nord's Southern Deserts

Meran Durante proved himself an obstinate young man. Not once in the last five days had he attempted to appease Leon but clung to his discontent. Leon let him pout. It made for a pleasant and silent vigil during the back-breaking work that travelling upriver necessitated.

Keeping the small craft to the edges of the Meith as much as possible, Leon navigated its course, heading towards the rendezvous with Tark. His muscles ached from the persistent and monotonous strain of paddling against the current.

Impressively, Durante had managed to keep up, wearying though his inexperience had made him. By the first day's end, his arms had flagged. His elbows clung at the level of his waist, his face set into a rictus of persistent pain that he looked determined not to give in to.

They made their way through an ever-changing landscape. The river glided from between high rocky slopes near the convergence to flat sandy plains. Reed-choked shores followed, merging into thick swathes of palms that stretched tentative daring fingers to the desert's border.

The days dawned dry and hot, but not near to the scorching heat of Draca in full summer. Nonetheless, they were forced to discard their tunics, the sweat bathing their skin, even as the heat kissed them dry. Leon could not wait for the loose tunics and britches that accompanied Tark and the provisions.

In the interim, Leon fashioned a makeshift scarf for his head to keep the fierce burn from his neck and shoulders. He would not risk sunstroke. Not even *Voce* magic held that malaise at bay. Amusingly, Durante followed his example. He also abandoned the use of his kohl and facial powders, the weather and their toil unconducive for keeping the embellishments in place.

The cairn Leon anticipated came into view, and he guided their craft across the current, making for the shoreline. From Durante's alert posture, it was obvious he had many questions, yet he held to his pique, remaining silent as they floated up against the gentle slope of the sandbank.

Leaping onto the shore, Durante reached out to accept the rope from Leon and proceeded to help him drag the boat up onto the small beach. Curiosity still burned in his eyes. Leon could have put him out of his misery, but it pleased him not to.

After taking their meagre possessions from the bottom of the small boat and carrying them into the shade of a thick cluster of palms, Leon dropped to his seat. Leaning back against the nobbled surface of a skinned trunk, he sipped from a canteen, grateful to whoever had tended the patch of vegetation.

He closed his eyes, cutting out the brightness of the midafternoon light, allowing the sweat to cool on his skin and his body to relax. He could hear the furtive movement of his companion, feel the blaze of his gaze sweeping him and the tingling buzz of his unquenched curiosity, and stifled his smile.

There was the clearing of a throat, the clicking of a tongue, the impatient shuffle of feet kicking up the sand. That Durante fiddled with the handle of the little dagger he had won, Leon imagined inevitable. Durante had taken up the nervous tick when he did not know what to do with himself.

The desire to tell the lad to find shade and quench his thirst before he sweltered into exhaustion tugged at Leon's lips, but he held back. It would come soon...

"What are we doing here?" The words came laced with impatience, Durante's voice croaking from disuse.

Without opening his eyes, Leon answered, "Waiting." The grin of triumph tugged at the corners of his mouth.

"For what?"

"When it happens, you will know."

Durante huffed out a furious breath, as hot as the weather surrounding them, but Leon refused to elaborate. He would not make the situation less *awkward* for the young fellow. No, when Durante put his childishness behind him, perhaps Leon would treat him as a man and an ally.

Leon satisfied himself with listening to the boy breathe through his irritation. Then the sound of his sandals crunching across the sand as he retreated to the water's edge. The rustle of footwear being discarded preceded splashing. Leon opened one eye to see Durante ankle-deep at the river's verge and inspecting his cargo. Three rundlets and three bottles of wine.

Durante had purchased them as gifts to allay their quarry's suspicions. Leon considered him lucky the cooler days of winter were on their way. At the height of summer, the wine would not have fared so well.

"Leave them be," he called as Durante began to drag them from the bobbing ripples of the river where they lay, fat and round and half submerged in a net. They had been a nuisance, dragging behind the boat, but it was the only avenue to keep them viable. "The longer they linger in the cool, the less chance you have of cooking the wine in them."

"Cook them?" Shock pinked Durante's cheeks, and the corners of his eyes crinkled with embarrassment. His life had no doubt thus far been sheltered from the logistics and pitfalls that accompanied trade. A timely lesson if he wished to convince anyone of his disguise.

Durante let the ropes loose and splashed again to shore before surveying his locale with indecision writ large on his face.

Leon said nothing. Closing his eye again, he relaxed his breath and sent out the farsight. He spotted Tark travelling by cart, but the distance between his clansman and the agreed rendezvous point remained indistinct. The day was hot, and there was nothing for it but to sleep the afternoon heat away.

After drinking near a full pouch of water, Durante settled in the shade, maintaining his sullen isolation while keeping Leon within reach. Not long after, exhaustion had done its work, and the deep calm breaths of sleep reached Leon.

A quick scan showed they were alone. The fauna of the desertscape slumbered, just as they did, through the hottest part of the day. Leon let himself settle.

He awoke to the caress of a cooling breeze and a sky streaked in fingers of blazing orange and brilliant purple as the sun sank below the horizon. The hum of life stirred about him. Leon scrubbed his face to shake off the residue of sleep. Again, he sent out the farsight. A wending trail amidst lush vegetation shimmered into view, along with Tark's cart juddering over its rutted and undulating course.

Rising, he edged out into the stand of palms, some thick with dead fronds drooping about their trunks like brittle skirts. The small cairn fell behind him, and soon he mounted a knoll of sand and stared into the twilight. Flickers of movement disturbed the distance.

Leon lit a wooden torch, the flames dancing in the breeze and casting garish shadows. He waved the brand back and forth, signalling Tark. The sounds of hooves and the rattle of wagon wheels grew louder and louder. A mule brayed a greeting from the darkness.

Warmth flooded Leon's chest as his clansman finally came into view, and spotting his black silhouette, he raised an arm. Tark presented a hulking figure. No rival for Leon's height, but equally as muscular.

A smile split the bearded face as Tark jumped from the cart and moved to clasp Leon's arm. His cheeks shone rosy in the torchlight, his eyes sparkling with obvious pleasure.

"By the gods, man. 'Tis a wonder to see ye again. It has been too long."

Emotion ached through Leon's jaw and down his throat as he wrapped his clansman in an embrace of long-anticipated welcome. "That it has, old friend. I have missed you."

Tark squeezed him with affection, administering a rapid tattoo of harsh slaps to Leon's back to cover the threads of emotion echoing in his clansman's eyes.

Leon pulled back. "Were you able to secure all that I asked for?"

"A'course, man," came the smiling reply. "That you doubt me stabs me to the quick. If you have the money, I have the means. Mind you, when that fat pigeon flew in, you could have knocked me over with its feathers. Never did I expect to see that broad scrawl of yours ever again. May I ask what brings ye to these desolate parts?"

"You may."

"And?" Tark encouraged, ignoring Leon's attempt at humour.

Leon flicked a quick look around. The farsight revealed Durante relieving himself by the river's edge. Time enough. Leon pulled Tark into the cover of a thick clutch of vegetation, vulnerability brewing in the cauldron of his hope.

But of anyone, Tark would understand its magnitude. "Word has reached me that has piqued my curiosity. Something of great import has been uncovered. Something that perhaps we have been seeking for many a long year."

Tark's eyes bugged, his skin ashen. "Ye cannot mean...?"

"*Amplion.*" Leon whispered its name reverently. "Aye. That I do."

"But how? Where?" Shock reverberated through Tark's voice. "Who told you?"

Leon hesitated to admit to Tark that he based his hope solely on Durante's mystical narrative... "A young fellow of Velkor who also happens to be of my acquaintance. An affiliate of Prince Rane and a budding merchant who has overheard murmurings from those of the coast north of the Meith. Word has filtered down that a certain object of interest has come to light."

Mouth slack, Tark gripped a hand to his nape, his other arm folded defensively across his chest, his expression one of stunned disbelief. "Pray, where? When?"

"I know not for sure. Some six moons or more ago, as far as can be placed, and on the plains of Southern Draca." Leon lay a reassuring hand on Tark's shoulder. "Tell me, have there been any incidents or altercations between the folks in these parts? Anything memorable that might offer a clue?"

"In the last six moons? Seems to me the whole darn lot of them have been antsy for some reason or other." Tark pursed his lips, his brow a thunderclap of concentration. Leon could almost see the memories mulled over and discarded...until the colour returned to Tark's face, his eyes sparkling as if alighting upon such a possibility.

"He called a moot," he said before he shook his thoughts into order. "I'm bound that you seek a man known as Keija."

"Keija?"

"He is catana of one of the larger Outlier in these southern parts. Possibly the largest since the pox afflicted many of them when I first came to these lands. I was travelling the floodplains near where his people trekked down from the high desert about eight moons back. Following an altercation between them and a village of the Bengay, an ally of mine living with the Outlier begged me to come to a rescue—"

Surprise piqued at Leon. "Of whom?"

"A Bengay boy and a big fellow, name of Sem."

"Sem?" The man that shadowed Mot's every step sprang to mind. "Is he the one that travels with Mot's crew?"

"Aye. She brought him to me." Tark's voice softened, his eyes momentarily brightening with fond sentiment.

Leon's eyebrows shot up, but Tark did not entertain his curiosity.

"She thought of me when he found himself a slave and at the mercy of a hellish master and thought life no longer worth living. There is nought more to it than that."

Leon doubted Tark's sincerity, but he left him to his secrets.

"I have met him. He does as well as can be expected." The man's heartache was far from over, but Leon hoped the street urchin's fast attachment offered Sem a feeling of worth and solace.

"I am glad. As for *Amplion?* I'd thought little of it back then, for Keija ever was a snake, and I'd not put him past the thieving of anything. But later, I heard that he and Catana Tane were up to something, and his holy man, Venner, insisted he call an assembly. Tane's Outlier is acting emissary, seeking out as many of the other Outliers as can be found."

"What is the significance of this?"

"A moot between the Outliers is almost unheard of. They keep to their own except to wage petty wars over camels and goats. Little concerns made large, but this gathering speaks of an undeniable change."

"How long since?" Leon's heart thudded with excitement.

"At summer's end, two moons back or so. As soon as the two Outliers abandoned their summer grounds, they parted ways."

Leon sighed. "Nord curse them."

Tark's broad shoulders slumped. "If Keija's found…" He faulted, taking a deep swallow. "I have failed my task tenfold. I deserve my exile."

Gripping both Tark's shoulders, Leon shook the disconsolate man. "As did I. As did any that Ivo sent to discover the whereabouts of *Amplion*. It was not the time…"

"Lives would have been saved." Guilt riddled Tark's eyes, his voice dropping low. "*His* life."

But nothing could have saved King Carl Voltan. He had made the sacrifice. The magic required to put an end to the conflict between Aleia's snake people and those of Locurnia had been the greatest ever expended by a single *Voce*. Only he had the hope of achieving it. The king had gone to his death to save all their lives. "What is done is done. Choices were made and we all must live with them."

"He speaks aright. You exile yourself for no reason." Said in Velkor, the voice interrupted their privacy, and Tark threw his head back like a stallion startled by a lightning strike.

Leon followed Tark's wide-eyed stare into the veiling darkness. There amidst the trees stood Meran Durante, again powdered and primped and looking slender and regal; and passing judgement where he had no right.

CHAPTER TWENTY-ONE

At Meran's interruption, Ricci's expression grew stony, but for once, he kept his own counsel.

Lord Ricci's companion shook off his surprise and stepped forwards. "Now, who might this be?"

The stranger's hand shot out, gripping Meran's in the formal way of Velkory. Forearms twined, palms together, knuckles facing each other.

Polite interest overlaid the man's features, the deep emotion, evident when Meran had come upon them, buried now beneath a stoic mask. "I am Tark of Clan Ricci." Tark's Velkor bore only a slight accent. "I come with provisions at the behest of my lord here. And you are?"

"His travelling companion."

As the perceived outsider, Meran already felt the depths of his isolation. Sometimes his disguise worked too well, but now that they were on Dracan soil, he had little choice except to maintain it.

"I am named Zachary the Fisher, from down Atena way."

Meran studied Tark, noting the big bones and chiselled features common to the Ricci's. Scars latticed the biceps of his left arm, forging up beneath the shoulder of his tunic, speaking to a time spent fighting in the Serpent War.

A warrior.

But Tark's lips were full and quick with the easy smile missing from Ricci himself, and his darker blue eyes and blonder hair created an aura of softness. Even in his unkempt state from travel, this clansman lacked the feral, animalistic demeanour worn by his lord.

And yet, his mere presence seemed to forestall Ricci's irritation at Meran's intrusion. Meran looked from one to the other, curiosity trembling on his lips, wondering at Tark's place in Ricci's plan.

Tark released his arm with a friendly clap on the back. "Zach'ry, eh?

'Tis a fine name. I have heard of the Fishers of Atena. You are of the Northern Merchant's Guild?"

"I am. A new member this year gone." Meran cleared his throat, at a loss on how to proceed. To bring *Amplion* up again would reveal he had overheard and understood some of their private conversation. Even if all he wanted was to reassure Tark that his guilt was unwarranted, as a Velkor, he could not know the prophet's teachings. That the scrolls made clear it would remain concealed *'until the coming of an abomination'* to awaken it.

Tark pursed his lips. "Ah. Come to seek new endeavours, have ye? The far north being a market not easily encroached upon."

"Aye. The Ballan has it all in hand."

"So, you would conquer the south?" Tark gave an amused laugh.

Meran offered a quick nod and shook off the surging feeling of guilt. If he accomplished what he wanted, war would come to Southern Draca.

"Well, you have picked uncertain times, my friend. The natives are restless. Still, nought ventured…"

"…nought gained," Meran finished. "Too true."

Tark fixed Meran with an assessing stare. "How came ye to know my lord? You must be a persuasive fellow to have secured his company on such a foray. Or wait…" A spark of insight flared in deep blue eyes. Tark gave him a studious perusal from his feet to his head. "You are his latest swain. Is that it? He always did like them finely put together, though I have never known him to go for one of Velkory."

Meran choked on his own spit at Tark's familiarity in his lord's presence. Even Ricci scowled and placed a restraining hand on who Meran guessed must be a kinsman.

"Enough. This is not the time nor place for such sharing. Come, show us what you have brought, and let us settle for a bite to eat; afterwards, I will tell you what goes on."

Uttered in *Voce* and with greater resigned exasperation than any resentment, the gentleness of Ricci's reprimand came unexpected.

Tark offered a shrug, unperturbed by Ricci's words, and turned for his wagon and the milling animals. "This way. I'm sure ye will find everything satisfactory, and out of the goodness of my heart, I've included a bit of brandy to set fire to your belly. In the desert proper, you'll need it when the night chill sets in, I promise ye."

Realising Tark's arrival had been what Ricci awaited, Meran

followed. His curiosity spiked as he spotted a small wagon filled with provisions and pulled by a mule. Strung out behind, a line of horses milled, all inferior in size to those ridden by *Vocekind.*

"I managed to secure six of the wee buggers for ye," Tark said. "I know they don't look much"—he flicked Ricci a pointed glance—"but they be sturdy beasts and strong enough to carry even you. They'll do ye proud."

Meran gaped. The animals did not look long enough in the wither to keep either Meran's or Ricci's feet from dragging along the ground.

"Here." Tark began pulling the items from the back of the wagon. "No time like the present, so let's be getting it sorted."

"Ah, should we not do this on the morrow; give you time to rest?" Tark had to be weary from travelling all day. What was the urgency?

"You'll not be heading out soon?" Tark asked Ricci.

"Surely, you jest?" Meran interjected before Ricci had the chance to open his mouth. It was now pitch dark, the waxing gibbous moon the only illumination; that, and the pinpoints of stars. How could they hope to find their way?

"'Tis a long journey ahead of ye to reach Becchus." Tark shrugged as if such a course made perfect sense. "That is where Keija's Outlier overwinters while their young-men-in-training go through their rite of passage. Though they will not be vacating anytime soon, it is still a significant trek betwixt here and there."

A spark of excitement lit deep within Meran at the mention of the catana's name. This man knew who they were looking for and where to find him. "You speak of an oasis? One bound by a winding river and slashed through with abundant greenery amidst barren red dust and sand?"

"Aye, that it is, and a big 'un."

Meran tried to recall any oases he had seen from the map at the Shimmering Fields's library which bore such a name. There had been several such formations noted on the dry and crinkled parchment, and he thought he recalled a larger one, centrally located. But the map had been little more than a stylised sketch and drawn without scale.

Eagerness to be off bloomed, although travelling in the dark seemed impossible. Meran turned on the lord marshal, his brow raised in question. "How can we travel at such a time?"

Instead, Tark answered, with an encouraging pat on Meran's shoulder, "Fear not. The lord marshal has all in hand. These beasties will ensure your path. That is what they be bred for." And with that, Tark continued to divest the cart of the provisions.

With the clansman's help, Meran grudgingly spread the supplies between the horses while Ricci, at Tark's suggestion no less, started a fire and, of all things, began to cook. Meran had not known Ricci had it in him. Up until this point, they had been subsisting on breads, cheese, dried meat, and raw fruit. Not that Meran had been looking forward to something hot, but the prospect now tempted his taste buds.

The way Ricci sliced and diced exhibited his expertise. That he had not shared his proficiency tightened Meran's lips.

When they came to the last animal, Meran burdened it down with the three rundlet barrels and a saddlebag carrying the bottles of wine. He padded it with clothes to stop the bottles from clanking together.

"Aw! These are from the Teff Valley, are they not?" Tark asked, slacking his curiosity as to the bag's contents. "A gift?"

"Aye. A peace offering of a sort." To keep within character, Meran intended to extend the same graciousness common to Atena.

Replacing the bottle in the bag, Tark pulled the strap tight about the horse's middle. "I did have me some when last in Atena. There is none the better. Ye start your negotiations off on the right foot, lad, I do not doubt it."

"Then it is only you?"

"You might wish to give his lordship a moment."

"He treats me as if I am a buffoon."

"Surely not." Tark peered into his eyes, his own glittering with earnest. "Look, lad, ye are a mite younger, and more exotic than is his normal fare, but no more loyal a man can be found once ye are one of his."

Scepticism curled Meran's lips.

"True, he is not easy to know, but if ye ask me, it is always a process…" For a moment, melancholy etched Tark's features, his eyes distant and glazed by memories. "Always." His voice softened. "But the gods' willing, it will come right."

Meran had no curiosity for whatever story was there. Tark Ricci had gotten the wrong end of the stick and Meran's hackles rose. "Sir. I insist, there is nought between us. There can never be…"

"Ah. You Velkor count him a hard man. The Hell-spawn! Aye, I've heard it said more than once. A lord without remorse or compassion."

Tark cast him a conciliatory gaze, his hand coming to rest against Meran's wrist, "but you would be wrong."

The gesture surprised Meran, but still he shrugged. He did not need to hear Tark Ricci's bias. "I can only go by what I see, but we have not been in company long." And despite everything he thought he knew, he realised he perceived very little of the real Lord Marshal Ricci.

"You know his legend, I am sure, but you cannot know everything." Tark's reproach echoed. "Do you even know how a man of *Voce* came to be a part of the games and tourneys of your people?"

Did Tark know the incident that had set the young Ricci on his course? Meran had always assumed Loni's ghost revealed a secret known only to her, one of the reasons for her shade's continued captivity in the dreamlands. Could he have been wrong? Those of Atena, of course, could have no idea that her dying had caused the young Ricci to run. "I do not."

"And yet you still keep him...*company?*" Tark's knowing gaze fell on him. "You are a sensitive man. You must see beneath this legend to the wounded heart that beats within, or you would not be with him."

Wounded? Impossible! There was no room in Ricci's psyche for vulnerability. "I am not *with him*," Meran said with a shake of his head. That Tark persisted in the supposition stirred an unwilling unease in his chest. A mixture of exasperation, want, and panic. "To me, he is a man of many contradictions, but tenderness is not one of them."

The memory of the boy and his sister at the Broken Sword, rescued from the attentions of Belton, came back to prick his conscience. Witnessing that, he had thought Ricci could not be all bad, and he had not been. He was a hard man but interspersed between those savage and fiery moments had been passionate and disconcerting ones. Ones he did not want to think on too closely.

Tark dismissed Meran's denial. "He is fierce, impatient, undiplomatic and e'en querulous, but he is also strong of heart and unfailingly loyal to his own. I think you may dwell overmuch on what Atena has made of him and not who he really is. The boy then is not the same as the man now."

"I have seen little difference." Tark's tenacious steadfastness stirred Meran's irritation. "I saw him fight at the events at the Shimmering Fields, and only law kept him from slaughter. The consummate warrior hides beneath his skin and cannot deduce friend from foe should he be let loose. That I have witnessed."

"My lord is a warrior. That I will never deny. But he does not wallow in slaughter like wine. Does not crave it—"

"Are you sure?"

"Does he rape as he slaughters? Does he torture with cuts that will bleed a man slow, while emasculating and disfiguring him? I know of one who does."

The spectre of Bas's abused body rose to haunt Meran with its greying flesh, waterlogged and lifeless. Had that been what the butcher had done? Meran squirmed in some discomfort, unwilling to believe anyone so vile. Nevertheless, the wounds he had seen evidenced the monstrousness of Bas's attacker.

"A man whose appetites and deeds are without honour," Tark continued. "Yes, Leon is a warrior, but he fights with honour in both the field of battle and in competition."

"Dead is dead, honour or nay." Petulance had Meran reason. "He has killed many a Velkor for nought but fortune." The Mavish had revelled in his slaughter at the arenas in Atena. He was no better.

Tark's eyes burned with a flare of disgust. "And you think this makes them one and the same? His lordship was a boy when he fought those battles, a boy racked by guilt and self-loathing that had become a death wish, but he did not murder the innocent. He did not take by force those who were not his and defile them."

Recognition of how personal this was for Tark struck Meran. Had such a murder dared to touch one close to him?

An apology trembled on his lips, even as Tark finished. "Every man who stepped into that arena knew the risk and had traded their soul for the value of the purse. Every man!"

Meran crumpled beneath the onslaught of Tark's affront. He had seen nothing of that part of Ricci's life. Though the woman's death may have been accidental, he had assumed its happenstance had sent Ricci on a killing spree. The desire for which he had managed to curb but never to cease.

Becoming a warrior and returning an earl at the death of his sire, Meran had presumed changed Ricci's base temperament not one jot. He had mollified his aggression in the tourneys in Locurnia, barely adhering to the rules of engagement, and he had beaten Lord Marshal Belton to a bloody mess. Yet Meran knew of no incident where Ricci had tortured an innocent victim.

Tark interrupted his churning thoughts. "Pray, tell me, Zach'ry?

Why trust such a man with this task, for trust him you must, or you would not head alone with him to such a destination."

"I-I have need of him. His skill. There are dangers I cannot navigate, people I cannot…" *Confront.* He trailed off, his throat clicking.

Meran's hypocrisy spilled over him like a flood of shame. Had he not proclaimed that this very temperament was why he needed Leon Ricci's service? He had used these very words to persuade Ricci to his side. Meran had even revelled in the delicious danger of such pleading. To pit his voice and authority as a seer against such a foe had been exhilarating.

But he had also lied. By omission, he had allowed Ricci to think the prize was *Amplion* when the visions told Meran it could not be. Blue, not white. That he would not rectify this misconception for fear of the consequence made him the least honourable of all.

Tark pursed his lips, the look of disgust vanishing as quickly as it had come. "Before you use him further, I think you should ask his story."

There were many things to glean from the spaces between Tark's words, not the least of them being that this one man knew of Leon Ricci's secret. Curiosity burned like a coal, fanned by the breath of Meran's frustration and shame that he had never considered Leon's side in the matter.

"Would you not deign to tell me? I fear he will not be disposed…"

"It is not mine to tell."

Meran's hope of taking the easy path flickered out.

"But the knowing may go some way for you to understand the Leon that is, and not the one that was," Tark continued. "He deserves more than to be used as your weapon. He would prove a good and stalwart man should you not spurn his friendship. And do not scorn him if you are lucky that he offers you more."

Tark's words sent a cascade of denials, wants, and inquisitiveness swirling in turmoil through Meran's brain, enough to leave him speechless.

Tark Ricci slung an arm about his waist and encouraged him from the wagon and the burdened horses. "Come now, let us eat. You have a long road ahead and, no doubt, many a fraught adventure on your path. Might as well commence it on a full belly."

CHAPTER TWENTY-TWO

Two nights later, Meran knew that night travel was the only answer. But in the darkness, the dire climes they headed into were as a wave of menace that rippled over his spirits. He missed the sound of the river and the green foliage along its bank. He missed the day.

Meran also missed Tark's easy company, though he had given him much to think on. He had assumed Tark would join them, though he had never been a part of Meran's visions. However, he begged off when it came time to depart. Something about an errand he could not put off, though it was said with a note of contrition.

True or not, Meran missed the effect that having this kinsman close had on Ricci. The camaraderie that sparked between the pair over their dinner had Meran rooted to his seat, wondering where the surly lord had disappeared to. Ricci had laughed, for the gods' sake, a sound that made him appear almost approachable...

But with Tark's departure, the lord returned with a vengeance. They had scarcely spoken more than three civil words together.

"Give your horse its head," Ricci ordered as Meran again tugged back on the small beast's rein, reacting to the looming shapes rearing out of the night. Ghostly forms morphed into spiked flora, and sand-blasted formations of rock littered their course.

"Easy for you to say." Not so easy to do.

Ricci had taken the lead position and their only torch. "I assure, its instincts are far superior to yours." His tone bled impatience.

Meran readjusted his situation on the snug saddle and tried to loosen his grip. The dry, dusty stink of the horse's coat plumed up to tease at his nostrils, his eyes watering. He barely held back a sneeze and cursed as an allergy tickled his mouth and throat.

The short, smelly animals were intolerable to ride. Either his legs stuck out awkwardly, or the shorter stirrup cramped his knees. He could walk faster than their laborious pace. What would take a horse bred in Locurnia mere days, he lamented, would take these beasts a week.

"How long until we reach our next stop?" he managed to cough out.

"After another full turn of the dial, I shall reconnoitrer the area. I will know then."

Frustrated at the lack of congenial conversation, Meran kept his silence. He itched to know Ricci's story, but since they had left the Meith, he felt kept at arm's length.

When Ricci finally called a halt, Meran dropped from his horse with a groan as his legs protested and his spine clicked into place. Stiffly, he lifted his mount's saddle and set about tethering the little caravan together.

Once done, he wandered over to watch Ricci breaking off some of the lower branches of a dry bush.

"Here." Ricci pushed the bundle into Meran's arms. "Gather more and light a fire. We could do with something warm, so set the water to boiling." He stopped for a moment, feigning mockery. "You do know how?"

Meran rolled his eyes. "I think I can manage."

He had enjoyed cooking while hunting with his friends in the forests of Ellom's ancestral lands, and he had proven skilled enough not to poison any of them.

"Good." With that, Ricci disappeared on foot into the darkness, leaving Meran to get on with preparing the victuals.

Meran chopped root vegetables, onions, and herbs and browned them at the bottom of a pot with a slick of oil. His stomach gurgled in anticipation as the aroma rose to tempt his nostrils.

Water added, he stirred it with slow sweeping strokes and awaited its boiling before dumping in a handful of grains.

He sat back, arms clasped about his torso to ward off the chill of inactivity. *Damn, the desert night was cold!* Meran silently thanked Tark for providing the boots, coat, and loose clothing. Yet this night, not even the soft scarf draped about head and shoulders proved sufficient.

Meran retrieved a blanket from the provisions and wrapped it around himself as he huddled by the fire.

Time dragged, and Meran's lids grew heavy. Being nigh on midnight, the need to sleep still hounded him. He would rest his eyes and listen to the simmering of their victuals and the furtive sounds of the desert as they drifted on the slight breeze…

Meran jolted upright. The sleep fell from him as he stared straight into a heavy mantle of fog, the desert gone.

He planted his hands to his chest, the feel beneath them insubstantial. Even as his heart pounded, he recognised his shade form and the surrounding ether.

The mists of the dreamland edged back to reveal a vision all too familiar. Meran had seen these stars, the panorama of the distant horizon, the eerie loneliness of the flat plain on which sat a campfire, a mere glow of coals.

Crushing isolation flooded him. Loss hounding him and carving out his insides. Fear rose like nausea, and Meran surged to his feet. His shattered nerves could not stand to repeat the vision's course. To run and find himself so close to what he had lost, only to be met with the disturbing winking of a myriad of eyes.

Darkness grew suddenly, encompassing his world; a night without stars, yet a glow emanated from behind him. A beam of eerie light fell across his shoulders. He turned; a brilliant orb of white burned his gaze. Not a moon, but something more dreadful.

He shivered, hands digging into his face as he closed his eyes. He filled his head with thoughts of feathers and snow and Sofie's childish laughter, all things that had brought him back from the brink before. Power flooded him, beckoned by his determination, and he took back control. He broke free of the dreamland's hold like a man breaking the surface from a deep dive. The cursed pull fell behind him and vanished into its mystical cloud cover as he came awake.

He gave a bark of triumphant laughter, well pleased with himself. "All is well." *Thank Holy Janus!*

Yet, he was alone. Wariness shadowed him. His previous hunting expeditions had never been solitary.

Meran sent out his farsight, scanning the near terrain for any signs of life. All about him gleamed with small, bright auras that frolicked amidst the skeletal structures of the desert's plants and slithered and stalked low to the ground. Some disappeared into the darkness beneath the desert's crust. A crust he had considered barren.

Regret welled that he had not better used his time in the Shimmering Fields, or even earlier, to study the desert fauna. He had no idea of what predators roamed Southern Draca. Ellom's forest had teamed with game and the solitary bear or two, along with small packs of timber wolves. But the desert?

He should have forced himself to question Ricci earlier, no matter how ambivalent their connection. Or asked how long it would take them to reach Becchus and what might lie in wait along the way. But that had seemed tantamount to pulling teeth.

Ricci brought out the worst in him. Now, all he wished for was Ricci's return. A man, no matter how intently Meran concentrated, no matter how far he threw out the farsight, he could not find. *What by all that is holy?*

A shudder of terror pressed down from the vast, lonely expanse above. *No, no. He did not need to take on so.* Ricci could be exploring some cavern or canyon where Meran's magic could not follow.

That certainty seeped away with the flight of time. The fire burned down, his stew bubbling and near to ruin. It had been too long. *Where was he?*

After rescuing the food from the fire, Meran strode to the edge of the firelight and squinted into the darkness, his mind roiling at the impossibility. Further out, his magic rolled over a herd of large animals, each shimmering beneath a pale lemon halo. Beasts of some unknown kind hunkered down and sleeping. And no threat.

Ricci had to be out there somewhere. No one could hide from the farsight forever.

Pacing the campsite's perimeter, Meran weighed up his options. To strike out on his own seemed folly, but was to stay any less? Vulnerability tightened his chest and destroyed any thought of hunger.

Hurrying to their provisions, he gathered his bow and quiver and set it down beside him as he returned to his vigil by the fire. It would keep him company until Ricci returned…

But what if he did not? What if some mischief had befallen him? Or he had come to the attention of some other nocturnal predator.

Or, what if his erroneous conviction that the treasure was *Amplion* tempted him to forge out on his own? To forget their agreement. Ricci had, after all, sought this prize before. The finding of which would cement his preeminence in *Voce* society.

A chill of fear trickled down Meran's spine. Was Ricci the kind of man to leave him to the desert's mercies? Tark would have him believe not, but Ricci had always been unpredictable, and knowing their destination, he might consider he no longer needed Meran, covenant be damned. He should have made him seal it with blood. Ricci was of

Farnham. The benighted highlanders, for all they bowed to Ivo and his new regime, still adhered to the old ways.

Shivering, Meran tried to tamp down his rising panic. Pulling the blanket close about his shoulders, he hunkered down beneath it as he set up watch.

A myriad of squeaks and chittering noises floated to his ears, along with the dry rustle of the horses' hooves. At every sound, he tensed more, his knee jittering up and down. His skin prickled in a shimmy of nerves as he scanned every movement around him with the farsight.

A presence loomed large and sudden behind him, an unexpected weight landing on his shoulder.

With a terrified squawk, Meran leapt to his feet, and out from beneath Ricci's hand, his own clasped to his chest as if holding his heart in place. "You bastard!"

Humiliation goaded Meran to pummel that familiar, egotistical face as the lord stood there smirking. That he would come off second best had him unclench his fist before it met Ricci's cheek.

Nevertheless, profound relief mixed with Meran's fury.

Ricci rumbled with dry amusement.

"There is nought funny about it!" Meran's heart rate began to return to normal. "How did you do that?"

"Pray, what?"

"Hide from me."

Ricci paused a beat. "You were spying on me?" He seemed surprised, but the glimmer in his eye turned taunting. "Did you miss me so much?"

Meran's hackles rose, not alone for the gibe but that Ricci sidestepped the issue. "You were gone for over two turns of the dial. What was I to think when you tell me nothing?"

All the anxiety and anger welled at Ricci's complacent expression, but Meran's concern had not been purely selfish. He had feared for Ricci's safety too. "This is beyond the pale. What if aught had happened to you?"

Ricci made a derogatory noise, such an outcome apparently beyond his comprehension.

"No! No!" Meran's voice rose. "I am not a child to be kept in the dark. Why do you keep me ignorant? Is it all in the name of petty vengeance?"

Ricci's brow dropped into a thunderous scowl. "I need no such reproof."

"Yes, you do." The floodgates opened. "We have a covenant. This is not your quest alone, but ours together. We must both play our part, or we fail. Failure is something I will never allow. Never!"

"Because you are a seer?" Ricci asked, his derision ripe. "Enough of that drivel. Was it seership that led you to threaten me? Was it visions that told you this avenue would make me compliant?"

"Must we dwell on this again?" Maddened, Meran threw his palms to the sky. "Tark has verified everything I have said."

"You gave me water and palms. Generalisations all. What nomad would choose to settle anywhere other than an oasis? A name would have been preferable—"

"I do not need these things, for pity's sake."

"What need have I of you when Tark pinpointed our destination? He warned us of the dangerous undercurrents pervading the south. He told us of Catana Keija's mood. Of Joram's implacability. Take out the father and you still have to contend with the son. You enlightened me of none of this."

Meran's affront escalated. "Damn you, man. I have no need to. The prophet guides me—"

"Delusions all."

"—to the river," Meran's voice rose as he stepped in close and poked Ricci's shoulder. Defiance was as foolhardy as poking a bear, but still, he dared, matching his sneer to Ricci as they came eye to eye, "and there, the visions tell me I have you at my disposal to fill in all that is blank."

Ricci's nostrils flared as they stood foot to foot, nose to nose. "I am at no man's disposal but my own."

Meran's chin came up. "Do it then. Leave me." Fuelled by irritation and foolish bravado, he shoved Ricci away.

The next second, Meran found himself soaring through the air and landing with a reverberating thud that left him breathless and gasping on the ground.

Looming over him, Ricci dropped on Meran's chest, his wrists captured above his head as he found himself straddled. There was nothing of desire or willingness in the hold, only control and force. Meran's face heated, his body straining with the need to take even one breath.

Sharp blue eyes glared into his as Ricci leaned close enough for the warmth of his breath to brush over Meran's lips. "Trust me, if I thought you would survive what the Draca have in store for you, I would be on my way. But see this, my young fool. If you cannot defeat even one man, how will you contend with many?"

"Trust you? Fuck you!" Meran finally gasped out. Tears of fury etched his cheeks as a weighted silence crashed down upon him, and Ricci's eagle gaze burned him to his soul. He closed his eyes, unable to bear the intensity, bitter defeat digging deep. "How can I trust you when all you are is a tyrant."

"Tyrant?" The word breathed across Meran's lips, a blistering caress of heat. Meran's eyes sprang wide. A fiery stare met his, so close he could see the silver flecks inhabiting Ricci's pale blue irises, the pupils blown large and black. "You say tyrant," Ricci's voice throbbed with feral intent as his gaze sank to Meran's lips, "I say master."

One hand released Meran's wrists to take up residence about his jaw, fingers curling. Ricci's brutal mouth descended on his, taking away Meran's mind and promising fulfilment of every expectation.

Fury and emotion converged in a dance of dominion, Meran's mouth captured in a roar of scorching passions, sucking him under, his resistance overwhelmed. The kiss hammered him, Ricci's mouth ravaging, demanding, and mastering him. The tumult of Meran's exasperation succumbed to the roar of his blatant desires, the power, the pull of possession. Capitulation became his only recourse.

Gushing like unstoppable geysers, the fervour of their joining smashed into the ether. It crashed down upon Meran with power so potent it set every particle of magic, every nerve he possessed, into a ferocious blaze. The passions that with Willard had grabbed him by the balls and yanked his seed from him were a flicker in comparison to the onslaught of magic that now drenched him.

Meran sank into it, groaning beneath the assault. The feeling of triumph thrilled through him, the fight having vanquished Ricci's disdain. Meran revelled in it. Answering with feverish intensity, he jerked a hand free and plunged his fingers into Ricci's locks. Dragging downwards, he scrabbled over Ricci's shoulders. He held on, not pushing away as he knew he should.

Ricci moved to imprison him in place and at his mercy. Bodies aligned to perfection. Meran pressed up into Ricci, gripping on for dear life, fearful his sanity would float free on the upsurge of wanton craving that threatened to consume him. To be taken and ordered and claimed.

Ricci's abrupt withdrawal left Meran's mind spinning, his mouth tingling and his tongue following, desperate to get another taste. "Leon?"

Leon lay rigid. His breath held, and his eyes sparking surprise, turmoil, fury...

Only then did Meran see the shadow of movement over Leon's shoulder. He, too, froze at the flash of light on metal. A blade held to Leon's nape.

Meran looked into a stranger's eyes, as black as night and afire with equal parts indignation and glee.

CHAPTER TWENTY-THREE

"Do not move, slaver." The words hissed in Velkor growled from behind him. The Dracan warrior's blade dug into the lower section of Leon's neck, threatening his spine.

Leon stiffened, staring down into Meran's confusion, his mind racing. Where had the bastards come from? His reconnaissance had revealed only a herd of sleeping dromedary to make him wary, but he'd not taken them for a caravan. Yet here the Dracan were, like locusts rising from the desert to plague them.

He threw out his farsight. It came back with nothing. *Impossible!*

Frustration roiled through him as great as Meran's must have been at not finding him earlier. But Leon's ability to evade the farsight was intrinsic to his magic. This he did not understand. Draca possessed only a few magic practitioners, and he'd not heard their earth magic could foil that of *Vocekind*.

Leon dared not lift his head as the warrior called to another of their number, the pressure of his blade unwavering. Varying voices took up the dialogue. Three, at least. *Not a swarm, then.* But how many, Leon could not guess.

He prepared himself for any eventuality.

One of the warriors turned on his heel. Knowing enough Dracan, Leon realised the man had been ordered to inform their lock that foreigners had been caught, if not red-handed, at least on Nord's soil.

The Dracan showed no mercy to captives suspected of slavery; the ways of torture and death at their hands were reputedly vicious. They could not afford to be taken, or their journey would be over ere it began.

"Come now, scum. Get up. Slowly."

Leon looked deep into Meran's wide, fear-filled eyes, bile rising at the thought of Dracan hands on him. A bright and passionate soul; courageous, obdurate, driven. And one who had teetered on the edge of a most beauteous and all-consuming submission.

The Dracan's vile crystal venom could never be brought to bear against Meran Durante. Leon had no choice but to risk all. And of all the *Voce* who found themselves in this situation, he had the one advantage.

He cautiously lowered his hands as if he meant to follow the scout's direction. Instead, Leon gripped Meran about the head, forcing his face into his shoulder. "Put your arms and legs around me. Now!" Confusion and a flash of curiosity answered him, but Meran's legs tethered themselves about his hips, arms about his back.

Magic flared. Like a wave, it billowed from Leon's core and flowed free.

He grabbed for the light, for the dark, distorting, manipulating, bending, blanketing. The night fragmented, reformed, and clung, and straightway he slipped beneath the fabric of his own concealment, taking Meran with him.

A shout of confusion joined the burst of chatter from more than one direction. Leon rolled them over, even as the knife plunged. Pain sliced into his shoulder, his teeth clenching against the cry.

"When I release you, go for cover." Leon stopped close to the fire and leapt free, leaving Meran visible and to his own recognisance.

Both the knives at his belt unsheathed and in his hands, Leon leapt for the bemused and flustered warriors. They would never see him coming.

Alert, though wild-eyed, still the Dracan held their ground, as if they heard his feet and smelt his advance. The pair crouched back-to-back, their arms circling, blades extending. "Demon! Show yourself," one called. "We know you are there."

In no mood to play, Leon ran.

As if synchronised, both warriors turned to face the churned dust as it plumed beneath his feet, heads thrown back, and ears searching. The pair's steadfastness was impressive in the face of what they took for a display of devilry, but soon they would be dead.

His knives moved in circles. Incredulously, he found his blades blocked, as if his was not the only witchery going on. He danced back and froze in place. The men's gazes swept the terrain, their ears straining, heads turning, trying to pinpoint his location before his next attack. Their muscles remained taut, ready…waiting…

Leon sent a powerful kick into one of the Dracan's solar plexus.

The man's defensive blade branded his ankle, even as Leon sent him sprawling. Straddling him, Leon went in for the kill, flesh parting as his knife slashed across the warrior's exposed throat in an expeditious move before he leapt aside…

Too late.

An arm snagged him from behind, encompassing his neck as if he were not invisible. Pressure squeezed.

Fingers tugged his hair, binding through the strands, imprisoning him as the force strengthened. The Dracan growled his determination and vengeance, even though tension rippled over every fibre of his being as he clung on. "Die, foul wraith," he ordered.

Leon began to see stars. Pain throbbed through him at the crushing weight.

No breath.

But the Dracan would not win.

Rage built a shield against defeat; the Mavish's indifference to pain, to life and limb, surged to the surface.

He drove the blades backwards, sinking them deep into the Dracan's thighs. His attacker grunted but held on, squeezing tighter. A strangled, defiant roar seared the Mavish's throat.

A meaty whump followed a whirring sound.

His blades free, the Mavish slashed a cut from the Dracan's elbow to his wrist. Glorious, pain-ridden air scoured into his lungs as the grip loosened and the warrior fell away.

Ignoring the urge to cough, the Mavish crisscrossed the knives' edges through the felled man's throat. In a gush of gore and blood, he almost severed the Dracan's head.

Blood sheathed Leon's face in a hot and liquid fist, his clothes drenched as he panted through the power of his feral urges. The death had been righteous, necessary.

Only then did he note a fletched shaft imbedded deep in the Dracan's shoulder. He turned blazing eyes on the scene, scorching a trek across the campsite on the lookout for further foes. It landed on a tall man, bow still in hand and looking like some kind of glorious avenging angel.

Leon slipped free of his magic's mantle, fierce pride welling at the sight.

Meran had not lost his head. In his place stood a warrior; defender; a keen and vicious hunter. Grinning through his bloody mask, Leon rushed Meran, hands gripping either side of his jaw and lips crashing against his.

Every sense swelled with the need to possess, to slack his vibrant aggression on one who had finally proven himself worthy of the Durante name, of being a defender of Locurnia. He pulled back enough to ravage the youth's face with his gaze, blood painting those luscious, parted lips with Leon's own barbarity.

"This," he said, laying a kiss on each of Meran's cheeks and mastering his own need for the hard fuck that followed a vicious fight. "In this are you worthy of being the brother of Beorn."

Despite the answering fire blazing in Meran's eyes and the obvious need to pick up from where they'd left off, Leon recognised the nausea that suddenly warped Meran's features. By choice, he had taken part in a brutal slaying. Turning away, Meran emptied his guts, his shoulders shaking as shock overtook him.

It had been an age since killing had sickened Leon, but he recognised the fragility clinging to Meran like a blanket as he righted himself. Pale and clammy in the firelight, tears glimmering unshed in his eyes, Meran wiped his mouth with the back of his hand and offered Leon a look of chagrin.

A welter of unexpected emotion welled in Leon's chest and filled his throat, as if…as if empathy threatened to choke him. He ached to draw the young man into his arms, hide that look of pain against his breast, and stroke his hair.

Leon shook the intense feeling free as a dog did water. Cosseting was the last thing a warrior needed.

He would not allow Meran to wallow in self-pity. His defence of Leon had ensured the victory and their escape, and it verified Meran's loyalty. And that elation spread like warmth through his blood, Leon chose to ignore.

They had to be on their way. While there had been only three scouts, a messenger headed back to his Outlier's lock with the news of them. The presence of a lock indicated a large hunting party, that much Leon knew.

"Come along." He drew away, though to let Meran go left a chill aching through his body. "We must break camp now."

"But you are bleeding!"

Like a stuck pig. Leon scanned his body. Not all the blood that soaked his tunic came from his enemies, but he would live. He shucked off the stained garment and used it to wipe his face.

"That will have to wait," he said.

"Of course." Meran shook his head as if in understanding, though in reality, he knew nothing. "It is rather grievous, the healing of which would put anyone on their arse."

Leon fought a smile. "Which we can ill afford. We'd best be from here ere they return."

"Shouldn't we go after the messenger? Stop him before others are alerted?"

"That would be a good plan if we could find him."

Meran cast a pensive gaze out across the desert. "How do they do that?"

Leon harrumphed. He did not know, but before they finished this quest, he would find out. Draca could not be left in possession of this advantage.

"How did you?"

That question again.

"There is no time to bandy suppositions." Leon gestured to the pot of victuals. "We'll need to either eat that on the run or when we find decent shelter." Quickly, he washed his face with a handful of canteen water and then pulled a clean tunic from his saddlebag.

A tentative touch imbued with concern stopped him in his tracks.

"At least let me bind your shoulder before you put that on." The look Meran offered came soft and shy. "And your ankle too, or you'll do nought but leave a trail of blood drops for the Dracan to follow."

Leon sighed. He appreciated the concern, but urgency prodded at him.

Before now, except for down in Aleia, he had considered the farsight an advantage that *Vocekind* had over all their foes. Reliance on such a gift now revealed its own peril. Few *Voce* were taught how to track. The same could not be said of the Dracan. "Make haste then," he said with gruff impatience.

A flash of hurt darkened those brilliant blue eyes as if Meran heard only a reprimand.

Leon had not meant to sound ungrateful, but they had to hurry. *Lords! Was he going soft in his old age that a mere look made him hot with guilt?*

Yet Meran's lips tightened as if he accepted it as inevitable.

No, no. It is not...

Taking the bloodied shirt, Meran tore the cleaner parts deftly into strips. Evidence he had done something of this nature before.

Fascinated, Leon watched those elegant hands, roughened from weather exposure and callused from his time aboard ship and at the oars. They were abraded and the most beautiful hands Leon had ever seen. They spoke of Meran's conviction. His devotion. Even if he were misguided, they revealed his steadfastness, his dedication to *Vocekind*. That he would endure anything for his people.

Leon could not repudiate it, and yet he drew back. He could not be caught up with such sentiment. He was here for *Amplion*. He was here to ensure the perpetual safety of his people through its possession.

He let Meran bind his ankle and wind the strips over his more awkward shoulder wound, yet he felt hungry, hollow. Like a starving man that had missed his only opportunity to eat.

It stopped the blood dripping but little else.

In the time it took, Leon could have healed it and they would have been on their way, but this was another of his secrets he hesitated to reveal. Already vulnerability tormented him. He would divulge nothing more this day but affect a slow and subtle healing as they rode. Meran need never know his administrations were not needed.

Still, once Meran finished, the voice of remorse urged Leon to offer his sincere thanks. And the pleasure that brightened Meran's handsome eyes at his words had Leon's hard edges soften even more.

CHAPTER TWENTY-FOUR

Leon led Meran north. Travelling a twisting and diverting course, they finally came across the mouth of a gully that had been his initial destination. A safe haven the last time he was in Draca, its entrance was almost invisible in the night.

Now, if only the Dracan were unaware of it. The hollow, nauseous feeling in his gut told him not to trust that hope. But what choice did he have? They had to hide somewhere, and this could be their temporary salvation.

They kept their caravan to the centre of the dark strip that ran the ravine's course. The horses' hooves clopped through the water like reverberating drumbeats in a hollow night.

Leon's nerves tightened with every indeterminate sound that floated down from above. Between the high walls, his farsight was useless, keeping him alert and on edge for any telling movement.

He abhorred travelling blind, but the scoured country the gully precipitated in turn offered them a superior concealment from their enemies.

As the sun breached the horizon, they reached his intended haven. A cave. And as luck would have it, uninhabited.

Once settled with the horses attended to and hidden at the cave's rear, they bedded down for the day, Leon positioning himself closest to the cave's mouth.

Sleep alluded him. Self-reproach demanding he keep a close watch on Meran curled at his back warred with Leon's need to ensure nothing breached their sanctuary, his anxiety simmering unrepentant.

He closed his eyes and lay staring at the red shadows seething behind his lids and waited for Meran's restlessness to relax into sleep. Silence followed the sun's stifling cloak as she swathed the land in her damning rays, and he strained to hear anything.

A breeze whispered of its journey across the searing desertscape, hot puffs as of a dragon at rest. Water rushed across stone, seeking with fearful and tinkling steps its escape from extinction. Meran breathed deep in his exhaustion, long and slow and trusting...

Leon cast a furtive glance behind him, a plethora of confusing emotions inundating him, not the least of it relief.

Why? Mere inches from him, Meran lay sprawled out like a feast of possibilities. All those acres of warm, tempting, malleable flesh. But the small distance between them might as well have been a chasm.

Leon's inattention had been the cause of their near captivity, his distraction inexcusable. His carnal desires could not come before their safety nor his gaining of *Amplion*. Nothing could stand in his way, certainly not this wayward craving to assuage Meran's desires.

The sudden surge in his yearning proved a weakness he could ill afford. Once, in the past, he had craved a man so desperately. His failure to keep Eain had led to tragedy and spawned a hopelessness tantamount to a death wish. Leon had run from his responsibilities and wallowed in his own misery. Until Tark had come for him.

Leon had been granted time to allow experience and obligation to clan and country to teach him a different lesson. He had found worth in his hard-won prowess and natural abilities; he had found his place and his purpose in the leadership of his clan and his small family.

Now he felt himself drawn again down a similar, reckless path. One he could not afford to traverse.

What should he do with his unremitting attraction? Shove it to the back of his mind where it would wither while he attended to the far more pressing matter of keeping them from being found.

Leon rose and returned to the cave mouth, seeking a distraction from his unceasing thoughts.

Seated at the entrance, he scanned the deep gully, boulder-strewn and striped in shades of pale yellow to warm ochre. Less cluttered with vegetation than he remembered, it still offered shelter from the sun's rays as it glided across the sky.

A shuffle of sound alerted Leon to Meran's presence as he exited the cave and seated himself on the ground. He had that startled, owlish look of one that had woken too early to feel refreshed. A look so reminiscent of Neve as a child, a protective affection infused Leon's chest, and he had to look away. *Ah, so young, so pliant, and ready to be shaped.* Another reason Leon needed to stay well clear of any libidinous thoughts.

"Do you see anything of them?" Meran rubbed his eyes.

"No. I had not thought to due to the height and depth of the gully." The farsight's limitations were a damnable frustration. "Still, I will keep watch. You must sleep while you can."

"Unfortunately, I have not learned that art, and now that I have managed an hour, seems my body is convinced it has rested the day away."

Ah. To sleep where one dropped took long years of soldiering. Something Meran would never have had to be.

"Do you think they will find us?"

"There is every possibility." The Dracan would not give up if they thought them slavers. Even though they carried none of the trappings, the borderland tribes would still give chase. "At least our guise is intact if that Dracan murdering the tongue of the Velkor was anything to go by."

"That is little consolation if they come upon us again." Meran tried to smile, though anxiety rode his brow and pressed his lips. "What can we do to avoid them?"

Leon considered their options. "I think this eve, we will head northeast. The Barrens is about two days' journey from here. They will be less inclined to traverse that plain, and it could be our saving grace."

"Barrens? Does nought grow there?"

Leon snorted, stifling his own hesitance. The name in no way reflected the region, but he shied from thinking on some of the fauna that dwelt there, the barest hint disgusting him. "There is plenty there to be wary of."

"A-a-and that would be?" Tension rang loud in Meran's request.

Guilt needled Leon that his previous pejorative silences and blatant condescension had caused such cautious uncertainty.

This had become their first and most agreeable interaction since leaving the Meith, unless he counted that kiss and the promise of what might have followed.

Leon's gaze flicked to those beautiful lips that Meran nervously chewed on. Before he could stop himself, Leon cupped Meran's warm and unshaven jaw. He followed up with a gentle touch to Meran's nape, curling his fingers through the soft hair that lay there.

How he ached. He leaned forwards to incite, taste, take.

Meran's lips opened, unresisting, beckoning. Leon's mouth met that luscious, generous softness and fell into a slow invasive exploration.

The kisses dropped tender and reciprocated, satisfaction stirring as Meran leaned in. Tongues swirled in lazy, delicious arcs interspersed with the sounds of their mouths lapping. Sucking kisses ended only to resume with an insistent supping beat until Leon could think of nothing else.

Capturing Meran's face in both hands, the intensity of Leon's excitement surged, his kisses lengthening, imbibing, savaging, as the thrill tore his judgement to shreds. To lose himself in the moment tempted him with fantasies of the bliss they could afford each other. His strong, generous demands plumbed the depths of Meran's unfathomed surrender. Until Meran gripped Leon about the waist and stones scattered. Leon's senses jarred back into place.

He tightened his hold on Meran's face and drew back, struggling for his normal self-possession. That sound could easily have come from above. From the pressure of encroaching feet...

Meran looked punch-drunk, reeling, and ready for plundering, his eyes glazed, pupils blown wide. A temptation Leon found alluring. Urgency swelled through his body, begging for him to give in, but he could not. Not here, not now...maybe never. It was dangerous, not least for Leon's flagging self-control.

"I should not have done that," he said, forehead bumping against Meran's.

"Why?" The protest came breathlessly. "I did not mind."

This divergence from Meran's initial reaction back at the Reach was not lost on Leon, the germ of which had been obvious since Tark had taken his leave. But in regard to his own reaction?

He swore softly, nose grazing against Meran's, unable to stifle his craving for the minutest of contact, even relishing the brush of Meran's warm breath. He could so easily fall to that enticement again.

Leon pulled away. Leaning against the rough sandstone, he shook his head. This was his weakness's return. One that he had hoped would never touch him again.

Avoiding Meran's gaze, he fell to scanning the terrain, but the intensity already burned up the back of his neck and induced a scorching blush. He bit back the snort of irony, his own behaviour spurring the perplexity of their situation. "Scholar, I came outside to keep watch—"

"For the love of the gods!" Irritation tightened Meran's tenor. "It's Meran. Call me Meran."

Leon's gaze swung around, taking in the sight of Meran, his cheeks redolent with heat, his brow furrowed, and his eyes flashing with anger. *Meran?*

Since the altercation with the Dracan he no longer thought of Meran as anything else. Yet he had never said it aloud. He would not do it now.

Tightening his lips against the urge to taste that intoxicating name on his tongue, Leon said, "I am here to keep us both safe, not to seduce you."

Meran spat a foul curse and surged to his feet, his fists clenched and the back he turned to Leon rigid. "You are all the fucking same."

It took some effort to keep the demand, "Who?" from Leon's tongue. Had someone caused Meran pain enough to have his entire body vibrate with fury and embarrassment as he compared Leon with them?

Had he been toyed with before by a man with a dominant hand and then rejected? Anger flushed through Leon at the affront, and yet his own behaviour could have Meran think nothing less of him.

Meran did not realise his temptation. How he drew a man against his better judgement with the overwhelming need to fulfil every one of his wanton desires for domination. Comparable with the need to breathe.

As much as he wanted to know what had happened, Leon hesitated to force such a confession.

Taking in Meran's tense frame, muscles quaking with the imperative to run, regret tinged Leon's every feeling. He could not allow him to retreat. Even if Meran sought distance only to find his equilibrium, he could be putting himself in danger. This was not the time to indulge in such emotions, and this was no place for any distraction. Something Meran had to learn the hard way.

Bounding to his feet, Leon banded his arms about Meran. The kiss fell fierce, a ferocious clashing of mouth, tongue, teeth; bodies coming together in a tussle for superiority.

Furious, Meran fought to pull free from the shackles of Leon's greater strength. His indignation scorched the inside of Leon's mouth, the bellow vibrating the length of his spine.

Water churned beneath their feet as Meran tried to stumble back from the clench.

Leon grasped Meran tighter, an arm bound about his waist, the other about his head, fingers diving into the short locks, imprisoning him in place to be plundered.

A strike landed hard against Leon's shoulder. Another thudded into his ribs, eliciting a grunt. Leon's pride swelled. His Meran was submissive, yes. But not impuissant.

Nonetheless, Leon could not concede; Meran had a lesson to learn. Still, the feverish power of lust stoked a fire through his body. The consuming spark dared Meran's capitulation. Leon surrendered himself to the beauty of passion's craving.

His lips softened the onslaught to a consuming exploration, to taste, to feed…to be fed on. He gave of himself, his moan, his mouth. The evidence of his arousal pressed against the man in his arms. He gloried in heat meeting heat and the undeniable answering hardness.

Meran sank against him and into the fervour of their kisses, tasting of victory and sweet assent.

Leon palmed down Meran's shoulders, down his arms to his wrists, and pulled them together behind his back. He encountered no resistance. Meran's body shivered with expectation and excitement, even as Leon bathed Meran's jaw in kisses, trailing them down his throat to nip at the skin beneath his ear.

Meran threw back his head, his neck a vulnerable offering, his moans stirring the unfathomable well of Leon's desire. Regret welled at what he must do next.

While one hand shackled both Meran's wrists, his other moved with graceful speed, the knife pulling free from Meran's belt.

The blade's point dug deep enough into the flesh beneath Meran's chin to have him freeze in Leon's grasp. "Wha—"

Leon stared into deep confusion. "This is what such distraction will get us, boy." He held the point in place for a moment, letting the situation sink in. "It will get us dead."

"What? No!"

"Oh, so you saw my intent? Saw the knife coming?"

"Fuck you." Meran struggled to break free.

Leon let him go, taking a step back, but despite his clasp on the knife, Meran barrelled at him, shouting, "Are you fucking crazed?"

"Hold!" Leon took in the young man's fury, his free hand meeting Meran's heaving chest.

"I fucking trusted you. You bastard."

"That is as it should be." Leon stifled the urge to placate, ignoring the hurt swirling deep in those accusing eyes. He did not want this, but it could be no other way. It was too dangerous for both of them.

He swallowed, his throat thick, his palm aching for the touch of those fiery cheeks to heat them. Leon reached again to cup one and feel the softness, juxtaposed with the roughness of a day's growth of beard as he attempted to rationalise. "Meran…"

"Don't touch me." The prohibition came not unexpected.

Leon licked his lips, his attention drawn to the deep swallow that savaged Meran's throat. The skin moved. The shadows danced in a mesmerising motion that stirred a longing in Leon's loins.

He threw up his hands and hardened his voice. "I teach you nothing more than that you must keep your wits about you. Never let down your guard. Never lose sight of the enemy. That, and only that, is how you will survive."

"Oh, so now you are my enemy."

"I am not." Leon rubbed his face and then wrapped Meran about the shoulders with little intent but to appease the aching emptiness of his arms. "In all I have done here, I have not lied. Not in any part of it. But now, it is crucial I step back from the brink, or disaster is likely to strike at us again."

Meran's throat clicked as if he were ravaged by disappointment. "I don't want…" That swallow came again as he caught himself.

Leon watched Meran suck in slow, calming breaths, paring back his emotions into a semblance of serenity. His voice came low and lethal, daring Leon to stand his ground if he could. "If this—whatever it is— may not prosper, do not shut me out. Speak to me. Include me. Treat me as an equal, for I will not go back to how it was."

How it was? Protest rumbled in Leon's throat. How could Meran demand equality when they were not equal? Even should they be lovers, a lord marshal far outranked a scholar. What did he expect?

"You have left me ignorant. I know not what dangers lie before us. The lands we traverse, the tribespeople, even down to the native fauna. You have withheld these details from me. And for what? And please do not insult me with accusations of my having known this already. That is not how the visions work."

The truth of it stabbed Leon. Social status and obligation had nothing to do with it. His silence had been meant to ridicule Meran's claims of seership and put him on the back foot. "You have the right of it," he said, as close to an apology as he could give. But the oversight could be rectified easily. "I promise, no more."

He would relinquish the stranglehold of his authority, considering Meran had demonstrated his loyalty. It would hurt nothing if they worked closer together. Their ultimate goal to ensure the superiority of *Vocekind* was one and the same.

He offered back the knife.

Meran took it, his expression solemn, even as an awkward silence descended.

"What now?" Meran asked, finally breaking it.

Leon stroked the wayward locks curling at Meran's nape and caressed the smooth, warm skin of his throat, trailing across his jawline with the pad of his thumb. The scruff rasped against Leon's skin. He almost sighed with relief that Meran leaned in.

He lost himself to the stir of his blood at the small gesture of supplication. *Fuck! Fuck!* How he had ever denied Meran anything was beyond comprehension. He licked his lips. It had never been a prerequisite that their faith be of a match; only the outcome mattered. On this page, they were the same.

"Though we may never agree on the semantics of seership, I will not leave you in peril. On this, you have my word." His final on the subject, and he meant it.

CHAPTER TWENTY-FIVE

Two nights swept by Meran in a haze of silent self-flagellation. His dissatisfaction hammered at the back of his throat and twisted like a ball in his gut as they rode. He wanted to hurt Leon as much as he wanted to captivate him.

More, he craved communion in every facet, not Leon's protection. This had been the underlying meaning of the prophet's instruction. As Jon had pointed out, it had not been enough to just *find the man* but to gain him in every respect.

The possibility of total immersion with each other, in body, mind, and purpose, had hung like a ripe fruit ready for the plucking. Meran had given in to Leon's overtures with the eagerness of the naïve.

He should have known better.

Flashes of anger burgeoned at the trust he had offered Leon, only to have it turned against him. Leon had put all possibility beyond reach and, in so doing, had wrenched open a wretched and much-loathed wound.

He recognised Leon's demonstration for the necessity it was, yet a part of him still dared to plumb passion's depths. With those kisses, Meran had felt the rightness of it. In tenderness or savagery, it did not matter. They were all moments as beauteous and sharp-edged as gems. Fragile or hard, he guarded them with the same greed as a dragon did his hoard.

He wanted to beg Leon to ignore their peril for a moment more of rapture, but he could not. Leon stood between them and mortal danger.

The want might be a void on the edge of which Meran teetered, the desire to succumb filling his world, but Leon also stood on a precipice. One of duty and obligation. Denying himself what he thirsted for.

Moments of gentle fulfilment.

Meran had inspired those light touches, those caresses of affection so unexpected in the lord marshal, the want of which glimmered in those light blue eyes. He could be that for Leon. More than he could be a companion worthy of guarding Leon's back.

The altercation with the Draca reminded him of his own hesitation and left him blushing. Phantom shivers still wrecked his insides at the brutality of the death Leon had dealt out; the grotesque images seared to his mind.

Panic, not bravery, had made him lift his bow in Leon's defence, and if confronted again, Meran did not know his worth. Would he freeze? Would he shoot? Or would his instinctual reticence for violence leave them in jeopardy?

He flushed hot at how his gorge had risen in reaction to the blood that had painted both man and desert. He was no warrior, and he had no right to distract from his task the one who was.

Meran said nought, nor did he do anything to make Leon aware of how he held himself back. And as they pulled up at the edge of a high mesa, a plain stretching out before them like an empty sea, he judged it for the best. They could not lose themselves at this juncture.

"This is the Barrens?" he asked instead. In the far distance sat a ridge, a slash of darker black against that of the clear, crisp obsidian of the star-spattered sky.

"Aye. We shall make camp once we have reached the bottom," Leon said. "It will give us shelter and a chance for me to reconnoitre the area."

How Leon pinpointed their apparent pursuers with such confidence, Meran little understood. But they had made it thus far without encountering further Dracan. For that, he was grateful, although he could not rid himself of resentment.

But for their threat, the potent tension firing between him and Leon, demanded Meran chase every possibility. With every inflection, gesture, and furtive gaze shared, the loss of what they could become ached through him.

Once they reached the lower plain, Leon called a halt, and Meran set up camp. Yet concern and restless suspense distracted him.

While the fire crackled to life and Meran prepared supper, the lord forged out on another reconnaissance. Worry grew for Leon's safety when time eked past the perimeters of Meran's expectation.

Though he tried not to send out the farsight knowing the futility of it all, he could not stop himself. Hope beat an undeniable tattoo in his mind. During that first desert encounter, ethereal power had showered down on them both. While Leon had become invisible to the naked eye and their contact broken, Meran had seen the ghost of it shimmering about Leon's person.

Unfortunately, the aftereffect had melted back into the ether within a turn of the dial.

He should have kissed Leon before he'd headed out this time. Perhaps Meran's farsight would have something on which to latch.

Between berating himself for his timidity and knowing he would be lost without Leon, Meran's anxiety only eased back at the sounds of his return.

Ease rode Leon's shoulders as he came into view, his usually furrowed brow smooth as he went to the pack that held Tark's amber brew and broke its seal.

Offering Meran a dram, he toasted the air, saying, "To finding not a trace of them." And sank down at Meran's side with a satisfied smile.

"But is that not the problem?" Scepticism kept Meran on edge. "How do you know they are not close when they can hide from our farsight?" He refrained from adding, *"Just as you can."* Perhaps to Leon's farsight, the Dracan were not hidden at all.

"I do not look for them," Leon replied, dashing Meran's supposition. "I look for the humped beasts they ride."

"Beasts?" Meran glanced around. Once more, with the wide open space spreading away from the cliff face, his farsight soared. The moon hung, large and round in the distance, casting silver beams across the land that spread before them like a becalmed sea. As usual, a myriad of auras glowed, but of something the size inferred by Leon's words, Meran saw nothing.

"Aye. Dromedary. They are ungainly creatures, all lumps and bumps, long legs, long neck, and large feet."

"That would be something to behold." Meran could not imagine.

"It stands about a man-and-a-half tall at the apex and can run the desert like a ship glides through the sea. However, it would appear we have put some distance between us. Those I see are still southwest of here, about half a day's ride away."

"But would the Dracan not leave these beasts to find us on foot?"

Leon shrugged, rocking his hand. "Mayhap. There will be scouts on the hunt who do not ride. Should they get this far, they will hesitate to cross onto the Barrens without the permission of their lock."

"Lock?"

"The sworn sword-hand of an Outlier's catana."

Anxiety rode over Meran. "Here! And why would they hesitate to follow us?" What would frighten them enough to deter them from venturing onto this plain? And why did Leon risk heading out where the Dracan feared to go without the say of their sword-hand?

"Pray that you don't find out."

"Leon?" Horror sank to the pit of Meran's stomach as he sent out a sweeping gaze. What by all the hells lurked out there?

Ignoring him, Leon cleaned the plate of his meal and gestured at Meran. "Finish your stew, and we will be on our way."

Hours churned by, the distant ridge remaining out of reach. Meran's arse ached, though not as painfully as it had before he got used to the shaggy horses. Still, he could not wait for Leon's command to dismount once shelter from the day had been reached.

"Pull up," Leon said. "Let's set another camp here."

"Pray?" Meran scanned around the area as he followed Leon to the ground. Flat and exposed, it looked nothing like any of their previous camps. "What goes on? Is something wrong?"

"I had thought to reach a place called Ferrora's Gulch by sun up, but..." Leon hummed a discontented breath. "The day quickens, and we have not travelled as far as anticipated. We will need a shelter closer to hand. I shall be back anon..."

With that, Leon passed his torch to Meran, firm, reassuring hands cupping over his as he took it. The warmth of Leon's palms penetrated even as Meran's mind reeled with the possibility of being caught out beneath the blazing sun.

"The Barrens are anything but barren. Build a fire and perhaps make us supper while you wait. The flames will keep you safe..." Leon's eyes became distant, distracted "...they shy from it."

"Pray, what?" Meran asked, almost breathless as he looked into the unfamiliar pensive gaze of his companion. "What is out there?"

Leon shook off his melancholy. "Oh, the usual suspects. Snakes, scorpions, sand leopards. But if you must do your own reconnaissance from the safety of the fire, then best you keep an eye out for the wild dogs. The big cats are solitary creatures and shy from our stench. Not so the desert dogs. They roam in packs and have no fear. Keep your bow close and your quiver full."

Before Meran had the chance to protest or plant a marking kiss, Leon took off at a brisk pace and disappeared into the darkness.

The sudden and inexplicable feeling of abandonment settled over Meran, but they needed shelter. He may not have liked it, but Leon's actions made sense.

Assuring himself nothing untoward stalked him, Meran turned his attention to the horses. As Tark had promised, they did not seem to need much.

Gathering provisions for the meal, Meran set about fixing a small firepit before settling to make a dough. Stick bread and hard cheese would have to make up their small feast.

He sat with a blanket warming his back and the flames heating his face as he awaited the dough to rise. Like picking at a scab, he sent out his farsight. Of Leon, he saw nothing. One kiss and he felt certain he could have found him. Why hadn't he grasped the moment? Disappointment ached in his throat. *Damn.*

Meran shivered, a chill breeze playing with the edges of his headscarf. He drew into himself just as power slammed over him. His shade flew from his body. It fell, slumped in the middle of a beam of ethereal light like a small, curled husk.

"Come," Philo's disembodied voice commanded.

"Master?" A firm, familiar hold captured his already outstretched hand, pulling Meran into the turbulence of the river, all his current concerns left in dust.

No longer did his master's call fill him with uncertainty or fear. As expected, Meran struck out across the surface towards a swirling maelstrom of energy.

The River of Time remained in flux, swirling and changing as it sped past the still-fountaining disruption that marred its course. Without hesitation, Meran dropped into a vortex of blindness, a darkness so complete the weight of it threatened to crush his fragile simulacrum. A whimper whispered through him as dread tolled in his mind. *Trapped.*

Darker than night, the closeness squeezed his chest in a fist so tight, he could not draw breath. Pain, so potent, seared like a poisoned lance into his belly. A fiery throb accompanied the cloying repugnant stench of rotting flesh.

Thunder rumbled about him, reverberating through every facet of his being, but no lightning pushed back the curtain of black that shrouded his eyes…until there was a light. A light he had seen in the dreamlands. A glowing orb over his shoulder.

The sounds of stumbling feet vibrated in his ears, jarring, tumbling steps humming up his legs. They could not be his.

"Who is it?" he called.

Except for the shallow gasping of breath, punctuated with soft heart-wrenching sobs, he heard no reply. Meran raised a hand to his chest and felt the contours of another. Cold, clammy, and dusted with soft hair. His shade wore a different body.

Meran churned with curiosity, yet as he stumbled from the confining hand of darkness, the pain fell away, and his essence slipped free. Hovering, he stared down at a youth who fell to his knees and began to drag himself to the water that ran like shimmering black veins of blood.

The lad drank deeply, then flopped to his back and stared skyward. Meran shivered, fearful he might be seen floating above. Warm brown eyes burned with a glassy, feverish heat, and his olive skin leeched to ash as pain rode his body and settled upon the furrowed wings of his brows. Even with his dark hair plastered to his head and tears streaking his cheeks, he was a thing of beauty.

Compact perfection, the youth's form was muscled and proportionate, his features a mixture of sensual softness and firm lines, full lips, and a shaded jaw. But his injury blared like a horn in the fog. Blood smeared from upper belly to breeches. These were the same style Sem had worn, a garment marking the youth from Draca, though he did not look fully Dracan. The cloth remained stained despite his soak in the water.

His heart filling with an undeniable tenderness and curiosity, Meran dipped lower to offer a gentling caress, the lad's pain beseeching him.

"Am I to watch him die?" Desperation to do something roiled through Meran as the pale Dracan began to shiver.

"Only the river yet knows," Philo whispered. "His fate is at this very moment being made."

"Then why am I here?"

"As always, as witness. You are a seer, and this is your calling. The course of the world stands on a knife edge. And here, too, the veracity of my prophecies will be determined. I know no more than that."

The inequity of it all surged through Meran. This youth's life hung in the balance, and the prophet's words struck him as too remote and inadequate to tame this injustice. "Get up," he commanded, grasping at the Dracan's shoulders with hands that lacked the power to affect anything.

The Dracan remained alone, wounded, and on the edge of death.

Meran shouted louder. "Boy, get up. Move. You must move. Now!"

The youth's eyes flickered, as if hearing him. Many slow blinks followed as they began to focus…not on Meran, but over his shoulder at the misted orb in its blanket of sheeting water. Dogged determination filled the lad's features, and weakly, he slithered on his belly, his attention snared by the fascination of the glowing light before him.

For the first time, Meran gave it more than a passing perusal. Familiar and alien both together, curiosity pulled him to the edge of the pool.

Darkness hid the vaulted ceiling, the cliff face cutting a swathe from both directions and trailing into invisibility. Majestic in proportion though it was, and the flow of water over the drop ear-shattering, the glowing orb still managed to outshine its magnificence. The youth struggled to cross to the foot of the cliff where the light sat, concealed in the vastness of its hiding place.

What was this thing? Meran could sense no menace within it, no intent or malice. It just was…until the youth reached out, and at the moment flesh met power, Meran knew with unwavering certainty. *Amplion.*

Bright lights like daggers pierced into his eyes, blinding him as power exploded outward. Heat tore his soul, lifting and flinging him. Time flashed by, colours blasting about him like shooting stars, and he slammed into darkness and into the chill grip of the desert.

Too stunned to move, pain grasped a hold of his chest, and Meran lay paralysed. The night above came into view even as he struggled to draw his first breath, thoughts of the youth still haunting him. Panic seared the edges of his consciousness. By the gods! Could the Dracan have survived?

The first tentative breath hurt, Meran's body struggling to gasp another and another until they came rapid as fire licking a path across sun-scorched grass. He panted for a moment, endeavouring to calm, the tension easing from him.

About him, the horses shuffled, and the fire warmed the side of his face. Relief flooded Meran, but he could not forget the implications of what he had seen.

It had to remain his secret. Leon could not turn from their destiny to find the brilliant white orb. The consequences for their people remained dire if they failed. And fail, they would. Meran had to have Leon by his side to fulfil his part of the visions. The blue stone and not the white, safe in his hand.

Yet, time had slipped by while Meran had been with the prophet, and there was no sign of Leon's return. *Not again!*

He swivelled about, casting out the farsight though it still proved useless. To the north, a thick blanket hugged the horizon. A roiling darkness, as if a storm gathered, billowed into the sky.

Turning about, Meran stared into a night that looked all too familiar. The brilliant shining face of the silver moon lit upon a flat ridge, complete with a protruding pillar of rock, and Meran's heart stuttered.

Déjà vu gripped him, along with the certainty that some ill had befallen Leon. Fear clutched at Meran, a black abyss of despair opening up to swallow him.

Nevertheless, he tried to laugh the damning certitude off. There was no more competent man alive than Leon Ricci. Sense told Meran his vision had to be a lie. *Had to be.* But—"Where, by the hells are you? Come on."

The vast vault of night rendered Meran small and insignificant. It was not the same as from the deck of the ship or from a window in some fine establishment. There, he could feel civilization pulse around him—people, buildings, cities. This was an overwhelming void that stretched on forever, punctuated only by the full moon's beams skimming a dire landscape. Destiny called to him. Demanded his action. That much Meran knew, and it terrified him.

But there were no more excuses, no more fearful anticipation. The moment had come. Meran knew now that Leon Ricci was that thing that he could not go on without; the mere thought of his loss gut-wrenching.

CHAPTER TWENTY-SIX

After dousing the fire and checking the horses, Meran set out. He took with him only a torch, a length of rope, a water canteen, and a bow and quiver.

Pacing himself, he set his face to the full moon and the landmark that speared into the sky. The weapon clutched in one hand appeased the knot of anxiety that threatened to leave him breathless as he ran.

Meran had not seen in vision any creature waylaying him, but Leon's words still rang as a warning. Something horrifying awaited him. Something that had defeated Leon.

Memories of a myriad of glowing eyes threatened to unnerve Meran.

And if it bested the Mavish, how would Meran ever overcome it? He was no warrior, no fighter. Good enough with a bow to hunt, but nothing more. What if he should fail?

Gods! He could not think. Only keep going.

His heart pounded with trepidation.

The ground raced by. His feet pounded across hard-packed dirt, risking life and limb as unseen cracks slashed his path. Stones and rocks littered his course.

Shade upon shade cut across the expanse.

A formation of rock punched into the sky, and Meran's mind shrieked as he ran towards it, the feeling more than the place familiar. It eclipsed his horizon until it submerged him in its moon shadow. Leon could not be far.

The crag to one side of him presented a terrifying montage of sharp edges and deep gouges; the earth at its feet shattered with black gaping fissures.

One of these had to be the cleft he sought.

He slowed to a walk, feeling his way beneath the overhanging darkness only to pinwheel as the ground gave out beneath his toes. As in the vision, Meran tumbled back as a small shower of pebbles disappeared into the void.

Ignoring the pain reverberating from his rear, Meran crawled on his belly to the edge. He held the flaming brand aloft as he peered into a sea of obsidian. "Leon?" his voice quavered. "Leon?" He swung the torch in tentative arcs back and forth, searching the scant scene it revealed.

Meran could make out rippling shades of darkness, a tide of motion without definition. Quickly, he scanned his surroundings, alighting on a cluster of feathery bushes. He needed light on the ground, and a branch or two would have to do in place of his own brand.

Each loud report as he snapped free the brittle branches had the nerves twitching up and down his back. Returning to the cleft, Meran dropped each lit stick into the depths. Scuffling and scrabbling followed as the flaming missiles descended, coming up short fifteen feet or so below him.

Huge, bulbous, dust-coloured creatures with hair-spiked legs roiled at the base of the cleft. Meran's heart thudded, his stomach churning. The size of small dogs, they were the largest spiders he had ever seen, their eyes reflecting the orange glow of the now-guttering flames. And buried beneath them, barely visible, peeked the stark white cheek and short dark sandy locks of Leon Ricci.

Facedown. Unconscious. Unmoving.

"Gods' damn!" The words hissed out of Meran, and quiet though he had been, the mass began to surge towards the wall beneath him.

One of the huge beasties skittered, lightning quick, up the sheer cliff face. Meran swung his torch down.

The hairs flew like a spray of daggers from the creature's legs.

Cursing, Meran leapt back, barely avoiding the shower.

The fire caught, the spider going up in a flash of flame and falling into the swarming sea below. As it hit, its bulbous body burst with a gush of black liquid.

Meran gagged, even as Leon's words returned to him. "...*They shy from it...*" Had Leon meant these spiders ran from fire?

Retreating, he gathered more of the branches and twisted bundles of dead foliage. Setting them ablaze, he kicked them into the churning mass as far from where Leon lay as he could. Some flickered out, but others blazed, and the spiders began to scatter, just as their smaller cousins did when their shade rock was disturbed.

Some caught fire, while others ascended and scuttled over the crevice's lip. Some hurried past Meran, making for the dark edifice behind him. Others streamed onto the plain.

Meran stood shaking.

Gathering his wits, he peered over the edge to ensure the fires did not endanger Leon. A few of the beasties lurked at the base while they burned, but most of the swarm had dispersed, leaving Leon prone and unresponsive.

Meran swore again. *Gods!* What if Leon had been bitten? What if he were dead?

A sudden and violent explosion interrupted his panic. One of the creatures burst in a flash of splattering innards and fiery pieces of exoskeleton. Meran instinctively ducked.

"By all that is h—" The curse back-jammed in his throat at the realisation some of the creatures were still close to Leon. If they blew apart next to him, he could burn. Injuries he could heal if he were conscious, but he was not.

The urge to do something had an arrow in Meran's hand and the bow pulled taut before he had time to consider. His aim rang true, with each creature put out of its misery before the heat could wreak havoc. Pierced by his arrow tips, the spiders splattered into puddles of slimy gunge as if by some unknown magic.

Despite it being gorge-rising, Meran affixed one end of his rope about a boulder, and after reassuring himself it would stay, he took that one fateful step over the edge. Teeth clenched, jaw aching, he awaited the pull of gravity. The rope tautened as he began to lower himself. One step after another, hand under hand.

"Leon!" he called as he scrambled over the gore-spattered ground to the prostrate figure. A thick web had already been fashioned about his lower limbs, while strands lay thick and white across his torso. Grimacing, Meran pulled the sticky mess free, rubbing the tendrils into balls and wiping them on the ground.

Gently he flipped Leon over, preparing himself for the worst. After a thorough examination, he could find no evidence of a venomous bite, only a pool of dark blood smearing the ground.

Leon had never looked so pallid, as if every drop of his blood had leached into the hard-packed earth. But in vision, Meran had seen his brother bleed out, and it had been a flood. This did not compare.

Nonetheless, a large lump swelled across Leon's forehead. With care, Meran touched the edges of the gaping, blood-encrusted wound that slashed its surface. No wonder Leon had not responded; no wonder the spiders had mistaken that for paralysis. "Leon, please wake up," he whispered, his lips trembling.

Leon did not move.

"Gods' damn you, man! Open your eyes." What Meran would give to have that piercing pale blue gaze, cool as ice and fierce as fire, on him once again.

He stifled the panicky fingers of dread and gathered himself. Faint tendrils of air caressed the finger he held beneath Leon's nose. He still breathed. Relieved, Meran touched Leon's cheeks, urging him to wake up. "Please, open your eyes. Please."

This was wrong, this vulnerability. Meran could not reconcile Leon's presence, strength, and unremitting vitality with the one lying here.

"If you don't awaken, I cannot get you from here." He could not carry Leon and ascend at the same time. But Leon did not stir.

Covering Leon with his long coat, Meran checked the wound again. Dust and blood smeared Leon's cheek, and dark particles infested the open flesh. "Here, let's get you cleaned up."

Retrieving his canteen, Meran flushed the wound clear. He rolled his tunic into a ball and placed it beneath Leon's head. Satisfied he had done all he could at this point, Meran turned Leon onto his side, cupping his cheek. "It's not long until morn. I'd prefer to be from here ere that happens, so now would be a good time to waken."

Expecting no response, he curled about Leon's back, saddened at the absence of his vibrancy. Memories of the last time they had been this close, and the kisses that burned him like a furnace, hollowed him out. That vital life force was now well-doused. A film of cool moisture sat on Leon's skin, grey in the advancing pearlescent light heralding in the day. Meran snuggled up to Leon's back, an arm pulling him tight, and offered whatever warmth he could.

All about them remained silent except for Leon's faint breaths. A comfort amidst Meran's turmoil.

Meran woke to daylight seeping down into the cleft. He rose on one elbow to check, but as far as he could tell, Leon had not moved.

Reluctantly, he abandoned his position and walked the length of the cut. Its walls were tall and straight, the rock blasted by a wound that left it gaping. It offered some shade, but with no overhang, it would not last the day long. They had to move or risk the parching noon-day sun.

Returning, Meran studied Leon's slack features, combing the short hairs at his temple and down the arc to the shell of Leon's ear. In the absence of the familiar harsh mask, a softness reminiscent of Tark blanketed that face. For the first time, he wondered what kind of man Leon would have been had fate not stepped in to harden his heart.

Regretfully, it would be one he would never know.

Sighing, Meran drew away to rest against the cold stone. A strangeness in the air settled over him, his senses on edge as anxiety rode his stomach.

He did not fear the great spiders' return—the heat of the day would keep them away—but something was coming. Something he had not yet envisioned. A prevailing pensiveness eased like a cloud through the ether as if every creature sensed a wild, momentous churning hovering on the horizon.

CHAPTER TWENTY-SEVEN

Darkness peeled back to a pounding ache hammering through his head, enough for Leon to wish to return to oblivion. Even through mere slits, the light jabbed into his eyes and pierced his brain, the avalanche of agony twisting his gut. His internals revolted, even as the lancing pain in his head insisted he not move.

His gut won out. Rolling onto the churned and stained earth beside his bedding, Leon retched violently. The effort shattered him, his skull from forehead to aft feeling as if it would split. "Fucking oath!"

His curses did little to help, and easing down, Leon nestled his head on the comfort of the rolled fabric at his back, determined never to move again.

Light played in red waves behind his lids as warm air caressed his face. The skin on his forehead felt tight; stretched. The copper stench of blood feathered through his nostrils. He connected with burst flesh as he reached to explore. Hissing, Leon drew his fingers away, covered in a thin trail of new blood. *Ah, ye gods!* He had an impressive bump on his head. Little wonder that he could barely see straight.

His memories danced behind a thick fog, impressions of darkness, irrational fear, and hysteria that swept all common sense before it. Even now, the very air rang with an ominous silence, the vague and indeterminate threat pressing against his entire body. Where, by all the hells, was he?

"Praise the holy prophet." A familiar voice floated down to him, breaking through Leon's confusion. Hand over hand, a shirtless Meran shimmied down a rope dangling flush against a cold grey rock face, a vision of lithe and defined musculature. He moved with such youthful beauty and grace, reinforcing his unwavering appeal…

Leon blinked away his wayward thoughts, his bemusement deepening at the daylight. Had he not meant to pass the day away at Ferrora's Gulch? This was not it.

In no time, that pretty face leaned over him, eyes wide and earnest as they peered into his. "How do you fare?" Meran grabbed Leon's hand between his and began to rub as if he thought Leon cold. "Can you stand? We must leave here with all haste. With what comes, I fear it is safe no longer."

A shudder of memory rippled free, shapes rearing from the darkness, skittering limbs dancing; enough to make Leon's blood run cold. "What comes?" he asked, his voice croaking.

Meran shifted his hold and began to tug. "A storm heads our way from the north. Can you not hear it?"

Leon listened for the wind—the roar of the razor-sharp particles of sand blown into a howling wall of destruction—and began to pull back. The slim gully would offer them superior protection than to go aloft.

"Hold," Leon commanded, a wave of brutal agony crashing through his head as he sat. "A minute, for pity's sake."

Meran froze at Leon's distress, but his urgency transmitted itself through their joined hands.

"Look, I need a moment to gather my thoughts and heal this damn avalanche going off in my head." Until then, he would not be going anywhere, tempest or not. Leon offered the dangling rope a baleful look. He could not climb it in his current condition.

"You don't understand—"

Leon frowned, even as he rubbed his temple and attempted to collect sense enough to command his magic. Sandstorms were to be avoided, but in a desert of this size, they were not unexpected.

"—I know what happens when such a deluge lashes hard, dry ground," Meran continued. "The land will be awash, and any gulch, gully, or cut will turn into a raging torrent. I've seen flash floods firsthand, and we cannot risk it."

"Pray, what?" Leon shook his head as Meran prattled, groaning as the thudding expanded behind his eyes.

"That drought we had some years back. Surely you must remember. It broke when storms washed down from the mountains and inundated the plains east of Dun. The village at Luz lost many."

"By the hells! I come from Farnham, up in those very mountain ranges." Leon cradled his head. He could not think straight, pain stoking his frustration. "For the love of Seus, calm yourself."

Meran's mouth twisted, words exploding out despite the impatience lacing Leon's. "If you go into a healing sleep now, there is no way I can get us to safety."

Leon ignored Meran's unease. He delved beneath the lightning flashes of agony in his head, trying to focus on the small glowing spark that represented the centre of his magic. He had been knocked on the head before. Fights in the arena could be brutal, and the quicker one could shake off such injury, the quicker one attained victory.

Like a caldron, he stirred the small kernel of power, letting everything within him radiate and swirl with expanding energy. Warmth, as vibrant as the sun, blossomed outward, eclipsing his world.

Tingling sensations coursed his veins and spun through every cell, his synapses sparking and fizzing with pure strength and vitality.

As always, the tide of ecstasy in the wake of healing threatened to inundate him. The pleasure of his newly pulsating particles throbbed in mind-blowing waves. Yet, he had control of himself. He was the Mavish. Nothing dared to master him.

Even as Leon forced the rush of rapture to subside, a streak of forked lightning crashed across the horizon, followed by the deep rumble of thunder. The distinctive crisp burn of ozone tangled in his nostrils, and he threw his head back, staring at the clear sky above. That was no sandstorm.

"Leon?"

Meran's warm hold clasped him as he surged to his feet, offering unneeded aid.

Leon ignored the surprise that flushed Meran's features as he pulled free and gathered up the crumpled coat and the wad of fabric. Realising whose they were, he pushed them into Meran's hands.

"How did you...?" Meran gaped before the obvious answer occurred to him. "You are a healer?"

Leon sighed. "Not by profession, but it has proven a welcome talent over the years, even should I not have been able to help others."

"I should have known," Meran chided himself. "At the Reach. There I was, almost swooning with the effort, and you just...just."

Leon gave a small laugh and cupped the back of Meran's head, ruffling his hair. A gesture bordering on affection. "Pray what? Popped my fingers back into place?"

"Yes! I'm such a dolt."

"Don't think on it. You had more pressing issues." Leon took the rope. "Now, let us get from here before that squall hits."

Leon pulled himself to the lip of the cleft, his heart warming as Meran hovered beneath him, arms raised as if to catch Leon should he fall. He appreciated the concern and the sentiment. Meran had said *us*. There had been no thought of abandonment.

"Take hold," he ordered as Meran pulled on his crumpled tunic and slipped into his coat.

Leon began to haul at the rope, pulling Meran up. Once on high ground, Leon wrapped it in a loose coil from shoulder to elbow as he scanned their location, familiarising himself.

The near horizon swelled with a huge surging black cloud, the colour bleeding to streaks of pounding rain from its underbelly. Leon's stomach lurched. He had never seen the likes, except maybe for a storm he had once experienced on the high seas many years back. A storm that had threatened to wreck everything in its path.

With care, he forced his features into a semblance of normality, hiding the shock at the power and foreignness of the mass rolling towards them. If he were a religious man, Leon would bet the very gods waged war in the heavens. Thank them that he was not.

"We should find cover of some sort," Meran said.

Agreeing, Leon searched for their caravan, a strange disassociation leaving him off-balance when he found nothing. "Where are the horses?" Where was anything?

"Where we left them last night. I felt it expeditious to leave them when you did not return."

Return? Leon strained to remember, but memories did not emerge because he had healed his physical trauma.

"I'm sorry, but we'll not reach them before the storm hits."

"Gods damn!" Leon could appreciate Meran's decision, but that left the beasts and their provisions to the mercy of the rain. It would bode ill for their own survival should it all be lost or the beasts scattered. "Are they secure?"

"As they can be. But some of the packs have been unloaded." Meran chewed his lip, contrition bright in his eyes.

"Better there than if we had reached the Gulch," Leon said. "Besides, there is nothing to be done about it now. So long as they can huddle into each other, butts to the wind, they will weather their way through. We are best placed where we are, I think."

That was until he turned. The deeper darkness that spoke of a break in the stark, jagged rocks rising before him stole his breath. A sheen of sweat broke out beneath his nose and trickled down his back like the tickle of scurrying feet.

The cave. He had entered that space earlier, considering it as an alternative shelter from the heat of the coming day. But his gaze had been as ineffective at piercing the darkness as his farsight while rock-shrouded. At the strange scuffling sounds that reached him, the hairs on his nape had stood on end.

Fear had bit deep and familiar, and the depth of his unease began to klaxon for a retreat, but then something had fallen on him.

Leon's gorge rose at the memory, a convulsive shiver racking his spine and goosebumps puckering his flesh. It had shattered his mind and filled his soul with hopeless wretchedness then, even as it stabbed at him again.

Shades of that infernal cellar blanketed his mind, darkness so thick he could not see his hand in front of his face. Punishment fit for his crimes, *she* would always say. The crime of caring for his siblings, of defending them and himself from her frequent and unpredictable rages. A night in the dark, chill cavern they had used to store stacks of wine and barrels of ale would apparently teach him the lessons he needed to learn. Things…things had crawled over him as he sat, tears of fear and resentment streaming down his young face…

He took a breathless, stumbling step back.

A hand shackled his arm and pulled. "Leon?" Fright and curiosity combined in Meran's tone.

The edge of the cleft loomed large behind Leon, sparking a memory. Unmanned to the point of blind panic, he had fallen.

"I'm fine," he said, but the repulsive images refused to release him. Disturbed by his presence, the spiders—sand creepers—had swarmed around and over him. He clenched his muscles against the internal shudder.

The feel of their feet, their quick and unpredictable scuttling, and the brush of their hairy legs had revolted him. He had fallen beneath the sway of his one unwavering nightmare.

Even now, their phantom touches ghosted over his body. The memory of one threading its spiked legs through his hair as it navigated over his head had his fists clenching against a resurgence of his terror.

Stomping, flailing, yelling like a madman. He remembered it now in all its humiliating glory. Pure luck had been his only ally, a spider's mandible brushing beneath his ear instead of latching on before he'd had the chance to unseat the clinging beastie.

"What is it? Leon?"

"Nought...'tis nought." With effort, Leon shook the weight of his shame free and wordlessly turned his back on the most convenient of shelters from the storm. He would not risk his sanity again when he did not know where the sand creepers had gone.

Meran cast the cave as wary a glance as Leon and followed without protest as Leon set off to find an alternative.

For the most part, the land was flat and crazed with deep gouges and rocky cracks, but Leon recalled passing a singular knoll not too distant. Complete with rocky pinnacles, it presented possibilities, and if nought else, it could offer them higher ground from the coming onslaught.

Red dust crusted their boots as they ascended the slope, with patters of rain announcing the storm's arrival. Fat drops fell, slow at first, and Leon pushed Meran upward. "Run!" he commanded. They had little time.

Slipping and sliding, Meran obeyed, seemingly oblivious to Leon's hand splayed across his arse and urging him on. The momentum gathered as they clambered their way beneath a jagged outcrop and dropped to the ground as the heavens let loose their torrent. Water dripped from their nose, chin, and lobes, and plastered their hair to their heads and the clothes to their bodies.

Like a sheet of noise, sound hammered a deafening din in their ears, Meran's voice lost in the uproar. Leon pulled knees to chest as water sluiced the overhang above and cascaded down the knoll's sides in a river. They had little choice but to hunker down and await its passage, and hope the parched soil held together, at least until they could move on.

Closing his eyes, Leon attempted to calm his mind and rest on their precarious perch, but his thoughts refused to quieten. Meran's body, so close to his, brushed against his side as the young man tried to make himself comfortable and keep his long limbs from the downpour. Elbow, shoulder, thigh, all radiating reassuring warmth that kept Leon's focus on him and brought to the fore again the spectre of their kisses.

Hunger erupted inside, urgent and powerful despite their precarious situation. Or perhaps because of it.

Was an uncertain future and brief, barely there touches all it took to have Leon aching for more? While a tempest raged around him, another burgeoned inside.

Meran had again kept his head where Leon had lost his. He had bested the spiders if the patches of spattered gore were anything to go by. Leon's pride swelled, almost as if taking credit for Meran's bravery.

But here lay another mystery. How, by the gods' hairy balls, had Meran found him at all? It should have been impossible. Not alone had Leon been surrounded by rock, but his magic also shielded him against the farsight of others.

How had Meran located him? Even as Leon baulked, a niggle of suspicion set up a tremor and threatened all his long-held beliefs.

Five hundred years and nary a glimmer of such ability in all of Locurnia until now.

Leon had set his heart on the treasure he knew lay in Draca's south. He had chosen to believe Meran's word. Why could it not be seer-given? Did this miracle not prove that Meran might actually be gods-touched? That he was a true seer.

The roar, when it came, drowned any further thought. Rock crumbled. Mud sluiced. Meran's scream of terror hit Leon as a torrent washed him from Leon's grasping hands, the ledge giving out beneath him.

CHAPTER TWENTY-EIGHT

Tossed and tumbled like a fallen leaf riding the rapids downriver, Meran descended, buoyed on the surface of the mudslide. He careened towards the desert floor where the saturated soil churned like a tsunami wave surging onto a beach, volume and mass behind it.

Flailing, he reached out to grab hold of anything to save himself. There was nothing. Hoarse cries of terror ripped free, the sound drowned out by the roar of mud and sheeting rain.

Meran tried to throw himself to the verge of the landslide, even as his legs sagged and a surge of mud rolled over him, pushing him down. Hopelessness broke like a cresting wave of chill realisation. It had all been for nothing.

Time quickened. Nature tightened her monstrous grip.

Darkness. Panic. The downwards momentum did not ease.

Pressure crushed him from above, swallowed him. Stars burst behind his lids and his chest burned with the need to breathe.

He fought the urge.

Must not.

The constriction grew leaden, a tight fist clamping his chest motionless. Suddenly weightless, he soared, only to gulp air and realise it had done nothing to relieve the suffocating hold.

His eyes popped open. Night and stars shrouded him in thick mist. Beneath his hands, the insubstantial feel of his simulacrum tingled through his nerves.

Somewhere between the dreamlands and the Elysian Plain, his shade floated while his body lay dying.

"Philo? Please," he begged. Fear, not bravery, surged through him, tinged with humiliation at his failure to face his death like a warrior. As Leon would. But Meran had not even reached his third decade. He had too much to do, too much to experience. There was the quest…and Leon. He could not believe fate would snuff it all out in the flash of an eye. "Please, please… Holy Janus, no!" This could not happen.

"I am here." The prophet's blessed voice washed over and through him.

"Thank the gods!" Meran's panic eased back as the overwhelming sense of injustice and abandonment dissipated.

"Peace, little one," that rumbling voice said. "While I hold you in my hand, my power envelops your corporal form."

Tears squeezed from Meran's eyes, even as he realised he could not stay on the ethereal plane forever.

"Fear not. If luck holds, he may yet save you."

He? Leon? But what if the mudslide had taken him too? Meran sensed nothing of him. The fire of Meran's panic grew. What if…?

A tug at his shade's solar plexus yanked Meran into the depths of the river before he could demand further answers.

"Look to the river, and perhaps you will see."

Desperation drove Meran into the nearest luminous bubble as it drifted down the river from the fountaining disruption that had shattered its heart at the moment of Anigema's excavation. When its influence would dissipate, he had no idea, but he feared it hinged on his completing his quest. For that, he needed to survive…and he needed Leon.

Meran expected to come face-to-face with Leon's fate. Instead, he fell onto an open terrace. Stars studded the night, offering no clue to his locale, but there he saw a gathering. A few were seated, the rest standing. Himself included. All eyes turned to a cadaverous man. Dark of complexion, with fierce fanaticism burning in his gaze, he loomed over a young man.

A young man with high cheekbones, a strong nose, full lips, and scruff like a permanent mantle across his defined jaw. Soft brunette hair framed a thick brow and glinting deep brown eyes. Meran startled at the familiarity of that face. This was the wounded lad from his previous vision. The very one who had touched the white stone beneath the waterfall.

Alive—

Meran's relief knew no bounds.

—and kneeling at the robed man's feet. Above the youth's head, the gaunt Dracan held a large object aloft. Meran's attention drew from the stunning lad to the dark, familiar thing in the older man's hands.

His breath caught.

As intense as the last vestiges of twilight, the gem sat, black crust shattered by patches of deepest sapphire blue.

Meran swayed forwards, his gaze affixed. Its call thrummed through his ears and filled his veins with the need to touch. He could almost feel the vibrations of its attention and taste the hidden power within. As if in recognition, the gem flew through the air, piercing straight through his trembling shade.

Confusion erupted about him in a cacophony of noise and protest.

Meran swung about to see the great treasure land with a bounce. Rolling, it fetched up by the toe of a sandal. His own foot filled the leather. Bending, the other Meran reached for it…and the world shattered.

Bathed in opalescent light, every nook and cranny was laid bare. Its radiance spiralled into the air and exploded. Rapture and trepidation, exhilaration and danger wrapped about him in alternating ribbons. It sucked out the very air.

Darkness pressed at the edges of Meran's sight as the light display began to diminish to streaks, like the receding flashes of a dying lightning storm.

Gravity exerted a disturbing hold, the manacle of his body dragging his awareness back to the terror of his situation.

This could not be foretelling. He had not seen Leon in this future. Was this no vision at all, just the last desperate sparks of a dying mind?

"Philo. No!" He tried to maintain the separation of shade and body, dreading to return to his mud-soaked grave. The strands of sense began to loosen nonetheless as sensation reasserted itself.

"Master?" He thrashed and held out his hand for aid. "Philo. Philo, are you there?"

Meran opened his mouth to shout, a rush of water and dirt flooding in. He gagged and choked as reality hit him with the impact of a sledgehammer. Immersed in cloying mud, he no longer had protection between it and his body. He tried to flail to the surface, and yet pressure cocooned him, hiding which way was up.

Panic set Meran's mind on fire. He fought and thrashed, even as arms slid beneath his pits and grasped him, dragging him upward. He broke the surface into the cool downpour, a fountain of red muck spewing forth as his chest met solid ground. A huge hand planted in the centre of his back pressed hard, knocking both the air from his lungs and the vestiges of detritus from his mouth.

A fit of coughing ravaged Meran, burning in his chest and devastating his throat. The hand began to pat and circle in soothing strokes. His hacking turned to a groan, and Meran drew his first decent, glorious breath.

His muscles began to tremble and shake as gooseflesh flushed his body, and weakness stole over him like a cloud of lethargy. He had no strength left to resist the hands that turned him over and drew him close against the stalwart power of a solid body. Pressure ghosted the hair at his temple—*a kiss?*—as warm breath feathered his wet cheek and arms squeezed about him.

Fierce, possessive, and intimate together, the strong grip held him tight. Leon's arms.

Meran sank into them with a rush of gratitude.

The crushing hold loosened far too soon for Meran's liking, but the rain still lashed, and he felt the chill of it sinking into his bones.

"Come," Leon bellowed above the storm's rage. "We cannot stay here. The rest of the hillside could come down any minute now."

That had Meran stumbling to his feet and staggering away under Leon's direction, his faith unwavering that Leon would keep them safe. An encouraging arm stayed at his back as they skidded across the wet but solid earth. Water sprayed as they ran.

The flood about their feet began to rise, the tug and swirl of current dragging at the bottom of their breeches. The waters were lapping at their thighs by the time they scrambled up a rock face and onto a small ledge above its rising tide.

Meran's back suddenly connected with hard rock at the entrance to a shallow cave, forbidding hands clenched about his biceps and dragging him close.

As rain poured in chilling droves, heat exploded through Meran's entire body as Leon's lips crashed into his.

The kiss plundered him, needy and wild.

Lust enveloped him from the tip of his toes to the strands of hair that fell to Leon's fist, twining, holding, tugging. Every thought, every fear fled at the onslaught, and Meran succumbed to Leon's devouring force.

Rain bathed their faces and plastered their hair to their heads as the kiss stretched, breathless and unending. Meran's arms glided around the big body that pinned him. He held on to Leon for dear life.

And then it was over. Meran found himself pushed towards the back of the rocky hollow, his protests groaning from him, even as his feet stumbled. Exhaustion doused the fiery passions threatening to overwhelm loins and heart, and he staggered beneath its insistent pull.

Leon threw his sodden coat to the ground, and they both crumbled to their knees, as drained as each other. They fell asleep within minutes.

When next Meran awoke, his cheek was pressed into Leon's nape and the rest of him wrapped around Leon's body like a limpet. The urge to awaken Leon bore down on Meran like a hammer to an anvil, but Leon lay still bar the deep rise and fall of his chest.

The cloth of Leon's shirt clung in damp folds. Meran skimmed the lightest caress down the breadth of a shoulder blade and to the hollow of Leon's spine and stiffened at the ferocity of his want. His shaft, full and firm, ached for Leon's note.

This man was formidable, his form granite hard and chiselled, a fierce and fiery lover. Vital, dynamic…controlling and vigorous…and vulnerable. Power nestled beneath Leon's every solid curve, alive with strength and dominance. Meran's heart squeezed at the audacity of his longing, wanting to have it turned upon him again. If it were, he would offer himself in return.

Gratitude burst through the bubble of his simmering lust. Here lay his saviour, sleep easing the constant tension that held those muscles rigid, exhaustion shutting down any hope of the warrior's normal vigilance.

Meran eased back. He might wish to touch, explore, and have Leon master him. Direct him. Overwhelm him. Send the magic of their connection bursting into the ether with the power of a lightning bolt, but he would take his turn to guard them. To prove himself worthy of Leon's attention and ensure that they were safe while he slept. If nothing else, the energy Leon must have expended in rescuing Meran, combined with the residue of healing his previous head injury, demanded the courtesy.

Determined not to disturb him, Meran stared at the void above, wondering what the rest of the day would bring.

CHAPTER TWENTY-NINE

It brought the chance for Meran to stand on the ledge, strip himself bare and let the rain wash the residue of dirt from him. It allowed time for him to clean the last of the mud from his clothes. Even his underdrawers were not spared.

By midafternoon, the skies cleared as if the deluge had never been, and hearing Leon waking, Meran drew on his wet britches. Leaving the rest of his clothes to dry in the sun, he returned to the shelter.

Leon's hungry gaze licked up Meran's chest like caresses of fire, bringing a flush to his skin. Pleasure unfurled at the scorching heat of that look that begged he not dress at all.

Yet seconds ticked by where no command came. Instead, a war of emotion waged in those sharp, pale eyes staring Meran down until darkness shuttered the flames.

"How goes it out there?" Leon asked, his voice far from lascivious, the mantle of duty appearing to bank his fire.

Meran sighed, disappointment smothering his desire, but he would not give in to his tendency to impulsiveness. Patience might serve him best than succumbing to the passionate recklessness of his past. "You will not like it."

"That goes without saying." Leon stretched and pushed to his feet, his boots squelching with the movement. He yanked them off and took them outside to bake in the sun, as Meran had done.

Meran followed, his gaze roaming again the sprawling lake of black water that stretched from horizon to horizon, surrounding them.

Leon's lip curled in disgust. "Well, I see there will be no travel this night."

There would be no food and no fire either.

The fate of their horses sprang to Meran's mind. He sent out a probing search with the farsight.

The water stretched for miles, a cauldron of death. No flicker or glow graced its depths.

That he might have lost them the beasts and their provisions, their means of survival, turned Meran's search into a frenzy.

"Ah, seems some luck is on our side after all." Leon clapped Meran across the back, the abrupt gesture still sparking across his nerves though it lacked the desired intimacy.

Meran turned his gaze where Leon pointed. He saw little but water and more dirty water.

The tops of some of the desert's vegetation poked above the flood level. For the first time, Meran spied the movement of disturbed and homeless creatures, taking what shelter they could on the flora's limbs.

A snake slithered across the surface in a rippling motion of soft lavender light. But for each creature that lived bobbed a dark and pitiable carcass. Where rain normally brought life, this storm had been a curse.

"They are stranded by the looks," Leon continued with some satisfaction, "but it seems they have found themselves a knoll."

"You have found the horses? Where?" Before Leon could guide him, Meran's sweeping gaze landed on six blessed globes of pale warm light in a sea of nothing. Resigned to their fate, the horses huddled close with the patience of the wretched and awaited rescue.

A rescue that Meran could not see coming for any number of days unless they found some way to traverse the flood. "Lords have mercy. How will we ever reach them?"

"That is the question." Leon made for the lip of the ledge, squinting into the distance, his gaze raking over the scenery, his silence contemplative. He wandered the confined area, peering this way and that, the churning of his mind easy to discern. Yet what resolution he reached remained a mystery.

In the end, Leon said, "Let me ponder on it for a while," and ducked back into the shelter, leaving Meran to his own devices.

Resentment churned at the walls Leon erected, as if still believing Meran was not his equal, not worthy enough for consultation. But what more could he do to prove himself after all he had accomplished?

Meran sighed in frustration and seated himself upon the small ledge, his goal still out of reach. How could he secure someone that baulked at being secured? Was it only wishful thinking on his part that their potential be equal in depth and intensity?

He closed his eyes against his dissatisfaction and, for about a turn of the dial, let the warmth bask him into a better mood. Though not the usual searing heat—*praise the prophet*—it still managed to heat him through, drying the fabric over his thighs.

When he again opened them, light glinted off the water in vibrant fingers of orange and gold as the sky turned to navy twilight.

In the dying light, Meran noted small swells and eddies and the rush of currents as waterfalls poured from the far ridges. Uprooted vegetation swirled in drifts, collecting debris and the bodies of the drowned along its path.

As the sun sank below the horizon, a chill, now laced with moisture, breezed over the still-wet crotch of his britches, goosing his flesh. Hunger gnawed at his gut.

Stiff, damp, and now cold, Meran shook free of his melancholy, retrieved their clothes, and retreated into the meagre shelter. He dropped Leon's where he lazed against the shelter's back wall, eyes remaining closed, extending only a muttered thanks for Meran's trouble.

Leon's aloofness stung, but though it was hard-won, Meran had vowed patience. The lord marshal had the concern of their predicament to distract him. Meran understood; he really did…

He found himself a spot in the cramped confines, wrapping his dry scarf about his head and shoulders. Other items were still damp in places, and though the rain had tried its best to clean the thick fabric of his coat, dirt clung to its seams and hem. Nonetheless, he threw it over his shoulders to keep from freezing.

Mourning the lack of a fire, his teeth began to chatter. Meran hunched in on himself and closed his eyes. A cool silence settled, mists creeping into his mind like a lullaby…

"Come here!"

The command shook Meran from the strange, meaningless reverie he found himself sinking into. He looked over at Leon, a huge silhouette against the silver light reflecting from the risen moon beaming into their shelter.

Leon slipped from his clothes.

"Wha…?"

Meran's mouth fell open at the sudden prospect, excitement sparking in his nethers, despite his earlier disaffection. He switched on his farsight, but wrapped in the cocoon of their cave, it refused.

Leon loomed, a godlike rendition fashioned in black obsidian.

Meran could imagine Jon's dedicated fingers forming no more stunning a masterpiece.

"I can hear you shiver from here," Leon said, spreading something on the ground to which he lowered himself, a hand making a muffled thud as he patted it in encouragement. "Get over here so that we may both be warm."

Heat of a different sort curled through Meran's body at the memory of Leon's broad chest pressing against him. Muscular arms capturing him, holding him, and hands threading through his hair while Leon consumed him with that morn's unforgettable kiss.

He shivered harder, a combination of want and the chilling grip of damp clothes and cold air wrecking him. His breaths ramped to a rapid rhythm, his mind feverish with the desire to see that stupendous cock he had once lain hand on.

The thought of it, potent and naked but hidden in the darkness, had fire racing in Meran's veins.

Lurching to his knees, he crawled eagerly, stopping only at the command—"Bring the coat"—to grab it from where it had dropped and scuttle over to that reposed figure, moonlight feathering over its curves and painting them in silver and dusk.

Leon's thighs seemed forged of iron, darkness hugging the balls at their apex. Light caressed the half-hardened appendage atop them, revealing how much his further arousal could make it grow.

"Take those off." Leon slapped down hard on the seat of Meran's damp britches.

The command shivered through him, images coalescing in his mind. Of himself being manhandled and having those large hands rip the fabric from his body, baring him. Of being tossed on his back and held in place while Leon kissed him senseless and showed him how a warrior owned him.

Feverish with haste, Meran struggled to shimmy out of his clothes.

"There, now," Leon directed, his arm thrown wide, encouraging Meran to curl up against him.

Meran added his tunic and scarf to the pillow Leon had made from his own and lay back, his excitement excruciating. Heat radiated from Leon's body, and Meran's mind blanked at the feel of him spread out at his back, naked skin touching.

At first, Leon made no sound and no move, allowing Meran to settle on the looped wool lining of his spread coat. He then threw

Meran's coat over them and wrapped an arm around Meran, drawing him close.

Meran forgot how to breathe as silken flesh pressed against his buttocks, huge and hard. The feel of it eclipsed his world, want and fear stirring. Fear of the intensity of his desire, of the needy capacity for capitulation that shivered through his body. What had become of self-preservation? What had become of his mistrust? Leon commanded and he gave in.

Such behaviour would never garner the respect he desired.

He did not care.

He cupped Leon's hand as it pressed to his chest, caressing his palm over the back of it.

"Show me where you want it," Leon directed close to his ear. Meran almost convulsed with eagerness as he urged that large hand in a determined descent until a featherlight touch from Leon's fingers burned the length of Meran's shaft. There, that was his heart's desire, his loins full and afire with his own collusion.

A curious sound rumbled from Leon's throat. "You want this again, my salacious seer?" His fingers curled about Meran's erection.

Want it? Meran was parched for it.

Slowly, that hand set into motion, a deliberate and seductive slide the length of him. Meran's flesh goosed, no longer from cold but from the desire that surged to the very tip of him, leaking free to flush the flesh where they touched. Leon curved his body closer, the heat of his arousal pressing like a rod of warning between Meran's cheeks and threatening ecstasy. "Tell me."

Meran's breath caught on a sigh. To have those bold fingers stroke him to undeniable heights, to sate the immensity of the craving induced by the blessed movement about his flesh; he would never deny it. "I do."

CHAPTER THIRTY

Surrendering to the power of his desire, Leon nuzzled the warming skin of Meran's nape.

He had looked across at Meran sitting and shivering, bound in misery, and his resolve had crumbled. The reasons for his hesitation vanished beneath the plethora of his own wants. Here, in this isolation, no Dracan, no predator could disturb them. They were safe.

He would have had Meran bracketed between his arms and up against the wall that very morning, but for a different set of circumstances.

Leon had owned those lips, bruised them beneath the barrage of his elation at their survival, and feasted on Meran's escalating passions, imbibing them in a frenzy of relief.

But for the shaking of Meran's limbs and the feverish clench that felt more like exhaustion, Leon would have commanded him; bid him drop to his knees in the pouring rain and fulfil the first fantasy Leon had ever had of him. To feel that tongue on him, that mouth taking him down to the root of ecstasy... Even now, Leon growled at the power of the image that stirred his baser nature—an almost feral and ravenous thing.

Desire burgeoned, insistent, stoking the unappeased yearning deep within, firing in both flesh and mind. The need to own and take and possess thrilled through him.

The chill that hugged his back, where Meran's coat did not cover, brought his thoughts back to reality. He should not give in to himself, not allow those wanton feelings to rule him again.

Yet Meran's acquiescence honoured him with a little-deserved trust in the face of Leon's previous rejection. Here lay his chance to prove himself made of a different mettle than the one who had dared hurt Meran in the past.

A furnace of fire filled his hand, his own cock aching for attention, but he knew there could be no untempered copulation. They were limited by the cold and the meagre confines of the coats and to a closeness that forbade extravagance.

Leon bit the heated flesh of Meran's shoulder and, taking himself in his free hand, stroked a duet of fiery caresses over both of them.

Meran's breaths escalated. His buttocks rolled against Leon in a display of invitation before he jerked forwards into Leon's fist, fucking himself into that grasp with increasing urgency and abandon.

Releasing him, Leon traversed Meran's stomach and ribs to land on a pebbled nipple.

He pinched hard.

Meran gasped, his body bucking.

"Calm yourself," Leon said. "Or it will be over ere we begin."

"Please, Leon." Meran tried to turn beneath his arm. "Please kiss me."

He would like nothing better, but… "Shh, I will have your silence."

Leon grasped Meran in both arms, plastering the length of him against his chest and holding him steady until any struggle ceased. As Meran eased down, Leon rewarded him with a pepper of kisses across both his shoulder and neck, seasoned with nips and licks.

The muscles beneath Leon's hand tautened as he slipped lower, his fingers finding the still-dripping rod of flesh and encircling. The bud of nipple still trapped between his other fingertips received a warning pinch as Meran urged the silken warmth of his shaft through Leon's grip.

"You will lie still, my wicked seer."

Meran froze, but Leon attributed it more to surprised curiosity than obedience. "Oh, so finally, you admit it."

A silent snort escaped Leon. It had been long in coming but could no longer be denied. "The *seer* and the *wicked* both," he said, squeezing Meran's vulnerable flesh in his hand. "Now you will be silent as commanded, and you will let me attend to you, do you hear?"

Leon purred at the eager nod, noting Meran's lips pinch as he observed the mandate. The swell of satisfaction stoked an avid answering fire in Leon's chest, cascading the length of his body to land in his loins.

His cock, engorged near to the point of pain, sat against the tempting heat of Meran's crease. But he would not sate himself with the delicious grip of that gorgeous body. The ferocity of his satisfaction stormed beneath his skin, demanding a rough and rapid response.

He swayed his hips back, freeing his shaft, and aimed its tip low. Even as the hand twisting at Meran's nipple slipped higher to cup his throat, Leon lunged forwards, thrusting that insistent pleading piece of flesh between Meran's thighs. Sliding the length of Meran's taint, Leon sank against the soft firmness of his balls.

Meran shook in Leon's arms, the exquisite breath of bliss trapped in his throat vibrating against Leon's palm.

"Good lad." Leon squeezed Meran closer, slapping his groin against the firm, sculptured globes of Meran's arse. He repeatedly dove into the well of heat at the apex of Meran's legs. He ramped his stroking to a rapid pace to keep time with the rising crescendo of lust that prodded and hammered him into a frenzy.

Huffs of breath, mere minutes from turning into groans of ecstasy, escaped between Meran's lips. The cascade of his pre-release increased, painting prick and palm in a salacious slippery coating that sang a rapid-fire beat beneath Leon's hand. Thwack, thwack, thwack, thwack...

Sweat, and the slickness of his own pre-seed, smeared Leon's shaft, adding its own voice to the chorus of muffled moans, panting breaths, and slapping flesh. A chorus he revelled in, building the imperative higher and harder and more urgent until Leon lunged one last time. Ramrod stiff, he bit down on Meran's shoulder and luxuriated in the pumping, glorious thrill of completion as rapture streaked through him.

In answer, Meran held back the high gasp, teeth chewing lip— obedient to the end—as his member pulsed into the dark, the last of his pleasure dripping warm about Leon's hand.

Leon's eyes shuttered in the silence that followed, their panting breaths easing as they came down from the unimaginable height. Warmth crawled like a blanket of satisfaction, entombing Leon in blessed contentment. It had been long, and long since such bliss had dared touch his flesh, his mind...his heart.

The possibilities Meran offered stirred a craving so deep and hungry, Leon yearned for it all again. This and more... Want, need, obsession, hunger. The power of his feelings sparked along the very edge of his skin, and his arms tightened about the precious man held in their grasp. Foolish, indispensable, dangerous longing. Still, he held tight enough he could not imagine ever letting go.

Beneath his embrace, Meran sank into him, the tension in every muscle waning with the fulfilment of his surrender. He was the most beauteous, ethereal being. His body a pleasure, his submission captivating; young, malleable, magical. Leon gorged on the ego-stroking feast of Meran's lust, the tendrils of a dangerous craving biting at the edges of his psyche. He nipped those stirrings in the bud. That want, that pain and loss would not touch him here.

For the moment, they were both warm and safe in their isolated cocoon, spun of night, intimacy, and satisfaction. Leon let out a sigh and fell into its welcoming arms.

Sleep wrapped around him, darkness taking him into oblivion as completely as night overtakes the day. And yet, as the moon sent its shimmering beams into the starlit sky, a chiming bell of unknown magic stirred…

As annoying as a small itch, tendrils of fog-like strands, seeped past Leon's sleeping defences. Like a column of smoke rising from a fire and spreading its warning, billows followed on its heels. Shades of platinum and blue-tinged cool grey and white, all tarnished by a dirty ochre, began to smother his world.

Fear crackled, and deep in his subconscious, Leon grew restless. Enough to question what trickery this could be.

"Leon?"

A voice called, his memory of it thick with the cobwebs of time. Unease slithered through his entrails. He clutched his chest with wraithlike hands, the body beneath his palms horrifyingly insubstantial. "What abomination is this?"

No answer came.

The mists parted, revealing a place he knew far too well. A place he had not visited in more than threescore and ten years.

"There is a glade, an isolated spot amidst Farnham's thick forests, though within walking distance of your hometown. In summer, its verge is lined with tasty mushrooms; small, hard apples fall to moulder upon the ground from the gnarled fruit trees dotting its course. There is one spot amidst the tall grasses that bears a flush of borage. The seeds were in her dress—"

Drifts of blue borage now invaded the grass, and in their midst stood a figure dressed in grey-and-red-checked homespun. Just as she had worn on that long ago day. And just as on that day, a deep gash ran from above her right eye to her abraded cheek, her temple crushed between them, marring the symmetry of her face.

He still remembered how she had flown at him like a hellion, her lips peeled back at the realisation of what his bold request had meant. *"How dare you? How dare you? He would never. Never! Never! Never!"*

The sounds of her slaps to his face echoed in the air, and instinctively, Leon touched his cheeks, expecting to find the raking scratches left by her nails. There was nothing.

The ghosts of his indignation stirred at the memories. No matter her insistence, she had no idea what Eain had wanted, what he had done.

"How are you even here?" he demanded.

The real Loni had died that day. Her head collided with a tree as he had pushed her from him, rage and denial rendering him unheeding of his own strength.

She glided towards him, the grass parting from her way with a shushing sound as if to reinforce her reality.

A shiver ran the course of his back as she drew closer, her skin grey-tinged and more translucent than it had been in life. Her lips were like a streak of red paint, her eyes like subterranean pools. She was not real. Could not be real.

"This is my world, Leon Ricci. It is you that intrudes. But no matter." She touched his face with a hand as cold as the grave, flashing him a cadaverous smile. "You have grown old...and soft since last we met. And I see you now have designs on Philo's pet seer."

Leon clamped his mouth closed on the demand to know how she knew Meran. Ghost or nay, he would not let her terror induce him to confess his burgeoning attachment.

"I do not need you to speak, foolish man. I know all." Her laughter trilled, shaking him like the squawk of a buzzard. "Long and long have I awaited this moment, and here you stand, the coil of seer magic bound about you because you could not keep your hands from him."

Leon knew she goaded, and he tried not to react, though the inference made him squirm. No magic had ever overcome him before, and he doubted her veracity. This was a nightmare.

"Meran Durante is too much like my Eain, all doe-eyed and easily led. A particular weakness of yours. I knew it the first I met him. So, I am here to give you a warning. When you lose this one, what will your madness bid you do this time? Destroy the world?"

No! Madness had claimed him once, but he had grown and changed since then...

"I am not a child." Yet, what if he cared too much? Gave too much of himself and it was torn from him? Would the damning madness simmering ever beneath his skin dare to resurface?

"You deny it?" She let out a scornful laugh.

Leon clamped his mouth shut. He was nowhere near that point of no return. He would never love another with the same open-hearted fervour as he had his first. Even should he possess *Amplion*, the world was safe, and he with it.

"We will see. And I will rejoice when this one rips your heart out. Your pain will be to me as a night filled with ecstasy."

A knife flashed in her hand, and as her voice devolved into a cackle, the blade plunged into Leon's shade. There should not have been pain, yet the ripples of agony through his chest were a tidal wave, tearing him asunder.

Leon jolted awake to breathless panic. He jerked to his seat, waiting for his heart to resume beating. It gave one hard thud and began again its rapid tattoo. "What by all the hells was that?" he groaned into the new day as it crept into their shelter.

"The dreamlands," came the soft reply, a gentle caress feathering down his biceps.

Leon let the hand settle and followed its insistence as it drew him back down onto the makeshift bedding. He had not expected an answer. That Meran had given one set flight to his fear and curiosity. "Dreamlands? I don't understand."

Meran's breath brushed a soft sigh across his cheek. "I'm sorry. I did not realise she would be able to call you there."

"She?" Anger stirred the caldron of his fright. As seer, what did Meran know? What had he seen? "What was that infernal place?"

"It is the place to which seers are drawn and, if they are lucky, retain their sanity until they reach the Elysian Plain and the river. It is not a place meant for the living."

Leon watched Meran's nervous swallow, the urgency of his caress turning to a hold that captured Leon's face.

"When we...come together like we did last eve, the ether explodes with such wondrous magic, but I had not realised it was mine. I let it capture us both. I think Loni's shade used it to trap you while you slept."

Leon's breath caught. If seer magic subjected him to a place where such abominations dwelt, he would have nothing to do with it. "Unhand me," he said as if Meran's touch were poisonous.

"It will not happen again. I promise." Meran's hold tightened. "Now that I know what it is, I have it all in hand. Please. There is no need to spurn what we have begun. Please."

Leon saw glimmers of sincerity in those shaded eyes, but it could not appease him. Loni's words of warning rang true. Here before him was one temptation too many. "You have the right of it. It will not happen again."

Clasping Meran's wrists, Leon pushed them away and surged from the bedding.

"Where are you going?"

Leon had nowhere to go, but he dressed in what clothes were available to him and retreated to the entrance.

"Calm yourself." Leon let the command in his voice ring. "I have much to think on and wish peace in which to do so."

"But—"

"No. Stay. Get your rest. I have promised to keep you from peril, and nought on that has changed." But he would brave the cool dawn rather than fall in thrall to Meran again.

Already, Neve owned a piece of him, as did her mother. If aught happened to them, it would leave his heart fractured and irreparable. Selfishly, he attempted to ensure their perpetual safety. But he could not afford to give anything more of himself away. Not here. Not now, for unlike them, Meran headed with him into dangerous territory.

Distance was best kept if he dared not risk the grief that the ghostly Loni had foreshadowed. He could not let her win. Would not, despite what it might cost him.

CHAPTER THIRTY-ONE

Instinct urged Meran to follow Leon into the dawn, protests falling over themselves in his mind. He baulked that their assignation ended in such a manner.

What had happened to the feelings that had exploded between them? The closeness. The satisfaction. The beauty of Leon's commands and Meran's own willing submission. He had gifted Leon such pleasure. Him. How right that had felt.

His body had drawn Leon out from beneath the aloof mantle of the lord and into the lush intoxication of their shared delight. Meran's greatest desire in that moment had been to give Leon every part of himself, and he had, in turn, flushed beneath the benediction of Leon's instruction.

He had revelled in Leon's wants, in the satisfaction that they had given to each other. Leon could not have been ignorant of it. It had resulted in slumber so deep and satisfying, Meran never wanted to rise from it again unless to repeat the glorious encounter.

How could Loni have done such a thing? Attaching herself to his magic like some ghoulish parasite, only to threaten and taunt. It was not right. Not fair. Her shade had been relentless in her scorn and vengeance, though Meran knew most of what she had intimated had to be lies.

In spirit, he had witnessed it all. He had felt the trauma rippling through her shade and knew her incapable of considering Leon's state of mind and his youth at the time of the event.

It was easily done. No one considered a man as formidable as Leon could be vulnerable, emotional, or suffering. But Meran suspected that was the case. On the one hand, he understood her. Life, as she had expected, had been ripped from her grasp by fate and unforeseeable tragedy. But in the turmoil of the dreamlands where emotions were raw and savage, she gave no credence to how the situation had been a tragedy for everyone. Not alone for her.

Not that Meran knew the full story. The question of what Leon had asked of Loni teased at him. He doubted he would get an answer.

A soft shush of mass slipping into water followed by gentle ripples drifting off into a distance teased him from his musings. He listened harder, perturbed by the ensuing silence. "Leon?" Slipping from beneath the coat, Meran pulled on his britches and went in search of his errant companion. He found the ledge empty. "Leon?"

Meran cast out the farsight to, of course, find nothing. Irritation, mixed with concern, tore through him as he scanned the black waters. Where had he gone? Where, by all the gods, was there for him to go?

Before he could call out again, an erratic movement caught his eye. A large piece of driftwood floated towards their shelter. Bringing up the rear, a head bobbed, the sandy locks wet and coloured a deeper brown.

One tension eased from beneath Meran's frown, only to set up a roar in his belly as Leon drew closer.

Meran grasped the end of the flotsam, dragging it onto the ledge as Leon heaved himself up, water cascading from his muscular perfection.

Lust strummed back to life as Meran explored Leon's tempting and glorious physique until he met the sharp glint of pale blue eyes.

"Discard the breeches," Leon said, his words lacking even a note of lasciviousness. Shutters had fallen, the returning stare imperious.

Meran felt the distance yawning between them. "Pray, why?"

"There is a dam of logs that has fetched up behind this peak. I have a mind to fashion a raft so we may get from here as quickly as possible."

Disappointment dug deep at Leon's practicality. Was this to be the tenor going forward? No further discussion when so much more needed to be said? More than loneliness ached through Meran's heart. He should have known better. Again, his magic stood between them like an unbreachable barrier. This time not inciting Leon's scorn and disbelief, but his revulsion.

Well, Leon would not get the best of him. Meran, too, could present as stoic a mask and shrug off any regrets. The interlude had been a means to pass the time. Nothing more. It would be better that way. He may not have gained a lover, and with it unstinting loyalty, but at least his position was no worse.

"Why may we not walk from here?" He did not fear to wade through the transient waters to its far edge. Even if it proved pit deep, it would be better than trusting their safety to a cobbled-together raft made of driftwood from a desert whose trees were little better than brittle bushes. "I mean, how deep can it be?"

Leon gave him a grim smile. "You do remember the plain we trod before this deluge?"

"Of course."

"And where you found me?"

Ah, yes. The plain had been scoured by cracked clefts, open pits, and deep gouges, as if two giant mythical beasts had torn up the land in mid-battle. *Leon made a good point, damn him.* With the water so dense with debris, seeing what lay beneath could prove impossible.

He shucked off his pants and, with a wave of his hand, said, "Lead the way."

Meran lowered himself off the edge, a current brushing at his legs, and strove to feel the bottom with the tips of his toes. He felt nothing, only unseen things grazing him in the sluggish undercurrent. His skin crawled.

Shuddering, Meran gathered his resolve and followed in Leon's wake. By the time he fought his way around their perch to the accumulation of debris, Leon was already trying to wrench another log free.

Meran stroked over to help. Together they wrestled it loose and used it to float back to their ledge. An hour later, they had managed to gather enough wood to fashion a meagre craft.

The exertion had served to tame his desolation, his muscles weary and chilled. He dressed in haste, as much for warmth as to restore a necessary decorum.

Meran sunned himself and drank one last sip from his canteen. "And to think. So much water and none fit to drink." How fatuous now his suggestion to walk seemed.

Leon cast him one glance before turning his attention back to their project. "These will make the platform for us to stand on." He indicated those that were longest and about a hand's width thick. They were far from straight, but at least they had displayed the necessary buoyancy. "And these four larger, we will use to sandwich them together."

Meran watched as Leon used the rope to lash the logs that

underpinned the platform to those that lay over its surface.

Grabbing the last two branches, he handed one to Meran. "These we will use as paddles. Now let us see if she floats."

Meran eyed Leon's handiwork warily. Longer than it was wide, the raft had enough room for one of them to stand on either end. With gaps between the sticks of the platform, its appearance did not fill Meran with confidence. Nevertheless, he helped Leon lower the craft into the water, half expecting it to sink. To his surprise, it bobbed on the two logs underneath.

"Get the rest of our gear," Leon said, using his makeshift paddle to tether the raft close to the ledge as he stepped across onto its middle. The raft dipped but took his weight as he braced his legs.

Meran gathered their meagre provisions, draping both sets of boots about his neck and strapping the canteen and bow and quiver across his chest to press against one hip.

He joined Leon on the craft, grudgingly accepting the offered hand until he had found his balance. Pulling free, Meran self-consciously wiped the sparking awareness from his palm on the sleeve of his tunic. The vessel shifted lower with the added weight, water lapping between the logs, but it remained floating.

"I take off my hat to you. I fully expected it to go down."

"Let us not speak too soon on the matter. Gods willing, we will make it back to the horses this eve."

Meran hid his smile. For a man who believed in none of them, Leon swore by them most frequently.

It seemed hours that they paddled, stopping only to doff their coats and adjust their head scarfs.

"Why did we not cross direct?" Meran asked, the desire for a drink drilling from his mouth deep into his belly. They would have made it to the horses by now if they had. Instead, they had made for the closest escarpment and paddled around its steep rocky face. It offered some shade, but many a waterfall pounded down from the higher steppe, turbulence hounding their progression as water met water.

Meran guessed Leon looked for a way to ascend, but there seemed to be no easy access.

"The Barrens was reputedly once a lake, the plain now encircled by a band of high bluffs. Its centre is the lowest and most crazed of it, meaning the centre is now where the water is deepest," Leon said. "I'd not risk such a crossing. Should the craft fail, there would be no hope of swimming the distance."

Meran shook his head. "This is the strangest of lands that I have ever traversed."

"That is due to Nord's curse." Leon's smile quirked. "Or so Draca's holy men would have you believe. It is said that he sucked the water out from underneath them as punishment for the misdeeds of an errant prince."

"A prince? It seems all must suffer for the nobility's misdemeanours." Meran's tone sounded jaded even to his own ears. "Of course, you do not believe them."

"Would you?"

"Mayhap. That is if I knew from whence their fables and teachings came." He threw Leon an assessing glance, the desperation to reopen their morning's conversation resurfacing. "If their priests and practitioners tapped the dreamlands with their earth magic, I would be wary. Not everything there is as it seems."

Expression souring, Leon remained silent, concentrating on his makeshift oar and their destination.

"She lied, you know," Meran said, almost holding his breath. "She tried to make it sound inevitable, but nothing of the future is set. Not even in the river. It bubbles and flows with many possibilities. Those most likely to eventuate are closest to the surface, but I have to believe that they can be influenced, or what need is there of this venture? If I could not affect anything, not change the fate of—" He stumbled to silence, the enormity of what he attempted crushing his heart until it shuddered within his chest. Patrice could not die in a pool of blood. Sofie could not end in enemy hands. His friends could not be trampled beneath the feet of an invading army. This was his purpose here. To change the future. And if he could facilitate such a thing, Leon had to know Loni's words meant nothing.

Leon paused, his back rigid, the current gently tugging them through the water as they both stared at each other.

A sudden grinding roll, as of thunder, interrupted any possibility of conversation. A plume of water surged in front of them, white waves crashing and roiling, trapped in an inexplicable vortex.

The craft jerked. Leon swore, urgency escalating in his voice. "That way! Paddle that way, away from the ridge." He gesticulated wildly at Meran.

That made no sense. But the cliff offered no purchase, its sheer rock face rising like a barrier to their escape. White water roared downwards like a waterfall, as if a plug had been pulled.

"What is it?" His words disappeared beneath the barrage of sound. Heart pounding, adrenalin streaking through his veins, Meran paddled harder.

The current picked up speed, threatening to sweep them into the swirling maelstrom, despite their best efforts.

Leon's curses flew back over his shoulder. Muscles bulged as he worked his paddle.

Wonder eclipsed the fear pounding in Meran's heart at the split second of admiration that filled him. Leon, for all his faults, was impressive. He stood like a bulwark against the impending disaster as if nothing could touch him.

There.

Then gone in an eyeblink.

Unbalanced, the craft reared up and shot out from beneath Meran. His roar of protest snuffed out beneath a surge of water. He went down, down, down... The chill depths gripped, and darkness swallowed him...

Pressure crushed into his back. Breathless, all-consuming pain overcame him, so vast he could barely feel anything but shock's chill numbness. His head filled with roaring echoes, gushing, pounding waters.

Paralysis gripped him, panic surging in waves.

The muffled thuds of racing feet teased at his ears, his vision swimming in and out of clarity. Uncertainty blurred time and sense. Devastated weeping echoed through what felt like years, stabbing at his heart... He was leaving... *"No!"* He still had too much to do, too much to live for...and something he must say. A warning?

It floated into darkness.

Firm fingers pinched his chin, pushing his head back, air caressing his wet face. The most glorious, welcome visage eclipsed his vision. Relief bound through him. "Leon." But a beard swathed the jaw of that familiar face, a face stretched with impossible grief, eyes reddened, and cheeks tear-streaked.

There was no sound, no breath, no feeling.

Confusion bubbled to the surface. White lights sparked across Meran's vision, clouding and burying everything before him in twilight.

He sped into endless night.

CHAPTER THIRTY-TWO

Warmth bathed Meran's face, red blanketing his returning consciousness behind his closed lids. The sounds of lapping whispered of peace, and the tugging of a gentle current lifted and lowered his body like he rode a soothing tide.

There was a cove not far up the coast from Dun, where such waves enticed swimmers with the promise of lulling away their every concern. The blue of the sea and the stark white cliffs filled Meran's memory. He smiled, and pain bit in.

Heat radiated from his skin, forehead tight, cheeks aflame, and he tasted a crust of salt as he licked his lips and let out a groan. Sense and sensation returned with a barrage of panic. Meran opened his eyes to a sky, blue and intense and blinding. Blinking, he tried to adjust both sight and mind.

His face hurt, head throbbed, and body ached, but dirt and sand scraped against his back. Ignoring the discomfort, he shot to his seat to find himself on solid ground. A burst of bright, incredulous laughter broke free. "Leon?"

Knowing full well he could not have survived once he hit the water, other than someone had saved him, Meran swept the terrain searching for Leon. Not gone, but there to drag his sorry self to the shoreline. A place Meran could not have reached alone, even despite fate's insistence that he live. That would be a twist of fortune unbelievable.

"Leon?" He swivelled about, scanning the shimmering landscape...and came up empty.

Fingers of doubt etched through Meran's confidence.

"Leon!?"

Surging to his feet, Meran fell to his knees as if slapped by a black wall of dizziness. Groaning under the weight of heat and exhaustion, he almost heaved, managing only to grope his way from the water and onto shore on his knees.

The comforting weight of hands on his shoulders did not come. "Leon!" he bellowed. "For the love of the prophet, show yourself."

His own voice echoed back.

This could not be.

With dogged determination to overcome whatever magic Leon had, Meran filled his mind with those familiar rugged features. He threw out the farsight as if the intensity of his desperation would have him win.

Nothing!

A wretched cry broke from Meran's lips, despair running roughshod over him. Had the maelstrom truly taken Leon down?

Every corner of Meran's mind echoed with disbelief. Nothing could smother that bold spark of life that was Leon.

Meran's farsight danced off the cliffs above a whirlpool raging at the escarpment's edge. The waters about it churned and swirled, captured, and sucked down into darkness. He had somehow avoided it, had ended up miles from its destruction, but what of Leon?

Had Philo intervened for Meran's sake but left Leon to his fate?

Morbid and indistinct, a vision lingered, but he could not pluck it free of the dark abyss that consumed the memories of his recent past. Worst still, he had received no warning of the impending disaster.

"Philo?" he shouted to the sky, muscles tense with accusation, awaiting the prophet's response. The blue expanse rang, empty and still. No voice came.

"Gods damn you! Philo! I need you." How else would he find out what had become of Leon?

But more than that, how could he go on?

Panic welled, bright and heart-constricting. Despite Leon's emotional withdrawal, Meran knew that something had sparked between them. Something that, with time and nurture, could blossom into a strong, powerful, and mutual aligning of passions and loyalty, of value and worth…and…and beauty. What could they not do with such an alliance? But now all that promise was dust.

"Philo?" His voice broke, small and forlorn, and echoing into the void.

No answer came.

Meran curled in on himself, back to the sun's glare, alone and bereft.

The cool touch of night, and a raging thirst, woke him from his fugue. His face throbbed, afire with sunburn, but he did not have the energy nor the inclination for healing. A pathetic husk, he clung to life by a mere thread, so parched no tears came, his misery overwhelming.

Nought has changed. Trust yourself, the pale voice of reason echoed on a sigh.

Philo?

How could he trust anything, least of all himself?

If Leon were gone, he would not be there to fulfil his part of Meran's prophecy, and all would be lost. Locurnia would be overrun, and the *Voce* annihilated. His sisters... No! He would not think on it.

Despite the wretchedness that tried to leach the strength from his heart, his quest could not be denied. He, Meran Durante, would not turn into a snivelling lump of useless humanity flailing in the mud. He needed to pull himself together.

Not knowing the exact location of his quarry could not stop him. Meran had seen himself on that open terrace in what must have been Becchus Oasis. He would get there, prophet willing. He had to believe in himself.

Resolved, Meran gathered every miserable emotion and forced them into submission. He would do it, and he would succeed.

Purpose or not, he now found himself without coat, weapon, canteen, or shoes. He needed to find the horses. As Leon had reminded him, they were his best resource, and with them, he would find the balance of their provisions.

A twinge of regret caught his throat. When it came to the horses, his farsight did not falter, yet of Leon, there was nought.

Sense told him no one could have survived what must have been a breach in the rocky crust at the foot of the escarpment. A crack opening into which the water drained, to the gods knew where. Yet he clung to hope. If Meran had not drowned, by the same token, Leon could have survived. That their paths were fated to cross was a belief he clung to like a light in the darkness.

Meran set out to bring his feet and the vision of the horses together.

With a burst of joy, he located them. Warm to his cold, he hugged the small beast that had been his mount, even burying his sore face in its now-dry coat. Life in a sea of lingering despair, despite its stink.

Tears of relief and mourning wet his cheeks. For that one moment, hopelessness won out over his belief.

Coming back to himself, Meran found that the packs were now dry despite having a faint lingering scent of mildew. The provisions themselves had fared as well, apart from the satchel of flour, dried spices, and what had once been a hard loaf of bread.

He drank long and greedily from the one full water bladder and then cobbled together a small feast of root vegetables and strips of jerky. A swig of Tark's brandy fired in his belly, and he settled down to heal the cursed sunburn blistering his skin. His eyelids were now puffed to the point he could barely see.

With the horses for company, peace settled over him, and he curled into the warmth of a spare coat and blanket. He gave himself up to the rejuvenating sleep that followed on healing's heels.

Revitalizing joy rang through him even when he awoke some hours later. His skin, now smooth and damage-free, tingled softly beneath his exploring fingers. *Thank the prophet he had been born Voce. He could do this.*

Closing his eyes, Meran brought the map from the Shimmering Fields back to mind in as much detail as he could. An emblem of a waterfall and palms, drawn at the centre of the vast space representing Nord's southern desert, sat stark but ever hopeful. Beyond doubt, Leon had been heading for this destination. All other oases were dotted either further west or to the far east. The only one within reach was this one, though gods knew how close it might be. Gathering his courage, Meran recommenced the journey.

Doggedly, he headed northeast.

His saddle lost to the flood, Meran found himself walking as much as being drawn to ride Leon's small steed. This saddle had cradled Leon on their journey, the lord marshal sitting ramrod straight and awkward, even as Meran was now.

He swallowed down pangs of loneliness and longing, though his lips twitched with a smile at the memories of this shared experience. The discomfort that they both had suffered. Like a secret he could squirrel away to comfort himself with on the dreaded days of solitude he knew he faced.

Walk, sleep, feed himself, feed the horses. And thus, the days passed, a repetitive cycle of dread silence so deep he had fallen into talking to Leon's horse; meaningless ramblings, even singing it snippets of songs learned in his childhood.

Still, the thudding of the horses' hooves seemed to plod through an unending night.

Meran lost count of how many he endured. Caught in a war with his despondency the longer Leon remained absent, he climbed to the top of the escarpment once again. The arid desert, to his astonishment, had burst into a verdant pasture, feverish in its attempts at procreation before the blistering sun laid waste to it again.

Pools of water lingered under rocky overhangs, and streams rushed down gullies. Frogs stirred, their croaks like a crescendo filling the twilight hour, and insects swarmed. Herbivores took their fill, and predators revelled in the abundance. A far cry from the cesspool the storm had made of the Barrens.

Vegetation burst with flowers of brilliant cerise and yellow. A rich carpet, the last of which Meran saw each morn before exhaustion took him, and the first he observed each eve before the night bled all the colour from the world and his journey began anew.

Meran now travelled gripping the hilt of his dagger. The night creepers were a terror that haunted his sleep, but they were not the only things on his mind. A plethora of other threats plagued his overactive imagination.

High buttes riddled the landscape, the edge of a vast mesa falling afoul of the eroding blasts of the desert's harsh storms. Pockets formed in the landscape, impermeable to his farsight. Canyons and gullies walled in unforgiving rock. His head throbbed from the effort of maintaining a watch with both his mind and his eyes, and still, the darkness left him blind and vulnerable.

He began to ache as much for the sun as for the end of the journey, though he still had no idea of how far he had to go. Tension ever rode between his shoulders.

Breaking free of the fractured landscape about midnight one night, Meran stopped his trek, sighing his thanks for the open expanse of star-studded sky. From here onwards, his farsight could soar.

Adhering to Leon's pattern, Meran attended the horses before building a fire to heat his dwindling supply of victuals. Even as he worked, he sent out his magic with a rush of relief and pleasure.

He saw little more than the glimmering hubbub of normal activity. The blue auras of small creatures skittered back and forth, seeking their own food, and hoping to avoid the ever-watchful eyes of their enemies.

The rolling vibrations of a night snake slithered in waving undulations; scorpions stalking, pincers and tails raised; spiders of every size and shape reared, pounced, and scuttled. Creatures died, and life proliferated. Just as it ever had.

And then shapes skulked through the eroded landscape at his back. Sleek streaks of pale green light, their eyes glowing like red fire, flitting in and out of Meran's farsight. His heart almost stopped as he clasped the knife harder, his grip slick with sweat. Desert dogs!

Indecision racked him. Should he break camp and be on his way? But the horses needed rest and food, as did he. For an unsettling minute, he paced back and forth and found himself once again trying to find what he knew he could not. *Lords.* Where was Leon when he needed him?

Oh, for the sight of him. Meran missed him with a never-ceasing ache that throbbed like a fresh wound. He would even welcome his acerbity, his condescension, for the comfort of his stalwart presence. But even Meran's belief flagged in the mire of Leon's continued absence.

Was the world without Leon Ricci now?

If so, it was the poorer for it.

But perhaps, he should worry for his own situation with as much diligence. His best guess placed the dogs about a league away. Plenty of distance to afford a distraction from his trail. At least, he hoped.

He busied himself reheating a stew of pulled meat and chunks of shrivelled white carrots while keeping his farsight attuned. He would eat with all haste and be off.

The glowing shades wove a winding path before disappearing like wraiths into a void. Meran took a breath, waiting for their reappearance.

The passage of time seemed endless though no more than a half turn of the dial had passed.

Though he had no appetite, Meran ate his stew, forcing it down.

Where had they gone? Had they found more suitable prey?

Snorting, the horses began to mill, tossing their manes and pushing against each other. Meran rose, grasping a brand, and tried to sight the menace, even as he drew closer, intent on calming the beasts if he could.

A step away, the shades reappeared from between the rock.

Meran counted five of them.

By the gods! He had not anticipated their speed.

What use was a knife against the pack advancing on him with such intent steps of stealth when he needed his lost bow.

Even as the beasts glowed in his farsight, dark shadows stalked the edge of the firelight, the horses dancing in a burgeoning frenzy.

One broke free, eyes white, mouth open and screaming, as teeth nipped at its heels. It kicked out, a hoof connecting. The sound of a wounded dog echoed in the dark. Confusion swirled. The horses scattered, ropes dragging, dust pluming as they surged away.

Leon's mount struck out, hooves pounding, four of the dogs on its tail.

No!

Brand in hand, Meran gave chase.

Out of the darkness, a beast appeared, bigger, darker, ears twice the size of its head, and eyes glowing.

It leapt.

The horse went down.

No!

The rest converged, a growling, yipping mass, pouncing and tearing at the terrified animal.

Meran's torch flung end over end, landing on the now-silent horse. Hair melted, its stink pluming. Sparks flew. The dogs yipped their protest and dispersed, treading cautious steps beyond the flame's light, eyes affixed to their kill, jaws foaming.

Meran ran, yelling, arms spread wide, knife ready.

Thundering darkness launched from his periphery. A hefty weight dropped him to his knees. The snap of jaws preceded pain lancing through his shoulder.

Fear whiplashed through him, adrenalin spiking as he screamed. Bodies ringed him. Darting and growling.

Lashing out, the tip of his blade bit. The pressure on his shoulder released.

Yelling and kicking, he stabbed again and again as he tried to gain his feet. Darting in and out, the beasts' teeth nipped and tore at his legs.

An open mouth lunged; a dark abyss of horror consuming everything. Teeth pierced his throat.

Pain flared like fire in his belly, his scream silent and breathless, consumed in terror.

A whirlwind of darkness was coming for him, his protests shrieking into the night. *No!* This could not be the end…

CHAPTER THIRTY-THREE

Like a fist clamped around his body, the force of water grasped Leon in a suction impossible to break. Water replaced air in a single heartbeat.

The shout of surprise slammed into the back of his throat. The battering rush silenced him; every conscious spark of life smashed beneath the torrent's unwavering hammer. No breath, no sense, no light. His eyes clamped shut as the world dropped away.

Panic surged, hot sparks that pierced his brain. Out of control, Leon plunged down, down, down. Caught by the heedless implacable hand of nature, his flesh, blood, and bone were as nothing.

Thought became futile, consciousness fruitless. Breathless darkness cascaded over him, through him, until the need to breathe tormented his lungs and drilled at his soul.

What worth were his muscles, bearing, and stature? What worth were his schemes, title, and position? They were nought in the face of such dark and tumultuous terrors.

With negligent disdain, the power of nature put all his vanity in its place.

Helpless fury warred at the back of Leon's lids and clenched his teeth, chest, and hands.

Relentless, fate tore at his sanity and laughed at his machinations. Curses floated into nothing as he sent silent pleas to the gods in whom he did not believe.

What felt like a free fall into certain death changed from weightlessness beneath the anvil of torrent, current, and sound. Pressure pushed him down. Even should he wish, he could not breathe as he tumbled and rolled like a stone beneath the flood, honing him into a fine grain of sand.

Leon flailed against fate, against the power of a watery grave, battered by the sharp edges of ground, rock, and debris that stabbed and scoured. Pain flamed through him, blood leaking, his hands grasping for anything…and broke free.

Chill air caressed his fingers with the cruel touch of hope, and he kicked to the surface and to blessed air. Cold, stale, pitch-black.

Echoes of distraught tears flittered through his memory of the cold hole beneath his childhood home, and isolation so desolate he felt it ring in his soul.

Leon fought against the surge of panic, the sense of himself crumpling beneath the burden of an irrational fear. As ever, he reached for his magic, the one Meran coveted. The one that wrapped him in mists and rendered him invisible.

Normally, he would take the ribbons of colour that flooded the world and bend them to his will, submersing himself in the comforting glow of his magic. But here, darkness ruled. He grabbed on to those ebony strands and bound them tight like a second skin, coating himself in a sheath of obsidian. Better that than to succumb to the frenzied hysteria that poured through his body and threatened to breach his lips with a hollow cry of terror and rage.

His eyes opened to nothing, his mind filling with dark corners and shimmering jet-black ghosts. Leon scrabbled against a face of smooth rock and fought a persistent current that dragged him along. Rumbles of sound pounded his ears, hollow and gurgling as he bobbed intermittently beneath the surface of the still-rushing torrent.

He spat and gasped and grabbed. Still heading downwards, the flow took Leon further away from the chasm that weight and water had broken through the rocky crust at the edge of the Barrens.

His hand snagged on a deep gouge, pulling him up short. Limbs shaking, Leon clung with chilled fingers and tried not to let his hopeless situation overwhelm him.

Trying to take deep breaths to calm himself, Leon took a moment to peer around, confused by what he saw. Like a blindfold, darkness shuttered his eyes. Yet the magic tolling in his mind echoed with shades of grey, from charcoal to raw iron, to slate, lead, and silver.

In the light, this same power, turned his vision to crystal prisms. Colour so bright and piercing it had taken him many years to tune them down to see enough to avoid a pounding headache. Here in the darkness, Leon struggled to focus the grey pallet into eerie shadows, enough to see more than feel the weight of the rock pressing down from above.

It should not be possible. The very fabric of the earth, its bones impenetrable in any of its forms, muted the farsight. But this magic seemed to scream from his skin and back to his brain, like the high-frequency sound echoing back to a bat's sharp ears.

Before him spread a vast cavern, water rising and churning as the floodwaters flowed down the cleft from the inundated Barrens. He had to get out before the cavity filled and drowned him. Yet that, too, felt impossible.

Lacking rocks to climb back to the new opening, he could not return the way he had come. The only way was forwards.

As soon as Leon edged out into the water, it grasped hold and tugged him on. The cavern trended downwards and defied him to disbelieve the old stories. Not a god's curse, of course, but a drop in the water table and the lake draining away through a vast array of underground caverns.

The echoey flow of water and deep silence surrounded him.

Minutes ticked by. Moments stretching out dark, uncertain fingers. Moments where dread and panic vied for supremacy against all hope. Hours or days, for that matter, could pass, and he would not know.

Threading through the air came the continuous boom of thunder, growing ever louder. Leon had mere seconds to grab a lungful of air before the force dragged him down again and tumbled him over the edge of a pounding fall. His dying brain sparked its demand for oxygen, instinct screaming that he breathe, though doing so would inundate his lungs with water.

A wave of helplessness turned all thoughts to pleading, to whom he knew not, as gravity sucked him down deeper. A swift current took hold of him, like the hand of a god reaching down. It slammed him forwards, lights flashing behind and through his eyes. He hit the surface, spluttering, coughing, and gasping both water and precious fresh air.

Blessed light flooded through and over Leon's magic, turning the dark strands into rainbows, blinding him before he managed to let them go. Yet the underground river's indefatigable hold barrelled through channels lit by a dim glowing mist and not the glorious brightness of the desert's day.

Still beneath rock, the water flowed its relentless, churning course, throwing him this way and that. It smashed him into any and every protrusion in its path. Despair demanded he form an immediate plan or succumb to the battering current.

Rounding a bend, the rumble and vibrating of the flood eased back, the channel scouring its way through a flattening landscape; a vast, low-hung cavern.

Taking the chance—mayhap his only one—Leon struck out with the last vestiges of his flagging energy. Finally, the ground scraped at his knees as he clawed and crawled his way up on to a tumble of strewn shale, hard and jagged under his hands. He fell beneath the combined weight of his misadventure and the hammer of his weariness and lay gasping and panting until the exhaustion took away every sense.

How long he lay vulnerable, he could not know. He opened his eyes to squint against the piercing rays of light slipping through a broken cut in the cavern wall. Lacerations and bruising set his skin to fire. His body thrummed with pain, the throbbing of his muscles bordering on agony.

"Stranger," a deep voice rumbled in Dracan.

Leon sprang to a crouch.

Pain flared like a supernova, and he cried out, even as his adrenalin spiked, overriding his body's every protest.

His gaze swept the cave's rocky ground for danger, only to land on a tall, lanky youth. Dusted with ochre and red sand, from gangly shoulder to the tip of his large sandaled feet, the lad clasped a chunk of rock in hand.

Leon lashed out, and the weapon went flying.

The lad gave a startled yelp, his face a mask of shock, and the darkest of brown eyes glimmered at Leon with astonishment. "Hold, stranger. I sav—"

Leon grinned, he might be battered black and blue, but a skinny lad such as this could not best him. He leapt to the attack...

The boy buckled beneath his aggression and his domineering weight as they wrestled. Much squirming and bellowed protest ensued, fright enlarging those young liquid eyes as they stared up at him in panic. Eyes that held fear and a flash of indignation yet lacked any belligerence.

But Leon could not risk the ruckus bringing others of the Dracan's companions. One strike. Not too hard. Not too soft. The boy's head jarred to the side with a shudder, his eyes rolling up in his head, his resistance over.

The effect of the fight reverberated deep into Leon's bones as he rolled away, but he had to get free of the cavern. Had to ascertain his situation…had to find out what had happened to Meran. *Ah, gods! He had to have survived.* The alternative drove a spike of fear deep into Leon's belly. Urgency hounded him as he stumbled to the low entrance, almost falling to his knees as he hauled himself outside.

He found himself in a narrow ravine set between two sheer cliff-faces. It ran parallel to the underground fissure through which the river churned its inexorable way into the distance.

He spat curses. If he wanted to see anything with his farsight, he needed to climb. The very thought sent his body into paroxysms of shivering. He collapsed to the ground, arms wrapped about himself as if to hold himself together by sheer force of will. Hopelessness nipped at his heels, threatening to cut him down.

Only then did Leon feel the cloth beneath his hands. Not his tunic, but swathes of bandages bound around his chest and encasing his right shoulder. Blood-soaked strips. He dug his fingers in deep, eliciting a gasp at the tenderness of his flesh beneath.

A quick perusal confirmed multiple strips of Dracan fabric binding him. Perhaps torn from one of their strange and voluminous pantaloons. *"Fuck me."*

A pang of guilt assaulted him as Leon realised what the young Dracan had done for him. He eased cautiously back into the cavern and made for the boy's side. A dark cheek, sweaty and warm, filled his palm as Leon brushed a moist thumb beneath the lad's nose, feeling the heat of slow breaths.

A small mercy. Leon slumped back on his arse and scanned the area, wondering what had brought the lad to such a place and where his fellow tribesmen were.

While he awaited the lad's awakening, Leon spent some time satisfying himself with his surroundings and the lad's small camp. A scraped-out firepit sat at its centre, dried dung smouldering. Propped against a larger boulder, a leather backpack rested, accompanied by a bow and quiver and a long, sharp knife. To the other side sat a capped goat horn, complete with a glowing ember. A firestick? Though Leon also found flint and a node of pyrite.

A round of dried and almost inedible flatbread sat wrapped in a cloth. Perhaps the lad intended on toasting it. There was also a pile of dead locusts awaiting the baking. The boy had obviously been here for some time. Yet, doing what?

Dracan seldom travelled alone, except for their rite of passage, which they had to complete on their own. Tark had mentioned now was the season for it, and the youth seemed the right age.

At the boulder's foot lay a small cache of the same type of stone that the boy had held in his hand. Grey rock-like pieces of granite shale. Some were chipped and broken to reveal a rainbow of differing colours within their hearts, from green to yellow to red. All much smaller than the one Leon had knocked from the lad's hand.

It had not been a weapon, after all. The lad had not been intent on attacking but only offered him much-needed aid. Overcome by instinct though he had been, Leon thanked the gods he had done no more than knock the young fellow out.

Leon reached for his sodden tunic laid out across another boulder as if left to dry. Dull patches of crimson marred its surface where he had bled, the fabric as torn and lacerated as his own body. Injuries of which he could make short work.

His body tingled with the flare of his magic, nerves sparking and surrendering to his inner administrations, the aftermath overwhelming and euphoric and harder to resist in his exhaustion. He closed his eyes, his head wilting forwards as he breathed through the healing.

Strength returned along with the urgency to be on his way, his internals already tied up in knots of concern for Meran's survival. The consequences if he had not bound Leon in fear. Terror he had no time for. Impatiently he tamped the riot of his emotions down.

Retrieving the rock he had slapped from the Dracan's hands, he knelt beside the lad, placing it on his chest. The biggest of those the youth had collected, its hardened crust encased the red fire of opal. Light caught at its heart, flickers of yellow, orange, red, and blue playing as the boy's chest rose and fell. A precious gem, and perhaps one of great worth, but not a talisman.

"Be well, young warrior. I thank you for your mercy. May your god bless you with success in your quest."

Leon took a risk, for a gesture of mercy here could mean disaster in the future. The youth could become a fully-fledged warrior and pit his strength against the *Voce*. Who could know what lay ahead? *Except for his seer...* But to dispatch the youth in cold blood tasted of ingratitude. Not a half turn of the dial gone, it had been him that lay here vulnerable.

Leon would not commit such an offence.

Young and far from battle-hardened, the youth had sported that determined fragility of the untested. Like a sand leopard, dangerous and vicious if pushed, but beautiful with all that latent potential.

"Forgive me, this one thing," he said as he pushed to his feet. Pilfering the bow and quiver, he headed out to the ravine without a backward glance. The lad would rouse and find himself one weapon less, but Leon left the means for self-defence and to hunt if necessary.

Pangs of guilt no longer hounded him, only an overwhelming sense of dread.

That dread did not dissipate once Leon reached a height to survey his location and send out the farsight. As the crow flew, so did his roving inner eye. It streaked across a broken and cracked landscape that ran for miles. To the north, a break in the desert's crust marked its termination, a plain falling away to roll like a burnt red carpet to the horizon.

Turning his attention east, and almost to the extent of his vision, his farsight landed on a speck of what looked like shimmering white dust. A caravan at rest and the glorious familiarity of Meran sheltering beneath a makeshift tent deep in sleep. Six horses stood resolute in the shade of a lone acacia.

Leon's relief was enough to drop him to his knees. *Yes! Yes! Yes! Praise Meran's holy prophet.*

Meran lived, his location some three days' travel northeast across a huge plateau stretching from the edge of the Barrens. Leon's pride swelled that despite what had befallen them, his seer had not turned aside.

Securing their reunion would be hard, each step made taking Meran further from Leon's position. It would require he travel both day and night.

"I am on my way," Leon called as if his voice would travel the distance between them. Would offer that reassurance that he lived also. But neither he nor Meran possessed that particular magic. More was the pity. For once, being undetectable by the farsight proved a disadvantage.

Banking the urgency that bid him hasten, Leon took a moment to study the landscape rolling out before him. If only he could run across the ridges, peaks, and troughs as a bird flew, but the crazed land forced him to follow its dictates. It might have seemed a longer route, but heading straight north would have him reach the red plain and easier ground sooner. He could then work his way around to the east.

Having determined his course, he slithered from his perch and back to the coarse, stucco-like ground. His bare feet would be shredded within moments if he tried to run.

Doffing his tunic, he unwound the bandages the Dracan had bound him in and, sitting, dressed his feet. It would not do in replace of his boots, but they were lost to the floodwaters, and the lad had none spare that he could have appropriated. That he had the wherewithal to heal them as necessary was his saving grace.

That necessity proved to be near on every hour. At what he calculated to be a full turn of the dial, he clambered the rock face and took his bearings. Afterwards, he sat and healed his abraded soles before binding them again and descending.

Thus following this pattern until darkness rendered it impossible, Leon headed towards the north with unrelenting purpose.

Having left the fire-making equipment with the Dracan, Leon swallowed his regret. He refused to let his offer of mercy hound him. That there would be no warmth for him this night, nor a brand to light his way, he would endure for the sake of his humanity.

Hand over hand, Leon scrambled up what he thought to be his last possible climb before the night stole his sight. He sent his inner eye soaring. It landed with the weight of his anxiety on Meran, awake and saddling Leon's own steed.

Seeing Meran address his beast set Leon's longing free. To hear that amazing voice, to feel heat and closeness and the fellowship of their shared purpose, sawed at him. But mostly, he yearned to experience again the awareness that thrummed between them. He longed for that undeniable sense of sexual potency, despite his sudden reticence for further exploration after his tangle with Loni in the dreamlands. He would sort this when they were once again in company.

Which would not be soon enough for his liking. Descending, Leon cursed the rugged, unyielding terrain he headed back into. Becchus beckoned, and the seer could not face it alone. Fear flashed through Leon like a visceral shiver as night's obsidian mantle wrapped about his world. High rock walls loomed, tethering his sight as easily as had the cave.

But the cave had not been able to bind him, had it? The magnitude of his gift had broken free of its chrysalis and pushed back. And it still resonated power within him. He summoned the ability.

The landscape came into focus.

Again lacking the colours of the day, the night revealed itself in depths of shade and tones of grey, black, and navy. Clear enough to keep him on track.

A feral pleasure unshackled the bounds of his impending despair, and with a grin stretching his lips and aching in his cheeks, he forged on again. No matter what the desert threw at them, he and Meran would conclude this quest together.

Days passed, more than he cared to count, but his resolve never wavered. The silver moon set, and the winter one finally reddened the night sky. The Outlier's Season of Rites would be over now. He had to wonder how long before Keija moved his people.

Three days after that propitious rising, Leon calculated he and Meran had been out in the desert for twenty-four days.

Leon's anticipation ratcheted higher as the distance between them closed. His spirits flew when Meran broke onto the plain to set up camp, allowing Leon's farsight to pinpoint him. *Not far. Not far.*

And then the beasts came skulking.

Fear set Leon's heart hammering. A roar of outrage, feral and brutish, blasted the night as he ran to intervene. His strides ate up the distance. One hand grasped his bow, the other nocked the arrow even as growls and yips and one terrified scream rent the air.

Leon's heart stopped even as his protest cleaved the night. A shout against the horror of the inevitable. Still, he kept running.

PART FOUR
A Meeting of Ways

INTERLUDE THREE

Becchus Oasis, Southern Draca

Nairo's eye followed as Joram paced his mother's tent, arrogance and condescension rife with every swish of his brother's long robe. Elder brothers were imperious bastards. Especially half-brothers, Nairo decided.

That night, the red moon had risen, bringing the Moon Rite to its official close. Joram had come at the behest of the elders to deliver Nairo their judgement. Of course, they had seen fit to give the duty to Joram, Keija's heir, a position attained by nothing but the randomness of birth. Nairo's anger simmered.

His father should have undertaken the responsibility.

Nairo had only done what they all should have near on a year ago. If his plan had succeeded, the stinking half-breed would no longer walk the earth, polluting it and the people with his presence. That they let a slave become a man, a warrior, weakened their Outlier, but the elders were all blind to its preposterousness.

"Are you listening?" a demanding sneer threaded through Joram's words.

Nairo looked up from his contemplation of the intricate rug on the floor. A reminder of what he stood to lose if the Quorum considered his behaviour imprudent.

"As if I would be so foolhardy not to."

"I can see from your expression that you do not know the reprieve that you have been given."

"I understand it perfectly." His scowl deepened, but he refused to hide his displeasure. "I am to be forgiven my interference in the *half-breed's* rite of passage because the Holy Nord has blessed him with success." Falric had made it back in time with that blasted Grypheon feather. "Venner has declared the slave-boy a warrior now, and by that token, we are sworn brothers." Anger curled Nairo's top lip, disgusted

231

they were now thought of as equals.

Joram came to a standstill. "Not yet," he said. And for the first time, Nairo noted a hint of dissatisfaction. Could they both abhor what their father condoned?

"Pray?"

"Oh, I assure, that would have been the case but for the agreement between the magos and our father. But he is to pass a further trial to ratify his position in Nord's eyes." The darkness in Joram's own hardened. "His elevation is unprecedented. There must be no question of his worthiness."

"He is not considered a man yet?" Nairo's spirits lightened at the wonderful news. Falric and he were not sworn brothers, and if he had anything to say on the matter, they would never be.

Hmm… What trial would be set? He might yet be able to influence the outcome. The storm of Nairo's anger dissipated enough to twist the edges of his lips into a smile.

"He is a man of Draca. That is not in question," Joram answered.

Nairo's euphoria vanished as quickly as the desert sun licked away moisture.

That meant the abomination would be able to mate, to fill the bellies of Dracan women with his tainted seed and dilute the tribe's purity. Nairo did not care for fucking women himself, but the privilege belonged to fully-fledged and proven men. It infuriated him that he would have to share the obligation with a slave—*that* slave in particular—a liar and a murderer. No one cared to recall what the half-breed had done to Raeden, but Nairo would never forget.

Ignoring the growl of disgust and anguish Nairo let escape, Joram continued, "The oaths have been sworn and all are aware of this further stipulation." Chastisement, however, burned bright in Joram's dark eyes, once again confusing Nairo as to his brother's loyalties.

Joram stepped closer, crowding Nairo and offering him a baleful look. "May I remind you, it is Nord who chooses the worthy? It is not your decision to make, and Father will not tolerate descension."

"You need not preach. I am aware." His brother sounded like Venner, the priest who had Nairo's father in the palm of his hand due to the discovery of Anigema. Even though the magos claimed the find was Falric's, any of sound mind knew Raeden must have found it down that well. The half-breed's interference had cost Raeden his life, and none heeded Nairo's need for vengeance. Well, that situation would change.

"You are free on Beric's recognisance." Joram brandished a finger in Nairo's face before he could rise from his seat. "You will not interact with Falric Mislan. You are not to go near him, nor are you to challenge him. Do you understand?"

Nairo's nod came curt and reluctant, though he wished to punch Joram's sanctimonious face.

"You have escaped the punishment of crystal venom by the skin of your teeth, little brother. Prove faithless again and lose all such leniency."

Nairo shuddered at the chance he had taken, risking his life in the name of vengeance. He had to think smarter.

"Now, if you want from this tent," Joram continued, "you will swear."

Defiance clogged Nairo's throat. He had already indicated his agreement.

The slave had not only caused Raeden's death but had also caused Nairo broken bones when he'd sought to set things to rights. A pain he would not soon forget. Nor would he forget that Falric's mother had refused to heal him and sent an acolyte to treat the son of her catana instead.

He would visit the sins of the mother on the son for her disgraceful display of contempt. Falric deserved to pay. Nairo would make sure of it, but he had to be free.

"If I must, then I swear, and on the life of my mother, no less."

"You swear you will not approach, interfere with, or challenge Falric Mislan?"

"Of course." Annoyance broke through Nairo's feigned temperance, impatient to taste freedom again. "I have said it, have I not?"

Lording it over him and annoying Nairo with the vast difference in their heights, Joram waved towards the tent entrance. "Beric awaits you. He will return you to the Tent of Warriors."

Nairo's gaze flickered to the tent flap. "Is he to follow me around like a prick up my arse?" He could do without the older man being a permanent tail.

"I assure, he has mastered the art of discretion."

Joram might as well have added, "Unlike you." Nairo grit his teeth, unable to suppress a dissatisfied growl.

"Only should you step from the bounds of your oath will Beric interfere. Do not break it, and you will see neither hide nor hair of him." Joram reached into his robe and pulled out a blade, the handle recognisable as Nairo's own.

Nairo took back his weapon, sliding it into its sheath and regretting that it would never slip between Falric's ribs. *Oh, to see the lifeblood flow over that insipid olive skin.* It would be ecstasy. With a grimace at his loss, Nairo followed his brother's directive towards the tent opening and the guard that awaited him outside.

The grizzled warrior said nothing as he followed Nairo like a silent shadow to the large Tent of Warriors. He did not follow him inside.

The tent housed ten-and-eight men lounging about the firebox in the large open section at its centre. Complete with rugs, cushions, and low tables covered in an array of food left over from the night's celebrations, the men ate and chatted; a low rumble of noise that turned to silence at his entrance.

Nairo scanned their faces for judgement but found only curiosity. Jayden, Shay, and Baban's, in particular, held expressions of relief. So they should. They had escaped punishment based on his lie. They owed him.

He stepped in, head held high as he strode past his tentmates. With a nod to Baban, he made for one of the curtained-off areas devised to offer privacy for sleep…and other things.

Dropping onto a low divan, he demanded, "What do you know?"

Baban grinned and spread himself over a bed, hands behind his head and feet crossed at the ankle. Ignorant, dangerous, and sadistic, Baban was still a loyal ally though he oft fell into familiarity. Nairo would remind him again who secured his place in this very tent, but not today. He needed to hear what information Baban had gleaned.

"Oh ho, do I have some tasty titbits for you. Enough to make you want to suck my prick."

For that to happen, Nairo would have to hear that Falric Mislan had met his end. But more than that, there had only been one man for whom he had bent the knee and offered his mouth. "Do not think you will take Raeden's place. You are nothing compared to him."

Slapping Baban's booted feet from the end of the bed and forcing him to sit, Nairo settled opposite. "Pour us a drink and tell me all."

Baban passed a goblet of wine, and Nairo sipped, letting it settle his impatience.

"After the ceremony, I followed them," Baban said. "He and the goat-turd took off for a bit of privacy with a bottle of tek. They went up onto the plateau east of here. I thought if they were off to fuck, I might use a pale arse as target practice for a few well-aimed stones."

"I assume they did not."

"Mayhap they indulged later." Baban shrugged. "They let their tongues wag first, enough for me to hear something of great interest." He paused for effect, his expression encouraging Nairo's curiosity.

"Man! Out with it." Nairo had no time to drag the story from his informer, bit by painful bit.

"*Gah!* Fine, fine." Baban rolled his eyes. "But you take away all my fun."

Nairo growled.

"Ah, very well. The half-breed had some interesting things to say of Magos Eno. Mainly accusations of charlatanism."

"How is this new? Some of the Outlier do the same thing, except that more oft than not, his visions prove him true."

"Aye, but slave-boy told goat-turd that those visions were his mother's. That the witch has an all-seeing eye. And…he boasted that one had opened up to him too, during his Moon Rite."

"Pray? What?"

Baban pointed to the centre of his forehead, speaking insolently and slowly, "He. Has. An. Evil. Eye."

Nairo baulked. "Preposterous." No one in Draca had ever heard that *Voce* had this magic. The ramifications of it were too frightening.

"Well, that is what he said. Told goat-turd he could see his mother with that eye as she went about her business before he'd gotten even three days from here."

"And you believe him?"

Again, Baban shrugged and supped his drink. "I am yet to be convinced. Because if his eye had seen I was near, he would never have admitted what he did next."

Curiosity replaced Nairo's sudden disconcertion. "Go on, you bastard. Out with it."

"Guess who I heard had assistance with his Moon of Solitude?"

In context, Baban could only have been talking of one person. At the spike of Nairo's interest, Baban's smile broadened into a malicious grin. "Guess who led our half-bred slave-boy from the ledge, out of our reach, and into the maze of Rahm's Warren? Guess who returned his pack to him and gave him a note with directions?"

Nairo leaned forwards. Two birds, one stone. "Goat-turd."

"Aye. Falric Mislan received aid on his Moon Rite from Jaro Raei. Which is forbidden."

Nairo swore in delighted disbelief. He had the little bastard now. He could lay out the evidence before the curia and both upstarts would face the crystal venom. At last, justice. "Give it to me."

Baban looked confused.

"The proof." Nairo's patience bled away. Why was every man such a fool? "Give me the proof of this?"

"Ah." Baban hesitated. "I do not have it. They burned it—"

"For the love of Nord!" Nairo let out a bellow of frustration. "And you took no other witness?" His last hope, dashed as Baban shook his head, the idiot devoid of even a look of contrition. Sometimes, Nairo found it in himself to detest his fellow man. "Then it is hearsay, and those two little turds will never, never admit to it."

Hissing expletives, Nairo pushed from his seat and began to pace, his fists clenching so hard, nails gouged into his palms. "Gods' balls!" He could see no way around it if they had no corroboration from a source acceptable to the Quorum. His word or that of any sycophant would be discounted out of hand.

"No sucking my prick then," Baban said, flopping back onto the bed, pouting.

Nairo raced at him, his fury a wild and fiery thing that refused to be stopped. Grabbing the dolt by his clothes, he headbutted the imbecile. That would teach him to think of his prick at a time such as this.

Yet, even as his own head rang, an idea bloomed bright and clear amidst the pain, and he dropped the groaning man. "That's it. Of course." There were obvious ways to hurt someone, and then there were other ways to *hurt* them. Surreptitiously and deeper...and he had thought of one that might even prove to be pleasant. Not for Falric. No, not for him. But for himself, definitely.

Ignoring the blood splashing from Baban's nose, Nairo returned to pacing, his mind whirling in a flurry, his excitement ratcheting higher the more his epiphany gained possibility. "Yes, yes," he said. He turned back to the wounded man, Baban pinching the bridge of his nose, his fingers beneath his nostrils covered in blood. Nairo threw a headscarf at him. "Wipe your face. I have an important task for you."

"Fucking bastard! With this for a reward, you think I will do anything more?"

Nairo shook his head. His apology came in the form of a harsh tousle of his minion's long hair and the promise, "I'll not suck your prick, but if you do this for me, I might fuck you."

Baban glared as if finding the offer offensive, but he also knew those to whom his loyalty belonged.

With a grudging huff, Baban gave his agreement. "What do you want of me?"

Nairo's eyes brightened. "I need to be rid of my tail. I need Falric out of the way," he said. "I want you to whisper a little something in Adon's ear."

"Aye? And what, pray?"

"Keno has yet failed to return, is this not so?"

"Again, aye." Baban squinted in some confusion.

"I want you to tell Adon of this miraculous gift Falric Mislan has come into. I want you to tell him that the half-breed can find Keno…with his newfound evil eye." He knew his grandmother would not have the failure of one lad to complete the rite destroy her celebration. "The lock will take a search party out as soon as possible, and Falric must be with them."

Despite the wince of pain from his dripping nose, Baban grinned as if catching on. Yes, this would prove Falric Mislan the liar he was. No one—not even *Voce*—had that kind of power. Keno would remain unfound, and the slave-boy discredited. But Baban would never know the true turn of Nairo's mind. Not until he chose to reveal it.

As if to prove it, Baban asked, "And what will you do while he is gone?"

"There is more than one way to exact my revenge." Nairo smiled viciously. "I have a proposal to make to our little goat-turd. One he will find he is unable to refuse." With his plan, Nairo would inflict pain. Falric Mislan had best watch his back. Fate was coming for him, and it was going to hurt.

Nairo had never felt better.

CHAPTER THIRTY-FOUR

One by one, Leon slaughtered them, arrows skewering. First, the beast at Meran's throat, and next, the one at his belly. Others went down as easily, though more fled, yapping. His arrows pursued them as he raced to Meran's side.

If the dogs had killed his seer, they could all rot in the deepest of hells.

Shallow punctures serrated the upper edge of Meran's throat, the alpha bitch having failed to get a proper hold and crush his windpipe. Death had taken her between one breath and the next; instant, final.

Regardless, blood soaked Meran's tunic, the pool beneath him expanding even as Leon placed a hand on Meran's chest and leaned close. Breath thready and barely there sent panic racing through Leon.

He swore and cursed every deity that entered his head. "You will not die, you sorry bastard. Do you hear me?" But if Leon could not tap into that part of himself that held the power to heal others, Meran would die in the next few minutes, his command rendered moot.

Meran needed his blood. Now! With no time for hesitation or doubt, Leon sliced his palm and, with a shaking limb, pressed it to the wounds across Meran's throat.

His will, indefatigable, forced a pulsing invasion. Blood, rife with energy, life force, and healing, squirted from his gashed hand, mingling with that which dripped down Meran's neck.

Enough had to leach into the dog's punctures before the swelling closed Meran's throat. Leon willed it so. Willed it with every fibre of his being. This man had to live.

Leon had not spent days scrambling through the cracked lands, risked a dangerous water-crossing, and traversed a plain vibrant with the storm's aftermath to find Meran in time only to lose him. "Live, gods' damn you."

Hands to Meran's shoulders, Leon gave him a teeth-rattling shake.

Breath bubbled through Meran's nose and wheezed through those beautiful, parted lips…and settled into a gentle rhythm.

Everything within Leon collapsed with the strength of his relief. But in spite of that, he had much more to do. At Meran's back, the pool of blood flooded the hard-packed earth like an ocean. He pushed away the muzzle of the dead dog collapsed across its own handiwork and blanched at the twisted and bloodied flesh beneath. The blue coils of Meran's entrails mixed in a crimson soup in the exposed cavity.

"Fuck!" Leon wiped the sudden sweat beading his brow with his forearm. Did he have the power to do this? It would take many cuts to his body. It would demand his concentration, his commitment. It would drain him…and it should come with sustaining words and rejuvenating chants of magic, most of which he had lost to the mists of time.

But what Leon did know was that he would give. He let instinct draw him again to that warm, throbbing power that banked at the back of his mind and stoked it into a furnace. He fed it with every desire, passion, and need that burned in his heart. Anger, fit for a man known as the Mavish, fuelled it to a blaze. It roared to his command, a fierce force of determination.

Blood poured from him, from wound after wound. Meran needed cleansing of dog and the befoulment of sliced gut. He needed the slashed viscera mended, muscle, tissue, skin. Layer after layer knitting together.

Exhaustion edged Leon's mind, but he could not give in. Only once the band of pale untarnished skin met across Meran's belly could he let himself go. Slowly he buckled, his cheek pressing against the newly born flesh of Meran's abdomen. Unexplained tears wet Leon's face and blurred his vision.

He did not want to see the gloves of red that coated his hands nor the stains that bathed flesh and earth. He closed his eyes against them, but his responsibility nagged. It was an affront to let Meran lie in the pool of his own congealing blood.

Ignoring his weariness, Leon lifted Meran in his arms and headed back to the small campsite. Quick and measured movements lent Leon purpose as he staggered to his seat by the flagging fire, his limbs threatening to give out, but Leon did not let go.

For long minutes he cradled the unconscious man, lips brushing across a brow turned warm and dry. Numbly, he breathed in the scent of sweat and dirt, the dusky tang of dog, and the thick odour of horse, mixed with Meran's unique scent. His slow, regular breaths lulled Leon, even as fatigue fogged every thought.

Leon's eyes closed.

He woke with a start, curled over Meran filling his lap still in the clutches of healing sleep. Snuffling sounds accompanying the dull tread of hooves alerted him to the presence of at least three of their horses, returned and milling at the edge of the firelight.

One carried Meran's damnable rundlets. A smile tugged at Leon's lips. Meran's gift was still intact. He would be pleased.

How much joy the notion gave him brought Leon's gaze back to Meran, confusion swirling in his heart. None of what had transpired would have satisfied the Mavish's crude, brutish cravings, nor would it have affected the lord marshal's obdurate sense of duty, but it captivated Leon Ricci, the man. That face was a vision in pale beauty, even without the stunning eyes to complete the picture. A combination of strength and frailty carved those features in softness and resolute persistence.

Respect welled fulsomely. Look at how far Meran had come.

A delicate caress across cheek and jaw evidenced Leon's longing, revealing every betraying tenderness. What was obligation in the face of this? And yet, was it not everything? His people, his purpose, the future of *Vocekind*? They both fought for this. And they had a long way to go.

On every front and in every possible way, Meran Durante needed to be safe from the possessive beast that lurked in his heart. Safe from the predictions of a ghoul and his own baser nature that had the capacity to rend the world.

Until Meran opened his eyes, glazed gaze fixing upon Leon, and for a breathless moment, he felt undone.

CHAPTER THIRTY-FIVE

Meran floated free of the darkness, opening raw and gritty eyes. They were met with those sharp and pale blue, surprise sparking in their depths. Relief jostled with Meran's consciousness. Leon leaned over him—a vision of wonder—warmth brushing his cheek from that man's very fingers, gentle and considerate.

"Is this the Otherlands?" Meran asked.

Leon huffed out a laugh, lips stretched into a fleeting smile. Stunning in its normality, amusement equalled by relief. "Does this look like heaven to you?"

Meran did not know; only darkness reigned where memory should be. He fought against bone-weary tiredness. How had he come to be here, held in Leon's arms, the man covered in dust and streaked with drying blood? "You look like hell."

Again, Leon laughed but offered only mild reproof, "Close your eyes, seer. Healing's sleep has not yet had its way with you." Blood-stained fingers swept down Meran's lids, delicate in their encouragement.

Yes, now he could feel it, someone's healing power overwhelming him until blackness overshadowed thought, and he sank into it as commanded.

Down it took him until his consciousness hovered at the edges of the dreamlands. Visions tugged at his senses, insistent and perilous, calling to his magic. Visions of war, desecration, and death that would tear him to his very core.

Spirits whispered, bound in their misery, beguiling, acerbic, vengeful, and crazed. Fears clamoured beneath the shattering fatigue that rendered Meran vulnerable.

He did not need further incentive to follow his cause. Resisting the maelstrom, he tried to awaken, needing to keep his wits and stay alert for more immediate dangers...

...Lithe, supple, black-and-tan bodies rushed him, teeth, sharp and lethal, flashing. He fell, crushed beneath them, his voice wailing...

Meran's lids fluttered open to the shadow of a shelter, the pounding of his blood and the thudding of his heart out of step with the stillness that settled over him. Two blankets lashed to sticks formed a primitive lean-to against the sun's glare above his head.

Testing his senses, Meran's gaze danced over the loosely woven fabric that let a muted light filter through. Crushed vegetation and the malodorous reek of northern horses filled his nostrils, underpinned by the subtle aroma of sweat and man.

Peace sank through him. Calm blanketed him.

The crackle of burning wood teased his ears, and the tempting scent of stew cooking set his taste buds alight. He felt the brush of fresh clothing against clean skin, his body alive and hale. But, best of all, his magic hummed vigorously within him. And that was because of...

"Leon?" Balancing on an elbow, Meran scanned the vicinity. There Leon sat, larger than life and impossibly whole, the travails of his journey scrubbed clean. Irritation followed Meran's heart's leap of elation. He had been waiting so long, hoping, wondering, despairing... "Where have you been?"

The spark of relief lurking in Leon's expression faded beneath his customary frown, his response reticent. "Here and there."

A dull sense of loss clenched in the centre of Meran's chest. Had he only dreamed of a warm and vulnerable conversation shared between them? Of eyes looking down at him with softness and compassion and arms that held him safe? Had they only been the yearnings of a befuddled mind?

No, no, no, no. Meran would never forget the joy that look had given him though unconsciousness had tried to rob him of it.

Leon must have used his healing magic, given his blood. A thing neither the Mavish nor the lord marshal would ever stoop to do for a man not of Clan Ricci. But Leon was not only warrior or leader but man; and even if he hid it well, that man had a heart big enough for mercy.

But now Leon sat by the fire, channelling the lord marshal as he stirred the contents of a pot; phlegmatic and resourceful, authoritative, and aloof. Meran's heart sank, shades of loneliness looming. He craved that connection birthed between them in the cave before Loni's apparition cleaved it asunder.

He tried to ignore his disappointment. Meran had no great inclination to share the turmoil, drudgery, uncertainty, and terror he had been through either. All that mattered was that Leon had returned. "Mayhap, one day we will speak of it."

Hiding from the forlornness of his tone and avoiding Leon's knowing gaze, Meran perused the area taking in the lush surroundings. Their five horses stood beneath a stand of acacia, tails flicking at nipping flies, feathery lashes blinking over patient eyes. To the west rose a line of unfamiliar buttes, and he realised he recognised nothing. "Did you move campsite?"

"I thought it for the best."

Of course. What was he thinking? Blood everywhere because...*of the dogs*. Meran shuddered, gooseflesh rippling across his skin. He threw out the farsight, but in the daylight, the desert slept.

"Here." Leon loomed over him, bowl outstretched. "This will aid your full recovery. Eat."

Leon joined him in the shelter, his presence keeping Meran's dark memories at bay. His internal shaking subsided, the silence congenial as he assuaged the growling hunger in his stomach.

"You managed to round up the horses," he said once nearly finished.

"For the most part, they rounded up themselves," came the response. "All but one came back on their own. The fifth had not wandered far and would have rejoined his herd-mates given time. The sixth, well, it makes for a nice stew should you cook it long enough."

Meran looked into his near-empty bowl, stomach churning. *Ye gods!* He had eaten Leon's horse.

Yet why should its death go to waste? Because it had not fallen to his arrow did not make its bounty any less. "And the dogs?"

"Mostly dead and thrown into a ditch downwind. The others ran off," Leon replied with a noncommittal expression that said he thought Meran would prefer horse to having dog served up with carrots.

Memories dared dance in with sharp stabs of alarm that had Meran cringe. *Fierce and ferocious growls, followed by excruciating pain.* They had almost made a meal of him.

He tried to blank out their clarity for the sake of his own sanity, but his appetite flagged. Lowering his bowl, he attempted to clean his palate with a drink of warm water.

Heat from those intense, considering eyes followed Meran's every move, the grim lines returning to Leon's mouth. "Are you all right?"

"I don't know." Though he discerned the potential for lingering terror, given the circumstances, Meran felt blessed…alive. "I'm better than I should be, I think."

He frowned, throwing Leon a questioning look. "I once witnessed a healing of equal magnitude as you must have given me. Ellom was saved by one from Dun's Healer's Guild. They warned me it would cause him a storm of emotions, and it was as if everything he had been feeling up to that moment magnified tenfold, but I feel none of that. Oh, I still feel afraid, wary, anxious"—emotions still awaiting the right moment to pounce, should Meran let them—"but that is no doubt to be expected after what I-I went through."

The frown on Leon's brow deepened, but he nodded. "I still possess the talent, but I am unfortunately ignorant of the lore. I can give you no explanation."

Despite Leon's diffidence, gratitude welled through Meran. "I do not need one."

Leon's efforts had been stupendous. If not for him, where would Meran be?

Meran swayed forwards, as if drawn like a moth to a flame, his hand reaching for Leon's, eyes glued to his saviour. Again. Those fingers, ofttimes so strong and unforgiving had lain on him, offering healing and hope and life. "I cannot thank you enough."

A caress of breath brushed his lips as Meran eased closer, Leon's mouth calling to him. He reached for it with gentle reverence. Everything within him yearned for the kiss, for Leon to hold his ground and accept his gift.

Warmth met warmth, the mouth beneath his, soft and yet unyielding.

Meran's heart jolted at Leon's resistance. Had Loni's deceitful decrees cost Meran everything? Any chance of warmth and closeness; of the ability to express his sincerest gratitude; to offer his affection, his body, his pleasure?

Then pressure and wetness traced the seam of his mouth, Leon's tongue teasing, urging him to open. A cry of relief wrung from him, tears threatening the corners of his eyes, even as the taste of Leon exploded over his senses and the ether erupted with swirls of power.

The kiss grew long, and yet not long enough, as Leon eased back, his hand slipping from Meran's grasp to land on his cheek. Control edged with a gentle distancing touch. "Not here, not now."

"Pray, why? You will not be subjected to the dreamlands again, I promise." Meran's protest rang desperately. He had never tried to wrestle with this power before. Either the dreamland's denizens had shown no interest in his previous lovers, or coitus had not produced that breathtaking spark. But surely he could keep the effect to himself.

If he wanted intimacy with Leon, something both his body and soul yearned for after that one euphoric taste, then Meran's determination would have to win out.

Unease shifted behind Leon's eyes, yet his expression remained unmoved. "'Tis more than that. We need our wits. Three nights' hard ride and we will be at our destination. I will not countenance any distractions when our goal is within reach. Do you understand me?"

Disappointment and protest filled Meran's mouth under that demanding look, even if Leon had the right of it. He swallowed back the pangs at his rejection. He would not behave like a child. He took a breath and, with a nod, said, "My lord."

"Not lord." Emotion roughened Leon's voice. Meran looked up sharply, taking in the pinch of Leon's lips, the ragged swallow. "As surely as you live in my heart. If I could, I would swear my life for yours, an oath on my blood that runs through your veins. But this comes upon us ill-timed when a barrier of malignant magic stands between us that I cannot broach."

"No." He would ensure Leon's safety from any malevolent spirit... "I swear—"

"Can you?" Leon asked with simple candour while his eyes commanded the truth.

Meran almost shouted yes, but guilt gripped him by the throat.

When release burst in shattering plumes and his mind and body revelled in the resultant bliss, could he truly keep that promise? He could not risk Leon's sanity for the sake of his own desires. "No." Anguish wailed through the word even as he clamped his hands to his face to hide the magnitude of his devastation.

He heard nothing beyond the raged breaths of his humiliation, the heat of falling tears, but he could not stop himself. Perhaps the healing had affected him more than he thought.

Cool pressure encircled his wrists, Leon's fingers dragging his hands away. Meran could not meet that condescending gaze as heartbreak made a fool of him.

A finger caught his chin. "Look at me."

"No, no, no, no." But how could he not? Leon had given him a command. He looked into eyes reddened with equal regret.

"There are but two beings in this life that I love unreservedly." Voice rough, the confession seemed to rock Leon with its truth as much as it did Meran.

Who were they? Meran cringed as jealousy stabbed him.

The fingers firm about his jaw held him in place.

"You'll be glad to know I am intimate with neither. Love, Meran Durante, is more than base desire. Passions can be quenched without the need to engage the heart."

To this point, that had been true for Meran. The faces of his many partners, those little remembered and those that had turned into lovers—Ormand, Ellom—flashed through his mind. But none had afflicted Meran's feelings in the same manner as did Leon Ricci.

"But Loni was not wrong; love is more dangerous," Leon continued. "My wife, my child, they are my Achilles. For them, I would destroy the world. Should anything happen to you, I begin to think I would obliterate it."

"I had never thought to hear such words from you." So profound, so emotional, so unexpected and welcomed. It grasped Meran's heart and squeezed, warmth overwhelming him. Not that he wished the world destroyed, but the power behind Leon's words spoke of a depth of feeling he had never thought to experience.

Leon's snort, downcast eyes, and the wry curl that tugged his lips spoke of his own embarrassment. "Many a man has considered me gauche, impolitic even, but still, I will speak as I see, though it mortifies me. Lack of clarity has only ever led me to disaster. I will not have that between us. So I will speak plain. Never will I demand fidelity of your body—"

Despite the urge to protest, relief flooded Meran. Leon might possess a zealous soul, but Meran had suffered enough from jealousy, though Ellom had never physically retaliated.

"—but I will swear my loyalty and devotion, offer my protection, and sacrifice. I will be your weapon, your vengeance should justice demand it, for you have become as family to me. A Ricci in all but name."

"But don't you want it all?" Meran protested. The need for it dragged at him. To be able to have coitus with anyone was all well and good, but he wanted that intimacy, that command and direction from Leon. The lack of possibility inflicted a grievous wound to his soul.

"Beyond measure."

Meran found himself enveloped in Leon's embrace. Hard, wanting, and heartsore, he buried his hot face against Leon's neck and wept silently, the loss hitting him like a child whose pain was unexplainable.

He revelled in the comfort of Leon's strong arms, his solid presence and the oaths that still reverberated through his mind.

"We will find a way, have no fear." The words brushed Meran's ear, drawing him from his fugue, and Leon set him on his heels, hands bracing his shoulders. "But first, let us fulfil our covenant and save Locurnia."

Meran gave a shaky laugh, his mind thudding back to reality. He wanted to make everything about this new and enticing relationship, but fate waited for no man. His sisters were still threatened by foreshadowed war, as were Leon's beloved family. As were all the clans of Locurnia. The needs of many were counting on them. This was no place for regrets, for childish impatience.

Wiping his face, Meran stepped from reach and gathered his composure. "What do we do now?"

Leon gestured to the shelter's shaded interior. "Stay here for the duration and set out again this eve. Consider reinstating your disguise ere we leave, but in the meantime, I suggest taking your ease while you may."

Ye gods! Leon's announcement came back to him. *"Three nights hard ride and we will be at our destination."* The full implication took hold.

So close and yet so far.

No matter whether he considered himself emotionally spent, anticipation rioted through him. He would have to shave every surface, retouch his hair with the balance of the servant's potion, and paint his face. He would need to resume speaking only Velkor so that it became second nature again.

Urgency boiled in him, but Leon pushed him back. "The night's journey will be long. I'll not have you fall from your horse for want of keeping awake. Rest now."

Resuming his place in the shelter, Meran closed his eyes. The end was in sight, and once reached, a whole new world lay before him. Opportunities unseen and unknown. New alliances to forge, and others to be tested.

And what of this wondrous but fragile connection between him and Leon? What of its future?

A chill thought struck. How long would it last when Leon found the gem was not *Amplion*? That Meran had known...and said nothing.

CHAPTER THIRTY-SIX

Meran chewed on that worry for about a half turn of the dial before it threatened to drive him to distraction. Licking his lips, he sat, flipping Leon a quick and assessing glance. By the fire, Leon was heating each of his arrows and working to straighten them in turn.

"You know," he began, plucking at a pull in the blanket on which he sat. "I once read an interesting passage from the word of the prophet. One that mentioned the touch of an abomination. In my life, I have heard it as a term used for many things. What say you?"

With a sneer on his lips, Leon gave Meran a condescending glance that reflected his distaste for all things theological. "If, as you say, it is part of a sacred text, it will refer to one thing only: a half-breed. You should know this."

Shifting to play with the edge of his tunic, Meran offered a glum nod, again avoiding Leon's eye. "That I do." Raising his voice, he continued, "Do half-breeds have magic, do you think?"

"Why do you ask?"

"Well, I know the primoris' offspring do not, but I wondered—"

Leon made a rude noise at the mention of Ivo Dee's issue. "Some do, but most do not. Any magic they may have is wild magic. Untameable and aberrant. It is a risk not to be taken and the reason few live past their birthing day. The world is best off without them."

"Ah."

Wild magic! And now Meran knew the meaning of his visions all those days ago. A handsome young man, a half-breed, with the touch to awaken a power unbelievable and unseen in these lands in millennia. Destiny intended he meet this intriguing lad and that it would precipitate Meran's claiming of Anigema, but not *Amplion*.

If all went according to his plan, they now stood on the precipice of the unknown. The actions and reactions of others, the decisions and choices of those at the fulcrum of change would dictate what lay ahead.

That *Amplion* might have been discovered stood to muddy the waters of Meran's purpose. For who knew whether this particular vision lay in the future or the recent past. The only thing immutable was that Leon's hand must take hold of the elusive blue sapphire. It alone led to Patrice's and Sofie's salvation, to Clan Ricci's, to Locurnia's. The blue, not the white.

But what would Leon do when he learned the gem at Becchus was not *Amplion*? He had placed so much stock on his assumption. Should Meran warn him? Meran's nerves squalled at the possibilities. Leon might rescind his oaths and suppress his newly confessed feelings.

His heart shrivelled at the thought. But then he had never encouraged Leon in this belief. While Leon might hope it was the treasure long sought, would he not take the disappointment in his stride? Especially when Anigema proved its worth. Of course, any who knew the myth of *Amplion* knew that it could be used to magnify any magic coming within its sphere, but Anigema's potential promised to be unlimited.

He had witnessed its power and Leon would see how much more precious this gift was. Meran's conviction on that score remained unwavering, yet agitation had him on the verge of pacing. He needed a distraction. "I think it time I became Zachary, if you will excuse me."

Taking himself off for a little privacy, he did the best job possible with blade and soap and his shaking hand to divest himself of every pale hair. The few cuts he inflicted, he healed quickly and surreptitiously. Focusing on retouching the silver halo that hugged his head beneath the covering of dull brown strands finally brought calm.

Returning to the tent as the sun coasted towards the horizon, he used the firelight to apply the makeup that turned him from *Voce* to Velkor. From Meran Durante, scholar and seer, to Zachary the Fisher, intrepid explorer and budding merchant. And with it came a sense of relief, of burdens lifting.

Night enclosed them not long after, and Leon set about packing up the campsite, moving away to load the horses under the acacia.

With Leon occupied, curiosity got the better of Meran. Knowing that Becchus was now in the range of his farsight, he focused on what he remembered of the Outlier from his vision. His magic landed easily on tents, encircled by a profusion of date palms and surrounded by dark running water.

The unknown hordes of bipedal figures, bound with the aura of life, fluttered like fireflies in the night. None were familiar as he had never seen any of them in real life to give them any clarity, but excitement for all other prospects mounted until—

A sudden howl snapped him back to reality. *By the gods!* Meran leapt to his feet, his heart in his throat. "Leon!"

The dogs had returned, and Meran's mind fogged with the intensity of panic's grip, his knife sliding from his frozen fingers. Stomach clenched and muscles shaking, he stood paralysed sheathed in a cold sweat. They had come back to finish him off.

Terror blinded him and silenced his ears, leaving him nothing but the fear of death lurking beyond the campsite. Any minute, teeth would tear into his body and kill him even as they feasted.

He awaited the lancing pain that accompanied their attack.

Pressure gripped Meran's neck, and warm breath smothered his face, vicious growls filling his mind. A blinding white eclipsed his vision as urgency rocketed through him, the immediacy of impending danger reverberating across his skin and through every flaring nerve. His muscles tensed, readying him to bolt.

"Meran!" A commanding voice pierced his paralysis. "Look at me."

A hand squeezed tight beneath the wayward strands of hair at his nape, fingers harsh, hard, and oh-so reassuring. The spiralling panic snapped back, Leon's visage filling Meran's entire view. He could see his wild fear in the reflection of Leon's eyes, so close and intimate. Their foreheads touched in Leon's attempt to ground him.

"They will not hurt you, that I promise. Do you hear me?"

The deep, resonant declaration pushed its way to the fore of Meran's mind and thrummed through his being. He shuddered. But how could he believe such a promise?

Yet before him stood a warrior, a fighter, hunter, survivor, his saviour. His kin in more than just brotherhood; Meran knew it, felt it. He let out a rasp, "I-I d-do."

He found his cheeks encircled, strong fingers holding him steady. Firm lips owned his, the claim blistering and shaking him further from his fugue into the reality of Leon's presence. Meran sank greedily into it, taking what he could. Even in his desperation, he kept the mists of desire spiralling as a fiery cloud into the ether to himself.

The kiss was bold, possessing, savage…and far too brief. A chill edge threatened to overwhelm Meran again as Leon drew back, hands still cupping his face, expression implacable. "Promise me you will stay here, and I will deal with them," Leon whispered. "Promise me."

"I-I promise…" But how would he stand alone with Leon gone? How could he continue if something happened to him?

"That's my brave seer." A satisfied grin slashed Leon's features, sending warmth through Meran despite the concerns threatening to devour him. He took what comfort lingered as Leon's fingers threaded through his hair and a last touch of lips burned across his.

Leon backed away. Grasping his bow and clutch of arrows, he headed to the boundary beyond the fire's light and onto the flat plain to the east.

Meran's gaze clamped to the familiar back, his farsight latched firmly as Leon stepped into the darkness and disappeared. Blindness was the price he paid for keeping the ethereal magic to himself as promised. He could see nothing but glowing marauding shapes in the distance, slinking closer.

The shivering resumed, and he peered into the night, trying to glimpse anything, his heart thudding an increasing tattoo even as a cry preceded a startled yapping. He flung his head up and lurched one step in the direction Leon had taken when, to his alarm, shadowy forms rose like ominous ghosts from the ground.

Not dogs, but men.

CHAPTER THIRTY-SEVEN

Chaos erupted across the landscape, dogs scattering and yipping for no detectable reason. Scanning with his farsight did nothing to enlighten Leon of what was happening, and the distance between him and the fleeing pack defeated his newest talent.

The hairs on his nape crackled. Something unseen strode the darkness with him.

Turning on his heels, Leon raced back towards the campsite. In the eye of his farsight, Meran stood, the glow of his aura hugging tightly to his body.

As Leon neared the acacia trees and the milling horses, his heart stuttered. Five Dracan, grim, and hostile, had arrow tips raised towards Meran. Another stood at his back, sinewy arm about Meran's neck, squeezing a dark blush into his cheeks. The blade at Meran's ribs kept him from contemplating further retaliation.

How dare they? Rage roared within Leon. He would end them for this. But cold clarity cut through the haze of his offence. These were Dracan, and mayhap from Becchus.

Banking his desire to see them all dead, Leon nocked an arrow against his bow, aligned his sight, and let the shaft fly. A warning, not a challenge.

The sound of whirring preceded a meaty thud and yelp of surprised pain, Leon's arrow sticking from the Dracan's biceps. His offensive blade fell at Meran's feet, and satisfaction warmed Leon as the tribesman jumped back, hissing a string of expletives.

Meran dropped to his knees, gasping and wheezing but alive.

Knowing they could easily kill him, Leon advanced. A further arrow sat nocked at the ready in case he had misread the Dracan tradition of respecting a warning.

"Step away." Leon's command, spoken in the Dracan tongue, had Meran rear back in amazement, those bluest of eyes glittering with awe.

Undeserved, unfortunately, though Meran's admiration warmed him. Leon knew enough to string a few sentences together, and that might be enough to survive this confrontation.

With a wave of his weapon, Leon directed the wounded warrior to join his countrymen. He obliged with a sneer, eyes blazing unbridled rage and promising vengeance. Well, that would keep until Leon had taught their current leader a lesson. Not in diplomacy but strength. They understood that, and he was perfect for the task.

But first, he helped Meran to his feet, nervous energy vibrating beneath his palm as Leon scanned him for injury. *None, praise the gods.* Relieved, he leaned close, whispering, "Do you trust me?" And caught Meran's instant nod.

"Good, then I bid you step back and let me handle this, no matter what it takes. Understood?"

Again the nod.

After guiding Meran back to the makeshift tent, Leon advanced to stand before his adversaries and perused them, seeking their leader.

He and Meran impinged on Nord's territory, and respect had to be earned. Tradition demanded they extract the name of a Dracan leader ere they, as strangers, could go any further.

His attention snagged on an older tribesman who exuded a sure and natural authority. Wiry, hard, and endowered with a granite stare, his presence commanded deference from the other Dracan as he took his place in the circle.

This was the one. It was now or never.

"Earn the right to our names, Dracan. Best me, little man, and I will give them." Leon bellowed his challenge.

That Leon knew of this ritual had speculation dawn in the wiry Dracan's eyes. A swelling rumble of outrage rolled out from the rest of the tribesmen, their expressions pulling taut.

The wiry man threw up a hand, silence following immediately, confirming Leon's suspicion. But it behoved him to tread carefully. This warrior might be diminutive in stature, yet he would not have earned this place nor received his men's respect without just cause.

Perusing Leon from top to toe, the wiry Dracan took in his height, his breadth, the confidence, and aggression writ large in his expression and let out a bark of command.

Rolled together, the words came too fast for Leon to understand them, but one of the Dracan sprinted into the dark. Unease kicked at

Leon's gut. He had to test his stamina against their leader. What were they doing?

Silhouettes appeared. Two figures. One, short and agile—the messenger returning—the other twice the size of any of the Dracan already present. Big and heavy with muscle, the newcomer's face was etched in a grim mask, obsidian eyes flashing, nostrils flaring.

Leon rolled his eyes. *Well, fuck!*

The wiry Dracan had authority, perhaps a lock or a second, but Leon guessed this behemoth led this band of warriors. This man had to be bested.

In stature, they were near equal, yet this would not be so easy. However, the challenge was thrown and now accepted.

Discarding his tunic, Leon squared his jaw and widened his stance. Plastering on a feral grin, he waved the Dracan forwards. "I dare you," he called, flexing his fingers. "This day, you have met your match." Though said in Velkor, Leon knew the warrior understood his condescension.

Word after word, Leon threw out, jeering as they circled, taking each other's measure. A flare of irritation sparked in the warrior's dark eyes. Leon's grin widened as his opponent succumbed to his taunting.

The warrior came at him like an angry bear. Leon danced to the side, landing a strike against the Dracan's kidney. The blow reverberated up his arm as if Leon had slammed his fist into a wall, the Dracan barely registering it.

The warrior turned, revealing an unexpected agility. He struck, the blow landing to the right of Leon's chest with the force of a sledgehammer. Sinking to his core, it almost rendered him breathless. He let it roll out of him, the pain dissipating with the strength of a hardened will and a touch of healing magic.

Using his amazing strength of shoulders, arms, and hands, the Dracan warrior proved himself a vicious fistfighter. With his opponent's reach longer than his, Leon stood less of a chance. To win, he would have to take the defensive position. A prospect he did not relish. Not oft did he need to wear his opponent out before his attack had any chance of success.

The contest became a dance of sidesteps and feints. At first, the warrior sneered with derision as if believing Leon's tactic evidence of cowardice. The longer Leon persisted, the more aggravated the Dracan became, his swings wilder. Leon met the repeated lunges with the ball of his foot slamming against the Dracan's ribs.

The warrior roared in rage as a further kick hit, air panting faster through his teeth. Leon dodged in. Strikes landed in rapid-fire. Throat, ribcage, and groin; and then he danced out again.

His opponent shook off the blows. Leon gritted his teeth. *This was no man but an ox!*

Ducking a retaliatory punch breezing past the top of his head, Leon sent a sidekick aimed for the warrior's knee and struck the lower curve of his thigh muscle.

Gods' damn!

It had to hurt, but it did not take the warrior down. The other Dracan jeered.

Gritting his teeth, Leon skipped left, right, and then lined himself up for a snap kick to the chin.

Searing pain jerked him back, tearing the balance out from under him. Fists curled beneath his ears, broad chest against his back, and a tight band of leather about his throat, cutting off air. Disbelief flared through him. He scrabbled to pull the garrotte free, pain and fury exploding. *A-a plague on them all. Dishonourable bastards.*

The Dracan leader advanced to where another held Leon captive, a vengeful gleam in his black eyes and a snarl on his dark lips. His arm reared back. Agony blasted through the bridge of Leon's nose and reverberated through his head.

The man's fist collided with his face once more. Darkness danced behind Leon's eyes, and he sank into oblivion to the accompanying wail of Meran's disbelieving, "*No!*"

CHAPTER THIRTY-EIGHT

Meran's lungs refused to work. Leon lay facedown, blood drooling from mouth and nose. Was he alive or dead? He could not tell...until he caught the subtle rise and fall of Leon's chest.

His rage surged. "Leave him!"

Scrambling towards Leon, arms outstretched, he ordered the enemy back. "You will not hurt him." Yet the Dracan had shown themselves contemptible.

Meran readied himself to give battle.

The big warrior pushed, and Meran went spinning.

He scrabbled on the ground, trying to get his feet under him, even as the tribesman injured by Leon's arrow advanced on the fallen man, eyes blazing with a vengeance.

A brutal kick thudded Leon in the ribs. Air whistled out between his teeth.

Meran bellowed, his protest inarticulate.

More strikes followed. Again and again, the tribesman lashed out, hitting Leon's body.

Meran threw himself between the pair, his skin alive with the expectation of a sandal-clad foot smashing into him. He would not allow them to beat Leon to death, even if he had to take it in his stead. "Stop! Stop!"

Unforgiving hands gripped his shoulders and tossed him clear. "*Gah*! No!" Willard's words came back to him. *"Hear me Draca, I invoke the Protection of Nord."*

The announcement sat heavily in the air as stunned faces turned in his direction. Meran anticipated retaliation, but the Dracan lowered every weapon, excited mutters chattering like a flock of agitated birds at the invocation of their god.

Meran swapped to Velkor. "Does any here speak the language of Atena?"

Most expressions remained blank, but the elder of the tribesmen, the one Leon had first addressed, let out a startling bellow over his shoulder. An answering baritone responded from the darkness.

Incensed, Meran glared into the void beyond the firelight. Had someone else held themselves aloof? Someone who could have interpreted for them and stopped this debacle from happening?

Rage tightened Meran's chest. He cared nothing that this Dracan was probably an elder, a learned man, revered and cherished by his fellow tribesmen. He could have done something.

A young man stepped into the light...

Meran lost his breath. Here stood the youth from his vision—*hair of soft brunette waves, sparkling brown eyes, and a scruff-covered jaw. Short, broad-shouldered, perfection*—his reality snuffed out any resentment. A silver halo of energy, unlike anything Meran had ever seen, shimmered through the ether about the youth...but along with him came a familiar touch. *Voce* magic.

Someone watched the youth from afar with their farsight. The essence of it spread over the gathering like a wave, a distinctive but unrecognisable prickle inundating Meran.

It tingled weakly, as if at the extremity of the unknown *Voce*'s ability.

Earlier, Meran had felt something. A barely tangible touch that darted in and out of focus as he awaited their departure, but he had dismissed it as anxiety playing tricks on him. Now he was not so sure.

He knew the Draca had their own form of magic, but it seemed they might also have a *Voce* back at the oasis. One that may have felt the touch of his own farsight from earlier. He shuddered at the possibility he had given their ruse away.

The newcomer stopped beside his fellow tribesman, and at the first's gesture towards Meran, the pair fell into a low argument.

Now that they stood close, Meran could see how much lighter the young man's skin was compared to the rest of his companions. Beneath the swirl of symbols embellishing all their skin in ochre and dust, the newcomer's shone a rich chestnut tan to their hickory.

A half-breed, indeed, but a mingling of what? With the evidence of magic clinging to the youth, Meran had assumed Dracan and *Voce*, but he also had the distinct look of the Summer Isles about him. A Velkor mix then, and presumably, one with an understanding of the language.

The elder Dracan's impatient growl tore Meran from his musings, his tone as sharp and brutal as a slap. Defiance squalled across the half-breed's features, but he did not retaliate. He took a deep breath and strode towards Meran. If the half-breed harboured curiosity for those who shared his heritage, he buried it beneath his disgruntlement.

As he neared, the waves of silver magic reached out. Static caressed Meran that he could appreciate even from where he stood, though no other seemed to notice it.

"What is names? What is...doing?" he asked.

"And I say, what is this?" Meran flung his arm wide to encompass the standoff. "That you greet a potential ambassador of trade in such a manner is despicable!" His anger grew the more he thought on it.

All eyes turned to the young interpreter, his flashing back agitation. "Slow. Much fast speak."

Though he bristled with impatience, Meran revised his opinion. If the half-breed's origins were part Velkor, he certainly did not use the tongue often. But if he wanted to be heard, Meran had to temper his rage.

Taking a few long, calming breaths, he recommenced in a low, slow, and considered rhythm. "I know that we are not of your kind, but my companion has attempted to adhere to the Dracan way of greeting. Is this not so? But you have used it as an excuse for foul play ere you know our purpose."

Maintaining a defensive gaze on Meran, the half-breed directed his words to the elder man and not the big warrior—*the dishonourable bastard*—who had withdrawn to the edge of the firelight. As the two conversed, Meran chanced a glance behind him. His gaze swept over Leon, agitation growing at the sounds of his rattling breaths. *Hold on.* He would get through to them soon, and then he could assure himself of Leon's survival.

Until then, Meran kept his body between the Dracan and Leon, determined to protect him with his life.

"Adon say folly walks with you, Atena man," the half-breed said. "Nord likes not...invasion."

"We are hardly an invasion. There are but the two of us. We are travellers. Merchants—"

"Him is merchant not!"

Meran raised a conceding hand. Any seeing Leon fight would know that. "He *was* a soldier, but no more, I assure. We are two friends seeking new places and people with whom we may establish trade. We heard of this land and its unique bounty and wished only to experience it. That is the truth, I swear."

Scepticism painted every face, as if they knew he kept secrets.

"Adon want proof."

"That we are merchants? That I can do." Meran gestured at the pack animals. "If Adon will allow, I will show him. I have with me the best of the bounty of Atena."

"Adon say you have name. He have not name. No name, no…ah," the youth tapped his head, "agree?"

Meran hesitated. From what he could tell, Leon had fought the *dishonourable bastard* to earn his name as spoils. Should he so easily capitulate?

But he knew Adon's name. Perhaps the only name that mattered belonged to the big warrior. Meran threw him a cautious glance. He would certainly not be challenging for it. He looked back. "Gift me yours, and I will give mine."

The youth looked taken aback. His warm brown eyes tinged with the cold hard frost of suspicion. "Why?"

Meran affected a shrug. He had merely given into his intrigue for the half-breed. His magic. His circumstances. What he meant to the Dracan, to Meran's plans, to the unknown *Voce* who watched from afar. Introductions were a necessity to initiate any dialogue. "I am but curious."

"I small." The youth lifted his chin, his lips curled with belligerence. "Adon big."

As the pair were of similar height, Meran assumed the half-breed compared their importance. The elder warrior's proud expression certainly promised offence if Meran held out much longer. It seemed only fair. "Zachary. I am known as Zachary the Fisher."

"And he?"

Do what they liked to him, Meran would never reveal it. It remained Leon's alone to give. Meran shook his head and set his jaw.

The youth offered him an unfathomable look. Considering? Surprised? Impressed? Tension tightened Meran's chest as that gaze dug deep, demanding he bare his soul, before it switched again to assess Leon's slumped form.

"Him you honour." The half-breed nodded as if recognising Leon's inherent authority. Even so, he gnawed on his lower lip as if this were unexpected.

Perhaps the Dracan were taught Velkory had no honour.

Understandable if the Velkor were a part of the slave trade on their southern border.

"He is a good man," Meran said.

Squinting his eyes, the half-breed offered Meran a brittle stare. Without breaking eye contact, he shared Meran's details with those clustered behind him.

Even as the palpable tension eased back, Meran's attention remained on the youth, his voice soft, reasoned. "And now you know who I am, will you give me your name too?"

Although he raised his chin high, his eyes piercing and aloof, the half-breed appeared unwilling to risk discourtesy. "I Falric. Falric Mislan."

Mislan? Definitely a *Voce* name, although not of his own clan or Leon's. Where had he come from? How had he come to be living in Draca's south? Who were his parents that he harboured such potent magic? *Wild and untameable magic.* Why had his family not culled him?

So many unanswered questions. And yet Meran recognised Falric's acquiescence for the gift it was. Curiosity lit large in Meran's mind, even if neither his hand nor smile were returned. At least he had not worsened their current situation.

"Adon say go," Falric reminded him.

"Oh, yes." Meran shook himself. But now that he had permission, he hesitated. He would not leave Leon lying on the ground and vulnerable, not even for a minute. He threw the big warrior a suspicious frown before shackling Falric about the arm. "I beg a boon…"

The boy stiffened, the silver aura shocking Meran, like the sting of a thousand bees. He dropped his hand, but his resolve did not lessen.

"I meant no offence," Meran said, his gaze affixing to Leon, "but I will not leave him. So, I beg a boon of you if I am to appease your clansmen."

Those brown eyes flickered between Meran and Leon, glimmering with intelligence and suspicion. "Him is more than honour? Him is…*heart*."

Meran marvelled at Falric's intuition. He had seen the truth. Leon was not just a lord, nor Meran's hand, nor his voice, nor his minion to command and use. They were more than any covenant, more than lovers. They were inexplicably tied together, not alone by prophecy, but by the ties of chosen family. Leon held Meran's future in the palm of his hands.

He nodded. "And now that you have my secret, what will you do?" Would he betray this confidence, allowing the elder to coerce Meran using this attachment?

Yet, what would be the point? They already possessed all the power.

Falric waved at the campsite. "Tell me, where is?"

Meran breathed out a sigh of thanks. "In the saddlebag of the last horse, there are three bottles of wine…" Doing his best to ignore the sting as skin met skin, his palm tingling with a jolting power, Meran grasped Falric's biceps. "There are also three rundlets of the same…a gift for Catana Keija and his Outlier at Becchus." It was imperative they were not squandered.

"Him, you know?"

"I know of him. They are in his honour. Will you tell your master?" Fascinated, Meran watched the youth's scepticism and suspicion fall away.

"Nah, nah, nah. They honour. We Keija warrior all, and him is heir." Falric pointed to the big warrior still standing silent and aloof.

Meran almost hissed, "Joram?" Tark's assessment now made perfect sense.

"Aye." Falric left Meran to approach Adon and fell into a quiet conversation. At a nod, he made for the horse and brought back only one of the bottles and a small metal cup. It seemed they were allowing Meran to keep the remainder.

Taking the offered items, Meran poured a sample and offered it to Adon.

Joram intervened, his expression menacing. Meran caught himself before he shied away, knowing how easily he could be broken. He held to hope Joram would honour the invocation of Nord's Protection, though he had already proven himself unprincipled. Perhaps he eschewed their traditions only because of the gem and the idea—and not a wrong one—that others would seek to steal it.

"He say drink, Zachary," Falric said.

"Pray, what? Does he think I would offer something tainted?" That would be pure foolishness when he feared for both his and Leon's lives.

Falric shrugged, giving no opinion.

For the love of the prophet! These Southern Dracan were a suspicious lot. Still, to do Joram's bidding was no hardship. The woodsy flavour flowed down Meran's parched throat. To his delight, it tasted perfect even after the distance it had travelled.

He refilled the cup and offered it to Joram. The Dracan considered it for a moment before lifting it to Falric's lips. Meran did not miss the flash of outrage in the youth's eyes nor the flare in the silver aura. Emotion and magic seemed inextricably linked, untethered power waiting to be tapped.

The urge to teach Falric gnawed at Meran, but he could not. He was meant to be Velkor and, as such, would have no magical ability.

Meran watched as Falric took a disgruntled sip.

Minutes passed.

Witnessing no adverse reaction, Joram took back the cup and drained it.

The world stilled, hushed in anticipation.

Tension mounted in Meran's back and shoulders as he searched for a response on Joram's sullen face. It came as a subtle lift of his brow and a slight easing of pressure at the corners of his mouth. The other Dracan stepped forwards, their chatter suddenly animated.

Relieved, Meran smiled, first at Joram and then at Falric. "Perhaps a further few cups and another bottle to quench the thirst of my new friends," he said.

Once each held a drink in hand, all except for Falric, whom Joram sent back into the darkness, they gathered about the fire to enjoy the unanticipated bounty. In Falric's absence, and no longer able to communicate, Meran found himself ignored.

He cared little. Grasping the opportunity, he sank down by Leon's side. Gliding hands over that dark sandy hair, he sent out a silent plea for him to wake up and prove himself whole after what had been done to him.

CHAPTER THIRTY-NINE

Leon roused to a plethora of pain assaulting his face and neck. Throbbing aches echoed through his chest and belly. As he rolled to his back, nausea rose, his stomach threatening to rebel.

"Lie still." The command came in a whisper, and offsetting Leon's misery, the gentling caress of fingers teased the strands of his hair, offering a comforting counterpoint. The need to hollow his insides out ebbed away.

Even so, his breath rattled wet through his nose, and he opened his mouth to gasp. Dry and sore, his throat rasped. *Fuck!* Where was he?

The warm pressure of a thigh brushed against his shoulder even as memories flooded back, prodding at his instincts. He had to protect. He had to win. And he would have... The sight of feral eyes and a huge fist flooded his mind, pain cinching his throat... *Treachery!* Leon's muscles tightened, ready for any eventuality.

"Hold. We are no longer under threat."

Leon's eyes popped open, gaze latching to the earnest face leaning over him. Meran's palm fell from Leon's hair to cup and hold his jaw, the pressure meant to steady him. A streak of awareness shot from Leon's skin to the very core of his being. Proprietorial and needy.

For a glorious instant, Leon revelled in it, but his sense of duty reared its head to drown out every soft feeling. He did not need coddling; he needed a clear head. He groaned as he sat, pushing Meran's gesture aside even if he laced their fingers together for the briefest of moments before reaching for his shattered nose. *By the gods!* "What happened?"

Leon wiped the blood from his face with his own discarded shirt as Meran quietly enlightened him. A storm of anger swirled to a vortex of outrage as Leon listened to the report of the tribesmen's perfidy.

"But they heeded your entreaty?" To go from disdaining a known custom to accepting mere words seemed impossible. Leon's suspicion thickened into a formidable cloud.

"They heeded the use of their god's name more than they heeded me. And mayhap the tradition and spirit in which I used it." Meran's mouth twitched deprecatingly, though Leon could see the delight he took from knowing something that Leon had not. Something that had gotten his seer further than the tourney had gotten Leon.

Where Meran had heard it, Leon did not know, but after perusing the distracted and celebrating tribesmen about the fire, he had to admit it proved worth its salt. He shook his head in all disbelief. He dared to go with it to see how long the peace lasted.

"That is Joram, Catana Keija's firstborn," Meran continued, surreptitiously indicating the bastard that had knocked Leon down.

Leon's lip twisted into a grimace. So he had been bested by the very son of the catana they sought. How fortuitous. The very man Tark had warned them of. The unwavering, resolute defender of all Catana Keija held dear, his possessions and his Outlier. A bull and an obstinate man. And a cheat. And yet... "You managed to get his name from him? How?" That should have been impossible.

"I did not fight him, if that is what you ask." A shiver vibrated through Meran's shoulders.

He repeated the conversation he'd had with the young half-breed. "He had a passing smatter of Velkor and revealed it to me, thinking I must know of him because I knew Keija's name. I was no fool to advise him otherwise."

No, that Meran was not, and Leon began to see the worth of it. There was more than one way to achieve their goal. And for the first time, he could see their combined strength. His unwavering, brutish physicality—a match for any Dracan—and his previous experiences, and Meran's capacity for diplomacy and his miraculous foreknowledge. Their possession of *Amplion* seemed imminent.

"He made a mistake. One on which I do not wish to play," Meran continued. "At least not at this time."

Leon quirked a curious brow.

"I do not think Joram will behave well should he realise that we have this information when they still do not have your name."

Well, well, this could prove interesting. Perhaps they would demand another contest. At least once he had healed his injuries.

"I'm sorry, but you can't heal that. At least, not now," Meran said as if reading his mind.

Leon cast Meran a baleful look, though he conceded. "Ah fuck. This I know, but I don't have to like it." A rebroken nose loomed in his future no matter what he did. He pressed at it, grounding himself with the sharp spike of pain. He could live without that, at least.

The healing magic reached out, tingling and heady, but as always, Leon mastered it. The heat of it surged through his internals from groin to chest. The wet whistling of his breath passing through mutilated cartilage and broken bone silenced as he knitted it together, his relief palpable. An imperfect solution as he'd had no way to hold it in place, but it would do to satisfy everyone.

"Did you just heal yourself?"

Leon huffed at Meran's outraged expression. "A little, but never fear. They will never know. I've left the swelling and bruising to do their work upon my skin."

Meran's disapproval quickly turned to concern as his brilliant blue gaze settled on what must still be an unsightly mess. Warm hands cupped either side of Leon's face as Meran came to his knees, and a gentlest of kisses pressed to his forehead and then to his lips. It spoke of his fear, of his resolution, his bravery, his boldness. In Leon's absence, Meran had proven himself a wonder.

For once, Leon let a man have his way with his mouth, soft caresses, needy lapping, a slow exploration around and in. Until he felt the shaking of Meran's limbs. Leon reached out, his hands firm about Meran's ribs, offering reassurance and balance. Whatever he needed.

Meran pulled back far enough for their lips to part and to see each other with focused clarity. "I see you, Leon Ricci, and I was sore afraid. Afraid they would take you from me. That I would lose you when I had just gotten you."

Leon swallowed. The lord in him did not know what to do with such intense and sweet declarations, the warrior in him scorning them as weak, but the man quaked inside.

Despite the threat of the ghostly Loni's pronouncements and the fear he still harboured for Meran's own unknown power, he could not deny the intensity of his attachment since declaring his oaths. This man was not Eain. Not driven by the need to conform or to bow to the dictates of others. He was brave, dedicated, strong-willed. He bore the true spirit of a Ricci. "I see you too. And you will never."

CHAPTER FORTY

Those words rang with such sincerity Meran felt light-headed, a grin aching through his cheeks. The prophet had demanded he "*find the man,*" but in Leon, he had found much more.

Jon's sage advice came back to him. *"There is more to a man than just the finding of him. You must also secure him. And what better way than he fall for you."*

Meran knew he could not have ever been so disingenuous. But from the first, his attraction had been piqued, even during the turbulence of their first meetings, though Leon's feelings had not been of a match.

Now, they had a melding of more than just purpose, of hope and enchantment. Together was their way forward. Meran hoarded Leon's declaration in his heart to treasure, the strength of his response tolling his own utter captivation.

Warmth flooded him, along with the desire to demonstrate the power of his devotion with further kisses. Begging, supplicating declarations to induce Leon into a frenzy of hard, hot passions that, apart from their current audience, he could not indulge in. Not until they found an answer to the ethereal magic that threatened to subject Leon to the perils of the dreamlands.

Meran settled himself as close to Leon as he dared until that churning magic resolved into the air and dissipated. His gaze landed on their *guests* as the Dracan drained the last dregs of the bottles.

Some eyed the horse on which the rundlets were packed, only to receive a withering scowl from the catana's son. A man with whom none presumed to argue.

At Joram's direction, they all began to pack the campsite, loading the horses with a practiced hand.

It seemed they, too, preferred to travel at night.

Meran revised his assessment. "They are not as barbaric as Locurnia labels them."

"But not to be trusted."

Leon had the right of it after what they had done. "We have a working peace, currently," Meran said, but still, he recognised the necessity to tread warily.

Finding the man had not been Philo's only command. Now that they were in the presence of the Dracan from Keija's Outlier, Meran knew the quest must transition into *freeing the gem* from their erroneous possession.

He and Leon were in a vulnerable position. With Falric's departure, they found themselves isolated. It would be easy for misunderstandings to erupt. "How much of their language do you understand?"

Leon seesawed his hand. "A little. Perhaps enough to keep us out of more trouble."

Perhaps it would be sufficient for this last leg of their journey, but what of once they reached Becchus? The oasis heralded the unknown and, amongst them, a *Voce*. Fortunately, the tingling touch of farsight had retreated along with Falric, suggesting he and Leon were of no interest to him, their disguises remaining intact.

But how could that *Voce* see the half-breed when neither Meran nor Leon had seen any of the tribesmen coming? How had they accomplished that? Earth magic?

Fiercely curious, Meran sent out his farsight, drawing on his memory of Falric's handsome face…and found nothing. He grimaced. There had to be something that the *Voce* focused on. Something to undermine whatever spell the Dracan had cast to keep them invisible. It could not be something physical. All life had a force that the farsight could latch to…except for Leon's.

Only when Meran had shared the ethereal magic of their connection had he been able to spy Leon out. So, what if he tried to latch to magic that flowed into the ether? He sought the youth's silver emanations. Fulsome and bold and beautiful and chaotic. Meran tried again. Quicker than lightning, his farsight latched onto the aura that glowed like the brilliant beams of a full moon in the darkness.

Meran watched as the young man's lithe form flowed across the ground like a pale ghost. He could run like the wind, stopping only to hurl rocks with amazing accuracy at the gleaming eyes of a few curious beasts, scattering them before him. It took Meran's breath away.

Yet these Dracan were a cold and menacing bunch. Joram, in

particular, sending Falric off alone and unprotected. *Such callousness.*

"They sent Falric out on his own. He is so young…" Despite the scruff, straight carriage, and pronounced muscle, he could be no older than ten-and-eight years. "If they can do this to one that they call theirs, that begs the question as to what our treatment will eventually be, even with this invocation in place."

"I fear they have changed since my last sojourn here," Leon said.

Meran rose from the sea of his own concerns to see Leon's pale eyes piercing the Dracan with an assessing stare, his familiar frown returning.

"They had been so noble, so forthright, predictable. I had not anticipated they would deport themselves with such dishonour."

"What need do they have of honour? They have a powerful talisman now," Meran shrugged, "and they have a *Voce*…"

"Pray, what?" Leon's scowl deepened.

"Aye. One watched Falric very closely. I felt their touch sweep in from the east…"

"From Becchus?"

"That is what I assume." Despite Leon's obvious prejudices, Meran would not keep the youth's heritage a secret. This was their quest, the next step theirs to succeed or fail in. He enlightened Leon of all that he had seen of the youth, of his appearance and the billowing, silvery aura.

"A half-breed and one with magic?" Leon's scowl turned to thunder. "The situation is even more dangerous than I had thought."

"How so?"

"I told you. If he is a half-breed, his magic is wild. No wonder the *Voce* keeps track. If the Dracan have somehow tapped into it, that might explain—"

"No, no. Neither the youth himself nor his fellow Dracan has any inkling."

Leon grunted. "They don't know?"

"That is how it seems to me."

Meran held his breath. He did not want a lord marshal's judgement to fall on the young Dracan. He could not say why, other than that he yearned to turn the tide of that unruly, effervescent power and give the youth a chance at control, at life.

"So, we have a traitor on our hands. A *Voce* who has sold our secrets."

Meran gaped. He had not thought of that. But somehow, the Dracan had seemed to know *Vocekind* could detect them with magic, and they had found a way to circumvent it.

Meran stared at the tribesmen, his mind in turmoil, studying them closely for any clue to their secret. The strangely painted sigils each man wore in bands of ochre, brick, obsidian, and other earth tones were the only things that stood them apart from all other men. These symbols extended across cheeks, chest, and arms and disappeared beneath the waistbands of their strange baggy britches. Could these symbols be the anchor of such a spell? "But even should they know, how can they possibly overcome our magic?"

"That is one thing I intend to find out," Leon replied.

Meran swallowed a nervous flutter. They were still heading for the oasis and the gem, but to succeed in their theft, they would need to know what power the Outlier had at their disposal.

If only he had a quiet, solitary moment to consult with Philo for direction, any direction the river could give…but his hope faded when a pair of the Dracan warriors advanced. Like herding sheep, they urged Meran and Leon to their feet and onto a horse each with gestures and urgent shouting.

Meran's peace lasted as long as three days. Longer than expected, especially after two of the Dracan had peeled back at Joram's behest, taking the horse bearing the wine with them.

Anxiety weighed Meran down. Leon too, if the stoic expression he wore like a mask was discounted. Leon channelled the aspect of a lord of Locurnia, the façade of a warrior who would much prefer to slaughter all who stood between him and his goal. But he held himself aloof and in check, allowing the future to play out as if handing Meran his faith.

Was Meran worthy of it? He did not know. He had not admitted to Leon that one fateful thing. Anigema, not *Amplion*, awaited them.

And yet, as that final eve spread fingers of fire across the sky heralding in the night, Meran felt the first tentative touch of success. Of welcome. He could sense it. The closeness of the gem, the glorious pull of power emanating from their destination, though it lay as a green swathe across the skyline.

Closer, closer, closer they drew, and fingers of anticipation wormed their way deep into his being. Yearnings not his own, a tumultuous welcome, a guarded happiness, as if his coming were recognised. Not by man or beast or any other living being, but by an entity beyond his imagining. A force that lay latent and on the very edge of revelation.

Philo! Philo! I am here. This is it.

Excitement encapsulated every particle, Meran's magic alive and fizzing and reaching out to be joined, consummated...

The small party cantered both on foot, horseback, and dromedary—the beast, as strange and unwieldy as Leon had led him to believe—until the outskirts of the large campsite spread out before them.

Lights flickered on sconces that trailed pathways from outskirt to centre. The party veered from the direction of the huge pavilion with its myriad of gregarious stripes towards a tent coloured a plain khaki and surrounded by grim-faced guards.

It appeared larger than most others Meran had spied, big and ponderous, but without flourishes of excess and elegance. With its squat and staid exterior, Meran wondered if they rode towards a prison, yet he felt heat and warmth and the accumulation of magic. The air sparkled with its untapped potency, thermals of it spiralling into the sky.

The wind picked up, chasing fingers through his short hair, surrounding him like a tentative, exploratory caress. It swept him, encapsulated him, pulsing and flaring as if it imbibed his scent, his being...and then swept free, taking the perfume of him with it.

Crossing the small gap between Joram's party and the dour enclosure, the wind whipped relentless fingers beneath the tent opening. The pegs mooring the edges to the earth flipped free beneath the harsh and persistent vibrations. Loud and concussive, the canvas protested.

The wind raced and curled, going to-and-fro like a swirling dervish, and beneath its storming breast, a voice called. One that rode those very thermals. One Meran had never heard and yet sounded like music and want and freedom and power and love... He yearned for it, unable to pull himself free. Perfection, completion awaited them. For him. For Leon. Without their unity, their collaboration, their bond, there was no hope, no success, no freedom...

His vision filled with a wondrous sculpture that embellished and framed the resting place of the gem. Not an orb of white, but an encrusted piece of ore of the darkest midnight sapphire, and at its heart, a raw and living power. It was. Right. There. Their prize, their goal...

"Ah, my gods!" Meran breathed in awe. "Do you feel it?"

From the tent's interior, a tall, gaunt man emerged and raced towards their party, his voice raised with fear and fury.

"*Curia Venner...*" Joram's voice echoed like prohibition.

Meran perceived the cudgel in Curia Venner's hands. Raised and menacing.

"Leon?"

Leon surged forwards with nothing but his body, his strength, and his determination to intervene.

"Stay back." Leon's command echoed in Meran's ears before pain split his thoughts.

Red fire assaulted his nerves. He fell into the deepest, most forsaken well of darkness, but with him remained the most glorious sight of that which would be theirs. The gem's recognition and its call.

He smiled in relief. They had made it, and now all that remained was to secure its freedom.

EPILOGUE

Pulling back the tent flap, the rumble of noise resonating through the thick canvas turned into an uproar as Vela stepped inside. Candlelight cast grim shadows as she took in a group huddled about a prone figure on the floor. Curia Venner looked emaciated and fragile.

"Step aside," she ordered. Keija's messenger had demanded her attendance, and she hurried forwards.

The overwhelming imperative to heal vied with twinges of dislike for the zealous priest. It was Vela's calling, the urges undeniable, as natural as the need to blink, swallow...breathe. But the man, no longer towering over the populace glowering at the ignorant and irreligious, had lost his superiority to unconsciousness.

The blatant condescension Venner harboured in his heart for her—for all women—necessitated she again adorn her healer's cloak of impartiality. A state of being she laboured under more and more often since experiencing the sentient touch of that cursed gem. A gem the priest believed to be Draca's fabled Anigema.

"This is an outrage," Keija declared.

Vela held back a derisive snort. She dared no provocation. She should not know the events that had precipitated her presence here. But as *Voce*, her farsight required she see these strangers in the flesh should she wish to keep track of them. From the shadows of the Tent of Worship, she had seen everything.

Dropping gracefully to her knees at Venner's head, she resisted any questions that would embellish her supposed ignorance. A quick scan was answer enough. The big stranger—his existence admittedly a surprise to her, having only detected one glowing aura amidst the search party—had knocked the priest senseless.

A sardonic smile twitched the corner of her lips. She bit it back. This was not the time for pettiness. Touching the swelling bruise beside the corner of the priest's eye, she marvelled at the stranger's

273

precision. His blow could have killed, and from the affronted rage burning across his demeanour, that had been his wish when Venner attacked his younger companion.

She had recognised a berserker's fire flaring behind the stranger's eyes, promising brutal retribution, and yet self-restraint enough to keep himself in check. Joram's proximity necessitated it, as did the fact they were but two strangers amongst the many warriors of Keija's Outlier.

A dose of smelling salts beneath Venner's beak of a nose roused him from his stupor with a screech of ill will, his face screwing into a mask of disgust. "What foul evil is this?"

Vela settled back on her haunches to await the end of his cursing fit.

Venner rose to his seat, hand across his face and glaring, fit to kill.

"Here, Curia, an ointment for the injury. Shall I administer it?"

For a moment, it seemed he would tear the small jar from her hand, but after a timid exploration of the area, he set his face and offered his temple.

"This will aid with the bruising," Vela said, smoothing the ointment over the contusion with a delicate touch, but it would not aid the deeper pain.

Once finished, she fished into her provisions and pulled out another container, this one filled with clear liquid healing. Vela need not have kept the potent elixir separate. She could have infused anything with it, but the tribe's expectations needed guiding away from the miracle that was her *Voce* magic.

She would not be here forever, and once gone, her acolytes had no way of reproducing her remedies. So she taught them the way of nature's healing with tinctures, oils, and potions and prepared the people for the future without her as best she could.

"This draught will dull the headache."

As if he deserved nothing less, Venner snatched it and threw it down his throat.

Instantly, he revived and pushed to his feet, dismissing Vela without thanks or further consideration as he faced those gathered around him. Catana Keija stood at the centre, his mother, Beata, to his right, and Joram to his left. Adon stood to the rear, expression stoic, his emotion unreadable. The shaman, Eno, lounged indolently on a low seat and sipped at a goblet of wine.

Vela eased back into the shadow to observe. None here would

dismiss her, but she was determined to avoid their attention now that she had completed the healing.

"Where are they?" Venner's attention turned to Joram. The only one in company that had also been at the site of the incident.

A flare of curiosity lit within the heir's eye. He was no doubt as mystified by the curia's behaviour as all those who had witnessed the spectacle. But something untoward had happened at the Tent of Worship. Something unprecedented.

It could have been nothing more than an errant breeze playing with the tent's canvas, but that Vela did not believe. It had boiled like thunderheads, forewarning a cataclysmic storm.

Venner had felt it, too. Fury and fear stretching his features into a rictus glare, he had charged forth. The young stranger had tumbled from his horse beneath that benediction, out cold.

"Separated," Joram replied. "Your attacker to the tombs, your victim to the Tent of Healing."

"He is no victim but a spy."

"How so?"

"He seeks what is not his."

Of course Venner would conclude that these strangers sought Anigema. Vela stifled the urge to roll her eyes. Since the men had been accosted out in the desert, she had been keeping watch. Though the farsight was silent, she had never found it difficult to read lips. When Falric had spoken in Velkor, she knew the glowing, bipedal figure he addressed had to be from Atena. In the flesh , the young fellow with the dull brown hair, golden skin, and brilliant blue eyes turned out to be one of their noble class. Curiously, his mysterious companion could have passed for *Voce*, but his dark sandy hair and dark weathered skin would not be misplaced amongst Velkor's nobility either.

Voice mocking, Magos Eno asked, "How would he know of it, Curia?"

Vela, too, found it difficult to believe they could know anything. Atena, a city lying at the Meith's delta, ruled a province that hugged Locurnia's western coast. Like a verdant barrier between Draca's desert and the western sea, few ever ventured from its lush pastures.

Those of Draca avoided it and its untameable waters. Nord did not command those waves. How could magicless humans even know of Anigema's advent? How could anyone beyond Draca's borders? No, they were wanderers in the wrong place at the wrong time, and she hoped they would not have to pay for it.

"I tell you, he does," Venner insisted.

"Oh, come now. We all know our greatest enemy is my own mother and her faction of Scroll Masters." Equal scorn for dam and priest dripped from Eno's tongue.

Though Vela considered the shaman despicable, a man made bitter and abusive by his own shortcomings, his dissenting voice gladdened her heart. The appearance of two Velkor felt like a ray of hope, a plan stirring in her breast. If she could achieve it, Falric might live free of the forewarning Anigema shared with her in the moment chill sapphire had met her flesh.

"She would never stoop to consorting with the Velkor," Eno continued. "How would sending perfect strangers into our midst forward her cause? She is canny enough to know we would be wary, especially after we have captured her spies already."

"Exactly. She but changes tack to deceive us."

Eno heaved a sigh while the gathering watched on with intense curiosity. Their two voices carried equal weight with the Outlier's Quorum of Elders. For all that Vela disliked them both, she could only hope this time Eno's would win out.

"They are a threat to our plans." Venner continued, demanding, "I want them dead."

"For the love of Nord. You go too far. Do you not realise that they must hail from wealthy families. Be they second sons of second sons, they have connections and are just trying to make their way in the world."

"No one will miss those who are so foolish as to step within our borders uninvited."

"Such dogmatism, my good curia. Anyone would think you afraid of a couple of merchants." Eno waved his goblet aloft. "Look at the bounty they have brought. It tastes magnificent. What could it hurt should they bring more in exchange for spices and a few baubles?"

"Devil take you, sot! More is at stake than slaking your thirst. We know nothing of their motivations. This is not the time for indulgence. Nord has a new path for his chosen, and when Anigema wakens to my touch as his new *candicio*, our blessed purpose will be unstoppable."

"The rest of Draca may have somewhat to say about that, do you not think? Despite how you scorn the old way and my dam as its advocate, she will not concede lightly."

"They knew the way of our greetings." Joram joined his voice to the conversation. "The young one invoked Nord's Protection when first we came upon them. The maki may have given them such advice."

Eno's expression hardened. "No. She is too stingy. She would share nothing with perfect strangers and risk them taking what she covets. I tell you, look for another reason for their presence. It cannot be Anigema. You are letting your paranoia rule over common sense."

"Well, no matter their purpose," Catana Keija spoke up, "beyond doubt, the big Velkor is a danger to all."

"Aye," Joram agreed. "He is trained in the art of combat, and his spirit soars with the love of it. The young one, not so much, though he gave evidence of a brave, stalwart heart."

"They impressed you then?"

Joram glowered at the smirking magos, but Vela could see the truth. Joram had taken the big Velkor's measure and not found him wanting.

"This Zachary insists they are merchants looking for fresh trading grounds and I am wont to believe him," Adon said. "His voice held no guile and his eyes sincerity. If it is not the truth, he has mastered the art of dissimulation to perfection."

And that said it all. Vela had seen few, if any, pull the wool over Adon's eyes, the divining rod of his suspicion unfailing. She needed to ensure their freedom and, in doing so, attain the same for Falric.

"Though they did not secure Joram's name, mine was sacrificed to them for good or ill," Adon continued. "But the big Velkor has kept his own close to his chest."

"Then they are not free to roam even under Nord's Protection until it has been secured." Beata, Keija's mother, said. "The celebratory games for our new warriors have been postponed long enough. Why not let them begin with a battle to the death. This warrior against our Joram. It will stir the blood of our people and whet their appetite." There was no doubt in Beata's voice that Joram would win. Brawny, aggressive, determined, unwavering, and bigger than the Velkor. Yet...

Whet their appetite for what? These games were a celebration of the Outlier's current *mentees'* success at surviving their Moon Rite. There would be fights, of course, competitions, and wrestling matches meant to allow the young men to prove their prowess. But it had never been a blood fest. The only difference this time centred on the further test for Falric. Because he was a half-breed, a slave, and her son. His becoming a warrior was unprecedented.

That he would have to endure this, Vela had kept secret, not sure how to share the egregious news she had agreed to. It was something he had only learned on his return from his Moon of Solitude and before he had been forced to join the rescue mission for Keno.

There had been no time for discussion, for him to prepare himself in either mind or body. The awakening of his magic had been of too much import, and still she'd had no time to teach him any control. If it was even possible.

Now betrayal bit deep. Vela knew she could never trust Falric's life to the machinations of Catanee Amata, an arch enemy and Keija's current wife, but Vela had trusted Beata to be fair. Yet, if a fight to the death was a precursor, what did the woman have in store for Vela's only son, and what could Vela do about it?

Coming 2024...
Seer Quest: Crucible
Description

A victorious rite of passage. A vicious trial by fire. Can surviving the first mean anything when death still beckons?

Falric Mislan is devastated. After surviving his Moon Rite, he finds his chance of rising from lowly slave to vaunted warrior has been set to nought. At the ceremony anointing his friends and peers to that coveted position, Falric is shattered by the reminder that he alone faces a last and deadly challenge.

Striking out with the search-party for the missing Keno, he hopes using his new-found magic will change the warlord's unfair demand. But two intrepid strangers await them, unleashing turmoil in the Outlier with their affinity for Draca's recently recovered sacred treasure. Falric fears even this last chance to prove himself will be lost in the chaos.

With all his hopes riding on a fight to the death, can he overcome the myriad hurdles in his way, and survive to stand amongst Draca's warriors?

Seer Quest Crucible is the heart wrenching second book in the Seer Quest – Legend of the Ancients Fantasy tetralogy. If you like a deadly challenge, an unscrupulous enemy, and a love deep enough to overcome adversity, then you'll love Deonne Dane's story of courage, determination, and deathless love.

Chronology of Legend of the Ancients

(As relates to timing of events, not publication dates)

Meran's Reproach
Moon Rite

Seer Quest Tetralogy
Seer Quest: Covenant
Seer Quest: Crucible *(Coming 2024)*

ABOUT THE AUTHOR

Born in New Zealand, Deonne grew up on a diet of genie's and witches and space adventure. Not vampires, not then anyway, they were too scary. Back in that day they definitely didn't sparkle.

She spent hours scribbling her version of fanfic in exercise books, on lined refill and coloured notepaper. But then she discovered epic fantasy; Eddings, Kerr, Donaldson & Brooks and felt she had come home.

Later, as happens with most people, she let herself be diverted by the mundanity of adulthood; marriage, widowhood, remarriage, children, separation and even lived through the Christchurch earthquakes, until she remembered the thing she was missing. Thus began her journey into the world of Locurnia.

With family in the queer community and her developing passion for all things MM she decided to marry these two loves together.

You can find her on: -
https://www.facebook.com/deonne.dane/
https://www.facebook.com/groups/KiwiAuthorsRainbowReaders
Or email to: -
deonnedane.author@gmail.com